‘A simple, funny and very engaging premise . . . Mulligan rewrites tragedy as a triumph, and turns the story into a neat way to explore friendship and tolerance’
Guardian

‘Mulligan certainly delivers in this extraordinary examination of grief . . . A highly original, emotionally-charged black comedy/thriller. A worthy successor to Mulligan’s excellent *Trash*’
Daily Mail

‘A poignant, imaginative take on adolescence’
The Times

‘Blisteringly funny, and sad’
Financial Times

‘Another blinding story from Andy Mulligan, which delivers the unexpected with superb imaginative qualities’
Mr Ripley’s Enchanted Books

Also available by Andy Mulligan:

Trash
Ribblestrop
Return to Ribblestrop
Ribblestrop Forever!

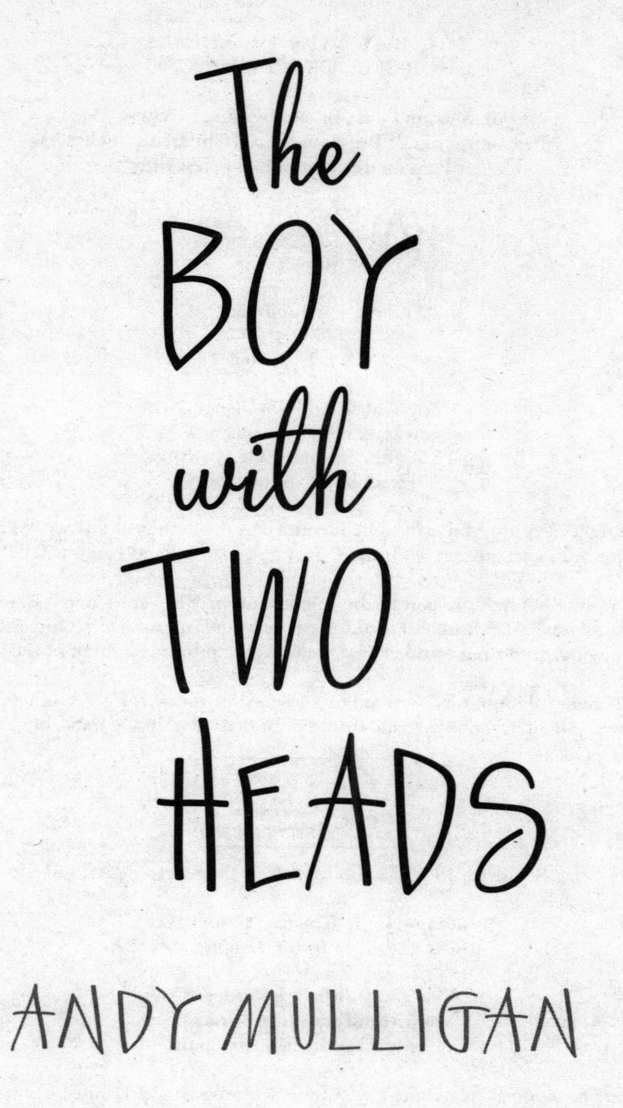

CORGI BOOKS

THE BOY WITH TWO HEADS
A CORGI BOOK 978 0 552 57347 4

First published in Great Britain by David Fickling Books,
when an imprint of Random House Children's Publishers
A Penguin Random House Company

This edition published 2015

1 3 5 7 9 10 8 6 4 2

Set in 12/15 pt Bembo by Falcon Oast Graphic Art Ltd

Random House Children's Publishers UK,
61–63 Uxbridge Road, London W5 5SA

www.**randomhousechildrens**.co.uk
www.**totallyrandombooks**.co.uk
www.**randomhouse**.co.uk

Addresses for companies within The Random House Group Limited can be found at:
www.randomhouse.co.uk/offices.htm

THE RANDOM HOUSE GROUP Limited Reg. No. 954009

A CIP catalogue record for this book is available from the British Library.

Printed and bound by CPI Group (UK) Ltd, Croydon, CR0 4YY

To Madeleine

PART ONE
NEWCOMER

CHAPTER ONE

Richard Westlake awoke, after a night of unquiet dreams, to discover a lump in his throat. It was no ordinary lump, for he could hardly breathe, and when his mother came to rouse him for school it was obvious that he was in no condition to get up. His voice was husky, and he was sweating.

The doctor arrived. 'Probably one of those fevers,' he said. 'But I have to say, I don't like the look of the swelling, and you can't be too cautious.'

He touched it gently with a finger, and the boy winced.

'Rather tender, is it, young man?'

'Mmm,' said Richard.

'It's got a rough edge, hasn't it? Right by the windpipe. I think we'd better get you checked up on.'

'But it's . . . football,' whispered Richard. 'I can't miss . . .' He had to stop, because the words wouldn't come.

'You can't go to school in this condition,' said the doctor. 'Football or not, a lump in the throat at your age needs to be taken seriously. Let me make a call.'

'He seemed all right last night,' said Mrs Westlake. 'We were packing his bag together—'

‘I don’t want any delay on this,’ interrupted the doctor. He put his thumb gently under the swelling. ‘I can feel it moving. Yes – I think we’ll get you an ambulance.’

So it was that fifteen minutes later, Richard found himself speeding through the city suburbs, siren blaring. His mother was holding his hand and there was an oxygen mask over his face. He was whisked along corridors and an elevator took him down to neuropathology. Within minutes he was in a tube that bleeped and buzzed. A number of levers held his head absolutely still while a dozen eyes stared down at him.

‘You say he was all right last night?’ said the consultant. He was a large man, with enormous glasses. They made his eyes bulge, and he had the unsettling habit of hardly blinking.

‘He was fine,’ said Mrs Westlake.

‘Happy as Larry,’ said her husband. ‘Out in the garden, running around.’

‘Really?’

‘Yes.’

A door opened, and a nurse entered with a ream of papers. The consultant set them on a desk next to a file full of photographs. The door closed, and Mr Westlake sat beside his wife, grim-faced. He’d come straight from his office and his suit was crumpled.

‘We’re pulling the threads together,’ said the consultant.

‘What threads?’ said Mr Westlake. ‘He’s a healthy boy – always has been. He was doing his homework as usual.

A . . . vocabulary test, I think. We watched a bit of television, and then it was cocoa, and off to bed . . . what's gone wrong?'

'What is it, Doctor?' said Mrs Westlake. 'Why's everyone being so secretive?'

'Nobody's being secretive, my dear.'

'Mysterious, then!'

'Where is he now?' asked Mr Westlake. 'Why can't we see him?'

'A few final tests—'

'Tests for what, though? Please!'

'We have to explore all possible avenues at the moment. Believe me, your son's getting the very best attention.'

'Can I introduce myself?' said a man from the corner of the room. He had been sitting in the shadows, observing, with his head on one side. He leaned into the light and smiled. 'I'm Doctor Warren.'

'Doctor Warren?' said Mr Westlake.

'And I understand exactly how you feel.'

'Do you?'

'This is a trying time, for everyone. It's an unsettling period—'

'All we want to know is what you've found.'

'Of course.'

He smiled again, and a zip of even teeth appeared above a neatly trimmed beard. 'I'm an associate psychiatrist here. I look at things from a purely psychiatric perspective. You've heard of the Rechner Institute?'

'Never.'

'We're a few miles out of town, specializing in neuroscience. We're always keen to assist with cases of this kind. Unusual cases—'

'Look,' said Mr Westlake more firmly, 'we just want to know what our son's got on his neck.'

'Then we must work together,' said Dr Warren. 'What's he had on his mind lately?'

'Nothing,' said Mr Westlake.

'No? No worries to speak of?'

Mrs Westlake put a hand on her husband's arm. 'Nothing major,' she said. 'He's not a worrier, as far as we know. I mean, he's no different from any other boy. He's got things on his mind, of course he has. His exams are coming up—'

'Important ones?'

'Yes, they're for the grammar school.'

'He's cheerful enough, though,' said Mr Westlake. 'Cheerful and normal.'

'They always are,' said Dr Warren, nodding. 'They always seem to be, anyway. I find that children of Richard's age can have a lot more going on in the old brainbox than we give them credit for. Tell me about his *emotional* balance.'

'Oh, for goodness' sake,' said Mr Westlake. He stood up and walked to the window. 'What are you driving at, Doctor? Because I have to confess I don't have much patience with this kind of thing.'

'No?'

'No.'

'You'd describe your family as emotionally stable?'

'Yes. I would.'

'Communication good?'

'Extremely.'

'Disappointments? Trauma of any kind?'

Both parents were silent.

'There was Grandad, of course,' said Mrs Westlake, at last. 'But that was . . . that was nearly a year ago, so I can't see that's relevant. We lived with my father, and he passed on – he'd been poorly a while, and Richard was with him when it happened. It was . . . well, we talked and talked about it, and he's a sensible lad—'

'Any counselling?'

'No.'

'Pity.'

Mr Westlake closed his eyes. 'Like my wife just told you,' he said, 'we talked it through at home – all three of us. It was a terrible thing, but Richard's a sensible lad, and everything got back to normal. He misses him – of course he does. They were close. But he puts his heart into school, as his grandad always encouraged him to . . . he's trying for one of the scholarships, you see. His friends rallied round and the boy got over it – like the rest of us.'

Dr Warren nodded wisely. 'How old was Grandad?'

'What?'

'Seventy-eight,' said Mrs Westlake.

'Right.'

'All we want to know,' said Mr Westlake, slowly, 'is what's wrong with our son. It's the neck we're worried about – not his mind! And you must have some idea, or you wouldn't be asking all these questions.'

The consultant stood up. 'Give us a little more time,' he said. 'We're talking to the whole team, and—'

'Is the lump getting bigger?' said Mr Westlake.

'Yes.'

'How big is it now?'

'It's grown considerably,' said the consultant. 'The speed of the growth is a major part of the problem, and Doctor Summersby—'

'Burst it, then!'

'Sir?'

'That's what we used to do. If it's a boil, or a . . . growth of some kind, you get a needle and—'

'Oh, it's not a boil,' said Dr Warren. 'We've taken X-rays from every conceivable angle; scans as well.'

'And you still don't know what it is?' cried Mrs Westlake. 'How can that be?'

There was a silence.

'We know a few things,' said the consultant quietly. He pulled the papers towards him and unfolded a chart. 'It's why I called the Rechner Institute. Doctor Warren here has been analysing the cranial data, so we are moving forward. It's a rare condition, as I said – but not unknown. Summersby's a neurological surgeon, based in New Zealand – she's looking at the results right now, because if we're right . . .'

The door opened again. A nurse appeared with another computer print-out, this one trailing to the floor.

She was white-faced, and nodded once.

'Confirmation,' she said. 'Really?'

'Yes. The surgeon's with us by satellite – she's positive. She'd like to see the parents. At once, if you can.'

They moved to an office. A laptop stood open on the desk, and two speakers were connected. On the screen was the head and shoulders of a serious-looking woman, with hair drawn tightly back from a thin face.

'That's Summersby,' said the consultant. 'She's at the cutting edge of neural science, and she's been observing Richard through monitors.'

'Can you hear me?' she said. She tapped at the microphone.

'Yes,' said Mr Westlake. He mopped his face with a handkerchief.

'I'm sorry I'm not with you in person.' She leaned forward and licked her lips. Two large nostrils seemed to sniff at the screen before she moved backwards and blinked. 'You must prepare yourselves, Mr and Mrs, er . . . Westlake. You have access to the counselling facility?'

'I'm right here, Gillian,' said Dr Warren. 'We're standing by.'

'Good.'

'What's wrong?' said Mrs Westlake, more frightened than ever. 'They've been testing him for hours. Can you tell us what's wrong?'

'I've seen all the results, Mrs, ah . . . Westlake – and the best thing I can do is explain the situation from a medical point of view. Your son's at a developmental stage, experiencing what we call a *larcedontal extrusion*, traumatic or spontaneous. It's a remarkable thing: your child has the cartilage, and the bone, of a respiratory organ, and that organ's ancillary to existing tissue – that's obvious. Now, as you know – as you've seen – it's located in his trachea, but what we've established is that it's outreaching the oesophagus, so we've got advanced compound cell division now. If you have any knowledge of basic physiognomy—'

'Stop,' said Mr Westlake. 'Stop.'

There was a silence. Dr Summersby came closer again, and stared. 'Can't you hear me?' she said.

'Yes!'

'You said you were going to explain,' said Mrs Westlake. 'I don't understand a word you're saying.'

'Well, as I said, medical clarity's essential in these cases,' said Dr Summersby. 'In a case of exponential cellular growth, where the brain—'

'We don't understand you,' cried Mr Westlake. 'You're going to have to speak in English.'

The doctor licked her lips again, and removed her spectacles. 'OK,' she said. 'I'll try again. Your son – Richard – has been developing, for some time, it would seem . . . a second . . . nose. The nostrils, as it were, are connected to the same airway as the existing one – and that's the main reason he's been having breathing problems. I want more time to observe, and I'll be over to examine him, as soon as I can. But I can tell you already that this . . . second organ is sharing your son's lungs, or trying to. It would also appear to be attached to the embryonic form of a skull, complete with cranium, forehead and jaw.'

'A head,' said Mrs Westlake.

There was another silence.

'What are you saying?' shouted Mr Westlake. 'What *exactly* are you saying? I'm still not clear.'

Dr Summersby blinked, but she held their gaze. 'I've seen a number of these cases, sir – rare as they are. I'm off to Vietnam tomorrow, to look at something similar. Your son is having the most extraordinary cerebral crisis. He's developing a second head. Yes. And it will emerge in the next twenty-four hours.'

CHAPTER TWO

Richard was unconscious.

The lump had grown significantly. It had gone past the walnut stage, and was now the size of a fist. Sticking up out of the lump was a sharp triangle of flesh, and above that were two red pimples.

'You can see it, can't you?' said the consultant quietly. He put a fat finger under Richard's chin. 'That's the danger-zone, there,' he said.

Mr and Mrs Westlake simply stared.

'Summersby's the expert. She's encountered similar cases before, but they've been hushed up – research has been terribly difficult. There's one she's been working on in Asia, which is attracting quite a lot of attention . . . but this is a rare condition.'

'And you can't just remove it?' whispered Mr Westlake.

'Oh, no,' said Dr Warren. 'Not yet. The heads share a brain stem. Same blood supply, so it would be fatal to amputate.'

'Then . . . what can you do?'

'We leave things be.'

'But surely you can deal with it in some way?' said Mrs Westlake. 'You can't just sit back and do nothing!'

'At the moment we observe.'

'Listen,' whispered Mr Westlake. His voice was trembling. 'You're telling us that our son now has a twin?'

'No, sir,' said the consultant.

'What, then – a parasite, feeding off him?'

Dr Warren shook his head. 'No, Mr Westlake. I need to emphasize this: as far as we're concerned, the second head will be Richard as well. A part of your boy, and we have to be ready for that.'

'So . . .' Mr Westlake paused. 'Oh, I'm lost,' he said. 'This is a nightmare . . .'

His wife took over, forcing herself to be calm. 'You're telling us that the second head will be . . . functioning, aren't you? That was the word you used. The new one – it will be able to think? It will have a brain – a mind of its own?'

'For sure.'

'It will have eyes? It will be able to see?'

A nurse leaned in. 'I think one's opening at the moment, Doctor. There's a growth-spurt, you can see from the monitor.'

Sure enough, the machine by the bed had started to bleep quietly, and a flashing light turned from green to red. The parents stared, and the right-hand pimple burst gently, the crater opening to reveal a tiny eyeball.

'Oh, Lord,' said Mrs Westlake. 'This isn't possible.'

'It won't speak, will it?' said her husband. His voice was

faint, and he held his son's hand gently. 'I mean, that's not possible, surely—'

'Both heads will speak,' said the consultant.

'In fact speech may be quite a feature,' said Dr Warren. 'The second tongue is well developed. Disproportionately large, in fact, so I would hope it's going to be quite a little communicator. We could all learn a very great deal.'

'It will feel things, then? It will have . . . emotions?'

'Yes. Absolutely.'

'How?'

'Well,' said the consultant. 'We don't understand the phenomenon as well as we'd like. But we suspect it's rooted in trauma. Latent trauma – buried and repressed.'

Dr Warren leaned forward. 'What we do know is that you're looking at an extra dimension of your son, Mr Westlake. The second head will share many of the likes and dislikes you're familiar with. It'll have Richard's memory, or parts of it – the memory's likely to be quite selective, depending on what's being ignored. You'll find that different things come to the surface at different times, so I'll need to work hard. What will be interesting is to see how the separate brains align themselves. Richard will need to stay at home for a while, but I would hope things will stabilize quite quickly and normal life will resume.'

'Normal life?'

'Yes. He won't be an invalid.'

'But . . .' Mr Westlake looked at his wife. 'He's got two heads.'

'And it's a rare condition,' said Dr Warren. 'Rare, but not unknown, and – as I said – it won't prevent him leading a totally normal life.'

'He's just finishing Year Six!' cried Mr Westlake. He stood up, and pressed his hands to his eyes. 'He's in the last year of primary school, eleven years old! He can't walk around with two heads on his shoulders, can he? Are you suggesting he goes back to school?'

'As soon as possible.'

'He'll be a laughing stock.'

'He'll need care, of course. We'll talk to his teachers—'

'Please,' said Mr Westlake. 'Cut the wretched thing off, now. Lop it off, now, before it gets a hold! One cut and this whole nightmare—'

'No, sir,' said the consultant. 'Death would be instantaneous – I can promise you that.'

'But he's a monster. Look at him . . .'

'Mr Westlake. That second head is Richard, as much as the first.'

'This can't be happening,' said Mrs Westlake quietly. There were tears running down her cheeks. 'I don't want this – look at him, look at our son . . .'

Mr Westlake drew his sobbing wife into his arms, and they stood helpless at the bedside. The little eye was now wide open, and it gazed up at them, sadly. The pupil was black, gleaming like a jewel. There was a crease of skin below the nostrils, and even as they watched it started to stretch slowly, and split. In seconds, two purple lips were forming, and a bubble of spit appeared. When it burst, the lips opened to reveal a line of delicate teeth. Between the teeth they saw the tip of a tongue.

Mr and Mrs Westlake stared. The second head turned slightly, and the first moaned in its sleep. The new mouth exhaled, and the eye blinked slowly, gazing up at its parents for the very first time. Minutes later, the second eye was open too, as wet with tears as the first. Richard writhed for a moment, and the alarm announced yet another growth-spurt.

Mr and Mrs Westlake were led gently from the room, bewildered and numb. The eyes followed them as the first, as the familiar head slept on, dreaming its dreams.

The transformation continued all night.

Fine hairs sprouted, and became eyebrows. By morning there was a black fuzz over the whole scalp, and the chin was sharper. The features were still close together, but they were expanding, taking on a marked resemblance to those by their side. The mouth was soon identical, and it smiled and frowned, as if practising different expressions. A junior nurse overheard the mumbling just before daybreak, and called the ward sister. Dr Warren arrived moments later.

The nurse washed the whole face gently, and patted it dry.

'Thank you,' said the head softly.

The ward sister stood back. 'That was speech, sir. Definitely.'

Dr Warren drew his chair closer. He produced a tiny

recording device, mounted on a silver tripod. He checked the focus and started to film.

'Can you hear me, Richard?' he said.

The eyes blinked. 'Yes. I think so.'

'Good boy.'

Dr Warren peered into the eyes. He checked the temperature on the monitor above, and wiped a bead of spittle from the lips. 'You're perfectly safe, young man. Perfectly safe.'

'Am I? Where?'

'You're in hospital.'

'Oh.'

'You're in good, capable hands,' said Dr Warren. 'You've got nothing to worry about.'

'What's happened then? I don't recognize anything . . .'

'Right now you're in the neurology ward, Richard. How do you feel?'

'Warm.'

'Yes? Comfortable?'

'Yeah. Wow . . .' The second head breathed out, and closed its eyes.

Dr Warren checked the camera again. 'I'm going to ask you to lie nice and still,' he said. 'You need to take it easy, OK? You've had a quite a shock and it's exhausted you. Can I get you anything?'

The second head smiled. 'I like the bed,' it said quietly. 'It's good to be still – I'm feeling pretty strange, though. I'm feeling . . . hungry.'

Dr Warren chuckled. 'You want food already?

That's a good sign – that's interesting.'

'What's it a sign of?'

'It suggests you're healthy.'

The forehead creased for a moment. 'You're filming me.'

'Yes.'

'Why?'

'Oh, just for the records. Can I ask you a question? How old are you? Do you know your age?'

'Have a guess, Doctor. Check my file.'

Dr Warren laughed again. 'I know the answer, Richard,' he said. 'Of course I do. What I'm wondering is if *you* have access to basic personal information. It's been a sudden arrival, so to speak. Do you know your full name, for example?'

'Westlake, Richard Arthur. Eleven and two months. A hundred and forty-two centimetres, thirty-seven kilos, just over. Holder of the Green Cross School long-jump record, and inside right for football. Bus monitor, too, I think. I know who I am, Doc.'

'Good.'

'Who are you? Because I'm not meant to talk to strangers.'

'Who told you that?'

'Everyone.'

'I'm a friend.'

The second head stared. 'I can read your badge,' it said. 'It doesn't say "friend".'

'Think of me as a counsellor.'

'So I need counselling, do I? Why is that, Counsellor?'

'We need to observe you, Richard. Run a few tests, check everything's working—'

'I'm not sick, you know. I'm fine. And another thing, before we go any further: I don't think I'm a Richard. That's not me any more.'

'You're not Richard?'

'No.'

'Who are you, then? You're Richard on the forms—'

'I think I'm a Rikki.'

'OK. That's cool.'

'Cool?' The Rikki head smiled. 'Everything's cool and fine, huh? – everything's safe. What's *he* like, by the way – sleeping beauty on the old shoulder . . . ?'

'He's a good boy. Don't you know what he's like?'

'I know he's polite. Please, thank you, how can I help you? He does all the right things, yes? We were in some school-debate team too.'

'Yes.'

'That might have to change.'

'Why?'

'Because I'm not a Richard. I just told you: I'm a Rikki.'

'What's going to change, though, Rikki? Tell me.'

The second head rose off its pillow slightly and the eyes narrowed. 'Doctor Warren, huh?' it said, squinting at the badge again. 'Psychiatric consultant, neurological team – wow. You think I'm of neurological interest?'

'I'm sure you are.'

'And you're here to help me.'

Dr Warren nodded. 'I'm with you all the way, Rikki, yes. I know we'll be friends and we're going to make discoveries, too. We're going to learn a lot together.'

'Friends? You and me?'

'I hope so.'

'I'm not sure I have any friends. We don't need any, Richard and me – we're pretty much independent now.' The head paused. 'Where are my parents?'

'They'll be back soon.'

The second head looked from side to side. 'I heard what they said, you know,' it whispered. 'About cutting me off – about parasites. But I think that is an understandable reaction, don't you? I'm not going to be hurt by that . . . I mean, I *am* a complication. I guess we're in for a rough, tough journey, but I can deal with rejection. I don't want you thinking I'm unbalanced, Doctor Warren.'

'You mustn't worry, Richard.'

'Rikki.'

'Everything's going to be OK. I promise.'

The Rikki head blinked, and stared. It licked its lips and grinned. A snigger emerged from the throat, and Richard moaned again in his sleep.

'Everything?' Rikki whispered.

'You're in good hands.'

'Oh, you're a liar . . .'

Dr Warren frowned. 'I hope I never lie to you, Rikki Westlake. I hope I tell the truth, always.'

'Then you'd better start over, because you just told me a bare-faced monster, didn't you? How can you possibly know anything for sure? According to probability based on evidence gathered so far, "OK" is the one thing life will never be. The world is not an *OK* kind of place, Doctor Warren – not any more. If it was, I wouldn't be in it. Do you understand that?'

'No.'

'You're not as clever as you think, then – are you? You need to work harder.' The black eyes narrowed again, and the smile turned to a snarl. 'We're all alone, man,' said Rikki. 'Every damn one of us.'

CHAPTER THREE

Time passed.

Richard and Rikki were moved to a small residential centre on the south coast – a division of the Rechner Institute for Neurological Studies. It contained just a handful of patients, who shuffled slowly along the corridors. Dr Warren visited as often as he could, and made careful notes. The second head continued to grow, and whilst a pair of physiotherapists worked on muscular control and movement, it was immediately clear that speech therapy wasn't necessary.

Richard's headmaster wrote to reassure the family that his place at school was being kept open. His best friend, Jeff, sent the most beautiful Get Well card. Richard loved aeroplanes, so he got every pupil in the class to draw one and sign it. 'See You Soon!' ran the caption, in puffs of clouds under a burning sun. Richard put it on his bedside table, and began to feel stronger. He wrote a letter thanking everyone, and he even dared to say that he hoped to be returning soon.

'By the end of the month,' said Dr Warren. 'I think you'll be ready.'

'I want to go home,' said Richard.

'Of course you do.'

'Has it changed at all?'

'I doubt it. Why would it change?'

Rikki smiled. 'You're lying again, Doc. Everything changes.'

Mrs Westlake bought new T-shirts, and made careful adjustments to them. She found a coat with an extra-wide hood, and a skilful tailor adapted the Green Cross school uniform. Mr and Mrs Westlake collected their son together, and soon he was walking up the familiar garden path.

It had been his grandfather's house, originally. Richard had been a baby when they moved in, and it had all made sense. His grandad could still manage stairs, if he was careful, so he'd had rooms on the first floor, overlooking the vegetable plot at the back. Beyond that was the lawn where his father had set up goalposts, and beyond that was the dangerously high tree house, with the swing . . .

Richard and Rikki breathed in familiar smells, and made their way up to the bedroom. They drew the curtains and covered the mirror.

The next day, a text from Jeff came through. 'We're waiting!' it said. 'We're keeping your locker tidy – nothing's been taken: DON'T WORRY!!'

'OK, thanks,' wrote Richard. 'What else is happening?'

'Football tournament. We need you!'

He visited, then: twice. Mrs Westlake apologized, but

kept him at the door. Richard was still too self-conscious, she said, and Rikki was settling. She was hopeful that things would improve.

Towards the end of the next week, Richard felt brave enough to pick up the phone.

'Hi, Jeff,' he said, after a pause.

'Richard! Is that you?'

'Yes.'

The second head said nothing.

'How are you, man?' said Jeff.

'I'm almost ready. I'm getting there. Do I, er . . . sound the same?'

'Exactly the same! When are you coming in?'

'Tuesday,' said Rikki. There was a pause, and Richard said, 'Tell me what I've missed.'

'Oh, everything!' said Jeff. 'Eric's in trouble again, and Bra-low's going crazy. We get tests every day, and Salome asked after you – so did Mark and Carla. You're really coming back? Let me call for you? We're dying to see you, buddy.'

'I'm not sure. Dad was going to drive us . . . Hang on.'

Jeff pressed his ear to the receiver, and heard anxious voices.

'That would be great,' said Richard, at last. 'We'll walk together, yes? Like it was.'

'Eight-ten, Tuesday. I'll knock for you – just like it was.'

'Can't wait,' said Rikki.

'What?'

'I'm looking forward to seeing you,' said Jeff. 'You nervous?'

'Yes.'

'Don't be nervous, Richard. It's going to be good.'

The next Monday, the headmaster called a special assembly in the dining hall. All the children sat in rows on the floor, and a number of parents sat on chairs around the walls. Dr Warren was on the stage – a special guest – sitting quietly to one side. He stroked his beard and stared at his laptop. The headmaster gazed at his audience.

'We have many things to be proud of at Green Cross,' he said.

The children were silent, cross-legged and straight-backed. Mr Prowse was a strict head teacher, who stood for hard work and self-discipline. They knew what was coming.

'I'm proud of you,' he said. 'And I hope you're proud of each other. As far as I'm concerned, there is no other school where children are as polite and tolerant, and I believe we are a genuinely happy community. Turn round, please, Eric.' He paused. 'One of the most important things in that community is the tradition of support and care. Any pupil here can expect support and care when things go wrong. Is that true, children?'

'Yes, Mr Prowse,' murmured the school.

'I hope so. Because my chosen theme for today's gathering is a proverb. A difficult word, that – can anyone tell us what it means?'

A hand shot up.

'Damien?'

'A famous saying,' said a small boy in the second row.

'A famous saying. Yes. A proverb is a famous saying that usually contains words of wisdom. And the proverb on my mind is one you may have heard before: "Two heads are better than one." Why have I chosen that self-evident truth? Because – as you are no doubt aware – Richard Westlake is coming back tomorrow, and I want us to be ready.'

He nodded to Dr Warren, and the lights dimmed. A large slide-photograph of Richard and his recent addition was thrown up onto a screen. There was an audible gasp.

'An unusual picture, children – I know. That's why I wanted to show it to you without embarrassing Richard. It was taken a few days ago, by his mother – and she sent it to me in the full knowledge that I would be sharing it. Er, number two, please.'

The photograph changed to a close-up. The two heads stared at the assembly, with blank expressions.

'Number three.'

There was a shot of just the second head, slightly thinner in the face than the Richard everyone remembered, with fiercer eyes.

'You'll notice something unusual on Richard's shoulder.' Mr Prowse paused, and the children stared. 'That is Rikki. Rikki, I can assure you, is Richard. Richard and Rikki are the same person, though they do, I'm told . . . have some little differences in character, some of the time. It's an unusual situation – I'd go so far as to say *rare*. But I have a feeling we're going to get used to it very quickly.

I am confident that Green Cross School will benefit enormously from the presence of both Richard and Rikki, because this is a school that embraces the new. Can any of you remember what special achievement Richard was so proud of last term? Hilary?'

Hilary's hand was straining. 'He won the long jump, Mr Prowse.'

'Yes he did. Joe?'

'He was bus monitor for the infants.'

'He most certainly was. What else? . . . Nicola?'

'He was runner-up for the *Kidspeak* prize.'

'Right behind Aparna, you're absolutely spot-on. And I will never forget his contributions to those meetings, because he was polite, organized and constructive, because *Kidspeak* could be rather important this term.' He paused. 'Rikki and Richard are going to have a wonderful time, aren't they?'

There was a loud murmur: 'Yes, Mr Prowse.'

'Two heads are better than one. To solve a problem, it is always wise to consult a second problem-solver. When we feel lost or lonely, how wonderful to have someone to turn to. That is why Richard is luckier than all of us. Never will he be alone, for he has a companion right beside him – and I suggest to you that when you get to meet that companion, you will have the pleasure of getting to know not one stimulating personality, but two.'

He turned, smiling broadly.

'Children. I want to introduce you to our guest. This is Doctor Warren, and Doctor Warren is a very important man – the Rechner Institute does ground-breaking work studying the human brain. He's agreed to help us, and you'll be seeing him around the school from time to time. Please make him feel welcome.'

'Thank you,' said Dr Warren, standing. He clasped his hands in front of his chest. 'It's really nice to be here, so thank you for having me. One thing I want to say is that Richard's first day could be the most important one. Does that makes sense?'

The children stared at him. Some nodded.

'Richard's been a good friend to many of you, by the sound of it. So he – and Rikki – are hoping that those friends will make a difficult time easier.'

He paused, conscious that his audience was scarcely breathing.

'My advice is, don't stare. After all, he'll be feeling a little self-conscious. Speak of him in the singular, and not in the plural – that means "he" rather than "they". Let's treat him as we would any other boy, and when you chat, look him in the eye in the same way as you would anybody else. He may not want to talk about his recent experiences, because . . .' He stopped and looked at the photograph. 'Because he's got so much to get used to.'

Nobody spoke or even twitched. The silence was absolute.

'Rikki's brain, you see, is newly formed, and has inherited only parts of Richard's memory. It's a fascinating situation. We will need to be understanding, and help him adjust. Shall we do that together? Let's make the resolution now: we're going to help Richard and . . . Rikki feel comfortable and secure. Is that a cool thing to do?'

'Yes, sir,' said the children.

'I do agree – absolutely,' said the headmaster, stepping forward. 'That's a first-rate idea, and I tell you now: this is going to be a test for all of us. A test to see how open and adaptable our community can be, and how we can all work with one another. Are we going to make sure Richard and Rikki are happy?'

'Yes, Mr Prowse.'

'Then let's say it with conviction. Will this boy be made welcome tomorrow?'

'Yes, Mr Prowse!' chorused the children.

'Very well. Good. Excellent. We will turn to page seventy-two and all sing together: "One More Step". And we have the usual end-of-assembly treat: Aparna, here, is going to play the piano. As you know, Aparna achieved grade two just last week, so we're very lucky to have such a talented young pianist playing for us. Aparna, take the stage! A round of applause, please . . .'

Aparna was a slim, nervous girl of eleven. She made her way to the piano-stool, cringing with embarrassment as the children clapped. The words of the hymn appeared on the screen, and everyone sang with gusto. Her hands danced over the keys, hammering out the chorus as the school gazed at the faces of Richard and Rikki, staring from under the text.

One was thinner, with back-combed hair and eyes that seemed harder than ever. The other was the face the children remembered, and he looked very slightly mournful.

The heads stared at their audience, as if they were listening to the music but unable to sing.

CHAPTER FOUR

The next morning, Richard's mother laid out her son's school uniform.

It was a simple set of clothes: grey trousers, a blue jersey and a blue shirt. There were two blue-striped ties. The shirt and jersey now sported two collars, and two V-necks.

'I can't wear that,' said the second head.

'Look,' said Richard patiently. 'We have to go to school. We tried it on yesterday, and—'

'I don't remember what we did yesterday.'

'Of course you do.'

'I'm adapting, all right? And this is the wrong style, totally.'

'It's the uniform, Rikki. It's what we have to wear.'

'It's baby stuff.' He peered at the jersey, with its golden trim. 'It's infantile, pseudo-military, identity-sapping baby stuff – you're letting them infantilize us. It's for kids.'

'I am a kid,' said Richard.

'I'm not,' said Rikki.

'It's what everyone wears, dear,' said Mrs Westlake gently.

'I know it's what everyone wears,' snapped the second head. 'I am not retarded. But if you think we're dressing up like a moron, you are mistaken. This is what I've been trying to get through to you people for the last month: we've moved on now and we're no longer morons—'

'You're going to have to mind your language,' said Mrs Westlake.

'Why?'

'You can't use words like that.'

'We're still at school,' said Richard. 'It's what we do – it's what everyone does, and it's what everyone wears.'

'That's always been the problem,' said Rikki. 'I've noticed it since day one – you don't have any fight in you, Richard! You wear clothes nobody normal would be seen dead in – colours that only a little girl would choose. You have a haircut like a vegetable and everything you say is a way of avoiding conflict.'

Mrs Westlake tried to interrupt, but the second head only raised his voice.

'Do I talk over you?' he cried.

He was the same size as Richard now, and though he had a similar hairstyle he made Richard comb it into a little crest. He had a slightly darker complexion too, and his skin seemed tighter. While Richard tended to relax and smile, the second head's mouth fell naturally into a frown. His eyes had a hunted look, as if he never got quite enough sleep.

'Do I?' he said, staring at his mother.

'Rikki, you have to mind your manners.'

'I keep a pretty civil tongue in my head, so how is it that whatever I say seems to get shot down before I even finish saying it?'

'You have to *listen*, Rikki,' said Mrs Westlake – who was always confused by the aggression of the second head. 'Richard's right: there's no choice in the matter, if you want to go to school.'

'Ah, Richard's right,' said Rikki. 'Richard's right again.'

'But he is, dear!'

'He always *is* right, isn't he? Richard never does a *bad thing* – how does that make me feel? And, oh – look! Hey, the debate's over, is it?' Richard was pulling on the shirt. 'So there's no discussion in this house? Let's just ride roughshod over the unwanted guest. I tell you something, there *needs* to be debate. Things are different now.'

'You think I don't know that?' said Richard. 'You think I'm under any kind of false impression about that?'

'You can't dictate to me!'

'I'm going to school. So are you.'

'You're going to have to learn negotiation. You've had it easy for eleven years, boy – and I never asked to be born, OK?'

'I'm being practical,' said Richard bluntly. 'I want to see my friends—'

'Friends?'

'Yes! And I don't want to stay stupid all my life, and these are the clothes we wear for school.'

'We look like a sucker.'

'I don't care. Life sucks, and I'm a sucker.'

Richard finished dressing in silence and stepped out of his room. He walked along the landing and up three steps. Then he turned left and took a deep breath. A door stood open, and through it – on the far wall – was a mirror, larger than his own. He had checked his appearance there every morning for years; now it was so different.

He'd stood there, centring his tie. He'd smoothed his hair, hearing the voice of the old man whose room he was looking sideways into. A bedsitting room, complete with kitchenette and bathroom. A long window that poured morning light in oblongs over the carpet, where Richard would stand, knowing his grandad was up and about, dressed and ready for the day.

It was an office now, for his dad, but the mirror remained.

'I am not a parasite,' said Rikki quietly.

Richard's jaw was clamped shut, and he could feel the same tension in Rikki. He could feel his heart beating, fast and furious.

'I know it,' he said, at last. 'You're me.'

'I am.'

'That's good.'

There was a stink of newness. The office had a new blue carpet, and the old smells of pipe tobacco were covered by the scent of shelves, straight from the showroom.

The walls gleamed white and bright, and there was a large, blond desk between two filing cabinets. There was a black leather chair and brightly coloured files. Only the old man's mirror had stayed, and Richard stared into it.

He adjusted his tie again. Rikki had his eyes closed.

A year ago his grandfather would have spoken from the corner: 'You'll do – stop looking at yourself.'

'I'm checking.'

'You'll crack the glass in a minute. You know what you look like!'

Richard would have turned and smiled and said, 'Are you meeting me?'

'If I can. Is that all right?'

'Right as rain.' The same words, every time.

'Rain's not right. I've told you that.'

'It's football till four.'

Smaller. His grandfather had lost weight, and his clothes were big on him now. His backbone was curved, and he put his head on one side, gazing out of bright eyes.

'See you at four, then. Get yourself gone – on the double!'

'See you . . .'

That was the ritual, every morning. That was the script they'd written between them, and the pips would sound on the old man's radio, which meant it was time to meet Jeff, who'd soon be at the garden gate.

'See you! Have a good day.'

Rikki said: 'Say it aloud, buddy.' The voice was soft in Richard's ear.

'No.'

'You want *me* to?'

'You're me,' said Richard. 'We don't have to argue.'

'I am not a parasite. You're me, as much as me – and I'm you. We're still part of this smashed-up family, boy, standing here in a room that used to be his. This was his house, you know. He owned it.'

'I'm going to put your tie on, Rikki. Is that all right?'

'Yes.'

'I can do that?'

'Make me look like you, brother. Make me happy.'

Half past three, or four o'clock. Every afternoon, his grandad would be waiting, and they'd walk home together. When had he stopped holding the old man's hand? When Jeff was around? Though he did hold it to cross the main road, because his grandad was slow and Richard had to help him.

'I'm on the edge too,' said Rikki. 'I've got tear ducts, you know – same as you. Don't ever forget that.'

Richard tied the second tie with trembling hands, and smoothed down his hair. The doorbell rang and he closed his eyes.

'Oh God,' he said. All four eyes were full of tears, and he had to rub them away hard with his thumbs. The ghost of his grandad flickered behind him, and Richard swung round to see his mother. 'That'll be Jeff!' he said. 'We're late already . . .'

'Be brave,' said his mother. 'Both of you.' She kissed the two heads, and hugged them hard. 'You look wonderful, do you understand that? You're a terrific boy, and you're going to have a good day, and see all your friends again. Everything's going to be fine.'

'I know.'

'I love you. So does your dad.'

CHAPTER FIVE

Jeff was standing on the doormat, eating an apple. He glanced at the two heads as if he'd known them for years, and smiled.

'Hi,' he said.

'Jeff, this is Rikki. Rikki: this is, er . . . Jeff.'

Jeff looked at Rikki again, and his smile got wider. 'Nice to meet you,' he said. 'I've been really looking forward to it.'

Rikki blushed. 'Hi,' he said quietly.

The boys stared at each other, and wondered what to say next. Richard turned back and waved to his mother, then pulled the front door shut.

Jeff laughed as they started off. 'You know, this is a hell of a relief,' he said. 'We're one down, so we really needed you back – we've got major games coming up.' He looked at his friend. 'You are playing, still?'

'Yes, of course. We're dying to play, aren't we, Rikki?'

'You bet.'

'You can, er . . . you can run like you used to?' said Jeff. 'No problems with balance or anything?'

'No problems with the running. We've been having kick-abouts with Dad, and if anything I'm faster now. Rikki's a good shot.'

'We're training hard. There's a cup match coming up against Morden Manor, so you'd better bring your kit every day. What happens when you, er . . . head the ball?'

'How do you mean?'

'Do you go for it with the same head? Do you kind of . . . clash in the air? – you don't mind me asking, do you?'

'No,' said Rikki. 'We . . . get along. We kind of just know who can get to the ball. Richard's a bit more timid than me.'

'Rikki's brave, I'll tell you,' said Richard. 'He's got the better reflexes.'

They crossed the street, and joined another clump of children. Nobody stared. It was a friendly neighbourhood and everyone had heard about the transformation. Clearly, there was an unwritten rule that everyone would behave as if there was nothing out of the ordinary: this Tuesday was the same as any other.

Richard began to relax.

Jeff kept the conversation going, and they were soon joined by two more of their old classmates: Eric and Mark.

'Hey!' said Mark. 'Good to see you!' He was a tall, thin boy in ill-fitting clothes. He had a slightly nervous, breathless voice and his eyes bulged. 'You OK, though, huh? You back for good?'

'I hope so,' said Richard.

'This is Rikki, then, huh? How you doing, Rikki? OK, are you?'

'All right, Rikki?' said Eric.

'I'm fine.'

'I'm Eric. You got the card OK? You see what I drew?'

'Yes.'

Eric trotted backwards, grinning. He looked from one head to the other, and Rikki nodded to him.

'What's that on your arms?' said Rikki.

'Tattoos.'

'Real ones?'

Eric shook his head. 'Transfers. I'm going to get one, though – a real one. Soon as I can. Soon as I leave this dump. In fact' – he rolled his shirt-sleeves down, to conceal the patterns on his skin – 'I get pestered if I even show these ones and they're only, you know . . . kids' stuff.'

'They're cool,' said Rikki. 'I think Richard needs one, right on his nose.'

Everyone laughed, and Jeff said, 'Eric's in trouble, all the time. Nothing's changed! So don't do what he does, Rikki.'

'They pick on me,' said Eric. 'They're trying to get rid of me – harder than ever!'

'He asks for it, though,' panted Mark. 'He's a rebel.'

Eric's smile got wider. 'You seeing Doc Warren?' he said.

'The counsellor?' said Richard. 'How do you know him?'

'I've been seeing him a year. He does my medication.'

'Medication for what?' said Rikki.

'They're calming me down. He was at the school yesterday, that doctor – telling us all about you, and what we should do.'

Richard laughed. 'He's a bit of a nuisance, to be honest—'

'And dead sneaky,' said Eric. 'You be careful what you say, 'cos he's always laying traps. I see him once a week and it's questions, questions – "How do you feel about this? Why d'you say that?" – on and on. I just lie my head off now, and boy . . . he gets excited.'

'What's he after?' said Rikki.

'Signs of madness, I guess,' said Eric. 'You been to the Rechner place yet? It's full of weirdos.'

'We're going next week,' said Richard.

'Don't trust him.'

'Are you smart, Rikki?' said Mark. 'Can you do maths and stuff, or what?'

'Rikki's pretty sharp,' said Richard.

'You'll be on the top table, then,' said Jeff. 'We do equations now, all the time. They're impossible.'

Eric laughed. 'I don't bother. I just colour stuff in, with Bra-low.'

'Bra-low?' said Rikki, as everyone laughed.

'You remember Mr Bra-low,' said Mark. 'He's our teacher. You have gaps, or what?'

'There's some things I remember,' said Rikki. 'Some stuff I really know about. But day-to-day stuff—'

'We'll keep you straight,' said Jeff. 'Bra-low's real name is Barlow, OK? But we call him "Bra-low" and he doesn't even notice. Oh, and by the way, here's another thing – you guys got re-elected for that *Kidspeak* thing! There's some big meeting coming up, and you're with Aparna again.'

'*Kidspeak*?' said Rikki. 'That rings a bell too.'

Richard sighed: 'I told you about this—'

'You didn't.'

'I did, but it's so boring you repressed it. We have to make speeches about what's important to us. It's a whole-school thing, and people talk about the environment or a hobby.'

'Which sounds OK,' said Eric. 'Till you realize it's crap.'

'So why do we do it?' said Rikki.

'It goes on your school record,' said Jeff. 'It helps towards the scholarship, but it's a way of brainwashing us. That's what my dad says, anyway. You end up saying what you're told to say—'

'But Richard was good,' said Eric, grinning again. 'He took all those questions at the end, with Aparna.'

'I hated it!' said Richard.

'You're one of the best, though,' said Jeff.

Mark fell into step beside Rikki. 'So what do you like doing?' he said. His eyes still bulged in wonder. 'You got hobbies and stuff?'

'Not yet. I'm hoping to get some.'

'You into planes – like Richard?'

'I can live without them.'

'Yeah?'

They had come to the school gates, and there were

lines of children pouring through. Clumps of parents stood waving, studiously ignoring the newcomers.

'It's just how I remember it,' said Richard quietly. 'Wow. I am so pleased to be back.'

'You're sitting next to me,' said Jeff softly.

'Great.'

'We didn't let anyone even move your chair. Every time someone tried we said, "That's Richard's seat. Leave it."'

'Rikki's too, now,' said Eric. 'We've been waiting for both of you.'

'How are you guys going to do it, though?' said Mark. 'Are you going to need two books, two pens, two . . . snacks?'

There was a short silence, and Rikki looked at Richard. 'You explain,' he said.

'It's hard to understand,' said Richard. 'We're actually the same person. We do stuff the same as we always did, but we kind of do it together.'

'Right.'

'What if you don't agree?' said Eric. 'I mean, in a test. If the question says, "Where's the River Nile?" – and if you think it's Brazil but Rikki says America, what do you do?'

'I suppose we argue,' said Richard.

'But what if there's a sleepover and Rikki wants to go but you don't, Richard? What happens then?'

Rikki said, 'Like he says: we argue. We thrash it around, and lay our cards on the table. Then I smack him one.'

Everyone laughed.

'Richard usually comes around to my way of looking

at things. We are civilized, you know – I'm not out of the jungle. Who's the weirdo, waving?'

'Oh, wow,' said Eric. 'That's the guy we were telling you about – our teacher. That's Mr Bra.' He laughed. 'Get ready for the spittle-show.'

'I *do* remember,' said Rikki quietly.

'He's nice,' said Richard.

'You think so?'

'Sure.'

'I think he's a cretin. Look at him.'

CHAPTER SIX

A tall, friendly-looking teacher had emerged from the school's main door, and was moving briskly towards the boys with his arm upraised. He wore a brown jacket, and though he had bushy hair over either ear, the top of his head shone pink and bald. He was smiling broadly, and calling: 'Richard Westlake! . . . Richard?'

Everyone was watching now, for the man seemed both anxious and excited. He dodged his way up the crowded path until he stood before the new arrivals.

He spoke quietly then. 'What a p-pleasure it is . . . to have you back.'

He put out his hand, and Richard and Rikki shook it. He had a curious, honking voice that seemed to come from his nose as much as his mouth. He also had the unfortunate habit of spitting, especially when he stuttered. He had weak eyes, and he dabbed his mouth with a handkerchief.

'You have been away too long,' he said. 'We n-n-need you. Both of you. You're Rikki, I . . .' He swallowed. 'I presume?' He leaned back and smiled again. 'If you're feeling n-nervous, my boy, just try to relax. These chaps will look after you – and if they don't, I – I will.'

He laughed apprehensively and wiped his mouth again. Mark and Eric had taken their own handkerchiefs out, and were wiping their faces. It was clearly a running joke, but Mr Barlow appeared not to notice.

'T-two minutes to the b-bell, so let's go in. Has Jeff told you about the football? I hope so. Come on, all of you – we've got a little sur-surprise for you. And you can t-tuck your shirt in now, Eric – school's starting.' He put his hand on Eric's shoulder. 'We run a tight ship here, or try to. Bit of a b-bore, but there you have it. Keeps everyone's minds off the important things – t-tie as well, please, Eric. Sort it out . . .'

Mr Barlow led the boys into the school and along the corridor. It wasn't long before they were in the classroom Richard remembered so well, and as he stepped inside, his classmates started clapping. A banner was unfurled: 'Welcome Back Richard and Rikki!' it said, and there were whistles and cheers from all around the room. A huge cake appeared on a tray, and a trolley of little snacks and drinks was wheeled through the bright furniture.

Richard turned red, and when he glanced at Rikki he saw that he too was pink and grinning, gazing around at a room bulging with artwork. Children came forward and introductions were made. The food was distributed as the chattering rose to shouting and laughter. Soon the carpet was covered in crumbs, and Mr Barlow called upon different children to explain the different things they'd been learning. When it came to clean-up he had to shout to make himself heard.

It had been the perfect start: the ice was broken, and the class was ready to work.

'Some s-start!' said Rikki, as everyone took their seats.

'What do you mean?'

'Hell of a p-party, huh? We're f-f-famous.'

'Shall we sit down?' They were standing at their locker. Richard swung the door open, and reached inside for his books.

'Oh my,' said Rikki, stopping him. 'What's all this about?'

'Our stuff. What's wrong?'

'You run a "t-tight ship" yourself. We did the decorations, did we?'

'Yes.'

'We should be proud. My word, what a little treasure-house . . .'

The lockers stood against the back wall, and the children were encouraged to keep them tidy, private and personal. Most of the class stuck favourite pictures around the inside walls. Some used them for toys and valuables as well as books, for they were secured by individual padlocks. Richard's was next to Jeff's, and they'd decorated them together. Jeff loved cars, but Richard had covered his with fighter-jets – the jets he'd loved since he'd first heard about them, and felt the engines throbbing through his dreams. He'd suspended his favourite from a nylon thread, and it was both diving and turning.

He'd made it with his grandad, of course, and their fingers had pressed the pieces together, then painted them carefully – pale green for the fuselage, and deep blue for the nose cone. The little pilots were protected under a clear canopy. They wore green, with brown webbing, and the tiny crash helmets were picked out in red. You could make out the eyes over the breathing apparatus, and they hung there – frozen – diving out of the sun.

Richard picked the model up with trembling fingers, feeling Rikki's breath on his cheek. It had been dusted, for Jeff and Aparna had a spare key. The de Havilland Sea Venom, with a top speed of five hundred knots, folding wings and a tail-hook. Pinned behind it was the most precious thing of all.

'Remember that?' said Richard.

'Oh my,' said Rikki.

It was a regimental badge. Two wings were embroidered in gentle blues, a fine silver thread picking out the detail. They had once adorned his grandfather's regimental jacket, and Richard had received them at the age of ten, as a special birthday gift. When he stared at them now, the tears came back to his eyes, and he heard engines howl.

His parents didn't know he'd brought them to school, and they would have been furious – they were irreplaceable and old and too, too special. He felt the weave between finger and thumb, then gripped them in his fist. They had been earned by a pilot who had once flown high above the world, and had, in later years, waited at the gate – it was just one of his trophies for courage and skill, and Richard had seen them in the old photos, too, stitched on the old man's tunic. He'd put the photos close to his nose and gaze . . .

'There! There, Danda! – just there.'

'Right again.'

'There!'

'And you can't fly without them,' his grandad had said. Then he'd handed them over.

Richard had fought for the words, and found only two: 'Thank you.' They were inadequate for such treasure.

'Look after them.'

'I will.'

Rikki laughed, and Richard was jolted to earth. Most children were in their seats, organizing books and papers.

'What's so funny?'

'*Danda.* What kind of word is that?'

'It's what we called him.'

'Did we? Baby days, boy. I'd forgotten all about it.'

The two-year-old Richard had found 'gr' such a difficult sound, so '*Danda*' had stuck. Now it seemed sloppy and foolish, and Richard blushed at the memory. He closed the locker door.

'Hey,' said Rikki. 'Doctor Warren's seen us. He was looking through the window, just a second ago – staring.'

'So what?'

'He saw what we were doing. He can't keep away.'

Richard looked towards the classroom door, but there was no sign of anyone. 'What's it matter?'

'He saw your eyes, I bet. We don't give him anything, all right, Richard?'

'I don't understand you. I don't know—'

'We don't give out secrets, that's what I'm saying.'

'We don't have any.'

'Don't we, Danda?'

'Shut up. No.'

Rikki looked at him. 'So, what do you want to do now? Is it time for more fun?'

'It's English. We sit down, I guess. Mr Barlow's waiting.'

'Story time, is it?'

'Yes.'

'I can feel it coming back. Shall we write a little story, Ritchie – like the other boys and girls?'

'Yes.'

'Just a normal one, huh? Not sad, or sick, or lost. Just nice. Normal. And if Doc Warren reads it, he'll get nothing—'

'Rikki . . . you've got to relax.'

'I'm about to.'

They took out their pencil case, and their English book, and went back to their table. Richard slipped the wings into his pocket, and saw that Jeff was staring at him.

'You OK?'

'Fine,' said Richard. 'I was explaining things to Rikki.'

'I don't understand anything,' said Rikki brightly. 'This is all so wonderful and new, and I feel so lucky to be here. When's the finger-painting? Oh, and there's Aparna! Hey, guys! I've missed her more than anyone.'

★

Tuesday mornings always involved a complicated writing exercise. The whole class was getting ready for exams, so everyone needed the practice. Before long, there was silence in the classroom, and every child was concentrating on the sheets Mr Barlow had prepared. Mr Barlow was a good enough teacher to know that the rest of the morning should be tightly controlled. He wanted a totally normal day, so that Rikki could relax into a firm but gentle discipline. When he glanced up at the boy, he saw that both Richard and Rikki were working hard, with their tongues protruding slightly through their teeth. Aparna was opposite, and Mark to the left. Jeff was close, on the right, and Salome had her back to them, sitting next to Eric. He let his eyes rest on child after child: Laura, Eleanor, Kasia, Sophie, Charles . . . twenty-seven children, working in silence.

He saw Dr Warren pause in the doorway again, with the headmaster.

Half an hour later, there was a gentle hum of friendly conversation. He noticed Rikki consult his neighbour, and Richard borrowed a pencil sharpener. When they got to the part of the exercise that involved illustration, and colours, everyone shared pens happily. The sun had come out and was pouring in through high windows.

Five minutes before break time Mr Barlow was working one-to-one with Eric. A loud voice called over the general chatter.

'Excuse me? C-can I be excused, please?'

Eric grinned. It was Rikki.

Mr Barlow looked up to find that the boy was staring

right at him. Richard looked slightly surprised, and Jeff looked anxious.

'Um, yes, Rikki – of course,' said Mr Barlow. 'It's actually n-normal to put your hand up. Then I'll ask you what you want.'

'Put my hand up what?'

'Up,' said Richard. 'Like this.' He raised his hand.

'Oh, I see,' said Rikki. 'Oh right, that's a kind of signal to attract attention, is it? I get it. What happens if the t-teacher doesn't see?'

'I think I usually do see,' said Mr Barlow. 'I t-try to keep my eyes peeled.'

'Yeah?'

'How can I help?'

'Can I use the bathroom, please?'

'Yes, of course.'

'So I didn't need to ask?'

'It's usual to ask.'

'Ah.'

Richard and Rikki got noisily to their feet.

'Though, actually,' said Mr Barlow, 'it's only about five minutes to break. Are you sh-sure you—'

'I really need to go,' said Rikki. 'I don't want to embarrass myself on my first day, so that's why I asked. If I stay in here I might flood the place. That's what I want to avoid.'

'Of course. Off you go, then – no problem.'

The class watched as Richard and Rikki made for the door.

★

'You don't have to be rude to him,' said Richard, as they stood at the urinal.

'How was I rude, Ritchie?'

'You know how. And don't call me Ritchie—'

'That guy's an idiot – how come you don't see that? Is he in league with Warren?'

'I doubt it.'

'He treats us like we're six. *Bra-low?* Who made that up?'

'I don't know, and it's not particularly funny.'

'Why is it some teachers are so dumb? He doesn't even notice it.'

'I know he's a bit . . . strange. But he's really nice. He runs the end-of-term residential trip—'

'Which is what?'

'The residential? We all go off on a kind of holiday. The whole class, at the end of term.'

'I'm not really a social person, Richard.'

'It's the last thing we do. It's what everyone looks forward to, and it's a way of saying goodbye.'

Rikki laughed. 'I'll say that now, if you want. How can you say Bralow's nice? He's gobbing on your face the whole time.'

Richard bit his lip. 'He doesn't gob,' he said quietly. 'The guys make a big thing of it, but it's not as bad as that. He had a stroke about two years ago, and he's got a muscle problem.'

'He should have retired. He's a health hazard – and he

doesn't get my sympathy just because he's ill. Weak people get no sympathy because they're weak. And who's the fat kid, by the way? Did you see her putting away that cake? *Our* cake.'

'How was that our cake? The class made it.'

'Bra-low made it, to give it to *us*. That's what kills me! You give someone a gift and then hand it round like it's yours. Eleanor, that's her name, isn't it? She needs exercise. You'd think her parents would do something.'

'Bodies change, Rikki. What's the problem?'

'People should stay fit. She's fat because she's lazy, and it's people like us that pick up the bills. She's obscene.'

Richard decided to change the subject. He stepped down from the urinal. 'What do you think of Eric and Mark? I'd forgotten how much fun they can be.'

'Yeah, I don't know about those two yet. The jury's out.'

'I don't understand.'

'Jury's out, Richard. It's the terminology of a law court, meaning "I am reserving judgement". Mark's a bore.'

'He's not.'

'Eric's cool – I like him. Mark's just plain ratty, isn't he? What's wrong with his hair?'

'Nothing's wrong with his hair, Rikki. Honestly, you're so critical—'

'You think his mother does it?'

'Does what?'

'Gives him a haircut?'

'I don't know. Probably – our mother cuts my hair, so it's very likely.'

'That's gonna stop. She's not coming near me. She brings scissors near me there's going to be a bloodbath. We have to break out, Richard – you're so traditional! Eric's interesting. But Mark's got some kind of growth problem. Or it could just be a genetic condition: bad hair, bad genes. Bad genes, bad trousers – you see his trousers? You can see all his ankles. Why don't kids do something about what they look like? He talks through his nose, as well, and his eyes . . .'

'He had an operation on his eyes.'

'They look like they're going to burst out of his head.'

'And what do we look like?'

'Huh? Normal.'

'You're sure about that?'

'I'm normal.'

'I'm not.'

'You will be.'

'Look,' said Richard. 'I like school, and I like my friends. I'm not going to be put off anyone by you. Let's just get back to class, and I'm not going to ask you what you think about Jeff . . .'

'Why go back? You heard what the Bra-man said. It's b-b-break time.'

'Yes, but the bell hasn't rung.'

Rikki snorted. 'Come on, Richard. Live dangerously, can't you? Where did you put the snacks? We need a sugar buzz, and then I want to see more weirdos.'

'The snacks are back in the classroom. That's why we've got to go back.'

'OK, Richard – I'm following orders, wing commander. Permission for takeoff!'

'Shut up.'

'Permission for landing, sir! What's the altitude?'

'Shut up, Rikki!'

'I'm joking, all right? And I am following you, again . . .'

CHAPTER SEVEN

They emerged from the toilets to find that the younger children from Years Three and Four were already in the corridor.

'You said the bell hadn't gone,' said Rikki. 'What's with all the riff-raff?'

'They let the younger children out two minutes early. Just to avoid a big rush.'

'I knew that. Wow.'

'Hi, Richard!' said a little girl.

'Hi, Maisie.'

'Little kids,' said Rikki. 'Don't you hate them?'

'No, I don't.'

'Hey, Richard!' said a boy, running past.

'They're all looking at us,' said Rikki. 'With their sneaky-freaky eyes.'

The children were making their way towards the playground, passing Rikki on both sides. Many of them looked up, fascinated. Many of them smiled and waved, because they knew Richard from his bus-supervision duties.

'They're thinking how weird you look,' said Rikki. 'Stop staring at us!'

'Just smile,' said Richard. 'They're bound to look. Hi, Mitch!'

'Hi, Richard – you OK?'

'Hi, Shoko! – be nice, Rikki. Relax.'

'You think they're looking at me? I think they're looking at that mummy's-boy haircut of yours. What's wrong with that one? – now, look at that! – he is *sinister.*'

'That's Salome's brother. Hi, Rolo!'

'Salome. Sure . . .'

Richard smiled. 'He's a nice boy. We help him.'

'Hey!' shouted Rikki. 'What's with the cap?'

'Leave it,' hissed Richard. 'You know Rolo! He's really friendly.'

'Oi!' shouted Rikki, more loudly. 'What are you looking at, pixie-boy? What's the issue?'

'Pardon?' said Rolo quietly. He had reached the door, but he turned and gazed with solemn eyes, surprised by Rikki's aggression. The child was small for his age, and he stood still, with one hand on the door handle. Other children pushed past, and scattered in the playground.

'You look lost,' said Rikki. 'You handicapped?'

'It's playtime,' said Rolo. 'I'm going out to play – hi, Richard.'

'Good to see you, Rolo,' said Richard. 'You OK?'

'I'm OK. I can't remember the name of your . . . I can't remember your name.'

'My name's Rikki. What's yours?'

'Richard just told you. Rolo. My sister's in your class.'

'What's with the hat, Rolo? You a goblin?'

'Rikki . . .'

'Shut up,' hissed Rikki. He turned back to the child, who stood blinking and puzzled. 'Nobody else is wearing a hat, Rolo – I'm just curious. You look like a gnome.'

'I get ear-ache,' said Rolo. 'I get this real pain in my ears.'

'You get finger-ache too?' Rikki had noticed that the boy was wearing gloves. Again, he was the only one. A crowd was now building up around the doors, listening to the conversation.

'Yeah,' said Rolo. 'It's a pain, but I have to keep warm. No cap, no play. No gloves – no play.'

'Why?'

'I don't know. I have to keep warm.'

'You a retard, Rolo?'

'Rikki!' said Richard. 'You better shut up, now. I'm warning you.'

'Retard?' said Rolo. 'I'm not a retard. I get cold easy – that doesn't mean anything. How'd you like it if I called you a retard?'

'But I'm not a retard, so it wouldn't bother me. How old are you anyway, cap-head?'

'Seven. And I'm not a cap-head.'

Rikki smiled. 'Bet you don't make eight,' he said. 'I remember you now, and I think you're dying.'

Those listening gasped, and the bell rang loudly above their heads.

Richard got Rikki away to their classroom, where they picked up their snack, and soon they were with Eric, Mark, Jeff and others, setting up for football. Five minutes later – just as the game had got going – Richard saw Rolo's sister, Salome, heading straight towards him. She was a powerful girl, and though Richard thought of her as a friend, she was not looking friendly.

He decided to move.

'What are we doing?' said Rikki.

'I think we'd better get inside,' said Richard.

'Why?'

'You know why.'

Richard trotted behind the old drama studio, and in through the nearest door. Ignoring Rikki's protests, he made for the library. It was pointless hiding from Salome, but if he could get somewhere close to a teacher, there might be a peaceful outcome.

Unfortunately, there were no teachers in sight.

He moved on, towards the cafeteria, where there was normally someone on duty. There were just a handful of juniors eating their snacks. Salome had come the other way, and emerged in front of him, cutting off the exit.

'Richard,' she said. 'Can I see you a moment?'

A small group had followed her. Jeff, Mark and Eric were all there, as were two of Salome's best friends – two girls called Lydia and Carla. Between them stood Rolo. Including the snack-eaters, it was quite an audience.

'Hi, Salome,' said Richard.

She looked furious, and Richard felt a curious lightness. It was that feeling of knowing exactly what was coming, and not being able to do anything about it. Salome was not just powerful, she was tough. She was well known for her fearsome temper, and she jumped to conclusions fast. Richard could not remember a time when he'd seen her this angry, though – and certainly not with him. She was so furious that her nostrils were twitching. Her brother, Rolo, had been pushed forward and was next to her. Her arm was round his shoulders, pulling him close.

'That's the one,' said Rolo. 'I didn't say nothing.'

'What did you call my brother?' said Salome quietly. She was looking directly at Rikki.

'I don't remember.'

'You call him "retard"?'

'No.'

'Yes he did. He called me "cap-head" too. Said I was going to die.'

'Salome,' said Jeff. 'It's his first day.'

'Stay out of it.' She looked back at Rikki. 'How long have you been at this school, that you think you can insult people?'

'He didn't mean anything,' said Richard. 'He's not used to things yet.'

Salome put a finger close to Richard's nose. 'You stay out of it too. This is between me and him.' Her voice was trembling. 'What do they call you? Rikki? This is your first day, isn't it? Like Jeff said.'

'Yes, this is my first day – I think you probably know that, being as you haven't seen me around before.'

'You call my brother a retard on your first day? You think that's wise?'

'He gave me a mouthful. He called me a two-headed freak.'

'That's a lie,' said Rolo.

'Your brother's out of control,' said Rikki. 'He spat at me, too.'

'Look, I honestly think there was a misunderstanding,' said Richard. 'We like Rolo – everyone knows that.'

'Yeah,' said Rikki. 'I don't know what we're doing here arguing about a kid. I think we've got better things to do.'

'My brother gets sick, all right?' said Salome. She was taking shallow breaths. 'He's got a condition where he picks up germs and bugs really easily, so one of the ways we deal with that is to make him dress up warm.'

'I'm on medicine too,' said Rolo.

'It's a pain for all of us, but we have to do it. He got really sick last year, so now he has a rule: "No cap, no play." You understand that now?'

Rikki nodded. 'It seems very clear.'

'Good.'

There was a silence.

'I'm going to give you the benefit of the doubt,' said Salome at last. 'It's your first day, like you said. So I'm going to assume you were just mucking about and didn't remember stuff. But I tell you now, you ever say anything like that to my brother again – you ever mention dying

– I'll hurt you bad. I'll put you back in the hospital you just came out of.'

Rikki smiled brightly. 'OK. I get it.'

'You've got it?'

'For sure.'

'Fine.'

Salome allowed herself to be turned round by one of her friends. She had her back to Richard and Rikki, and the confrontation might have ended there had Rikki not said what he said.

He spoke loudly. 'So just to be clear . . . Let me check this: I'm not allowed to call your half-dead brother a retard, even though he's clearly ready for the graveyard, chasing a box and a headstone, on his way to Jesus?'

Salome simply turned again and punched Rikki with all her might, full in the face.

She hit him so hard that he was knocked flat to the floor. Richard lay on his back, wide awake, gazing at the ceiling. Rikki was out like a light.

He was lifted up, blood pouring from his nose. Teachers arrived. The headmaster was called, and Dr Warren was beside him in a moment. Within thirty minutes, Richard and Rikki were back in an ambulance.

They did not go to the hospital this time, however: the ambulance was private. It sped out of town, and zoomed off to the motorway. Two hours later it was spinning down a leafy lane, then pausing before electronic gates. The gates eased open and a team of orderlies was there to receive them. 'The Rechner Institute', said a plate on the wall.

'Neurological Research and Observation Centre'. Another sign said, 'Strictly Private – Authorized Personnel Only', and cameras gazed down from every angle.

Richard and Rikki were loaded onto a trolley and wheeled inside. Dr Warren moved briskly beside them.

CHAPTER EIGHT

A number of things happened, all with remarkable speed.

Salome was put into immediate isolation, then suspended for assaulting another pupil. Her mother came to collect her, and the two of them were gone by lunch time.

Rikki and Richard found themselves in a white room, where everyone whispered and even the footsteps were quiet. Half of Rikki's face was black from bruising, and there was mild concussion. His skull and brain had so recently formed that the doctors insisted on forty-eight hours of observation, and extensive tests. Dr Summersby was called in by satellite and updated.

Mr and Mrs Westlake remained at his bedside. Dr Warren sat in the corner, listening, writing and recording.

'What did you say to her?' asked Mr Westlake.

'Nothing,' said Rikki softly. There was a patch and bandage over one eye, and he was attached to a dozen electrodes.

'I find that hard to believe. I know what a mouth you've got, and I know how provocative you can be.'

‘She called me a two-headed monster. I told her I was going to tell – and that’s when she hit me.’

‘Is that true, Richard?’ said Mr Westlake.

Richard had his head on the pillow, and lay with closed eyes. ‘No, Dad.’

‘Oh, here we go!’ said Rikki.

‘Keep calm,’ said Dr Warren. ‘Tell us what happened – in your own words. Take your time, OK?’

‘And you’re all going to believe *him*,’ said Rikki. ‘Aren’t you? Richard’s the favourite! Richard can do no wrong—’

‘Hush!’ said Mr Westlake. ‘I want to hear what he’s got to say.’

Dr Warren leaned forward. ‘This is not unexpected,’ he whispered. ‘There’s bound to be an internal conflict: we have to accept that. He’s at a very delicate stage.’

‘I can hear you,’ said Rikki.

‘Let Richard speak,’ said his father. ‘I want to know the facts.’

‘OK,’ said Richard. ‘It was pretty straightforward. Rikki called Salome’s brother a half-dead retard – I don’t know why. She told him not to, so he did it again, and she punched him out. We got what we deserved.’

Mr Westlake closed his eyes.

‘Were there other people there, love?’ said Mrs Westlake.

‘Loads. He was really rude – he’s been rude all day, and I can’t stand it.’

‘I was having a joke,’ said Rikki.

'Then why was no one laughing?' said Richard. 'And what are you going to do next?'

'No one stuck up for me,' said Rikki. 'Those are the kinds of friends we've got! Don't you see that now? Well, I say school sucks. I'm never going back. I'm going to write to the papers about that place, and about that girl.'

'You know what I think?' said Mr Westlake. 'I think you've got an attitude problem, and you have to do something about it, fast.'

Mrs Westlake took her son's hand. 'What did Danda tell you?' she said.

'Grandad,' said Rikki. 'Call him by the right name!'

'I don't know,' said Richard.

'Nor do I,' said Rikki. 'What did he tell us?'

'Be honest. Be courteous.' Mrs Westlake let the words sink in. 'If you manage to be both—'

'Oh yes,' said Rikki. 'He said that just before he snuffed it.'

'Yes, love. But—'

'We burned him up, as I remember. He was a skinny old bore, anyway – said all kinds of crap. We're better off without him.'

Richard's eyes were closed, so he didn't see his father clench his fists. His mother was struck dumb – her mouth opened and closed, and no words emerged.

Dr Warren stared, his pen poised over his pad. 'Rikki,' he said.

'What?'

'You were close to him, I think?' he said.

'Not really,' said Rikki.

'You were with him, weren't you? When he died?'

'Who cares?'

'Can we talk about it?'

'I don't remember. I'm confused. And anyway, if Grandad was so important to everyone, how come you emptied his bedroom, Dad? How come we don't ever talk about him, when it was his house?'

'Rikki,' said his father. 'We talk about him a lot.'

'No, we don't.'

'I just mentioned him,' said his mother. 'We can talk about him whenever—'

'You've forgotten he even existed! And a good thing too.'

'He's not forgotten,' said Mr Westlake. 'You know he isn't.'

'It's his house, still.'

'It's our house. It's the family home, love,' said Mrs Westlake. 'And as for his room, I thought we'd agreed all that. Your father needed the space.'

'I needed an office, Rikki – you helped me decorate it, remember? Grandad's been gone for nearly a year, and we agreed to make changes.'

'You've got no right to be in there,' said Rikki. 'No right.'

Dr Warren leaned in, and put his hand on Richard's arm. 'Let's try to go slow, shall we?' he said.

'Don't touch me,' said Richard.

'Listen a moment,' said Mr Westlake quietly. 'Just listen a minute – shh! There are issues here, I can see that – but Doctor Warren *is* helping us, and he's keen to chat to you, properly – one to one. I think it's about time we did that. Then, when you're back at school, you're going to deal with the damage.'

'What damage?'

'You've caused a lot of upset, love,' said Mrs Westlake.

'And what about the psycho who hit me? You're on her side, I imagine?'

'Of course not,' said Mr Westlake. 'But if you insult people, you can expect to be battered. Is that hard to understand?'

'Oh, so she can just beat people up if she wants to? How is that "courteous", going back to the wisdom of . . . of . . .'

Mr Westlake paused, and felt his wife's hand on his. He looked at Richard, and then at Rikki. 'I'm not saying violence is right,' he said.

'Grandad knew how to fight.'

'Did he?'

'He was in the war. He wasn't flying around for fun, you know. What do you think he had bombs for?'

'I'm sure that's true. But he didn't like violence, and nor do I. You provoked someone, Rikki, and got just what you deserved. I hate to say it, because I don't ever want to see you hurt. But you can't say things like the things you say, and not expect consequences.'

★

'He hates me,' said Rikki, later that night.

The machines buzzed and bleeped, and the ward was in darkness.

'Nobody hates you,' said Richard. 'Yet.'

'You do.'

'No, I don't. But you're making life so difficult.'

'You should have stuck up for me. Dad asks you what I said, and you dobbed me straight in. Not exactly loyal, are you, Richard?'

'You want me to lie?'

'Yes. You should be on my side. We're the same person.'

'And when Dad asks Jeff or Mark – or Salome? Everyone heard what you said. And anyway' – Richard turned to stare at his second head – 'I am not going to lie for you, ever. What you said, and what you have been saying about people, was really horrible.'

'Oh, you are such a dweeb.'

'OK, I'm a dweeb. I've been a dweeb for eleven years—'

'You wait till you get out into the big wide world, boy. It's not about being the blasted bus-monitor. Plastic planes, Richard – you're the half-dead retard, don't you see that? And I'm going to get that cow – what was her name?'

'Salome. She's not a—'

'I don't forgive. Ever.'

'She'll wipe the floor with you. She'll wipe the floor with *us* – and she's got three older brothers. If they come looking for us, we will be seriously dead. You know what her dad does for a living?'

'No.'

'You do. He runs the boxing club, Rikki: that's where Salome learned to punch like that. He makes our dad look like a . . . mouse.'

'Our dad *is* a mouse.'

Richard sighed. 'You are horrible, aren't you? And what you said about . . . Grandad was . . . Why are you so sick?'

'What did I say?'

'About him being . . . burned. The way you said it!'

'We put him in a furnace, Richard. You were there.'

'He was cremated.'

'Same blasted, bloody thing, so get used to the truth. We burned him up and sent his stuff off to the Oxfam shop: he's gone. You see him in the mirror but he's not there, do you understand that? So we've got some growing up to do now, and Dad is a mouse compared to him – he will never protect us. All your life you've known it: dead-end Dad, and a coward as well, and Grandad was . . . a hero! Remember? And it takes me to bring it out into the open. I'm not a soft, watery, dweeby little pansy, hiding from life, brother. I won't do anything physical to that girl, sure – I'm not dumb enough to fight her with our fists. There are better ways. And I'll warn you now – so far, you think you call the shots because you have muscular control. That, friend, is going to change.'

Richard stared. 'What do you mean?'

Rikki lifted his right hand and took hold of Richard's nose. He pinched it gently, and then twisted it.

Richard winced.

'Did you do that?' said Rikki.

'No. I mean . . . yes.'

'You squeezed your own nose, did you?'

'Well . . . you did it and I . . . kind of . . . I suppose I let you.'

Rikki started to laugh. 'You think you have control. You think life is all gold stars from lovely Mr Bra-low. It's about to get complicated. Retard.'

'We have to see that counsellor tomorrow, because of you.'

'Bring it on. I can't wait to be counselled by that schmuck. "We're going to be friends." That's what he said to me! "Life will be *OK* . . ." '

'My God, Rikki . . .' Richard stared at the ceiling. 'Maybe it could be.'

'Never.'

Richard felt tears prick his eyes. 'You know something?' he said. 'The only time I've had peace lately was when you were unconscious.'

'What happens when *you* go unconscious? I tell you what, Richard . . . there are going to be times when I'm on my own, and when things are going to be the way *I* want them. Times when you feel a little bit sleepy, and I'm in charge. I hold the keys, buddy.'

'Why do you speak like you're from America?'

'I don't.'

'What do you want?'

'Nothing. Metamorphosis.'

Richard looked at Rikki again. 'You think about Grandad. All the time.'

'No I don't.'

'You do, Rikki. What do we do – please? Are we going to . . . burn the house down?'

'Why not?'

Richard closed his eyes, and the tears ran down his cheeks.

Rikki said, 'I will trash everything. Nothing's worth anything, Richard, and that's what we've got to learn – or we just won't survive. That's why I was born, my friend: to make you strong.' He looked hard at Richard's profile. 'So dry your eyes, you little queer. And grow up.'

PART TWO
TREATMENT

CHAPTER ONE

Dr Warren's office looked like a playroom.

It was on an upper floor, where thick carpets made the world silent. Even the doors whispered as they closed, and there weren't any windows.

The counsellor was waiting for them. He wore a pair of spectacles that were on a loop of blue cord, and he sported a bright bow tie. He had a habit of putting his head on one side, as if he wanted to see the world from an unusual angle.

'Rikki!' he cried. 'Come on in! Richard – make yourself at home. How about a glass of juice?' He went to a small fridge, and displayed its contents with a smile.

'Thanks,' said Richard.

'No,' said Rikki. 'We just had lunch.'

'One yes, one no. That's cool – I can cope with that.' He poured out a glass of orange juice and set it on a low circular table. He poured some mineral water for himself and sipped it. 'I can't take the hard stuff,' he joked. 'Not any more! Now, sit down. What do you think of my room? This is the first time you've visited me here.'

'It's very colourful,' said Richard.

'Are you recording us again?' said Rikki.

'Yes.'

'Why?'

'Because these exchanges will be of diagnostic importance. It goes without saying that the material is totally confidential.'

'Sure,' said Rikki. 'So, just for the record – for anyone watching – what exactly is this place?'

'It's a private hospital.'

'A nuthouse?'

'No, Rikki. No. We don't use those terms any more. This is a research institute, looking at behavioural science.'

'Why all the signs saying "no admittance"? Why all the locks?'

'There are some sensitive areas here.'

'Like what?'

Dr Warren smiled. 'We like to think of ourselves as being revolutionary. Truly original and truly experimental. First and foremost, though, we're about *care*—'

'And what are your credentials, sir?'

'Well . . .' said Dr Warren. His mouth continued to smile. 'You are a direct-and-to-the-point young man, and I like that. I like people who are up-front – and to answer your question, I was an SHO in neurology – psychiatry too. I completed an MD study out in Colorado, and I have a research fellowship, of course – which I obtained in Kent. As for the Rechner Institute: I've been senior man for seven happy years.'

'And your speciality?'

'The patterns of the brain. Crudely speaking, I look at how the two hemispheres connect and function.'

'Wow.'

'Intervention. Reconstruction – drug therapy and certain forms of realignment. If there's damage.'

'Is Eric damaged?' said Rikki.

'Who?' The doctor frowned.

'Eric Madamba,' Richard explained. 'A friend at school. He told us you were his shrink. So what are you doing to him?'

'That's confidential,' said Dr Warren. 'Eric's a good boy, so we just watch from a distance.'

'You were watching me,' said Rikki. 'Am I a good boy too?'

Dr Warren paused, and winked. 'You're one of the most interesting people I've met, Rikki. Like your father said, a chat's what we need, to clear the air. You could teach me a lot.'

'We've been tested about a million times, you know. I was hoping to spend the day reading, and now—'

'Really? What are you reading?'

'What am I reading?'

'Yes. Reading's important to you, is it?'

'I'm reading a book. It's called *How to Answer Time-wasting Questions in Case Some Beardy Weirdo Keeps Asking Them*. I'm only on the first page because some weirdo with a beard keeps asking me time-wasting questions. People think kids have nothing to do, but we've got a lot to do. So

Richard and I – me and Richard – we'd like you to get to the point, so we can move on back to bed.'

Dr Warren stroked his chin. 'How do you feel about that, Richard? Is Rikki speaking for you?'

Richard sighed. 'I'd like to know why we're here. Rikki's right: we've been tested a lot and we're getting a bit tired of it. And we're not comfortable in this place.'

'You don't get as cross as Rikki, I notice.'

'Rikki's rude. I try not to be.'

'Courtesy and honesty, eh? But there's something on your mind, isn't there? Richard, Rikki . . . I think there must be a whole . . . range of things you want to talk about. But before we start swimming in the deep, I want to play a little game with you. It's a game called "the squiggle test", and I bet you have never been squiggled.'

Rikki and Richard both looked at him. Dr Warren winked again, and stood up.

'Your silence convinces me of my correctness. The squiggle test is a very useful diagnostic tool, and I use it a lot. We're going to draw some squiggles.' He fetched some crayons and some sheets of white paper. 'We are going to squiggle away, and then we are going to compare what we've created. I use it as an ice-breaker, and you do not have to be Picasso. Though it may help.'

'Isn't that a scandalous waste of paper?' said Rikki.

'Ah, you're an environmentalist?'

'No. I hope the world ends soon.'

'I read a speech you gave last term. *Kidspeak*: I know you're worried about natural resources, and that's good—'

'Like I said,' said Rikki slowly, 'I'd like to see the world go up in flames. But I don't waste paper, Doctor Weird – I like to draw on the desk. And as I'm here to express myself, I hope you won't mind.' He took a large purple crayon from the tin, and before Richard could do anything, he started to scribble on the pale oak table top in huge arcs. Satisfied that the crayon was solid enough, he drew a large, cloud-like shape and crossed it out. He gave it eyes and made it rain. He put a sun behind it, and a plane zooming out of that, and then wrote the dirtiest word he could think of. 'How's that?' he said. 'Have I cleared any air?'

'It's . . . dramatic,' said Dr Warren quietly. He paused. 'I'm going to use the paper myself, and . . . um, here we go – my turn to squiggle.' He drew a shape that could have been an amoeba. 'What's that look like to you?' he said, holding it up.

'Dinner,' said Rikki.

'A lake,' said Richard.

'A man with a violin who's been run over while sitting on your face,' said Rikki.

'It could just be a puddle,' said Richard. 'Or an amoeba.'

'Do you ever get punched?' said Rikki. 'I got punched yesterday, and it really hurt. I think it did me good, though.'

Dr Warren took his glasses off and let them hang. 'It's been known to happen, Rikki. I do meet people with a lot of anger. Sometimes I have been a victim of that anger.' He put his head on one side. 'Who are you angry with?'

'You.'

'Why?'

'Because you're a liar.'

'You said that before. How am I a liar?'

'I know why you wear your specs on a string. It's in case they go flying off, isn't it? If I were to punch you, what would happen to me? Would it mean pass, fail or disqualify?'

Richard could feel his hands curling into fists. He put them under the table.

'It would mean you're deeply upset,' said Dr Warren. He smiled, and put his hands up in pretend defence. 'Don't punch me, Rikki! It wouldn't be cool. Now: you drew an aeroplane. Would I be right if I connected that—'

But Rikki and Richard were standing, and the table was on its side. The crayons had exploded from their box, and the drinks had simply disappeared.

'I'm sorry,' said Rikki hoarsely. 'I suddenly felt lots of anger just bursting up within me. I needed an outlet, and so I've done something rather violent. I guess it was an eruption just waiting to happen, and now I feel so much better.'

Dr Warren stepped back and folded his arms. 'What you're doing, Rikki, is closing down a challenging question. You've made a strong point, my friend. So calm down.'

'I'm calm.'

'How do you feel about this, Richard?'

Richard shrugged. 'I can see where Rikki's coming

from, because this is all a bit boring. I wouldn't do what he just did – I mean, what *I* just did. Because we are the same person. But on the other hand, if you treat us like a little kid—'

He was interrupted by a furious cry, and before he knew it he found he was bent double, charging forward with both arms outstretched. His heads came together and caught Dr Warren full in the stomach.

The man staggered back into a large fish tank, and a potted plant smashed to the floor. Rikki turned, and lurched around the room doing his best imitation of an angry gorilla. He picked up a crayon in each hand, and Richard found that he was writing on the wallpaper. How Rikki knew such filthy words, Richard didn't know. He was writing in huge, curling letters, shouting the words at the top of his voice. Dr Warren had tripped over a beanbag. He struggled to his feet, calling out – but Rikki took no notice. He had turned and snatched a photograph from the desk.

'Who's this?' he shouted.

'Rikki. Richard. I must ask you to put that down.'

The door opened, and two nurses appeared, anxious and breathless. An alarm was sounding, outside.

'Doctor Warren!' said one. 'Are you all right?'

The counsellor held up his hand. 'We can talk about this, Rikki. Richard: you're over-reacting to a stimulus that you have found invasive and threatening. My authority has been challenged, and that's fine, but now, Rikki—'

'Who's the lady in the photo?'

'The lady is my wife, Rikki. Richard: I'd like you to put it down, and *calm* down.'

'Why?'

'Because it's made of glass and metal. You could hurt yourself.'

'Who's the kid in the pushchair, Counsellor?'

'That's Nathaniel, my son. We were taking him through the park—'

'Normal, is he?' said Rikki. 'Normal kid? Happy smiling face, huh? He's not gonna stay that way. Listen, Nathaniel . . .'

Rikki brought the photo-frame hard down on the back of a chair, and the glass exploded. He took the photograph out and ripped it quickly, tearing round the figure of the child so it was free of its parents – who fluttered to the carpet. Rikki held the smiling child up in a trembling hand. He grinned at Dr Warren and whispered: 'Nathaniel says, "Oh no! Oh, Daddy! No!" Nathaniel says, "Help me! Not even my clever father who I always trusted can protect me now. I'm alone, so what do I do? Who do I turn to, now my parents have gone? The world has cracked right open and the people I love most? – oh my God! – I can't see them any more!"'

'Rikki, I—'

'Do you understand me?' cried Rikki. 'That's what alone is!'

'I understand what you're saying.'

Everyone was silent. The fish swam calmly, and the

clock ticked. Rikki screwed Nathaniel into a ball.

'Alone,' said Rikki. 'Don't ever try to tell us we're not, because we are, and always will be, and nothing – ever – is OK.'

'OK.'

There was a long silence.

'I think we ought to end this first session,' said Dr Warren quietly. 'In many ways, it's gone well. But I'm sorry I made you so angry.'

'Do you want a hand clearing up?' said Richard. 'Do you have a dustpan?'

Rikki laughed.

'What's funny about that?' said Richard.

'What you just said,' said Rikki. 'I mean, what *we* just said. I make a mess, and you offer to clear up. You don't think that's funny?'

'Rikki,' said Richard. 'We've trashed the man's room. We ought to help him – and you had no right to tear up his photo.'

'We have not trashed his room. If we wanted to trash his room, we could do better than this. I should have turned the fish tank over, but, even in the white heat of this anger I'm supposed to be feeling, I felt some kind of empathy for the fish. So I restrained myself.'

'Can we sit down?' said Richard to Rikki.

'On a beanbag? Why?'

'Because my legs are shaking.'

'We can't sit here – it's for kids. This creepy little man thinks that if he makes his room child-friendly in this crass, unimaginative way, we're going to relax and pour out all our secrets. Don't you find that insulting?'

'No. Not really.'

'You want to tell him our secrets?'

'We don't have any.'

'That's why I'm inventing some.'

Dr Warren smiled. 'Let's finish it for now,' he said. 'But I'd like to see you again. Soon.'

'I want to go,' said Richard. 'I'm sorry about all the mess, Doctor. I think Rikki was just showing off, because he's not a psycho any more than me.'

Dr Warren nodded. 'I'm sure you're right, Richard. I'm certain of it.' He turned to the nurses. 'Would you help Rikki and Richard back to the ward, please? Make them . . . comfortable, would you? Point-two-five: one tablet each. No school for a few days, I think – we need a little observation time.'

Back in the bed, Rikki chuckled. 'He wasn't smiling when we left, you know. And he didn't threaten us: we threatened *him*.'

'Is that good?' said Richard.

'I've made us an enemy. You saw what he drew.'

'Just a blob. It was nothing.'

'It was a rope, Richard. It was a trap. It was a noose, even. It was a little lost soul in a big empty universe, floating.'

'It was a random squiggle.'

'He likes order, that's what he likes. He likes independent

thought, as long as it confirms everything he thinks. Ha! Did you see how he was looking at us? The one-eyed look. The head-on-its-side look . . . I think he's dangerous. What he wants is to close us down.' Rikki swallowed. 'I can see the future,' he said. 'He's going to end up trying to kill us.'

CHAPTER TWO

That afternoon, Richard was surprised to find that Rikki fell asleep.

They'd been given a number of painful injections, always in the neck. Whatever cocktail Rikki had received had knocked him out completely. Dr Warren came by, but didn't say anything – he just looked, and winked at Richard. Richard found that his second head lay heavy on the pillow, and nothing could rouse it.

Then, at four o'clock, as Rikki snored, Jeff, Eric and Mark appeared with a school bag full of gifts.

'Special permission!' said the duty nurse, drawing curtains round the bed. 'We don't usually have non-family at the Institute.'

'You guys know me,' said Eric. 'I'm harmless.'

'You'd better be.'

'I know everyone round here,' said Eric. 'I know the secret corridors too! You've got a pets' corner, haven't you? – for experiments . . .'

'You know a lot more than I do, Eric. You can have twenty minutes – no longer.'

'What?' said Jeff. 'It took us two hours to get here . . .'

The boys sat up on the bed and laid out their presents. There was a comic, some action figures, a carton of chocolates and a small plastic puzzle. Eric was soon busy with the puzzle. They'd all come straight from school, and Eric wore his tie round his head, Native American-style. He'd put in an earring as well, which was against the rules, and he was finding it hard to keep still. The nurse returned with a tray of drinks, and they were soon enjoying a party.

'There's big news,' said Eric. 'Salome's been busted. Kicked out of school.'

'No!' said Richard.

'We don't know for sure,' said Jeff. 'Not yet.'

'She won't come back,' said Mark. 'Bra-low's sad, but the head was furious.'

'It's true,' said Jeff. 'He told us that whatever words Rikki used – however insulting he got – she should have controlled herself.'

Mark nodded sadly. 'It's a shame, though, huh?' he said. 'She was funny. Is he really asleep by the way – or just pretending?'

'Asleep, as far as I know,' said Richard. He noticed how Mark's wrists stuck out of his shirt-cuffs, and how his Adam's apple bobbed in his throat.

The boy smiled at him, eyes bulging. 'He's going to get you in trouble, isn't he, huh?'

'He's ace,' said Eric. 'It was about the most hilarious thing, you've got to admit that – you went flying, man! That girl's got one hell of a punch.'

'I don't know what I'm going to do,' said Richard. 'He's just smashed up the counsellor's office.'

'No! Doctor Warren's? I like him even more . . .'

'The thing is though,' said Mark, sniffing and wiping his nose, 'you can do just about anything, huh? You can get away with murder now.'

Eric laughed. 'We were talking this over. You can blame anything that goes wrong on him. You can cheat, steal – bully the little kids. Puke on your homework, and if anyone complains, you just say it was Rikki.'

'I don't want to do those things,' said Richard. 'I like doing homework, and I want to get that scholarship to the grammar.'

'You should rob a bank!' said Mark, grinning. 'They can't put you both in prison, can they?'

'Hey!' said Eric. 'Do you have extra talents now, like a superhero? Can you do things you couldn't do before, like hear through walls?'

'I can do *less* than I could before,' said Richard.

'Why, though?'

'Because he's always with me, butting in. This is the first quiet conversation I've had in weeks.'

'So knock him out,' said Eric. 'Hire Salome – she's got time on her hands, now.'

'What if he knocks *me* out?'

Eric slapped his knee and laughed again. 'That would be worth seeing, man. Rikki without you to restrain him! I'd pay money to see that.'

'This isn't why we came,' said Jeff, noticing that Richard was about to get cross. 'We came to give you some *good* news, Richard. Bra-low's doing the Year Six trip again, OK? But he's changed where we're going, and you are going to love it.'

'Where are we going?'

'It's amazing!' said Mark. He dragged his legs up so they were crossed, and looked serious. 'It's a totally different place, thank God. 'Cos you remember last year? They got a week at "Lambs and Ponies", and everyone said it was the lamest place in the world? Well, for us it's going to be five days at an SAS Survival Camp!'

'Show him the brochure,' said Eric. 'It's unbelievable.'

'We've got to get slips back fast,' said Jeff. 'You've got it, Eric – you show him.'

Eric searched in his pockets, but brought out only sweets and a toy car. Jeff searched his, and finally found a crumpled, multi-coloured leaflet. Unfolding it, Richard saw a picture of grinning children in bright red crash helmets. He struggled into a sitting position, Rikki lolling against his ear.

'Wow,' he said. 'Is this serious?'

'We go all the way to Wales,' said Jeff. He pointed at one of the headings: *Can You Handle a REAL Adventure?*

'Let him read,' said Eric. He was finishing the chocolates.

Richard turned the paper over, and was bewitched in an instant. He didn't know where to start, because the photographs were all so captivating. There were children abseiling down savage cliffs. There were children in a canoe, rolling under great sprays of white water. A boy was being belted into some kind of paraglider at the edge of a precipice, and under that there was a girl squeezing through a dark cave, a torch strapped to her forehead. On the back of the leaflet stood a whole crowd of children, in green camouflage dress, with painted faces. They were screaming with joy, some leaping – and they held aloft an enormous banner: 'Who Dares Wins!'

'This is incredible,' said Richard.

'We've got to get into groups of five,' said Jeff. 'You're in our group: Tiger Team. It's a whole week of activities, and we spent all this morning going through them.'

'You sleep out in tents,' said Eric. 'They teach you how to read maps, and then one night they just dump you in the middle of a wood, no landmarks or anything. And you have to work out how to get back. Bra-low said you have to sign a form saying that if you die, your parents won't sue.'

'It was a joke,' said Jeff. 'But it does sound dangerous.'

'You got to buy the kit first,' said Mark, wiping his nose again. 'You get basic provisions, and then you're out all day – trapping animals, cooking them up. You learn how to skin rabbits—'

'When is it?' said Richard. His heart was thumping.

'End of term,' said Mark. 'Two weeks before.'

Eric hauled the duvet up, and threw it over their heads. In a moment, the boys were cocooned in an igloo, the brochure between them.

'Look at the picture there,' said Eric, pointing. 'That's what I want to be!'

'So cool,' whispered Jeff.

They were looking at a soldier in full battle-dress. '*The SAS train hard*,' said Eric, reading with difficulty. '*Because they know. That who dares wins. They know that when. You're up against it, it's true. Survival skills that are necessary.*' He paused, and it was as if they were there, in a foxhole. They could almost hear the wind racing over the plain. 'Clifden Adventure Centre,' said Eric. 'It's been recommended. By the SAS. But are you tough enough? *Will you survive?*'

'Oh God,' said Richard. 'We've got to get back!'

'Will your parents let you go, though, huh?' said Mark anxiously. 'Will Rikki be OK? 'Cos if he screws up, wow . . .'

Richard's mind was in a whirl, for he could see himself in every picture. He knew his parents would have to say yes: it was inconceivable that they wouldn't, and he felt every nerve tingling with anticipation. Rikki's head flopped against his, and he adjusted it gently.

'Mr Bra-low is sound,' he said. 'I vote we call him *Barlow* from now on.'

'I agree,' said Jeff. 'He's the best teacher in the school. When are you out of here?'

'Soon.'

'It'd better be by Tuesday, man.'

'What's happening on Tuesday?'

'Richard,' said Eric, turning to him in disbelief, 'I

think your memory's going. Tuesday's football practice. It's the cup match next week!'

'You said you were ready,' said Jeff. 'We're relying on you.'

'Yeah,' said Mark. 'You're part of that team too.'

CHAPTER THREE

His parents came to collect him the very next evening.

As Richard walked out of the ward Rikki's head was heavy against his own, blinking groggily. Mr Westlake was in earnest conversation with Dr Warren.

'We'll talk about it later,' said his mother, putting the adventure leaflet in her handbag. 'I'm sure it's possible, but there's a problem we need to deal with first.'

'What problem?' said Richard. 'Is it what we did to the office?'

'Well,' she said. 'We need to talk about that too. But the real problem appears to be your friend, Salome.'

'Oh.'

'Did Jeff tell you?'

'He said she's being kicked out of school.'

'Yes. And her father's coming round to see us. They say they want to have it out with us, face to face. I'm not sure what we can do, but that's the priority. He sounded very upset.'

Richard and Rikki had hardly finished their tea when the doorbell rang. Two minutes later, everyone was in the lounge. The television was off, and the chairs were full. Salome's father was a big man, and he used up most of the sofa. He appeared to have come straight from the club he ran, because he was in a thick tracksuit. Salome was squeezed next to him on one side, and her mother sat opposite, pouring the tea that Mrs Westlake had set on the coffee table. Salome was looking at her knees.

'I'll come straight to the point,' said her father. 'My daughter shouldn't have done what she did, and there's no two ways about that. She let us down, and the first thing we're here to do is apologize.'

'Apologize, girl,' said Salome's mother.

Salome looked up. She had clearly been crying. She licked her lips and said in a small voice, 'I'm very sorry, Rikki. I'm sorry, Richard. I shouldn't have hit you. I have to learn to control myself.'

'It's fine,' said Richard.

Rikki said nothing.

'Two things are happening to our girl,' the man continued. 'Three things. Number one, we as a family are punishing her. Big time. She is grounded. Phone, computer – she don't even get to look at them. And that, for Salome, is a big deal. And that is going to go on, and on, until she's satisfied us that she can behave. Number two and number three are the problems, though. Which is why we are here. You know the school is suspending her?'

He was talking to Mr Westlake, who nodded.

'Well, they tell us today they want to expel her.'

'I'm sorry to hear that.'

'They say she doesn't fit, and that means she's out, and that means she loses her boxing licence too. Salome's in the under-thirteens junior flyweight right now – you probably didn't know that. There's a tournament covers all this district, and the next fight is Monday, and she's been training two, three times a day. Got through the qualifiers, got a TKO in the second bout, won the next two on points.'

'That's very good,' said Mr Westlake. 'I'm amazed.'

Salome's father stared at him.

'You must be very proud,' said Mrs Westlake.

'I am proud. We are very proud. I'd be lying if I said I wasn't. She's a hard hitter, but she's also technical. Needs to work on her left – she's a jabber and that's OK up to a point, but I always say, "Salome, the jabs are preparation – you got to have a bigger *finale*." So we're working on the left, and we always do footwork.'

'She's been fighting since she was three,' said Salome's mother. 'Her big brother used to use her like a punch bag, so I guess it was inevitable. He don't do that no more.'

'She hits hard,' said her dad. 'That's what your boy got. That was a shoulder-right full-on to the nose and mouth, and that's a head shot we've practised . . . If she could do that with the left, she'd be made. But . . .'

'Rolo's different, of course,' said Salome's mother.

'We heard he wasn't well,' said Mrs Westlake. 'How is he now?'

'Oh, he's got a condition. He's never been well.'

'But he's a fighter in a different way,' said Salome's father.

'To be honest,' said her mother, 'I'm glad to have one child who stays outside the ring. Four boys I've got, and Salome. All they talk is training, weights, diet. It's nice to have a little boy who's normal.'

Salome's father interrupted. 'Listen, though, Mr Westlake. We're not here to tell you about our family. We got another agenda here altogether, and when she hit Rikki, Salome broke every rule in the book. She . . . I mean, those fists of hers, they are offensive weapons. Have I told you that, Salome? Sit up!'

'Yes, Dad.'

'Do I tell you that every time we train?'

'Yes, Dad.'

'Control is what it's about, and you would have thought she'd remember. But she lets us all down, and she forgets. What she did to your boy's going to cost her the thing she loves most. She's going to lose that licence – and it's like losing a loved one.'

There was a short silence, and Richard said, 'How would they know? We're not going to tell.'

'They find out,' said Salome's father. 'The school tells the Association.'

'That is the real issue,' said her mother. 'The school has to sign her licence, you see – so they sign up to say her behaviour and conduct are exemplary. She gets expelled, and they report it – they have to. And, Salome, you can cry as much as you like, my girl, but that's the fact.'

Richard looked at Salome, and saw a tear drip down her cheek.

'I see,' said Mr Westlake.

'That's why we're here,' said Salome's father. 'We would like to know where you stand on the incident, because we will mount an appeal, and where you stand is critical.'

Mr Westlake sipped his tea. Then he turned to Rikki. 'What do you think, son?' he said. 'You're the one who got hit.'

'She shouldn't have hit me,' said Rikki.

'You shouldn't have called my brother—'

'Shhh!' said her father. He stared at Salome, and she looked at her knees again.

There was a silence.

'I think she has to learn her lesson,' said Rikki. 'She can't control herself. That Association, whatever it was, needs to know what she's like. She's a thug and I want to see her go down.'

Everyone in the room stiffened.

'Rikki,' said Mrs Westlake softly. 'Salome is not a thug and you know it. She has apologized to you—'

'What's she going to do next time?' said Rikki.

'I will control myself,' said Salome.

'Which is what we all need to do,' said Mrs Westlake. 'You, most of all, Rikki.'

'Fine,' said Rikki. 'But what if I accidentally say something else she doesn't like? I might get a chair over my head. Or a knife in my back. I would not feel safe if she was in the school, so I think she's getting just what she deserves. She ought to be in a zoo.'

'Ouch,' said Salome's father after a moment of silence. 'You don't forgive, do you, boy?'

'Never.'

'Why not, though?' said her mother. 'You have to let things go, sometimes. If you don't . . .'

'What?' said Rikki. 'What happens?'

'You can't move forward. Nobody can.'

'I don't want to move forward. I'm going sideways.'

Mr Westlake licked his lips. When he spoke, his voice was soft. 'What about you, Richard? You feel the same as Rikki?'

'I don't know, Dad.'

'What don't you know?'

'I . . . Look, I didn't get hit.'

'You surely did,' said Salome's mother. 'I think you've got to have an opinion on this. We were all told you are the same person.'

'OK, then.'

'He thinks what I think,' said Rikki.

'Is that true?' said Salome's mother.

Richard closed his eyes. 'I think Rikki's wrong,' he said. 'Totally, utterly wrong.'

Rikki shook his head. 'You cannot back me up, ever—'

'Shut up, Rikki,' said Mr Westlake. 'Nobody interrupted you. So let's hear Richard.'

'Look,' said Richard slowly. 'I think that Salome was

in the right. I don't think she's done anything she needs to apologize for. What Rikki said . . . what *we* said, about Rolo . . . If anything, I think she should have punched us harder. Because if . . .'

'What?'

'If someone said that about me, then I think Rikki would get upset. Or even the other way round – I hope. He talked about *dying*.'

'I wouldn't get upset,' said Rikki. 'Not about you.'

'You would. If she insulted me, you'd be angry – but Salome would never insult me, because we're friends – good ones. Or we were.'

Rikki shook his head. 'We are such a loser,' he muttered. 'You get confused!'

'We should be the one apologizing,' said Richard loudly. 'Rolo's one of the nicest kids in the school, and I can't believe what we said.'

Mr Westlake sat back again. 'Listen,' he said. 'My view is very simple. Salome should not have hit you, Rikki. You should not have provoked her. You got punched, and Salome is now getting punished. But there is no way she should be punished three times over. I do not want her losing her licence, and I want her to stay at the school, with you.'

'Dad,' said Rikki. 'You are undermining me.'

'You are in the wrong, Rikki. Totally. I told you that.' He looked at Salome's father. 'What is it you want us to do, sir?'

'I want you to go down to that school, Mr Westlake.

I want you to say exactly what you just said, to the headmaster. That way, we might save the day.'

'I'm going to do that, Rikki. And you're going to come with me.'

'I bet I'm not.'

'I will take the morning off, and I will be outside his office as soon as the school opens. And you better learn from this, Rikki, that I will not tolerate you provoking people, winding them up and being a general . . . menace. You're the one who's going to get himself expelled.'

Rikki stared back at him. 'I hope I do,' he said.

Salome's father sat forward. 'Why?' he said. 'What's wrong with you, boy?'

'Nothing.'

'Salome's your friend – or ready to be. She was before this, wasn't she? That's what Richard said.'

'No,' said Rikki. 'Never.'

'She was!' said Richard. 'We were *good* friends, I know we were.'

'I don't want friends,' said Rikki. 'They let you down just when you need them most. I'm on my own, and that's how I like it.'

'Then you're in a lonely place,' said Salome's mother quietly. 'I hope you come back from it.' She looked at Mrs Westlake and smiled sadly. 'You got a fighter too, you know, dear? I hear it in his voice, so don't expect rest, ever. Oh, and Salome? – you're listening to this?'

'Yes.'

'This young man is going to need you, some time. Whatever he says – whatever he does—'

'I don't need anyone,' said Rikki.

'You say that,' said Salome's mother, 'but we know better. That's your duty, Salome – or part of it.'

CHAPTER FOUR

Time passed.

The football season continued all year round at Green Cross, and the next game was looming. True, there was a bit of cricket, and some rather feeble athletics. A parent ran a Saturday rugby club, which was well attended, and there was a karate class after school on Tuesday. But football dominated, for the simple reason that Mr Barlow loved the game and spread a real passion for it among girls and boys alike. In his youth he had 'tried out' for a London side, so he knew what he was talking about. He wasn't fit any more, but he pushed the children as hard as he could.

They had beaten Morden Manor three–nil, and it was during that first game that Richard and Rikki were exposed to the more hostile stares of other children. They quickly got used to being called 'two-heads', and soon discovered how those who insulted them always seemed to be the most stupid.

'Oi. Two-heads.'

'Yes?' said Rikki.

'You're a freak.'

'Thank you.'

That would usually be the end of it.

'Do you two snog?' said one witty boy, just before half time.

Rikki smiled, and Richard waited until the next tackle, then elbowed the boy so hard in the stomach that he was stretchered off.

Richard was astonished to find that he was getting used to his second head. From the beginning, he had been relieved to discover that Rikki did not prevent him sprinting, dribbling or shooting – in fact, he had turned into a much better player. His balance was as good as ever, and he found that in the course of a game, they worked together and followed just the same instincts. The next match was a quarter-final against their arch-rivals, Blagdon Road Juniors. In fact, every other school was an arch-rival, for Mr Barlow liked to whip up a real sense of competition when there was a cup involved.

'They're a quick s-s-side,' he said, spluttering slightly. 'But they're not so, so s-strong at the back. I've also . . . I shouldn't be telling you this, maybe, but I was t-talking to their headmaster and one of their strongest has got chickenpox. They've got a new f-full-back, and he's not experienced. That's why we've been w-working on the one-touch pass – I w-want to get that ball forward. Are you . . . are you with me?'

'Yes, sir,' everyone said.

Nobody made jokes in the training sessions, and Mr Barlow's spittle problem was never referred to.

'Eric, you're going to be key.'

'Sir.'

'I want to st-start with a lot of right-wing work, so Eric's our front man. Salome, I don't want you up front at all – I want you way back, p-pushing it up.'

Salome nodded. Her suspension was over. She'd signed a strict contract of behaviour, and she was due to have an anger-management session with Dr Warren, whose visits to the school were getting ever more frequent. He was keen to experiment with mild medication, though Salome's family was resistant. She and Rikki exchanged bitter looks over the desks – but kept out of each other's way. Even on the football field, they kept their distance.

When Blagdon Road Juniors kicked off, there was an instant hurricane of whistling and cheering. It was soon clear that the Barlow tactics were working, for Green Cross had most of the possession.

For twenty minutes it was nil–nil, but then Mark got the ball way out to the school's lethal weapon – Eric – and he hammered in the most gorgeous cross. Salome's friend Carla muffed it, missing the volley, so a defender booted it hard. Rikki was there: right place, right time. He dived sideways with extraordinary courage – and his forehead made full, glorious contact. The header was unstoppable, and the goalkeeper was open-mouthed as the ball shot straight over his shoulder into the net.

The Green Cross team rushed howling into a huddle,

and Richard and Rikki were carried shoulder high to their own half. Jeff, who was goalie, ran all the way from his goalmouth for high-fives, and when the game re-started, the team was solid as a rock. They held their lead through sensible defending, and at half time Mr Barlow congratulated his team warmly.

'Change of t-tactics, now,' he said, smiling.

'Why, sir?' said Jeff. 'They don't know what's hit them!'

'Six–nil,' said Mark. 'Minimum!'

'I think we have to surprise them,' said Mr Barlow. 'They know what we're about, now. They'll be talking about you, Eric, I'm sure of it. So I want to sh-shift the main play onto the left – it'll be just enough to confuse them. I want Carla supported, all right? I want to get her up f-front – left wing – c-crossing it in. Richard – Rikki. I want you even further forward.'

The two heads nodded.

'Get it to Carla, Eric. Can you do that?'

'Sure,' said Eric.

'I'm expecting magic. From all of you.'

Magic was exactly what he got.

The Blagdon Road Juniors team fell straight into Mr Barlow's trap. They had repositioned themselves to close down Eric, and it was a long time before they realized he was no longer the principal danger. Carla was now the mainspring, and everyone was pushing the ball in her direction. She was a forceful girl and had mastered some very delicate footwork. Soon, she was putting the ball in from all angles, seeking out Richard and Rikki. There were two Blagdon players who were particularly tall, and they dealt with some of her crosses. But Rikki and Richard could jump higher than they'd ever jumped before, and seemed to possess a far better sense of timing.

Fifteen minutes before full time, Richard found himself at the near post as the ball sailed in, long and hard. He leaped like a salmon, and Rikki nodded it straight through the goalie's hands. Five minutes later Carla found him again, and he got impossibly high to head it down to Mark. Mark chested it onto his right foot, and managed not to panic. He cracked it into the back of the net, and stood goggle-eyed with amazement. Then, in a final movement that looked more like dance than football, goalie Jeff found Salome, who booted a massive pass up to the strikers. Rikki received it on his temple, flipping way across the pitch to Eric. Eric was through like a whippet, and his final shot tore the goal net from its hooks. The quarter-final score was an unbeatable, unmistakable and totally uncompromising . . . four–nil.

They would play the cup-holders in the semi-final: the dreaded St Michael's Preparatory School, who trained in all weathers, every day. It was a boys-only team who'd toured Brazil the previous summer, and been coached by professionals.

When Richard and Rikki trotted off the pitch, they saw their father. He was standing, huddled up in a big coat, gazing at them.

'Dad!' said Richard shyly. 'I didn't know you were watching.'

It had been a sensitive family issue, because Richard's grandad had never missed a game – even when his health was failing.

His father said, 'I didn't want to put you off. I just sneaked in and stood at the back.'

'What about work?'

'Told them I had more important things to do. Sorry . . .'

'What's the matter?'

'Sorry, I'm . . . ooh. Something in my eye, son. You played so well. Rikki, that was—' He hugged his son to him, and kissed the tops of both heads. 'You're beautiful. You know that? He'd be proud.'

'Who would?' said Rikki.

'You know who. He'd have been dancing.'

CHAPTER FIVE

Meanwhile, the tests got harder.

Everyone in Year Six was used to the weekly papers, which were building to the scholarship exam – but Mr Barlow seemed to be setting questions that were impossible.

Only Eric seemed not to care, and he was sometimes absent altogether. Everyone knew that he had a complicated life. He'd missed a lot of school the previous year as well, and had come close to being sent away altogether. He was always vague about the details of his family, but his friends were fairly sure he lived in several different places. There was a mum, and an auntie, and also a friend of the auntie, and they all took charge and shunted him from one flat to another. There was an older brother too, nicknamed 'Spider', and Eric claimed that he spent weekends with him and his mates, doing wild and crazy things. There were rumours of stolen cars and house-breaking, but nobody was sure if they were true. Now, however, Eric was arriving late, and he was often unwashed, wearing only half his uniform. He was surrounded by the faint smell of liquor, and his eyes were wild and unfocused. If he took part in a class test, his results were shocking, and he told Rikki and Richard that his visits to Dr Warren were being increased.

'They say I got something wrong with my neurones,' he said.

'What are they?' said Jeff.

'I don't know. They want to laser them out, though. Cut out my bad bits, so I can get fostered or something. It would be three days in that Institute place, and the food's pretty good. Flatscreen TV, chocolate-chip cookies—'

'Eric,' said Rikki, 'are you talking about surgery?'

'Yes.'

'On your brain?'

Eric nodded.

'But you're normal. Don't let them near you, buddy.'

'They say they want to help me – there's Doctor Summersby, too, coming back from America or somewhere. It's research, so everything's paid for.' He grinned. 'Warren says I can't go on the way I'm going.'

'Why not?' said Mark.

'I don't know. They've been doing stuff on monkeys, so now it's my turn. They got a lab on the top floor, through secret doors.'

He was grinning as he said it, but Jeff looked worried. 'I don't know how serious you are, Eric,' he said. 'But that sounds bad.'

'What did you see?' said Mark.

Eric shrugged. 'I haven't been in, but you hear weird noises. There's chimps, I think, in cages, all kind of . . .

wired-up. I saw one, through the doorway – then they shooed me back out again.' He laughed and pushed his hair back. 'I don't care what they do – I'm joining the Army, and you don't need brains for that. If Warren wants mine, he can have it.'

Richard and Rikki had a different attitude.

They were taking their work very seriously, and so were their parents. There were only three scholarships to the grammar school, and they were awarded for academic excellence. As a result, the Westlake home was often silent with concentration. The television was on for a maximum of one hour per evening, and Rikki and Richard stayed up late memorizing facts and formulae. In the classroom, Mr Barlow panicked about what he hadn't taught, and the children got anxious about what they hadn't learned. It was an emotional time, and every day someone was in tears.

Richard kept tight hold of his grandad's wings. He often held them in his fist as he worked, and at the end of the day he'd replace them in his locker, letting them rest on the dangling Sea Venom. It was coming up to the anniversary of the old man's death, and he knew that day would be difficult. Nobody at home had mentioned it: the subject was too huge, so they trod carefully round it.

The two heads worked together, burying themselves in work. There had been a time when Richard had laid his homework out on the old man's table by the window, and breathed the scent of pipe-tobacco. Three steps up along the landing: the door to Grandad's room, which now smelled only of newness.

The photographs were gone from his walls, but Richard remembered each one: the long runways on wild islands, and the faded gatherings of men in uniform standing on the decks of vast carriers.

He could hear the voice. 'That was Terry. That was our commander.'

'That's not a Venom, though, is it?'

'That's a Hornet. That was state-of-the-art, then. Look at her . . .'

'How fast?'

'Four-fifty, I think. Slow, by today's standards—'

'You call that slow?'

'The first drops were over Wales, you know. In over the sea. Now that's the Baltic fleet . . . that's the Q-hut – remember that?'

His grandad's hands would be on his shoulders, and turn him, or shift him along. Such strong fingers, which he'd dig into the boy's shoulder-blades that little bit too hard, and Richard would grit his teeth, knowing the game.

Now and then, a smell or a sound would make him turn, usually when he was on the landing, and there'd be a flicker in the air. His grandad would be there again, and gone. It happened in front of the wretched mirror, as Rikki stood with his eyes tight shut, the scent of new carpet rising around them. Yet the changes were right and proper, for his dad had been working in the kitchen, which was always a nuisance. It had made sense to create an office upstairs, and they'd talked it through. They had repainted the ceiling and chosen new wallpaper. The pictures were wrapped up in the attic.

Why hadn't they moved the mirror?

It had a brass frame, and was screwed to the wall. It was the only thing that had stayed . . .

'Danda, you coming later?'

'If I can. Come back here.'

Richard would turn. 'You meeting me?'

'If I'm not busy.'

Grandad's chair had been there, in the reflection. Even when he'd been sick he'd made the effort to get up and sit in it, smartly dressed. Even as he withered.

'You wouldn't rather walk home with your friends?'

'I don't care.'

'You want to walk with Jeff, that's fine.'

'It's all right.'

'What did they teach you today, then?'

He remembered more silence than talking. Or maybe he prattled on – maybe they did talk, and he'd forgotten. What had they talked about, though – when his hand was in the old man's? Such a creased thing, and it had once held the controls . . .

He remembered planning the tree house, which his dad had said was way too high.

His grandad had laughed. 'If he breaks his neck, it'll be a valuable lesson. You won't though, Richard – will you?'

And the old man's shed, way below, that was still full of screws, nails, tools, glues, bicycle pumps, blunt saws and too much to identify or sort. Richard had found an old mug there, pushed onto a shelf and never returned to the kitchen – never washed up. It might have been his grandad's last cup of tea, set down before the last time he pulled his jacket on and changed his shoes, to walk the last mile ever to Green Cross School.

'See you later.'

'If I can. Come back here.'

Richard would turn. 'You know it's practice today?'

'You're getting taller, you know. Hold your hand out.'

'No, Danda—'

'Hold your hand out! Do as you're told.'

A two-pound coin, pressed in and closed in his fist, his grandad's fingers frighteningly strong. His pilot's eyes, weaker now behind bi-focals, but always bright with life.

'You keep it.'

'Mum doesn't like it—'

'Don't tell her, then. Simple as that.'

Richard was breathing hard. He crushed the wings, squeezed them hard, and he found that this time *his* eyes were shut. When he opened them, he was gazing into his locker and Rikki was staring at him.

'We're at school,' said Rikki. 'You've got to stop.'

'Stop what?'

'You know what. Remembering.'

'How? I just . . .'

'What?'

'I just want . . . to know where he is.'

'Dust to dust, buddy. No heaven – you know that. There is no heaven.'

'He's somewhere, Rikki. He cannot be gone.'

CHAPTER SIX

The same afternoon, the headmaster dropped a bombshell.

Mr Prowse didn't often smile, but that day he went from classroom to classroom, grinning broadly, and rubbing his hands.

He had astonishing news. *Kidspeak* – the debate project the school took so seriously – was going to be featured on prime-time television, and Green Cross School had been chosen as the venue. It was the culmination of months of hard, competitive work – and it had finally paid off.

'They confirmed it today,' said Mr Prowse. 'I am so proud of you all, particularly you older children.' His voice trembled with excitement and he waved a paper in the air. 'Sixty schools applied, children! Sixty! And they chose just two of us. Why did they select us? Because our speeches were the best. Just listen to this: "The ideas that emerged from Green Cross were some of the most stimulating we received, and demonstrated the pinnacle of sensitive and intelligent discussion." ' Mr Prowse smiled happily. 'You ought to feel very, very pleased with yourselves. You've shown that young people really do care about the world they live in – and these television moguls want to make that fact public!'

Mr Barlow's class burst into joyous applause, and the headmaster nodded.

'Dedication, you see. It's paid off again.'

When he went on to name the actual programme that would feature them, there was an audible gasp. Some of the girls squealed in disbelief, for it was the most popular, fashionable children's show on the network: *School's Out*, hosted by celebrity heart-throb Anton Dekker. Twice a week it went out, at quarter past four. It featured young people doing wonderful, inspirational things, and it had a huge audience all over the country. This was because of Anton, its super-cool lead-presenter, who had tripled ratings in his first month.

'When?' shrieked Eleanor. 'When?'

'Will . . . *he* be coming?' shouted someone.

'Who, my dear?'

'Anton! Anton!'

'Anton who?' said the headmaster. 'Who are you talking about?'

'Anton Dekker!' cried the children, and Eric immediately burst into one of his rap songs, while others demonstrated his dance steps.

The name was familiar to every child over the age of five, but the headmaster seemed unaware. Anton was in his early twenties, and was famous as a breakdancer, a rapper, and a tireless fundraiser. He'd saved tribes in the Amazon. He'd set up a hospice for whale-sharks, and he had his own boy band with a string of hits. He was supermodel handsome too, and wore a new costume every time he appeared, transforming high-street fashion overnight.

'I don't know who's going to be presenting,' said the headmaster. 'It's our top speakers they want to see – a feast of debate, with questions at the end. And I have to say I'm not surprised. It's going to put this school on the educational map, children – it's the most fabulous opportunity. Miss Maycock, you're co-ordinating things, yes?'

'Yes, Mr Prowse.' Miss Maycock was a young student teacher who had recently arrived 'on placement', supporting Mr Barlow. She was very keen – if a little nervous.

The headmaster continued. 'The winners of last term's competition will be the ones featured. You need to be thinking about new topics now – I don't want repetition. What we need are extra-specially good, *topical* ideas. It will be in the lunch hall, filmed in front of everyone, parents included. So I want those thinking caps on, and I want real ambition. What do you want, Rikki?'

Rikki had his hand up and was waving wildly. 'Can we talk about *anything*?' he said.

'The floor is yours,' said the headmaster.

'Wow.'

'That's the whole point, you see. It's just the six speakers, Mr Barlow—'

'Only six?' said Rikki. 'And that includes me?'

'Like I said, we'll have the six winners from last term, so that's a nice spread of ages. And totally new topics. Aparna did political prisoners, and as a result of that we had the fundraising disco, yes? Then there was Natasha in Year Five, and she spoke about, er . . . the famine in . . . somewhere. Africa, I think – and that led to the Design-a-T-shirt competition. Topical ideas, you see.'

'Right,' said Rikki.

'Mr Barlow will guide you. We want cutting edge, don't we, Mr Barlow? Be bold!'

'You said *Kidspeak* was for losers and dweebs,' said Richard, a little later. It was Thursday afternoon, and that was always given over to art.

'It is,' said Rikki.

'So how come you got so excited?'

'I want to change the world, Richard. I want to express myself.'

'Why?'

'Things need changing. The past must be destroyed, and we need to embrace a whole new way of looking at things.'

'Are you going to stop teasing Aparna about it, then?'

'No.'

'We have to work with her, Rikki: she's team-leader—'

'I tease Aparna because she has no personality. She's wet, she's conventional and she's Jeff's buddy. She needs teasing.' He looked up, and shouted: 'Hey, Aparna!'

'Shut up, Rikki,' said Richard quietly. 'Leave her alone.'

Rikki shouted again, louder than ever. 'Aparna – baby!'

'Get on with the drawing. Please!'

Aparna was at work at the far table. She was sitting

beside Jeff, who lived in the same street as she did. Richard had never got to know her well, because she was so shy, but *Kidspeak* had pushed them together. Everyone trusted her, and respected her cleverness.

Jeff was looking at Rikki now, and he wasn't smiling. Salome glared at him, but Aparna kept her eyes down, mixing her paints carefully. Miss Maycock was out of the room.

'Aparna!' shouted Rikki. 'You want a banana?'

This had become a favourite joke. He liked the fact that the two words rhymed. Aparna continued to ignore him.

'I've got a big bunch today, Aparna!' called Rikki, louder than ever. 'Why don't you come and get one?'

'Get lost,' said Jeff. 'You're not funny.'

'Leave her alone,' said Salome.

'Oh, guys!' said Rikki. 'Jeff's defending his girlfriend!'

'Shut up, Rikki,' said Jeff.

'Come on, Jeffrey. When's the baby due?'

Jeff went beetroot-red and threw his paintbrush down. Aparna said something to him and tugged at his shirt – but Jeff was making his way across the room. There was a smattering of laughter, and Mark whistled.

'Don't say any more, Rikki,' whispered Richard. 'We don't need this.'

'But Jeff's coming over, just to see us,' cried Rikki. 'Jeff's visiting his old friends! We hardly see anything of you these days, Jeff, now you've got a sex life.'

'I'm asking you to shut your mouth,' said Jeff. 'You're

not funny – you're just an idiot. And what you're saying is offensive.'

'Offensive, how?'

'You know how.'

'I'm just offering Aparna a juicy, big banana. How is that offensive?'

'Everything all right?' said Miss Maycock, trotting back in. 'Oh, that's a lovely picture, Rikki – why is it so black?'

'You need to keep this guy quiet,' said Jeff to Richard.

'Jeff, he's being stupid. Ignore him.'

'I'm trying to like you, Richard,' said Jeff. 'But that thing on your shoulder needs battering again. Someone's going to do it unless you make him shut his mouth.'

'Can you ask Aparna to show her picture, miss?' said Rikki. 'I'm always so inspired by what she does, because she's so wonderfully gifted.'

Miss Maycock smiled. 'Maybe at the end of the lesson,' she said. 'That's a very kind thought, Rikki. I want you to finish yours, first. What is it, by the way? It looks like a thunder-cloud . . .'

'It's not as good as Aparna's, miss. It never is.'

Aparna's artwork was outstanding – but then everything she did was outstanding. She excelled at swimming and gymnastics, and the previous year she had taken a major role in the city's semi-professional ballet. She was a very keen pianist too, playing in the county youth orchestra.

Somehow, she seemed to have been born without a mean bone in her body, and she spent most of her time trying to avoid the attention everyone wanted to give her. For example, she had painted a picture for a recent schools' competition, and had won second prize. The piece had toured the country, and postcards had been made of it. It now hung under glass in the school's main reception, and had featured as the cover of the school magazine.

Aparna had only been embarrassed by the fuss. She seemed to shudder, and writhe away from the spotlight – and yet it was continually trained upon her. The title of the painting was 'Icarus Descending', and it featured a landscape of crazily leaning crags that zigzagged into a blisteringly hot sun. The eye was drawn to a tiny lighthouse at vanishing point, and you got vertigo looking at it. As you gazed into the centre you felt yourself swooping to the ground, and it was as if you would crash-land any moment. Jeff had said it was the most beautiful painting he had ever seen – and that had been the beginning of what everyone assumed was a romance.

Eric had asked the question: 'What's Icarus?'

Aparna had been too shy to explain, but had at last been persuaded to say, 'It's what he saw.'

'When? Who?'

'When . . . when his wings came off.'

It was clear that very few people knew what she was talking about, so Mr Barlow called everyone together the next Friday afternoon, and told them he was reinstituting 'story time'. There had been cries of disgust at first, because the children all knew only the Year Fives and under were read stories, and they were facing the big exams. But they also knew that Mr Barlow was the best storyteller in the school. When he got into a story, his stammer disappeared, and it was a wonderful way of ending the week.

'You need to know about D-Daedalus,' said Mr Barlow. 'Oh, and you need to know about the Minotaur. I should have started this weeks ago . . . Pull the b-blinds down, please.'

They created a blackout, huddled onto the rug, and in minutes Ancient Greece materialized around them.

'Daedalus was imprisoned in a high tower,' said Mr Barlow.

'I remember!' said Mark. 'The bird-man, huh?'

'Shhh!' hissed several people.

Mr Barlow frowned, and continued. 'Up there where he sat, it was only the birds that kept him sane. He would watch them from the window, soaring and skimming over the sky. Sometimes they'd come and perch on the sill, and occasionally – of course – they'd drop a feather. Out of all that observation came his most remarkable idea. He offered the birds cake crumbs, and the birds got used to visiting.'

'Did he eat them?' said Eric.

'No.'

'Didn't they poo everywhere?'

'Shut up!' shouted Salome.

Mr Barlow raised a hand. 'They'd take the food from him,' he said, 'in return for a feather. Over the weeks and months, Daedalus gathered pillowfuls of feathers, and he put them all into sacks. "Are you making a duvet, F-Father?" said Icarus.

‘ “I’m not making a duvet, son – no,” said Daedalus.

‘But what he *was* making he kept absolutely private, waiting for his boy to fall asleep at night. Only then would he work on his invention. Feathers, wax, twine and the lightest straw. He was way ahead of his time, and he knew that the skeletons of birds must be almost weightless. He was studying aerodynamics because, don’t forget, nobody in Ancient Greece had ever flown.

‘Anyway, there came a day when his invention was ready. Icarus woke up, and there on the bed were two pairs of the most enormous, glorious wings. So many birds had contributed feathers that they were multi-coloured – and they were so big they spread right across the room. There was no time to be lost, of course. Daedalus strapped one pair onto Icarus’s shoulders, and Icarus helped him with his own. Soon, they had the window wide open and were ready to go.

‘ “There’s one thing,” said Daedalus.’

‘Don’t go near the sun,’ whispered Richard.

Mr Barlow smiled. ‘Yes,’ he said. ‘It wasn’t too strong in the early morning, but he knew the sun would soon get roastingly hot. “Stay below me,” Daedalus said. “Stay behind me, and stay low. These wings are just feathers and wax, and if we go too near that sun once it’s up . . . we won’t last long. Do you understand me?”

‘Icarus was the same age as you, of course. So the boy nodded.

‘With that, the old man leaped out into the abyss, turned head over heels – and was suddenly flying. Icarus did the same, jumping out as far as he could, and then one flap, and oh my goodness, the power in those wings. He shot up like a bullet, the breeze getting right under him. Now you can understand that both father and son were experiencing something that . . . well, only angels experience. They soared and whirled and looped the loop. But it was Daedalus who remembered that the whole point was escape. It was Daedalus who led, and they were soon over the coastline and then over the sea. Poor Icarus, however, could not control himself. *I have to go higher!* – that's what he thought, and who could blame him?

'Daedalus gave chase, and screamed out after him: "The sun Icarus! The wax!"

'The boy simply didn't hear. He flew higher and higher, and if he heard anything it probably sounded like a bird calling. In the end, all Daedalus could do was watch as his son turned into a speck, soaring upwards. Then, suddenly, the air was full of feathers, because, oh . . . the sun was indeed too hot, and Icarus had flown too close.

'Out of the feathers came the plummeting form of a terrified boy. His wings were in tatters, and all he had round his shoulders were a few bits of straw. He went headfirst past his father into the sea, and there was nothing the old man could do but watch him crash down into the water.'

Mr Barlow paused. 'That,' he said, with a sigh, 'is the story of Icarus.'

'Was he drowned?' said someone.

'He was drowned.'

There was a light smattering of applause, but most children simply gaped.

'How come there's never happy endings in your stories, Mr Barlow?' said Eric at last. It was his first appearance at school that week, and his hair was a mass of intricate dreadlocks. 'Why are they always so sad?'

'I didn't write it,' said Mr Barlow. 'It's not m-my ending.'

'But whoever did could have said . . . I don't know, "Icarus flew higher and higher, and then suddenly remembered: *Oh my God, I can feel my wings getting melted. Dad was right!*" Then he zooms back down again just in time, and they both get home safely, and live happily ever after.'

'And that would be a better story, though?' said Mark.

'Huh?'

'I just want a happy ending for once,' said Eric. 'People don't always have to die. If you're flying, you don't have to crash.'

'My grandad flew,' said Richard, before he could stop himself.

'Shut up,' said Rikki very quietly.

Mr Barlow nodded. 'You've told us that before, Richard. Tell us again.'

Richard licked his lips, and found that his voice was shaking. The little wings were in his fist. 'He was a Navy pilot,' he said. 'He flew Buccaneers off HMS *Eagle*. He flew Vixens too, but he loved the Venom best, so he stayed with jets. Usually out on the carriers.'

'That's aviation history, of course. He m-must have had some stories.'

'He said it was the best feeling in the world, up there, in control. They were still developing the planes then, you see – he was in one of the first squadrons that landed the old Hornets. So he did the tests for that, and then he did the aircraft carriers – the big ships. You drop in at about . . . I think it's a hundred and fifty miles an hour, and you line up on lights, and then you have to catch the wire – it's stretched across the ship's runway, and it brings your plane to a dead stop. You go from one-fifty to zero in two seconds, and as it catches you have to give full throttle, just in case you've missed it. Otherwise you wouldn't get up again. You come out of the sun, so it won't blind you. And there are three wires across the boat-deck, and there's a hook under your tail. It's called "assisted landing", and the best pilots catch the middle wire, first time round – every time. He got a medal for fifty perfect drops.' Richard looked up, slightly breathless. 'But he had to stop in the end, though – did I ever say why?'

'Stop talking,' said Rikki in his ear. 'Nobody cares.'

'Why?' said Carla.

'Did he crash?' said someone.

'No,' said Richard. 'He saw himself, on the wing.'

'Saw himself?' said Eric. 'What are you talking about?'

Richard looked at him. 'It's what . . . happens when you reach this point in flying. He explained it, but I didn't really get it. He was in the cockpit – it was a Seahawk, I think, and he was out over Wales, and everything was fine. Great visibility, and he was just getting ready to go back . . . when he looked to his right. And on the tip of the wing, he saw himself. Just sitting there, like a ghost. And he looked at himself, and at first, the guy on the wing was just looking forward. But then he turned, and Danda couldn't take his eyes away then. He was looking at himself, like there was two of him – two heads – and they just gazed at each other.'

The class was absolutely silent.

'What happened?' said Mr Barlow.

'Well, he managed to look away, just in time. And he looked down at the controls, and of course he was doing about three-ninety, so he was way off course, and he realized that he'd lost the rest of the squadron. He'd been looking at himself for maybe fifteen seconds, which could have killed him. So he turned back—'

'Was he freaked out?' said Eric.

'Yes. Totally. Because he'd heard of other pilots seeing themselves, and it was always a sign that you couldn't handle flying any more – you were no longer stable. You'd been too high and there was part of you that couldn't go on. So you have to tell your commanding officer, which Grandad did – he went straight in and told him that this had happened. And they, er . . . they did checks and lots of psychological counselling stuff. They made him draw pictures, and they kept at him and at him . . . and then they grounded him. So he stopped flying, and he taught simulations after that, and helped develop one of the simulators they still use. The Jameson simulator . . . but that was before I was born, before we moved into his house . . . Before.'

Again, there was a pause. In the end, Eric said, 'Well,

that's a happy ending. I thought you were going to say he crashed and burned.'

Richard shook his head. 'No. He invented things as well, and when he retired—'

'Why don't you bring him in?' said someone. 'He could tell us himself!'

'Shhh!' said someone else.

Richard became aware that everyone was silent, and even anxious. Aparna was staring straight at him, and she looked frightened. The class knew his grandad had passed on. Richard had been absent for six days, because it had all been so horrible, so terrible, so impossible – everyone knew, and the silence now seemed unbreakable. Every child knew the facts and nobody would ever, ever mention them. The boy who'd asked the question was new.

Rikki sighed loudly. 'Tell them again,' he said. 'It was a year ago, nearly.'

'Tell them what?'

'Tell them how he died. They've forgotten, you see, Rich? – it wasn't important enough, and they've moved on with their lives.'

Rikki turned to the class.

'Grandad died last year, guys. He was walking us home, 'cos he used to meet us from school. We were walking along and he had a great big, bone-breaking heart attack, right on the pavement, about five minutes from here. Took one hour to get an ambulance to him, by which time he was cold as a stone. It wasn't a problem, though, because the hospital said he would have died anyway, so the fact he died like a skinny old dog . . . even though he was a hero . . . like some dog in the street, well, that was just tough luck. He was always meeting me and walking me home, even when he was sick. And he was always buying me stuff – like chocolate, which of course he would always eat most of. He was greedy. Selfish . . .'

Richard was shaking his head. 'He wasn't. He so wasn't.'

'He had diabetes, you know?'

'I know.'

Rikki laughed. 'We'd watched him getting weaker, but he hated being in bed. He'd been active all his life, so he always came to get us. And this one day, about quarter past four, he suddenly stops, and puts his hand on his chest – just here. And we said, "You OK?" – and he said, "Wait." Just like that: "Wait a minute." "What's wrong?" says Richard. And he goes all white. Grandad, I mean – not me.' Rikki sniggered. 'Then his legs went, and oh-my-God he's on the pavement. Bam! Ha, right outside the newsagent, with everyone staring. One dead grandad, simple as that.'

He smiled.

'Second-hand clothes, yes? Funeral, and all this stuff nobody knew what to do with. Stuff left over – all the crap in his cupboards – man, we still haven't got rid of it all, 'cos it's a big house, and we'd moved in, to be with him, because Mum wanted to look after him more. It's our house now, of course.' He shook his head. 'But oh my God, you put it in boxes – the crap, that is. You shove it in the attic, but you don't know where to put it, and it drives you mad.'

Rikki was laughing.

'Oh, and even the ash – listen to this! After we burned him up, we put his ash in the wind at this ceremony thing, out on some airfield that all the old men came to, so . . . off he flew on his last flight – the pilot without a plane – and I heard someone sneeze, and I thought, *Wow, maybe they've got a bit of Grandad, right up their nose.* Gone with the wind, huh? Gone!'

He knocked his head gently against Richard's, as Richard stared at his knees. 'Life is cruel,' he added. 'Don't expect a happy ending, buddy. Ever.'

'But, Rikki . . .' said Mr Barlow.

'What?'

'He was a wonderful man.'

'How do you know? He wasn't your grandad.'

'Everyone knows. He was a hero, like you said.'

'Didn't stop him dying.'

'He's not forgotten—'

'Not that we're complaining – there's more room upstairs now, and we got rid of the smell. Everything's worked out for the best, guys. Life goes on, getting better. He was an arse.'

There was a silence, and then the bell went, sudden and shrill. The children got up to leave, and all Mr Barlow could do was watch, for Richard and Rikki bolted out of the classroom, pushing through the crowd long before he could get to them.

The teacher stood in the corridor as the doors banged, and Dr Warren was suddenly beside him.

Mr Barlow blinked. 'I didn't know you were here.'

'I'm glad I was.'

'D-did you hear that?'

'I recorded it. I came in just as you started.'

'You were in the c-classroom? You should have told me.'

Dr Warren nodded, and slipped a small metal device into his inside pocket. 'I got it all. I'm just gathering evidence.'

'What for? What do you mean?'

'He's at a critical stage. I'd say he's going to need a lot of help, that boy. Intervention, in fact.'

CHAPTER SEVEN

The TV people arrived the very next week.

The pupils were kept away from the hall until after break time, and then they were marched inside, in awe-struck silence. It had been transformed. The walls had been repainted, and a steeply tiered arena had been constructed around a drum-shaped stage. The stage was for the speaker-team: six children. Parents had already been seated and the pupils would occupy the main blocks. Now the platform seemed to hover in a carpet of fog, for the smoke machines were being tested. The lights went from blue to red to green, and there was a sudden blast of deafening rock music, which was cut just as abruptly when a man in head-phones waved his arms.

'Test level seven,' said an echoing voice. 'Nothing on monitor seven, Henry.'

'Level seven, check,' said someone.

Mr Prowse led the Year Four speaker to his seat at the table, and a man with a beard attached a microphone to his jersey. There were three cameras, and one of them could move right round the podium on a little railway track.

Engineers stared at screens, and re-plugged cables. Voices blared from different speakers, and the children sat, dazed with wonder.

There was no sign, however, of Anton Dekker.

'Hello there, I'm Mel,' said a girl, right in front of them. She spoke into a headset-microphone, smiling brightly. 'How are we doing today at Green Cross – are we having a party? How are you guys?'

Nobody spoke. The children were simply too nervous.

'Oh, wow!' laughed Mel. 'You gotta do better than that! Let's hear you, now!'

She held up a sign that read, 'Cheer!' – and the children cheered quietly. 'Laugh!' read the next one, and that was followed by 'Clap!'

'You're half asleep!' said Mel. 'This won't do, Green Cross! This is *television*!' She swung round to the podium, and froze. 'What the hell is that?' she said.

The children stared. She was gazing at Rikki and Richard, who had just moved to their seat on the stage, and it seemed to unbalance her. The headmaster was frozen too.

'Come on, guys!' she managed to shout. 'I want you to, er . . . raise the roof!' She held up another card. 'Can you do that for me? Can you do it for Anton when he gets here?'

She leaped into the air and waved the sign back and forth. 'Go crazy!!' it said, and the Green Cross children came alive at last, struck from their stupor by that magic name. Soon she was organizing Mexican waves, left to right and right to left.

Miss Maycock winced at the barrage of noise. She was laying jotters and pencils on the speakers' table, so that those making speeches were properly equipped. The technician still moved from seat to seat, sorting out wires, and a large boom appeared for the question-and-answer session.

'Richard?' said the headmaster.

'Yes, sir?'

'Didn't Mr Barlow speak to you?'

'I don't know, sir. About what?'

'About this.' The headmaster swallowed, and saw that the technician was staring at him. 'Mr Barlow was supposed to have a word with you yesterday.'

Richard and Rikki shook their heads. 'We were all quite busy,' said Rikki. 'He may not have had the chance.'

'Well, we need to have a chat, so . . . could you put the pencil down for a moment? There's a bit of a problem – I thought it had been explained to you.'

'No,' said Richard.

'Come with me. It's a technical matter.'

Rikki and Richard clambered down to floor level, aware that they were being gawped at by a number of technicians. The headmaster ushered them to one side, where the man with headphones was waiting. A woman with a clipboard full of papers stood next to him.

'This is, er . . . Richard,' said the headmaster. 'And Rikki. I asked Mr Barlow to break the news, but I fear he's avoided it. We've got a rather serious technical problem, you see, and . . . I need your support to resolve it. It's one of those wretched, last-minute glitches.'

'Right,' said Richard.

'Can we find a quiet spot? This is a bit embarrassing.'

They moved round to the back of the stage, behind a curtain.

'We spoke to the BBC some time ago, and . . . one of the things they asked for was photographs of the delegates. We sent them, and apparently they're a bit worried about picking you up properly on a microphone. The, er . . . signal won't be clear, and Tom and I were talking, and—'

'Who's Tom?' said Rikki.

'Hi,' said the man with headphones. He was looking at Rikki in wonder. 'I'm Tom, and I'm the producer. Look, guys – we've never had this situation before.' He tried to laugh. 'And from our point of view it's a bit tricky – I did explain to the boss, here. But the, er . . .'

'The message must have got lost in translation,' said the headmaster. 'Mr Barlow's normally very good, and I spoke to Jeffrey's parents last night. This is a wretched nuisance.'

'Sir, aren't we about to start?' said Richard nervously.

'Well, we're still waiting for the big man,' said Tom. 'Anton's on his way, but we've got a few minutes, and, um . . . we've got to resolve this. Where's the other kid? Jeffrey Rawlingson.'

'I don't know. I'll find him.'

'Look,' said Tom. 'How can I put this? We can't mike you up, guys – that's the size of it. It's a kids' programme, you see, so . . . the sound has to be extra clear. We're going to put Jeffrey in, and you can watch, with the audience.'

'We can have a hand-mike,' said Rikki. 'Would that work?'

'No,' said the headmaster. 'It wouldn't.'

The producer smiled again and shook his head. 'Look,' he said, 'you don't understand. It's not going to be possible to get a clear signal from the, er . . . two heads. We've just been running the sound-checks, and . . . it's not going to happen. We agreed this, we thought it would—'

'That's rubbish,' said Rikki.

'What?'

'Excuse me, Tom,' said the girl with the clipboard. She had a mobile pressed to her ear. 'Anton's here. We're going to do a test entrance, get the kids freaking out. Stand by, camera three.'

'I don't get this,' said Richard.

'They're talking nonsense,' said Rikki. 'You just put a mike on our chest, same as everyone else. We can speak clearly, so what's the problem? I've got things to say – you know that.'

'No,' said the headmaster. He spoke with icy calm. 'I'm not going to debate this. These things have to be faced, Rikki – the school's reputation comes first, and you have to take it on the chin.'

'So it's censorship,' said Rikki.

'Of course it's not!'

'You're telling us, sir, that you don't want us up on that stage—'

'We're on show!' hissed the headmaster quietly. 'Green Cross stands for a conventional education and . . . family values. Jeff is going to take over from you—'

'He doesn't do speeches!'

'He does today, and you're in the audience.'

Tom had turned away, and had pulled the curtain back. 'Stand by, lights,' he said. 'I want this totally spontaneous – just let them go for it, OK? Keep it rolling.'

'Sir,' said Richard. His voice was trembling. 'This isn't fair.'

'Well—'

'Rikki's been preparing topics—'

'I saw them. They are not appropriate.'

'What do you mean?'

Whatever else the headmaster said was drowned by an ear-splitting roar, which exploded into screams and whistles. Mel was leaping up and down again, and a dozen spotlights spun webs of colour all around the hall. The disco music blew in again, shaking the ceiling panels, and Richard and Rikki stared as Anton Dekker himself burst through the double doors.

'*Stamp* and cheer!' read the card. The hall started to shake.

Anton froze. He was wearing a purple leather jacket, and a make-up artist was putting final touches to a mane of dreadlocks. The smoke machines were pumping over his feet, so he looked like he was moving through clouds. He put his arms up, and all the cameras caught him from different angles as he pirouetted and removed a pair of skinny sunglasses. He had a microphone in his hand, and yelled into it: '*Howayadoing*, Green Cross?'

The crowd went even wilder, and an infant fainted.

'Do you know my name?' he shouted.

'Anton!' screamed the children. Rikki and Richard could only gaze.

'Do you know my name?' he repeated, and the echo machine bounced the voice from speaker to speaker.

'Anton!' shrieked the children. 'Anton! Anton!'

They stamped as they chanted it. The presenter twirled in a circle, and his feet were suddenly a blur in the smoke. He was down on one hand, then he was leaping upwards in a somersault. He whirled in the lights, and the music seemed to turn him faster and faster.

Richard looked at Rikki and saw that there were tears running down his cheeks. 'It doesn't matter,' he said into his ear. 'You told me that. Nothing matters.'

'This did,' said Rikki. 'This does.'

'We had nothing to say. It's all rubbish.'

'What are we here for if nothing matters? What *does* matter, Richard? He's not getting away with this – I have questions.'

'Come on.'

'No.'

'Yes!'

Richard made his way to the seating block, through the barrage of noise. He started the long climb to the back row, where he could see other members of his class, dancing and waving. Rikki had to use his handkerchief, and his eyes were glittering. They pushed past Mark, who was stamping with everyone else, and moved along to the middle. Miss Maycock had just that moment taken Jeff by the wrist, and was leading him towards the platform. Richard and Rikki took the seat he'd vacated, and watched as he was miked up next to Aparna.

Mr Barlow was looking wretched. He stared at the back of the seat in front of him, curiously still.

CHAPTER EIGHT

'Is this the best, or is this the *rest* of the best?' shouted Anton.

'Try it again, Anton. We're low still.'

'Is this the best, or is this *west* of the best?' repeated the host. His arms were crossed over his chest, and his fingers had splayed out into scissor shapes. There was a baseball cap pulled low over one ear, and instead of the leather jacket he now wore a green satin tunic, rather like a jockey. The make-up artist was still dabbing at him, and two costume assistants plucked and tucked.

'That's good,' boomed the producer. 'Can we go again from your entrance? The green's better.'

'Moves again?'

'Whole thing, please, Anton – it's lovely. Keep it safe.'

The smoke pumped over the floor, and as the cameras rolled, the doors burst open once more. The children leaped to their feet as Mel waved her card. Anton pirouetted and flipped, but this time he ran through the fog onto the stage. He twirled himself up onto the table, and stood frozen in a kung-fu pose as the six delegates clapped and the audience roared yet louder.

'Now we is far from London,' said Anton in his most gravelly voice. He lifted one eyebrow, and camera two zoomed in close. 'We is checking out a *cool-school* today, so no way is you gonna switch off till you heard what the kids have to say.' He winked. 'This is where the reel kidz is gonna take off the lids and do the biz-niz. It's a laugh, not-half, but we gotta start—'

'Anton,' said Tom. 'Nothing on three, I'm afraid. Go again with that, please.'

'Stand by, seven, Anton's intro,' said someone, and a man emerged with a clapperboard. 'Ready, Anton? It's gorgeous! Take two.'

Anton wasn't quite ready, and laughed. The producer laughed, Mel laughed and the children applauded.

'Go, seven, Anton intro. Ready, Anton? Take three.'

'Hey-o *lo*!' said Anton, with his hands up over his head. 'We is checking out a cool school today, so no way is you gonna switch off till you have heard what the kids have to say.' He winked again. 'This is where the *reel kidz* is gonna take off the *lids*, and do the *biz-niz*! It's a laugh – not-half – an' we gonna start with the cool head teacher-man, whosa baby this is! Is a-Green Cross a-Primary-*cool*!'

Mel waved her sign: 'Cheer and Whistle!' Then she put 'Silence!' up.

The children did as they were told, and camera one panned left to right as the searchlights turned pink and blue. The headmaster came forward, smiling, and Anton jumped down so he was sitting cross-legged on the table. Someone whistled, and Mel put her sign up again. Anton put his arm round the headmaster's shoulders and drew him close.

'Wassa wevver in this school, Mr Headman?' drawled Anton. Mr Prowse looked at the camera, and went to speak. Anton, however, took the microphone away and said: 'How is the learnin' layin'? The kids goin' or stayin'? An' whass this they a-sayin' in de *Kidspeak*-project? Ooooh . . .'

The headmaster swallowed. He hesitated, and Tom – the producer – raised his thumbs.

Mr Prowse cleared his throat. 'Here at Green Cross,' he said, 'we pride ourselves on a policy of inclusivity that we believe is truly child-centred. Established in the nineteen-seventies, the school originally served only the middle classes—'

'Cut!' shouted someone.

'You can't say all that,' said Anton in his normal voice. 'This is eleven seconds.'

'Eleven seconds?'

'I do eight, you have three.'

'Oh. I thought this was the interview.'

'Just say "hi". That's all you've got to do, man. It's a kids' show – for the kids.'

The headmaster nodded, and the next take was successful. He waved his hands as he said 'Hi!' and managed a two-second grin, front teeth visible. They cut, and the cameras were repositioned closer to the big table. Anton was taken aside for some cut-away nodding-shots, and the speakers checked their appearance for the last time. Everyone had received letters about uniform – there had even been a diagram detailing tie-knot sizes.

'Excuse me,' said Jeff to the headmaster. 'I can't do this.'

'Yes, you can,' said the headmaster.

'What's happened to Richard, though?'

'Read your speech, it's better.'

'But I don't—'

'Just do it! Aparna? You're looking tense.'

'Sir, Rikki was working on this—'

'Shhhh!'

Rikki and Richard watched in silence as Anton returned to the stage.

He stood in front of the table this time, and he'd changed again. He was now wearing a glittery crimson tail-coat, and a top hat. The producer had decided that the cameras would keep rolling as the speeches were delivered. The editors would then pick the best moments from whatever they got, including questions at the end. They only needed ninety seconds, because the programme would finish with the song Anton was releasing later that month – a charity-fundraiser called 'Every Kiddie Counts'.

'School debate, take one!' cried somebody. The clapper-board snapped.

'So!' cried Anton. He leered at the closest camera. 'This is where the issues get laid out and made out. Check outta kidz, heh? – they got stuff on their *mind*. Who's got the power in this tower? – nowyer gonna find out from one little wower called, ah, Miss Suzi Peterson!'

The first speaker – eight-year-old Suzi – immediately stood up. The producer signalled to her and she sat down again. 'My name is Suzi Peterson,' she said nervously. 'I am the Year Four winner of the *Kidspeak* competition, and I would like to talk about pets. Thank you.'

The headmaster nodded. Suzi had her nose close to her piece of paper. The hall was quiet. Mel was holding a card saying, 'Total Silence – Total!'

'Every year,' said Suzi, 'many of our four-legged friends suffer needless pain because of cruel owners. One man got annoyed with his dog for always barking, so instead of training it and being kind, he starved it and was cruel. Thankfully, he was caught and punished, but not all dogs are so lucky. Here are some pictures of cats and dogs that have not been so lucky.'

'OK, cut!' said a voice. 'No images, right? Move on, angel, that was great.'

'The pictures are on my laptop,' said Suzi. 'Shall I show them?'

'No need, Suzi,' said the headmaster. 'It was lovely. Do you want more, Tom, or is that enough?'

'Can we have the kid with the glasses?' said one of the technicians. 'We can do a nice cross-fade – sit him back, will you? – put his head up. He's going to catch the light.'

'Morris!' hissed the headmaster. 'Your turn.'

'My name is Morris,' said Morris.

'Wait,' said Tom. 'Take his glasses off.'

One of the make-up assistants removed the boy's

spectacles and drew his chair backwards a fraction. She sponged the boy's gleaming forehead.

'Go,' said a voice. 'Rolling.'

'My name is Morris Belgrave,' said Morris. 'My speech is about being a good parent.' He coughed, and squinted at his paper. 'Sometimes we think that our mothers and fathers are mean to us, by not letting us do stuff, but I want to ask a question.'

There was a loud whistle from the audience, and Mel hissed angrily – and waved the 'Silence' card.

'What . . . if . . .' said Morris. He stopped.

'Keep going!' said Tom. 'You're doing fine. Don't touch the mike.'

'I can't see my words,' said the boy.

'Oh God, I thought you'd memorized this,' whispered the headmaster. 'You were practising all last week – it's not that difficult.'

'I can't see, Mr Prowse. I need my specs.'

'Can we give them back?'

'There's too much reflection. What's the question?'

'I can't see!'

'Well, do it from memory!'

'I can't, sir.'

'OK,' said Tom. 'Let the girl at the end have a go.'

'We can edit this, can't we?' said the headmaster. 'Tell me we can edit this.'

'No problem – it's always tricky. What's your name, love? . . . What?'

Aparna whispered her name.

'Aparna, speak into your mike,' said the headmaster. 'Don't go silent on us.'

'What's your speech about, dear? Can you go from the middle?'

Aparna lowered her eyes. 'It's about how, er . . . food aid in Africa can do more harm than good.'

'What?'

'Because it can undermine the, er . . . local farming economy and skew the market.'

'More bananas!' shouted a voice. The headmaster glared out into the audience, but the lights were so strong he could see nothing.

'That's a bit heavy for TV,' said Anton, laughing. 'That's not going to work with the song, either.'

'Could you just read out some snippets?' said Tom. 'Or just do the beginning, with your name? What's the boy next to you got? The blond boy? Jeff.'

'Mine's about racing cars,' said Jeff.

'Let's go with that,' said Anton. 'That sounds cool.'

Again, there was a long, shrill whistle. Some of the audience were talking, and there was a lot of fidgeting. Mel walked up the aisle, and a whistle came again, from somewhere else. Mr Barlow had his head in his hands and was refusing to look up.

'Can we stop this noise, please,' said the headmaster. 'You can all just be patient for a moment. We're sorting out the order, and then we'll get going again.'

'Get the bananas!' called a voice, and this time some of the children laughed. 'It's banana time!'

'Look, who is saying that?' cried the headmaster. He tried to find the producer, but the cameras had moved again and all he could see were dark shapes. 'Do you want to give Hermione a go? Honestly, I thought they'd be better than this . . .'

'Sir, I want to hear what Aparna's got to say,' shouted a voice. 'Can we mike her up properly? She's so interesting.'

'Look, whoever you are, you're going to be in my office in a minute! Can we do something about the lights? – I can't see anything.'

It was Rikki, of course, and he was standing up. 'I'm just saying we want to listen to Aparna, sir. And Jeff. If he's taken over from me, it's bound to be good. I just can't wait to hear him.'

'We could do some questions if you want,' said Tom, reappearing at the edge of the stage. 'Questions should be easy.'

'Let's hear Jeffrey first. Mr Barlow, can you keep order up there, please? This can all be cut, can't it?'

Jeff was now visibly trembling. He started to stand up, and frantic gestures got him sitting down again. His right hand went to his tie, and there was a crunch as he twisted the microphone. Aparna was sitting absolutely still with her eyes closed.

'The Grand Prix,' said Jeff breathlessly, 'is the exciting most sporting event in history . . . and it is my, er, dream to go there – is this OK? Every year the nations of the world gather from all around the nations of the world . . . sorry.

Gather – to pit their wits and technical know-how, and skill – but . . . What very few people know is that sponsorship. Sponsorship . . .'

'Keep going. Slow down a bit.'

'Deals. Are being made in many millions of pounds, which is the fastest car, is the Ferrari.'

'Not true!' shouted Rikki. 'It's a Skoda—'

'Developed by Federico Ferrari. Here are some of the statistics about its engine, and—'

'I've got a question,' cried Rikki. 'I want to ask something!'

Jeff dried completely, and stared hopelessly into the lights. The headmaster shaded his eyes with both hands, and saw with horror that the microphone-boom was being hurriedly swung over the heads of the audience. In a moment, Rikki's voice was loud and clear.

'I just want to know something,' he said. 'Remind me, please: what is the point of this?'

'I don't think we should do questions,' said the headmaster quietly.

'We'll just do a few,' said Tom.

'Not him. Please.'

'We won't film him, but he's got a good, strong voice.'

'He's a menace . . .'

'Can you repeat your question, please, son?'

Rikki looked up and spoke slowly into the mike. 'I've got a few questions,' he said. 'Number one is why me and Richard got kicked off the panel. Number two is why we have to listen to puerile rubbish about racing cars.

What are you doing there, Jeff? How could you agree to this?'

Jeff gaped. 'Rikki,' he said. 'I didn't—'

'You just can't keep away from your girlfriend, can you?'

There was a gust of laughter, and a cry of 'Shame!'

'Move on, please,' said the headmaster. 'Richard! Will you sit down now?'

'You kicked me off the team, sir, but that's not going to stop me speaking,' said Rikki. 'You go on about it all the time, sir – freedom of speech. I don't see much freedom here, today. I only see people reading stuff you've checked and approved. I see a bunch of little kids pretending to be grown-ups, and worst of all it's your version of grown-ups. Look at them all! Look at us . . . you even make us wear stuff that takes away identity – like these stupid little ties, like we're all going off to the office. You want us looking the same and thinking the same, and that's one of the tools of control, Mr Prowse! That was what my speech was about, ladies and gentlemen. It was called "The Tools of Control", and it was about fear and repression and not being allowed to speak when you need to.'

'This is outrageous,' whispered the headmaster.

Rikki had won a smattering of applause, and Mr Prowse was now on his feet. Mel was making her way up the aisle, towards Rikki. Mr Barlow sat still, and his head remained in his hands.

'Let him talk,' said a parent.

'Shh!' cried somebody else. 'Get on with the speeches!'

'He's hijacking this meeting,' said the headmaster. 'Take the microphone away, and let's get back to the script.'

Rikki reached up and grabbed the boom. The next moment he was making his way towards the aisle, with the microphone cradled comfortably under his chin.

'Keep rolling,' said Tom. 'Camera three, stay on the panel. One and two, pan audience.'

Rikki laughed. 'You asked how I dare?' he said. 'Well, what have I got to lose? I mean, can you imagine how much trouble I'm going to be in? And what's my crime? I just want to ask questions – but not about stupid, dumb Ferrari racing cars, or dogs and cats that should be put down and fed to the homeless. Aparna, you were going to talk about Africa. Why? Who cares?'

The producer made hand-signals. 'Keep going!' he whispered.

'What I don't understand,' said Rikki, 'is where any of this is going, or why it's important. Schools just pump you full of stuff you either don't need, because it's irrelevant, or they turn you into a clone. We don't get taught important stuff.'

'Nonsense!' cried the headmaster.

'First aid,' said Richard. 'Why didn't we get taught that?'

'Good point!' said Salome.

'Chinese,' said Rikki. 'You're mucking about with languages nobody needs, when everyone knows the economic future is going to be dominated by China. We should be learning Mandarin for when they invade us, not finger-painting and writing stories. We should be sat in rows learning proper maths, but you waste our time telling stupid stories and doing stuff like this. Why are the cameras here? How has this dumb-arse circus helped us to think? This is a puppet-show, Mr Anton. We are being brainwashed.'

'Be silent!' shouted the headmaster. He was bright red.

'Why?'

'I do not tolerate rudeness!'

'Who's being rude?' said Rikki.

'You've been shouting out. You've been interrupting—'

'You interrupt us all the time, sir, and you're the one who's shouting. You're trying to shut me up, but what have I done wrong? I'm just being honest! Everyone knows you kick out kids who make your school look bad – you're trying to get rid of Eric right now, and what's wrong with Eric? He's a bit psychotic, but so what? At least he's a laugh. You didn't want Salome, and I know you don't want me. The only thing you're interested in is looking good yourself – which is why you've invited all the TV people here in the first place. And why did I get kicked out of the team?'

The headmaster peered into the lights, helpless and desperate. 'Can we stop this, Mr Barlow? Where's Mr Barlow?'

'You want a Fascist crackdown,' said Rikki. 'Plain and simple. You don't care about people's feelings any more than I do. Nobody does!'

'Can we cut, please?'

But Anton was grinning. The cameras continued to

roll as Rikki and Richard made their way down the steps towards the stage. Mel moved towards him, and tried to take the microphone. Rikki protected it and stood still, his eyes closed.

There was a deathly silence.

'Here are some proposals, OK? Real ones that I think about, because *Kidspeak* is about thinking, yes? Teach us about real life, please, sir. Teach us something useful, like about sex, so we know stuff and don't get scared, or pregnant, or sick, and so we don't get it wrong. Cut the stupid hymns in those . . . mind-numbing assemblies, and admit that God, if he ever existed, is now dead – or fled. He's not here now, that's for sure.'

'Hey!' shouted a parent. 'We didn't come here for this . . .'

Mel tried again to seize the microphone. Rikki held onto it and raised his head. 'Listen to me,' he said quietly. 'What are you scared of? I don't care about kids' stuff any more, or global warming, or . . . polar bears, or all the other rubbish we're supposed to worry about. Can't we just cut the environmental nonsense, because who gives a toss, really? It's all too late. If pandas are too dopey to survive, stuff a few and put the rest in a zoo. Castrate poor people so they don't have kids – stupid people too – and save money. Bring back the death penalty, and improve chemical weapons. Make it easier to buy guns, and that way we might start getting the population down and save the planet, if we really want to save it.

'What about fat people? I say, put them in cages and

don't let them eat, and give the skinny ones their food. Take us to old people's homes, and line us up in front of people that are dying – we need to know how scary that is, so we're ready for it. Cut the charity-days, because all those poor kids – how's charity going to help them? They're going to die anyway, from Aids. Or famine, or floods, or just from battering the hell out of each other with the bombs we all keep selling them. Let me finish! I heard Aparna's speech last week, and she's right – the only reason we send food to the Third World is to make a profit out of them, and get them addicted to the rubbish we can't sell to all the obese, retarded kids in our own country who can hardly walk ten paces down the street without needing an ambulance, which won't even come because there aren't enough of them any more.

'Tell us how to build nuclear shelters, Mr Prowse! So when some mad country nukes us, we might survive – if we want to survive. If we don't want to survive, give us a worksheet on how to kill ourselves painlessly, which you could do now if you wanted, because I'm not sure me and Richard want to go on much longer. How do we die, sir?'

There was another long silence.

'Why do our bodies fail, and where do we go? What's it like – dying? Why don't you ever teach us anything that's useful? Show me someone dead again. Tell me what happened. Tell me why the heart stops. There's no heaven, is there? There is no God, no afterlife, no point, no . . . sweet choir of angels, and we don't ever see the ones we love again, do we? Hell, I believe in, because I'm standing in it right now. But no heaven. Just tell us the truth. *Please.*'

Again, nobody spoke. The cameras rolled, and the audience gazed at Rikki, dumbfounded. A child started to cry, and Anton Dekker wasn't smiling any more.

'Ideas,' whispered Rikki. 'That's all they are, sir. You told us to put on our thinking caps. I spent a week working on that, but I can't go on much longer. Not like this.'

'Have we finished?' said Richard quietly.

'Yes.'

Someone in the audience started clapping, but nobody joined in. It died out, and the producer said: 'Cut, thank you. Cut everything.'

Nobody moved.

'That's a wrap, I think. Close it down.'

CHAPTER NINE

Jeff was waiting for Richard and Rikki when they got close to home.

The television people had packed up and gone, and the last lesson had taken place in a horrified, frightened silence. The headmaster did not appear – he had been seen in heated conversation with the producer, and had driven after him in his car. The rumour went round that he was offering money to get the whole item dropped from the schedule. Rikki and Richard got all the way to their own road, walking alone and not talking, when they looked up and saw Jeff blocking their way.

'Hi, Jeff,' said Richard.

'Why did you say that about bananas to Aparna? What if that goes on TV?'

Rikki looked tired. 'It was a joke,' he said.

'Why do you keep going on about bananas? How is it funny?'

'Are you going to thump me? You said I need battering. If you want to hit me, Jeff, just—'

'It's because you're racist,' said Jeff. His voice was

trembling. 'I know what you mean by it. She knows too. Bananas are for monkeys. Aparna's Indian origin – so you're just a racist, saying all she eats is bananas.'

'I'd never thought of it like that,' said Rikki. 'But I see what you mean.'

Jeff stared at him, so full of emotion that Richard thought he was going to cry. His mouth was working. 'It's filthy too.'

'Why?'

'You know why!'

'Are you going to spit at me?'

Jeff said, 'No.' Then he looked at Richard. 'It wasn't my fault you got kicked off the team.'

'I know,' said Richard.

'So why did you make me look so . . . stupid?'

'Because you are,' said Rikki, butting in.

'Am I? OK, I can't use lots of long words like you can. But at least I don't go around upsetting everyone. And you – Richard.' He shook his head, and tried to get control of his voice. 'You were my best friend, once. I don't know who you are now, or . . . what you are. You just make everyone feel bad all the time. Why don't you leave? Why don't you go to some institution where they can . . . sort you out? Aparna's a nice girl and she's worth fifty of you. You're a racist . . . slug. You're not even worth hitting, and if I could step on you, I would.'

He walked away, fast, and Richard heard his footsteps break into a run. He and Rikki plodded on towards their house. They walked up the path and then round to the back garden, past the shed, and they glanced up at the tree house. They moved past the vegetable patch, where nothing grew, and when they opened the back door, their mother was waiting.

'Mr Barlow phoned,' she said. 'I know what's happened. He says they probably won't show it – they've agreed to cut it.'

They watched the television together, and at four thirty-five Green Cross School appeared. Anton's routines dominated, but there was cleverly edited footage of happy, smiling children. Ten seconds was given over to fragments of the various speeches, and somehow the producers made it all seem sensible.

Moments later they cut to Anton's co-presenter, who was reporting from a seal sanctuary in Cornwall. The seal pups were doing well, but more aluminium ring-pulls were needed for the fight against flipper rot. Three minutes were devoted to a school that had collected a whole lorry-load. By the time the programme had finished, Richard and Rikki were lying back in the chair with their arms over their heads. Mrs Westlake served tea and there was no conversation.

When they went up to their room, Richard felt more tired than he had ever felt in his entire life. He tried to get on with his evening revision, but his eyes kept closing.

'Let's stop,' he said to Rikki. His head lolled and the papers on the desk were blurred.

'Why do you want to stop?' said Rikki. 'This is life. It's what we do.'

'I don't want to do it.'

'No choice, Richard. We learn stuff and we do stuff.'

'I can't think. I can't see the words. I can't remember what I'm supposed to remember. I just want to sleep, Rikki. Today was horrible.'

They were staring at a labelled diagram of a chrysalis. Rikki was colouring in the butterfly, bound up tight like a tiny parcel – like an Egyptian mummy. He made the body purple, and he gave the folded-up wings yellow stripes. He put spikes around the head, and drew lightning bolts.

'I'm going to finish,' he said. 'There's nothing else worth doing.'

Richard, however, was already dreaming.

He found himself up in the clouds, hurtling through mist. When his head was jogged, he suddenly burst through into a bright blue sky and found that he was sitting on a wing. Why he wasn't blown off he couldn't say, but it was as comfortable as a chair, and his hair was streaming out behind him. His hands held the hard, cold metal beneath him, and it was some moments before he thought of looking round at the pilot.

The pilot was Rikki, in a red helmet, his hands gripping the controls. He had his chin thrust forward, and he was concentrating hard. After a few seconds, however, he noticed Richard, and though he tried not to look, there came a point when their eyes locked together.

'Crash and burn,' he said.

The dream went on and on, as the plane skimmed through the air. Richard looked at Rikki, and Rikki looked at Richard, and Richard knew they were plummeting. When Mr Westlake appeared in the bedroom, he found Richard was snoring, and Rikki was colouring.

'Did you see the TV show, Dad?' said Rikki.

'Yes,' said his father.

'Were you proud?'

'No.'

'Oh.'

'I've seen the speech you made too. Doctor Warren made a copy. I was called in, which is why I'm late home.'

'We were kicked out of the team. For being different.'

Mr Westlake nodded. 'You shouldn't have been.'

'What did you think of me? Really?'

Mr Westlake sighed, and sat down. He looked into Rikki's eyes. 'It doesn't matter what I think. We want you to see the counsellor again.'

'Why?'

'Why, Rikki? How can you ask me that?'

'I'm asking.'

'Because you're not well, and he wants to change your medication—'

'Because I ask questions?'

'No. Because you're so . . . furious. Also . . . it's a condition of you staying on at Green Cross. Doctor Warren was there – we all watched it together. If you want to stay at the school, you have to see him and they're going to see what they can do. Drugs, perhaps, or—'

'I don't want to stay at school. I don't want to live.'

His father leaned forward and held his son's shoulders. 'How can you say a thing like that? What happened to the . . . to the—'

'To the Richard you knew?'

'No!'

'I guess you didn't really know him, did you? I'm so sorry to disappoint, Dad – but this is what we are now, and if you want to lop off my head with a knife, why don't you? I don't belong in this family. I don't belong in the world.'

Mr Westlake paused, then pressed Rikki back in his chair. He looked at him hard. 'I wanted them to, once, Rikki – to intevene. I'll be honest. They told me I'd be killing you, so we couldn't even think about it. But I can't stand much more of this, that's for sure.'

Mrs Westlake had followed her husband up with a tray of cocoa, and stood in the doorway looking at them. 'Don't fight,' she said quietly. 'We're not going to solve anything by another row.'

'What do you want to solve?' said Rikki. 'I didn't ask to be born. You were the ones who organized that.'

His parents stared at him in silence.

'Rikki,' said Mr Westlake, at last. 'Don't you want to be helped?'

'No.'

'You can't go on like this – you said that yourself.'

'So what? It's got to end sometime.'

'Doctor Warren can help. You didn't give him a chance, and we want you to go back to him. In fact, Rikki, isn't that the point? You don't give anyone a chance.'

'What is the matter, love?' said Rikki's mother. She came into the room and sat on the bed. Her husband put the cups of cocoa on Rikki's desk and sank back in his chair. 'I haven't seen it yet,' she said. 'But from what your dad said you sounded . . . you sounded suicidal. Why, love?'

'I don't know what we're *for*,' said Rikki quietly. 'Any of us. You, in particular – look at you. You just work and sleep and cook and make hot drinks that we don't even want or need. I don't know what this is about. You're strangers to me. I look at other kids' parents and . . . I mean, don't you look at other kids and wish they were yours, instead of me? I look at you and think, *These people I live with, in this crazy house . . . this old house. They're nothing. They're going to die, they're going to end up in the earth – or not even in the earth.* We'll be pushing you into the furnace like we did Grandad, that's what me and Richard will do, and then we watch the smoke come out the chimney. We put on black clothes and we go around sad for a bit – and that's the end of you.'

Mrs Westlake couldn't speak.

'We pack up your stuff. Give it away. It's all junk.'

His mother's lips were trembling. She blinked helplessly.

Mr Westlake said, 'Rikki, you've got to shut that mouth of yours. All you do is hurt and upset people—'

'Why can't we talk about dying? He lived right there,

just down the landing! He lived in your office, and it's not your office! How is that your office?'

'Is that the problem here?'

'No!'

'Then what? We're all going to die, son. Of course we are. I am, you are – is it Grandad you want to talk about?'

'Where is he?' said Rikki. 'Where did he go?'

'I don't know. People die—'

'There's no God, is there? I was right about that.'

'I don't know,' said Mr Westlake.

'You don't believe in one.'

'Don't I?'

'Do you?'

'Oh, my word. Sometimes. Yes. Sometimes, I do.'

'I do too,' said his mother.

'When? At Christmas. When you want something.'

'No,' said his father. 'The last time I really believed, if you want to know, was when *you* were born. I remember that moment and that was a miracle.'

'When Richard was born, not me,' said Rikki. 'I'm the monster from hell, remember?'

'No, no, no. To me you are the same now.'

'What made you believe in God, then – when I was born? Did you see those angels?'

Mr Westlake sighed. 'Oh, my boy,' he said. 'You ask questions, but you don't listen to the answers. No: I didn't see angels. I'll tell you something – we'd wanted a son for so long, and when you were born it was like our prayers were answered.'

Rikki laughed. He put his fingers into his cocoa, and gritted his teeth as the liquid burned him. 'That's just genes,' he said at last. 'Evolution – we do it at school. We're conditioned to propagate ourselves and we dress it all up as miracles – it's just science, Dad, and you wanting to prove your manhood and tell yourself some part of you lives on after death.'

'You know nothing about it,' said Mr Westlake. 'Nothing at all.'

'It's in the exam. It's in our science book.'

'You know nothing about birth.'

Mr Westlake paused for a moment, and Rikki stared at him. Then he sucked his fingers.

'I was scared,' said his father.

'Why?'

'I don't know. I didn't want to be there, I suppose – in the hospital, I mean. I was so scared, and I thought, *Why do they need me? – I'll be in the way* – but I'd promised your mother. You know, I actually thought I was going to faint I was so nervous.'

'Scared of me being deformed?'

'No.' He took his wife's hand, and held it tight. 'Of seeing all that mess, I suppose – and not being able to do anything useful. But I got there, obviously – and . . . it wasn't like that.'

'You weren't easy, Rikki,' said his mother.

'You certainly weren't. Not even then.'

'You weren't round the right way, for one thing. It wasn't drastic, but we'd been warned it was going to be difficult. We'd tried a long time for you – given up, almost. So everything was at stake.'

'When I saw you . . .' said Mr Westlake. His voice was soft. He had his eyes closed. 'When you emerged . . . I could not believe it. You had long hair, do you know that? Your face was all twisted, and your little fists were clenched. You screamed out – my God, you were strong. And you were so beautiful. You imagine – but you can't, Rikki. You cannot imagine what it's like.'

'Genetic conditioning,' said Rikki. 'So the race survives.'

'You won't know, for a while, what it is to see life . . . starting. Dying, you know about now, and I wish you didn't. But being born – you know nothing at all. Every time I look at you I am so glad, and proud – just as your grandfather was. He was! – don't look away. We phoned him so he was the first one to know. And I remember holding the receiver so he could hear you screaming away, and he was in tears, Rikki. He could not speak for joy. We lived up north, then, so it was nearly a week before he saw you. He was outside the house, waiting for us – that was the first time he held you, and you're named after him—'

'I know this,' said Rikki. 'I know all this.'

'Three months later we moved in, to be closer to him. You know all about it. He was ill, but he had ten years—'

'I've heard this, Dad.'

'And now you talk about ending your life? Rikki, you're just breaking our hearts. You think we're going to let that happen? Either of us?'

'He hasn't understood how precious he is,' said his mother. 'Maybe it's us. Maybe we haven't made it clear. Whatever you say, or do, Rikki – you are the most precious thing. And we're not going to let you go.'

Mr Westlake's phone rang suddenly. He let it ring for a moment, and then found it in his pocket. He checked the screen and said, 'It's Doctor Warren. Talk of the devil.'

'I don't want to see him,' said Rikki. 'He's not on our side and he's going to make it worse.'

Mr Westlake pressed connect, and said to Rikki: 'You're going to see him even if we have to drag you there and hold you in the chair. He is going to make you well, because we can't.'

He paused, and Rikki stared at him.

'Who else is there?' said his father. 'What else can we do?'

CHAPTER TEN

They made a four o'clock appointment for the following Saturday.

In the morning, they had shopping to do. Richard and Rikki needed all kinds of things for the Clifden Adventure Centre residential, which was at the very end of term. There were boring things to be found, like trousers and socks, but they soon moved on to the altogether more exciting 'Outback Survival' store. First, it was headgear, and Rikki wanted a baseball cap. Richard showed him the Clifden brochure, which assured the reader that 'the right choice of clothing could well be a matter of life and death. Bring balaclavas,' it said, 'or woollen hats – for nights out under the stars . . .' The shop assistant showed them the full range, and they spent several minutes trying out the possible colour combinations. She then brought out scarves, and a small crowd gathered to watch as she knotted a complicated figure-of-eight in vivid purple around the boy's two throats.

'Very nice,' said Rikki. 'Buy one, take one?'

'No.'

'You can have a photo. Think of the advertising!'

'Sorry.'

They bought a new rainproof coat with an extra-wide hood. They bought gloves. They got a two-man ridge-tent and a camping stove so small it fitted in your pocket. They bought a map of Wales, a compass and two beautiful penknives – Rikki wanted the bottle-opener attachment; Richard preferred the screwdriver. Then they chose walking boots, two head-torches, and an SAS-approved survival blanket that appeared to be made of tinfoil. Mrs Westlake put it all on the credit card, and they crossed happily to the local bookshop. They were disappointed, however, to find that the recommended handbook – *Alive and Uncaught*, by Chris 'Nailhead' McGinty, SAS Commander – was completely sold out.

'I've had about a dozen kids in here after that,' said the shopkeeper. 'Why's it so popular all of a sudden?'

Richard explained, and added his name to the order list.

They went to the barber's, then – though Mrs Westlake was worried about time. She had tried to cut her son's hair herself, but Rikki had been impossible and she'd had to give in. Richard had sat still, but Rikki simply waggled his head and squealed – it had been way too dangerous. Colin the barber had been delighted to oblige and he put them in the chair, utterly unfazed.

'Total head-shave, twice?' he said. 'Fancy the skinhead look?'

'You shave my head and we'll sue you,' said Richard.

‘I want a trim, please – just off the collar, and—’

‘Give him something decent, Colin,’ begged Rikki. ‘He still looks about seven years old – give him train-tracks – I know! Give him a little Mohawk!’

‘I want to look normal!’ said Richard.

‘That’s what I’m suggesting,’ said Rikki. ‘You never get it, do you?’

‘There’s not enough time for anything fancy, I’m afraid,’ said Colin. He was combing their heads simultaneously, flourishing two silver combs. Again a small crowd had gathered, and someone was filming on their phone. ‘Do you want to look the same, or different?’

‘Different,’ said Richard.

‘The same,’ said Rikki. ‘We are the same, so I think a left-parting for me, and a right-parting for him. There’s safety in symmetry.’

They arrived at the Rechner Institute at ten past four, looking neat, tidy and happy. Soon they were in the same bed on the same ward – fifth floor – with two nurses looking after them. It was Dr Summersby’s ‘special ward’, apparently, where she put her most important patients. After a snack, they were taken down for tests, and submitted to an hour of scans. They filled in a questionnaire, and looked at swirls of colour. They copied shapes and solved riddles, and then they were put on a treadmill. They had X-rays in a long, metal tube and for the last half-hour they were connected to headphones and what looked like car batteries. Strange photographs were projected onto the wall in front of them, and they were interrogated about what they saw.

After a warm shower they changed into school uniform, and it was time for the counselling session.

'Rikki, put your tie on,' said Mr Westlake. He had left work early to join them.

'No,' said Rikki.

'Do as you're told!'

'No. Dad, I'm not at school—'

'Come here! Do what you're told, and try to make this work – show the gentleman respect. Put your chin up . . .'

Rikki submitted as his father looped and knotted his tie, and when both heads were completely respectable, they went back up in the lift. Dr Warren's room was on the sixth floor, where the carpets were extra-thick.

'Welcome,' he said.

The place had been transformed. It had been cleaned since the last visit, of course, but all the beanbags, games and puzzles had been put away, out of sight. The counsellor had subdued the lighting, putting on a couple of desk lamps. He had also illuminated the fish tank. The sound of an aria floated in from a discreet hi-fi, and there was a smell of roasting coffee.

'How are you?' said Dr Warren, smiling brightly. 'A long day for you, I think – I hope you're not too tired.'

'No,' said Richard. 'We're fine.'

'How are you?' said Rikki. 'Wow, it's dark in here. Have you been sleeping?'

'No, Rikki.'

'Telling ghost stories? Scaring the nurses?'

Dr Warren smiled again, and shook his head. 'Sit yourselves down,' he said. 'It's really good to see you. Can I get you coffee, or tea, or a soft drink . . . ?'

'What's this music?' said Rikki.

'It's an opera,' said Dr Warren. 'It's a love story—'

'*Madame Butterfly*,' said Richard. 'Mum and Dad like this. We get this at home.'

Rikki laughed. 'What is it about you old people?' he said. 'You get all misty-eyed about nothing – guys singing about their love affairs. This one forgets all about her, doesn't he? So she breaks her heart and . . . what does she do in the end?'

'Madame Butterfly kills herself,' said Dr Warren. 'It's a tragedy.'

'People die,' said Rikki. 'That's not tragic, Doc – it's the circle of life.'

'Is it?'

'See the show. I'll sing you the song if you like.'

'I think life *can* be tragic,' said Dr Warren. 'You'll find, sometimes—'

'I wouldn't know,' interrupted Rikki. 'I'm just a boy with a simple outlook.'

'Are you?'

'Who wrote the music, by the way?'

'And you're answering a question with a question. Is that intentional? – it's certainly clever.'

'Can I have a coffee?' said Richard.

'How many sugars?' said Rikki quickly.

Richard looked at him. 'Don't you know?'

'Haven't we given up?' said Rikki.

Richard paused. 'Do you think we should?' he said.

They were both grinning, and they turned to look at their doctor.

'That's impressive,' he said. 'That's not an easy game to play – I am impressed.'

'Ah, we play a lot of games now,' said Richard. 'We amuse ourselves, now. We don't rely on others, because, now we're losing our friends.'

'Really?' said Dr Warren.

'He's lying,' said Rikki. 'In *my* head, I have tons of friends.'

'You play games against each other? What kind of games?'

'I-spy,' said Richard.

'Do you want to see us arm-wrestle?' said Rikki. 'It's very entertaining, but it can get violent. Chess, we can also play. But I always win, so Richard gets a bit tearful.'

'Why is that?'

'Well,' said Rikki, 'I'm a simple soul, and I don't want to get tangled in an argument about brains with a man of your experience. But I think it's because I'm smart, and Richard's dumb.'

'Not true,' said Richard.

'What's the capital of the Sudan?' said Rikki.

'Khartoum,' said Richard. 'How long is a chain?'

'Fifty metres. Who invented the aqualung?'

'Jacques Cousteau,' said Richard. 'Define "catharsis".'

'Ah, now, catharsis is a disputed term,' said Rikki.

'So don't get tricksy. But the majority of scholars would define it as the moment passion or emotion is purged while witnessing something massively distressing. One more question, Richard: are you gay?'

'No. I'm not sure about you, though.'

Rikki laughed, and kissed Richard on the cheek.

'That's quite a show,' said Dr Warren, sitting back and chuckling. 'I think those television people would be interested in that. They missed an opportunity. I was at the recording, by the way – I wrote down some of the things you said.'

'Yes. Dad got in a mood about that.'

'I can imagine,' said Dr Warren. 'Do I pick up a little bit of resentment towards your father?'

'Of course,' said Rikki. 'Our father's a well-meaning schmuck, and we want to kill him. But that's basic Freud, so we'd be crazy if we didn't.'

Richard said, 'I don't want to kill Dad, Rikki.'

'Yes you do, buddy,' said Rikki. 'You dream about killing him.'

'Interesting,' said Dr Warren. 'Are you aware of Richard's dreams?'

'Of course.'

'He's not,' said Richard. 'My dreams are totally private.'

'He dreams about flowers. Chocolate. Killing Dad. And . . . what was it last night? We were in the classroom, and you looked down and we had no trousers on. You woke up, and you turned to me and said, "Rikki, if that stupid shrink asks about our dreams, don't for God's sake mention the trousers." '

'Not a word of that is true!' said Richard.

'Richard,' said Rikki, 'you're a dirty perve: I read your diary.'

'It's your diary too, and you write much more than me. You're the one with dodgy dreams. Can I have that coffee by the way?'

Dr Warren stood up and went to the sink. He put the kettle on and prepared a cafetière. *Madame Butterfly* filled the silence, full of tenderness.

'Can I change the subject?' said the counsellor, once the drink had been served. He smiled broadly. 'Let's start again. I heard about the recent football match. You scored two goals, which is pretty fantastic! Congratulations.'

'Both headers,' said Richard.

'Next match coming soon,' said Rikki. 'We're training hard.'

'You must have felt good about the victory, and your part in it. I gather your dad was there, and saw the whole thing.'

There was another silence.

'Did you feel good, knowing he was watching?' said Dr Warren. 'I know your grandad used to like seeing you play. He played football in the Navy, I believe—'

'How did you feel, Richard?' said Rikki. 'Let's think back.'

'I felt pretty good,' said Richard. 'We scored good goals, so—'

'Your grandad used to watch, didn't he? Cheer you on? Play shots in the garden?'

'Four–nil,' said Rikki.

'You were remarkably close. You and your grandad.'

'Were we?'

'When you had trouble sleeping—'

'He was around.'

'I'm told he'd sit with you. For hours, sometimes.'

Rikki smiled. 'I just can't remember,' he said. 'Memory like a sieve. But as to the football, well . . . I have to say we'd been pretty anxious about playing, Doctor Warren . . . because – well, you know, there was the chance that other kids would say personal things – 'cos kids can be cruel. So when we scored two goals . . . yes. There was a sense of relief. Triumph. Vindication. Not vindication, that's the wrong word. *Validation*. Now, if that's what you meant by your original question, "Did we feel good?" then . . . yes. We felt good.' Rikki put his head on one side. 'This is "The Rectal Institute", right? Arsehole therapy.'

'We observe, Rikki. We try to understand people.'

'You understand me?'

'I try to.'

Rikki paused. He closed his eyes, and said, 'I don't want your understanding.'

'I accept your hostility. That's fine—'

'You understand it?'

'Of course. I'm trying to see where it comes from. There are things you don't want to talk about because they frighten you, and that's what hostility is.'

Richard said, 'But I'm not hostile. I'm honestly not.'

Dr Warren smiled. 'You're not, I know. But I was addressing a different part of your brain. Rikki.'

'Don't ignore Richard,' said Rikki. 'I warned you about that: he has feelings too.'

'I hope I'm not ignoring you, Richard—'

'I'm Rikki. This is me.'

'I was talking to Richard.'

'But I'm Rikki,' said Richard.

'What?'

'You're Richard,' said Rikki. 'Don't confuse the counsellor!'

'I'm not ignoring either of you,' said Dr Warren. 'All I want—'

'Who are you talking to now?'

'Both of you!' There was a short silence. 'All I want to know,' said Dr Warren quietly, 'is whether you think the situation you're in can improve.'

'Clearly not,' said Rikki. 'Unless you have a guillotine handy.'

'Rikki,' said Richard thoughtfully, 'I don't think I'm hostile. I think I'm quite . . . un-hostile.'

'No,' said Rikki. 'That's self-deception.'

'Is it?'

'You conceal your anger, and everyone thinks you're balanced. But a man of Doctor Warren's insight sees right through you. I tell you something, Counsellor: Richard beats me up. Do you want to see the marks?'

'He's lying,' said Richard. 'There are no marks anywhere.'

'Let's take off our shirt.'

'No.'

'What about last night? Who got angry last night?'

'That was you. You started it.'

'You finished it, and I got cut.'

Dr Warren stood up, and turned on the main light. 'If you're talking about the marks on your arms and shoulders, I do know about them. Your tests have picked them up, as you might expect, and your school has reported them as evidence of serious physical abuse. So yes, I would like to talk about them. Let's do it.'

'There are no marks,' said Richard and Rikki together.

Dr Warren smiled. 'I think you need to know something.' he said. 'We're close to what's called a "referral". If a child is deemed to be "high-risk" in any way, then the school keeps careful watch. You've talked openly about suicide, and your behaviour's deteriorating. So we have prepared what's known as an *Interim Care Order*.'

'An order for care?' said Rikki.

'Yes.'

'You care about us, do you?'

'Yes. It allows us to step in, before something bad happens, and we can protect you—'

'Lock us up. You want to lock us up, Doctor? Is that where this is going? You want to protect us with your infinite sense of care? What from? The world is a bad place, we all know that.'

Dr Warren smiled again. 'Look,' he said. 'I don't necessarily have the answers. I asked you about the marks on your shoulders, because we all know they're getting worse. What I need to know—'

'There are no marks on our shoulders,' said Richard quietly. 'Or on our arms.'

'Richard, please.'

'I'm Rikki.'

'Richard. I am not your enemy. We need to talk about where they're coming from.'

'We play football,' said Richard. 'We get bruised like everyone else.'

'But these are deep cuts, aren't they? Why don't you want to talk about them?' Dr Warren put on his glasses and leaned forward. 'I can take the pain away,' he said.

'Can you?' Richard and Rikki said together.

'I can make it better. If you trust me.'

'We don't.'

'Why not?'

'Because . . .' Rikki paused. 'We have come to understand that the pain never goes away. Ever. It is a condition of being alive.'

Dr Warren nodded. 'Then let's get on to the real subject. We've been avoiding it, and you know what I'm referring to. You can't block it out for ever, boys—'

'Sex?' said Richard.

'No.'

'Tooth decay?' said Rikki. 'Bad breath?'

'What?'

'That's your problem, Doctor Warren, so maybe we should talk about *that* – bring it out in the open. I mean, when you lean forward like you did just then. When you get all coy and intimate, it's like talking to a corpse – poison gas, man. Let's discuss dental hygiene, because I think we can help you. First of all, you need to floss more carefully and try an anti-bacterial mouthwash. I mean, how does your wife stand it? Or has she left you? And what about little Nathaniel – that poor kid in the photo? Does he puke when you kiss him?'

'Rikki—'

'I'm Richard, you freak, and I'm asking you about puke. Do you make everyone puke?'

The colour had drained from Dr Warren's face. 'Whoever you are – Richard, Rikki. You desperately need help.'

Rikki swore brutally.

'Urgently,' said Dr Warren. 'You need it. So I want to ask you, openly . . .' He spoke quietly. 'I want to ask you about the death of your grandad, and what you saw. I want you to tell me, in your own words, what happened. I want you to talk about how you feel.'

Richard nodded and stood up. There was a long silence. 'We've got nothing to say about him,' he said at last. 'Not to you, not to anyone.'

'Why?'

'He died, and it was a long time ago. People die.'

'Are you still dreaming about it?'

'We have to go now.'

'That questionnaire – that picture you drew. Everything you say—'

'We have to go now,' said Richard loudly. 'Goodbye. Thank you for the coffee. Have a nice day.'

He put down his cup and walked out of the room.

Dr Warren sat still for a moment, and then crossed his office to an inner door. He tapped in a security code, and it opened to reveal a long white corridor. He walked down it and came to a laboratory. A woman sat at a bench, hunched over a laptop from which cables trailed to a small silver junction box. She was in a white coat and her hair was drawn back tight from a pair of soft, watery eyes. She wore a name badge: DR G. SUMMERSBY, ASSOCIATE NEURO-SURGEON. She turned off the camera and removed her headphones.

'He's extraordinary.'

'Can you believe it?' said Dr Warren.

'Yes.'

She paused. 'He's what we've been waiting for, isn't he? Pure, unrestrained, unfocused fear.'

'He's almost frightening. And he's killing himself.'

'He's a sociopath. In its purest form – uncontrollable and self-destructive. We'll have to intervene. The drugs do nothing.'

They stared at each other. The silence was broken by the occasional chirp and gurgle, and the rustling of anxious animals in straw. A hamster chose that moment to jump into its wheel and run. The wheel ticked, on and on, as the rodent scampered to nowhere.

'He's extraordinarily brutal,' said Dr Warren. 'It's

competitive now: the critical stages – just as you predicted. The serotonin's down, obviously, but it's the absence of self-censorship . . . that's a hormonal imbalance quite beyond anything I've seen before. Bordering on psychotic, surely.'

'You want to see inside?'

'Don't you?'

'I have from the start. The question is when?'

Dr Warren smiled. 'Keep it slow,' he said. 'There's a crisis coming, isn't there? That's fairly obvious. We'll have a reason then, and after your recent experience in Vietnam . . . it will be rather attractive.'

'What would his parents say?' said Dr Summersby. 'We'll need them on board.'

Dr Warren said nothing. 'It was what they wanted at first,' he said at length. 'From the moment they saw the second head – I have that on record. The father asked me to chop it off – that's what he said.'

'And you said we couldn't.'

'It would have been fatal. But everything changes, and like I said, you've had the Vietnam experience. You're better informed. This boy's stronger, so we could keep the Rikki head here, let it stabilize – document the whole pathology. We might keep him going indefinitely, if we're lucky. Get him to the States.'

'Molly's still strong. Would Rikki last?'

'Yes, I think he would.'

'And you'd look after him?'

Dr Warren smiled. 'We'd learn to get along. He wouldn't complain.'

Dr Summersby stood up and moved to a wide glass chamber. It was in the corner of the laboratory, and a set of bars ran across the front. A monkey sat inside, secured to a frame so that its head leaned backwards. The eyes were glazed and couldn't blink: the pupils were moisturized by tiny tubes.

'Three months now,' said Dr Warren. They both peered through the glass. The noise of a motor puttered, and filters bubbled. The animal's brain gleamed pale grey, for the top of the skull had been removed. A collection of electrodes emerged from the tissue. Meanwhile, a ventilator was hard at work keeping the lungs moving. A pump sucked and sluiced, and tiny lights flickered. Fine wires were attached to a rack of needles that scratched their patterns on an uncoiling roll of paper, as Molly thought her silent, lonely thoughts. She gazed at the ceiling.

'She's doing well,' said Dr Summersby. 'You think Rikki's as resilient?'

'Possibly. Would Richard survive the trauma, though? That's an important question.'

'Probably.'

'Intact?'

'He'd be alive,' said Dr Summersby simply. 'He'd have basic processes – just like Butterfly.'

'If we could just get Rikki up here and . . . keep him conscious . . .'

'We have to intervene, don't we? The boy's cutting himself. We have recorded evidence: threat of suicide. What did he say? – "Unless you have a guillotine".

It's what we've been waiting for.'

Dr Warren nodded. 'I don't see any alternative. He's dangerous now.'

'I'll reserve a bed, then,' said Dr Summersby. 'Make sure we're flexible. You'd better speak to that headmaster again. Prepare him for something drastic, because . . .'

'What?'

'We'd have to move fast. Push the paperwork through, and assemble the team.'

'I'd better speak to the parents.'

'Present it as good news. Say it's the obvious thing now that the medication's failed. An opportunity for normalization, essential for Richard's survival.'

She closed the laptop.

'They'll sign. Why wouldn't they?

CHAPTER ELEVEN

Richard woke that evening to find himself sitting at his desk.

Rikki was asleep still, and he couldn't remember how he'd got home. It was happening more and more: their sleeping patterns were changing, and he could shut down sometimes out of sheer exhaustion. His diary was open between his hands. Small, spidery writing filled the page:

Richard no longer has the upper hand, and Dr Warren knows it. Richard can't keep up, and he is the one going down. He has to, for his own good – he is the weaker, and he is losing strength. It is going to be sad to see him go, because I've got fond of his dweeby ways, and I can understand that he is a baby still. But his time is coming, and we have to cut away from all that slushy sentimental stuff.

He is not strong.

In the great evolutionary struggle, he is going to be crushed like a bug. Already, he is trying to be like me, but he will only ever be a poor substitute. He is the one cutting us, out of fear and desperation. I intend to start cutting him back.

He is the one prepared to destroy us both: I am the survivor.

Next time we see Dr Warren I am going to have to tell the truth: Richard is haunted, night and day. He sees Grandad everywhere, and it's getting too much. There can be no progress until Richard is restrained . . .

Richard looked up.

He turned to the mirror, where his own face stared back at him. He had his grandad's eyes, for sure, and there they were, unblinking and steady as a pilot's. Rikki leaned against him, dozing.

Richard clenched his fist, and swallowed. Then he punched Rikki hard, in the left eye. The head jolted back, but stayed asleep. Richard wondered if he should do the right eye too, which would be a more difficult blow. He was still thinking about it, when his other arm flashed up and he was dealt a savage slap, right across his own cheek. Then his own fist jabbed him in the nose, and he had tears in his eyes.

Rikki was awake, looking at him.

Richard had a nosebleed. He looked down and let the blood drip onto the diary. Then he put both heads in his hands, balancing them – elbows on the table – and sighed.

'Crash and burn, buddy,' said Rikki softly. 'Crash and burn.'

Richard didn't know what to do, or what to think. There was no textbook, because Mr Barlow didn't teach this particular subject. There was no friend now, because Jeff had gone, and Eric was hardly in school. Mark was nervous about his work all the time, Salome ignored him and Aparna just turned her back.

On top of all that, the one man who could have helped had died, while the grandson he trusted and loved had sat helpless, trying to keep him warm. Saying things – saying foolish things that his grandad couldn't answer, because he was too busy dying. An artery blocked, and a muscle failing – an organ that had grown old and had never been replaced. That heart had pumped successfully for so many years, in cockpits, as Grandad flew in out of the sun and screamed to a halt under impossible pressure. On runways, in mess halls and out there in the garden, walking to school, watching from the touchline. And then one day it had stopped. The whole body had been left without an engine.

Richard had answered a question about blood in last week's test, and now he watched it drip.

'It's all right,' he'd said to Grandad. He had said it again and again. 'It's all right, Danda – they're coming. Don't worry.'

But his grandad had lain there, trying to breathe, and the old lips had gone blue. He was in a collar and tie as usual, and Richard had the tie, still, in his wardrobe – it was one of the things he'd kept, thinking one day he might wear it. The other clothes were too big, so they'd been folded and disposed of. Shoes, as well. Grandad had owned seven pairs of bright, shiny shoes, and they had been shaped to his feet: nobody else's feet would ever fit so snug. They had emptied out his sock-drawer, and in the one below that they'd found shirts still in their wrappers, because people had been buying him shirts every Christmas and there were some he'd never got round to opening.

Richard stood up, and crept along the landing. Three steps up, and the door stood open. The sound of television floated up from the lounge, and he could detect the scent of hot milk. He stepped across the threshold and turned on the light – the new desk sprang into focus, under the window, where Grandad's sideboard had been. Instead of the wardrobe there were the two filing cabinets. The pictures were absolutely gone.

The mirror offered him a perfect reflection.

'What do we want?' said Rikki quietly.

'Nothing.'

'What do you want to do? How serious are you?'

'Serious.'

There had been seven suits, and Richard had sat among them in the wardrobe. He'd let the jackets conceal him, breathing in the smell. A few days later he'd found the wardrobe empty, and the clothes were in a box in the car. His mother had cried, and he'd cried too, but they'd agreed to be sensible, and they'd taken them together to the charity shop on the High Street and even told the woman there a little about the old man who'd once worn them. To know that they still existed was good – they'd fit somebody, and they were far too well made to be thrown away or turned into rags. Somebody would buy them. Some grown-up might be wearing one of the regimental blazers now, as Grandad had on the last Armistice Day, at the war memorial with the Scouts, cadets, Brownies, St John's ambulance . . . Richard remembered him trying to march – trying to keep pace with the younger men in the town square as the wreaths were laid . . . trying to stand straight and tall when his back wouldn't let him.

Good clothes had to be recycled, even if they ended up as fancy dress – Richard knew that. And anyway, he had taken the things that he wanted – he'd been allowed everything and anything. He had his grandad's books on his shelves, and he had his spectacles case, and the silliest ornament too – a pair of Dutch clogs under a little toy windmill. The old man had bought it with the grandma Richard had never met, when they had honeymooned years ago, in Amsterdam. They had hung it on the wall, on the hook that now held the very modern clock.

The woodwork had all been repainted. He had helped his father sandpaper it smooth.

He put his hand in his pocket and pulled out an old leather wallet. He didn't take it to school, but he'd slip it into his jeans sometimes, because it had his grandad's smell. It had a picture of him – Richard – in the side panel, eight years old with the most appalling haircut, which had made Rikki laugh and laugh. The wallet gave up its scent, but it had no money in it any more. He had vowed he would never spend the banknotes he'd found in it – because they were Grandad's last. But he had. Of all the things he was ashamed of, that came back: the fact that he had taken Grandad's last ten pounds and spent it on some trash that he didn't need. But what did he need?

'What's money?' he said to Rikki.

'Nothing.'

Grandad wouldn't have minded. Grandad would stop and search his pockets for the gift of that two-pound coin, or a five-pound note.

The wallet had a hearing-aid battery in it. Grandad had been deaf without his aid, and he had owned a dental plate too – translucent with little wires. There were the photos in the album downstairs, which they had all organized together:

Photos of a slim pilot in immaculate uniform, from a world of black and white . . .

A grainy world, with Grandad in an old car – the first one he'd owned . . .

Grandad on the runway with two of his friends, impossibly young . . .

Grandad older and in colour, with a baby in his arms – and the baby, somehow, being a little, tiny Richard that had now grown and morphed and monstered into a boy with two heads . . .

Richard leaned on the desk and started to cry.

No photos of the funeral, of course – people didn't get their cameras out at funerals. So there was no record of the trip to the crematorium, and the slight delay as the preceding funeral finished and cleared. A white shirt, bought specially, because his school shirts were blue and inappropriate – the collar too big for Richard's neck, and the sleeves too long. No record of this, except in memory – and nobody needing to hear about it.

That was where the armchair had been. The old man might have looked up from it. 'You off to bed?'

'What's on the radio?'

'*Jazz Favourites*. Is it too loud?'

The smell of whisky, always. Strong, when he kissed his cheek. The hand squeezing his shoulder, just enough to hurt.

'No.'

'Shout if it keeps you awake.'

'Good night.'

'Good night, son.'

Rikki spoke, close into his ear. 'Is there a knife? To cut out what you're feeling?'

'No.'

'Is there a laser, then, to burn it away?'

'To burn it out? No, Rikki. There's no knife. There's no laser.'

'I didn't think so.'

They were quiet for a moment.

'I just want to sleep without dreaming,' said Richard. 'Every time I dream, and then wake up—'

'I know.'

'It's like, just for a moment, I forget. Not every day. But it's when we forget, and then remember – that's the worst. I can't stand that, Rikki. I just can't stand that.'

He felt inside the wallet again and found the book of matches. It was small and green, from the pub down the road. Grandad had gone there one or two nights a week, and smoked in the back courtyard. The cardboard was bent, and the matches broken, but it was still possible to break one off and hold the red phosphate clear for striking. You had to rub it against the paper, and when the flame flared it burned his fingers, and he dropped it at once. It fell, like a little comet.

Richard turned Rikki round and pulled a sheet of paper at random from one of his father's filing trays. Rikki adjusted it, so the corner projected. This time, when they lit a match, they took the flame straight to the paper, and the paper caught. It was easy then to draw the paper free and lay it on the desk. It was easy to take another sheet and feed the flames. The papers writhed and opened in flowers of black and orange, and the smoke rose up into their faces.

Rikki coughed and laughed. He pulled open a drawer, and they scooped the flames into it, and there they blazed more fiercely now that they had a nest. More and more smoke – it was amazing how much smoke a few papers made, and how much ash. There were more papers everywhere: reports and files – his father worked at home one day a week and was forever bringing more paper into the house. Rikki crumpled them, and Richard stuffed them into the drawer. The wooden sides were blackening now and there was real heat. The room became foggy so fast, and Richard's eyes were streaming with tears. Smoke was rolling up over the ceiling, and the inferno was beginning to breathe and crackle, coming alive. They added more fuel. They tore a cardboard folder into pieces and the smoke was black. The drawer itself was on fire now, for it was cheap chipboard: the desk was burning. Somewhere out on the landing, an alarm started to chirp: an urgent, anxious cry.

Richard closed the drawer knowing it was now like a bomb, the temperature rising higher and higher. It would all go up, with the curtains and the window frame, and then – if he was lucky – the house itself, from floorboards to roof. The drawer was cremating itself and would burst any moment: he could hear roaring. He was coughing, and so was Rikki: the heat was wonderful. Rikki was laughing too, and there was ash rising around them in curious slow motion.

Then, under it all, came the inevitable thump, thump, thump of feet on the stairs and there were shouting voices. There was a scream, and the door crashed open, and someone was there, hazy in the fog, waving his arms. The figure bounded forward, and still someone screamed – the smoke alarm was frantic now. Richard saw his father's face, the horror and fear – such a wild, twisted mask. He felt his father's arms around him and he was hauled from the room, and the shouting and the screaming beat like wings, upstairs and down.

Their father had a fire extinguisher. Dad was always organized, Dad was sensible, and the flames were dying. In a moment, the windows were open, and it was only boiling smoke. It was just mess, and stink – and then, for the first time in a long time, Richard knew his dad was going to hit him. It was almost a joy to feel a strength he couldn't fight lift him up and shake him, and take him back along the landing. A joy to hear the shouting louder than ever, and to feel a hand smacking down, so he didn't even protect himself. His mother was crying out, and his father was punctuating every blow with the words: 'Stupid! Stupid! Stupid!'

He was on his bed. *Smack*, across his shoulder. *Smack*, across his head – his mother screaming, 'No, Frank – no! Stop it!' Richard didn't want it to stop. He was putting his face up, and so was Rikki – they both leaned into the blows, aching to be hurt. When the door slammed shut, and he found himself alone, with his flesh on fire, it was a relief. It was as if something had been silenced. The boy with two heads wept properly, then, until his mother came, and then he wept in her arms, and was rocked gently to sleep.

In the morning, they found that the door to their grandad's room was locked.

Their father had gone out and their mother made breakfast, trying so hard to be normal. The whole house stank of burning, and her hands were shaking. Richard and Rikki were bruised all over and the shirt they wore could not conceal the marks. They sat at the table in unbreakable silence.

PART THREE
THE CHANCE TO BE NORMAL

CHAPTER ONE

The school term slipped by, inching towards its end.

Mr Prowse, the headmaster, could not bring himself to look at Richard or Rikki, and said nothing directly to them. Perhaps Dr Warren had advised against confrontation of any kind? The counsellor himself was often close by, adapting the boy's medication. His visits to the school became more and more regular, but the fire at home was never referred to.

Lessons continued, of course, and those in Year Six worked harder than ever. At last it was time to take the dreaded exams, and the children filed down to the hall where neat rows of desks awaited them. The papers were distributed, and the ink flowed. The papers were gathered in again and – suddenly – it was all over.

There was a strange sense of anti-climax, and a feeling of emptiness.

Luckily, there was football, and then the residential.

The semi-final against St Michael's was scheduled for the very next week, so Mr Barlow ran regular practices. A large calendar on the wall revealed that the trip to Wales was just ten days away, so that started to dominate too. Mr Barlow had to spend hours organizing and talking through the arrangements, for the children always wanted to discuss them. Deposits were paid and kits had been assembled.

They got onto the Adventure Centre's website, which had pages of photos and links, and pored over every detail. The special order for Nailhead McGinty's precious handbook had been delivered too, and Eric and Mark's copy was already so well-read that the spine had broken. They'd had to put elastic bands round it, and together they'd cross-referenced different sections with Post-it notes. Eric had memorized some of the great man's sayings, and would sidle up to his friends and mutter: '*A man has more chance if he's alone, you know.*' Then he'd narrow his eyes like the Nailhead photo, and smile, adding, '*Trust no one – only yourself.*' Mark just grinned happily, and wrote endless kit lists.

Transport details were confirmed, and every child received a letter. The coach would leave school at seven-thirty on the Sunday evening, and drive through the night. Clifden was a tiny village, nestling in a wild part of moorland close to the sea. The brochure revealed that it was right beside the British Army's Commando training ground – a restricted area to which Green Cross would have 'specially negotiated access'. Adventures would begin as soon as they arrived. That would be on Monday morning, so everyone could sleep on the bus before a day of paragliding. Mr Barlow announced that he was re-organizing the groups, as he wanted to ensure the right mix and gender balance. Everyone groaned, but Richard and Rikki were secretly glad, as they knew Jeff wouldn't want to be with them any more. That friendship had broken for ever.

Then things went badly wrong for Eric.

He was caught in school with cigarettes. He insisted that he'd been looking after them for his brother, 'Spider', but he was disciplined and sent home. No further action was taken. Later in the same week, however, he appeared with a devastating new haircut. His brother's girlfriend had shaved parts of his scalp, and woven intricate braids. He had a meeting with Dr Warren, and was sent home again to have the style amended. The very next day he got into a fight with two older boys, from another school. Eric did karate, and used a manoeuvre everyone knew was dangerous and illegal. One boy was hospitalized, and Eric was suspended properly this time – there was even talk of expulsion.

He was back the next week, though, having agreed to spend more time at the Rechner Institute. Surgery, they said, was now a real possibility. He signed a final 'good behaviour contract', and the reward he was offered for keeping it was his place on the all-important residential. It was the one thing he was looking forward to, for he hated school more than ever. Mr Barlow tried to stay close, and keep him calm, while Mark read him his favourite sections of the McGinty book. The two boys spent their time planning how they'd survive in the wild, should they ever need to.

Meanwhile, the football pitch was mown, and its lines were repainted.

St Michael's Prep School rolled up in a silver minibus, and the team disembarked in identical tracksuits. They had won their previous game thirteen–nil, and everyone knew they were determined to make the final and keep hold of the cup. Their trainer was a tall, thin man called Mr Merrett, and he would referee the game. St Michael's wore red; Green Cross wore midnight blue.

It was obvious straight away that Mr Merrett was going to be biased. He had a great lolloping stride as he ran up and down the pitch, but he also had the disconcerting habit of encouraging his own team even as he reffed, which was extremely off-putting for Green Cross.

'Come on, Phipps – get in there!' he'd shout, as one of his boys went in for a tackle.

'There at the back! Tolly! – What are you doing, boy? – Close him down, lad!'

He'd blow his whistle at some minor foul and say, 'This isn't what we practised, is it? Now get yourselves together! Three, five, nine – go! Go!' Then he'd blow his whistle and sprint after the ball as if he was going to take possession. 'Good pass!' he'd yell. 'Shoot! Shoot! Don't just look at it, boy – go for goal!'

At half-time, it was two–nil to St Michael's, and the ref had ignored a very obvious handball in his own team's goalmouth.

Green Cross were not happy.

'It's not fair,' said Salome. 'They're a bunch of snobs, and cheats!'

'Can't you punch a few out?' said Rikki.

Salome pulled a face and mouthed an obscenity at him.

'We've got to change t-tactics,' said Mr Barlow. 'I know what you're thinking, and I've got eyes myself. But they're not snobs, and there's no point getting upset about it: they're good in d-defence and we're not getting through. I'm going to suggest something controver-versial.'

His team listened carefully.

'Richard. R-Rikki. How would you feel about taking over as full-back?'

'I'm a striker,' said Richard.

'And a very good one,' said Mr Barlow. 'But haven't you noticed? They're better than us in the air, and they're winning the ball every time. I want you back with Jeff – and J-Jeff, you have made some cracking saves. But I think you need an extra line of defence now, and I think Rikki and Richard can help you. Salome.'

Salome looked at him.

'I'm going to put you f-forward. You're powerful, and I think some of those boys will fall apart when they see you coming. They're a timid little side in some ways – apart from anything, they're scared of their own r-ref. So my idea is to put you up front, put Richard and Rikki at the back. I just think we could change everything. Eric. Mark. I want you to use Salome as much as you can – push the ball towards her.'

Everyone nodded, and in a moment they were all trotting back onto the field.

'Five–nil, minimum!' shouted the ref as his boys lined up. 'This should be a walk-over and you're letting yourselves down. Radford!' he yelled at a small boy who was re-tying his laces. 'If you don't get a goal you're in detention, do you understand me? You're like a girl today. Now get your backside into position, and let's have some concentration!' Radford trotted forward, looking utterly terrified. The ref grabbed him by the arm and dragged him to one side. 'Not there, stupid!' he hissed. 'What's wrong with you? Outside right, supporting Tayler and Ballingal.'

The whistle blew, and the game restarted.

By coincidence, Radford took possession almost straight away, and surprised everyone by some very neat dribbling. He punted out to the right wing, and earned a 'Good show!' from the referee. Then came a beautiful cross, but Rikki – in his new position – caught it even more beautifully, with a powerful header. Unfortunately, it fell straight to another St Michael's player, who volleyed it hard. Richard and Rikki leaped again and deflected it wide. When the corner came, Jeff plucked it out of the air skilfully, and booted it into midfield. For the first time in a while, Richard, Rikki and Jeff smiled at each other.

Eric then took charge. He dummied neatly and got round his first opponent. The referee screamed, 'Take him out!' and two red shirts ran towards him. Eric back-heeled it to Clara, who put it straight out to Salome. Salome then broke, and Mr Barlow's advice was proved absolutely sound. Two boys came in for tackles, but Salome simply ran through them. She wasn't fast, but she was as strong as a truck – and she could not be deflected. The red shirts regrouped around her, but she hacked the ball through the lot of them, Eric screamed for the ball, and received it. He dummied again, and got it onto his favoured left foot. He shot hard, low and true, and it was two–one.

The referee – Mr Merrett – was white with fury. The game stopped for a moment as he went to have words with his goalkeeper, who hung his head and cried. Then Mr Merrett walked to the centre spot and jammed the ball down. He glared at Radford again, who fell back nervously. 'You're *worse* than a girl!' he said. Then he spat into his whistle.

Once again, the St Michael's side looked strong, and once again it was Rikki who won the ball in a fabulous jump. Mark passed to Eric, and Eric took it out to the youngest member of the team: ten-year-old Jason. Jason worshipped Eric, and imitated him skilfully. He leaped and weaved, and Eric was right there, supporting him. Eric took the ball over, and got it to Salome. Salome worked the same astonishing magic – she was more confident this time, moving through with some joyously clever feints and turns. It was Mark who received from her and found himself in front of the goalkeeper, his lanky body wobbling in panic.

The goalkeeper wasn't sure whether to come out or stay in the goalmouth – his face was a rictus of indecision and fear. He went as low as he could and put his arms out, and Mark just managed to keep his head. He weaved left and slotted the ball hard to the right.

The red shirts stood with heads bowed again, waiting for the horror of Mr Merrett's retribution. He pulled his team together, and the Green Cross children looked at each other as a stream of abuse poured over them. When St Michael's got back into formation, it was clear that instead of building them up, the referee had only succeeded in breaking them.

Their co-ordination went to pieces. If the ball came near one of them, it was a ball to be feared – and they'd do anything to get rid of it. They were clearly so frightened of making errors that everything they did was an error. Eric scored again five minutes before the final whistle. And then, to add insult to injury, Carla – who had been playing midfield – managed the most extraordinary lob, and the goalkeeper misjudged it totally. It bounced over his head, straight into the net. Worse even than that, in a last-minute scramble of confusion in the St Michael's goalmouth, the ball fell to poor little Radford, and his back pass to the goalie turned into the most horrible, hellish own goal.

When the teams shook hands at the end of the match, Eric noticed that Radford was hyperventilating.

'What's the matter?' said Eric. 'You've gone all white, man.'

Radford pressed his hands to his eyes. 'I know,' he said. 'He's going to kill me.'

'Oh, come on,' said Jeff. 'It's a game. You played well.'

Radford shook his head, and another boy said: 'I won't get food tonight, none of us will. We'll be out on a run till dark, and then freezing showers. Extra prep and everything.'

Meanwhile Mr Merrett had made his way to Mr Barlow. 'Not sure it's strictly within the rules, that,' he said coldly.

'What's not?' said Mr Barlow. 'Good g-game, by the way. Your boys work together nicely.'

'You know what I mean. I'm not sure it's legal.'

'I'm afraid I d-don't know what you mean.'

'You're playing an advantage that distracted all of us. I'm talking about him. Or them. What do you call it?' He was pointing at Rikki and Richard, who had their arms round Eric and Mark. 'I'm talking about two-headed players!' said the ref angrily. 'It's like having an extra man. No wonder we lost.'

'I'm sorry you f-feel like that,' said Mr Barlow. 'That's R-Rikki Westlake, Richard Westlake. One man. One pair of b-b- . . .' He fought for the word. 'Boots!'

'Well, it cost us the match. It was like being at the bloody circus, and I'm going to write to your headmaster.'

'Stop a minute,' said Mr Barlow. He put his hand on the referee's arm, and the two men stood opposite one another. 'Are you s-suggesting he shouldn't play?'

'I'm suggesting exactly that. We came for a game of football, and you play a . . . freak. It's bad enough using females – that's a . . . distraction too. But I would not have agreed to this fixture if I'd known about that creature.'

'Mr Merrett,' said Mr Barlow. 'Like I said, your b-boys were good. But they were outplayed. We beat you fair and square. Don't take it out on R-R—'

'You cheated,' said Mr Merrett.

Every player was now watching and listening. The two men were in a large circle of astonished children.

'You're out of order, sir,' said Mr Barlow quietly. He wiped his mouth with a handkerchief.

Mr Merrett smiled. 'There are special schools for children with that kind of disability. It's not on, and I'm going to challenge this result and have you disqualified. We train hard, and we don't expect the rules to be bent. My boys put their souls into this game, and they've been cheated.'

'Sir,' said Radford.

'Shut up,' said Mr Merrett. 'Get in the bus, the lot of you.'

'Sir?'

'What do you want? You shouldn't be here, Radford. You should be dead, in an unmarked grave.'

Radford licked a pair of very dry lips. 'You shouldn't speak about someone like that, sir. Nobody should.'

The St Michael's teacher twitched, and changed colour. 'Are you telling me . . . how to conduct myself?' he said.

'We lost the game, sir. But that doesn't mean you can—'

'Get in the bus!' roared Mr Merrett. 'All of you!'

The St Michael's boys didn't stir. They were all looking at their teacher, and then at Radford. The child put his head down, and then lifted it again to meet Rikki's eyes. Then he looked at Richard.

'I would like to apologize to you on behalf of my team,' he said. 'We were outplayed today, and you have been insulted. You have the match, and you did jolly well.'

The whole St Michael's team applauded for ten full seconds. Then they turned away, and the Green Cross children watched them walk to their vehicle.

CHAPTER TWO

Richard said to Jeff: 'Are you still mad at me?'

'Yes.'

'Can't we even speak?'

'What do you want to speak about?'

They had finished changing, and were just leaving school. The strange confrontation after the match had subdued everybody. Nobody knew whether the horrible Mr Merrett would be challenging the result or not – so a place in the final did not feel secure. They didn't dare celebrate. Many of the children were also extremely worried about what would happen to brave little Radford.

Jeff wouldn't meet Richard's eyes.

'I don't see why we have to fall out,' said Richard. 'If we can play football together—'

'You're still giving people a hard time. I don't like that.'

Rikki sniggered.

'See?' said Jeff. 'You've always got to be laughing at someone.'

'You've still got the hots for Aparna, haven't you?' said Rikki. 'Full-on Hindu wedding?'

'Shut up,' said Richard. 'Shut up! Shut up!'

Jeff looked at Rikki this time, and held his gaze. 'Why do people like you exist?' he said. 'You know, before you came along . . . I won't say this school had no problems. But it didn't have many. We got on pretty well.'

'Bad things happen, Jeff,' said Rikki.

'Bad things like you.'

'You want everything easy,' said Rikki. 'The world is not a nice place, and you can't control it.'

'Rikki,' said Richard. 'Just—'

'No,' Rikki interupted. 'Jeff's a big boy – he can take a bit of truth. The fact is, he's lived in babyland for a long time, and all that's happened, Jeff, is that you're finding out you're a bit of a loser. We don't need you as a friend.'

Richard tried to speak, but found that he couldn't. His jaw seemed locked shut. Then, more worrying, he found that his right fist had closed round Jeff's tie, and he was pushing Jeff backwards, hard. Jeff tried to get away but failed. In a moment, he'd tripped over a bag and Richard shoved with all his strength.

The boy might have stayed upright, but his feet got entangled and he was slammed to the ground. He landed on his elbow and lay there, stunned. For a moment nobody knew what to do.

Richard and Rikki turned, and saw that Aparna was looking at them – she had just emerged from the school gates. Jeff wasn't aware of her; he was trying to get up, but was in too much pain.

Miss Maycock appeared and crouched beside him. 'Anything broken?' she asked softly.

Jeff was holding his left arm, and his face was twisted in agony.

'Can you stand up?'

'Yes. No.'

'Let's try. Move on, everyone. Show's over.'

Jeff struggled to his feet, still nursing his arm. He let the teacher gently straighten it, and then he flexed it slowly.

'Move your fingers,' said Miss Maycock.

Jeff did so. There were tears running down his cheeks, and he was deathly pale.

'Nasty sprain, I think. But nothing broken. We're lucky. I'm going to sit you down for a moment – come back inside. Richard? Rikki? I'll see you tomorrow. Aparna, can you come with me?'

When Richard and Rikki got to school the next morning, they were both nervous. They'd said nothing to their parents, but they had the same fear that had been haunting Eric: would they now be kicked off the residential? It was obvious that people were ignoring them as they came up the corridor. Word had spread, and they knew they were in trouble.

'Take no notice,' said Rikki.

'This is your fault.'

'He had it coming.'

'You've lost every friend I had. You've made us hated.'

They went to their locker, and saw at once that it had been broken open. The little padlock had been forced, and it dangled from the catch.

Richard opened the door. Sure enough, revenge had been swift, thorough and horrible. The pictures of aeroplanes that he'd lovingly pasted to the walls had been shredded, and some of the pieces fluttered out onto the floor. There was a stink of fruit, and he realized that milk and banana had been rubbed over his books. The whole locker was soaking wet and stinking. The model plane was gone, but more shockingly, the precious wings – the priceless gift his grandad had given him – had been cut in two. The pieces lay in a puddle of white. He could only stare in horror.

'Oh dear,' said Rikki. 'We've been visited.'

The classroom was almost empty. The other children were not looking. In fact, they seemed remarkably busy doing other things.

'You swine,' whispered Richard at last.

'Someone's angry with us,' said Rikki. 'You think it's Jeff?'

'No. He's not even here yet. Unless he . . .'

'Unless he came and went. Sneaky boy. Where's his locker?'

'Let's get everything out. We are not doing anything about this.'

'This is going to need careful thought, Richard. We have been attacked. You're upset. You're going to blow.'

Richard started to arrange everything on the nearby

desks. He found a roll of paper towel, and started to salvage what he could. It was clear that a lot of his things would have to be replaced. 'We tell nobody, OK?' he said. His voice was shaking. 'We don't tell tales. We don't go crying to Bra-low—'

'Sure,' said Rikki. 'What we do is work out a counter attack so massive, the enemy backs off. I think it was Salome and Jeff together. Look at that . . .' He picked up a piece of the embroidered wings. 'What do we say to Mum and Dad about this?'

'Nothing.' Richard was taking deep breaths.

'It's only stuff.'

'Where's the model? Where's the Venom?'

'Stolen,' said Rikki.

'Oh God.'

'Don't cry. It's just stuff. You know that.'

'We made that together. Me and Grandad! Me and—'

'It's *stuff*. Richard! Stop crying!'

'I'm not crying. It's all because of you!'

'We'll fight them. We'll let them think they've won, all right? And then we blow them out of the water. That Jeff kid needs a serious battering – we should have stamped on his head.'

'Richard,' said a voice. 'Rikki?'

They turned, and saw that the headmaster had entered the room. He was staring at them, with an expression of cold dislike.

'Could you do that later, please? I need you in my room. Leave your things where they are.'

Richard and Rikki followed him up the corridor.

The headmaster turned. 'What's happened to your ties, by the way?'

'It's in my pocket,' said Richard.

'You look a mess. Have you walked to school like that?'

'Yes, sir.'

'I don't like it, Richard. Rikki – I don't put up with it. Get your shirt tucked in, and make yourself look presentable. I've noticed you more and more lately – you look like a ragged urchin. Now sort yourself out.' Richard and Rikki both looked at him. 'Things are getting very serious here,' Mr Prowse added, 'as you no doubt know.'

A minute later, Richard and Rikki stepped into the study. Mr Barlow and Miss Maycock were already there, sitting on wooden chairs. In the corner of a small sofa sat Dr Warren, with a sheaf of papers in his hand.

He looked up and smiled. 'Good morning,' he said.

'Doctor Warren was here about Eric,' said the headmaster. 'But I've asked him to be present for this, and Miss Maycock – as you know – witnessed yesterday's assault. Things appear to be escalating—'

'He's not our doctor,' said Rikki.

'What do you mean?'

'Doctor Warren. We don't want him here.'

'Keep a civil tongue in your head, Rikki Westlake!' said the headmaster. 'I've had about as much as I can stand. It was Doctor Warren who predicted exactly this kind of . . . horrible climax, and I have to say I'm at my wits' end.'

'We can still find a solution,' said Dr Warren quietly. 'I'm here to protect you, Rikki. Richard. And the school wants to do everything it can.'

'You're not our doctor,' repeated Rikki.

'Why are you so hostile?'

'You lied to me.'

'When?'

'The first time we spoke. When I woke up in bed, remember? *Everything's going to be OK.*'

'I still believe that, Rikki.'

'But I don't!'

'Look,' said Mr Barlow, 'I agree that things are getting c-complicated. Can I suggest, therefore . . . before we get t-tangled up again, that Richard and Rikki tell us what happened yesterday? In their own words?'

'Sure,' said Dr Warren. 'Good plan.'

'Happened y-y-yesterday?' said Rikki. 'How far are we going back?'

'You know what we're talking about,' said the headmaster. 'What led up to your fight with Jeffrey? The attack was witnessed by several people, and appears to have been totally unprovoked.'

'Jeff insulted me,' said Rikki.

'Did he?'

'Yes.'

'He d-denies that, of course,' said Mr Barlow quietly.

'He called me a two-faced freak. He's been doing it for weeks. I tried to be friendly with him, and he just . . .' Rikki wiped his eyes with his sleeve. 'He just makes it clear he hates me and thinks I'm an outsider. So do other people. He insults my family too.'

Dr Warren nodded. 'I wonder if we could ask Jeff to step in? Miss Maycock, would you mind?'

Miss Maycock left the room. The headmaster perched on his desk.

'I'm sorry it's come to this, Doctor Warren,' he said. 'I know you've done your best, and I like to think we all have. But things have been brewing for a considerable time – and perhaps I should have put my foot down far sooner. Physical assault, vandalism: we just don't put up with it here.'

'No, sir,' said Richard.

'That's what I tried to tell Jeff,' said Rikki. A tear rolled down his cheek. 'It's what I tried to tell Salome, as well, when she attacked me—'

'Let's leave her out of it at the moment. Explain the picture, please, Richard.'

'What picture?' said Richard.

Dr Warren said: 'Does the picture upset you? You mentioned it before, I think.'

'What picture?' said Rikki. 'I don't know what you're talking about.'

The headmaster stood up. 'Do you deny touching it?'

Rikki stared at him. 'I don't know anything about any picture,' he said. 'You're not making sense.'

'I'm warning you,' hissed the headmaster. 'You're this close to expulsion already, so—'

'What he meant—' said Richard. But he got no further, for Rikki interrupted loudly.

'What I meant, sir, was that I have no idea what you're referring to when you say, "Do you deny touching the picture?" Sir, I don't know how else to express myself! Sir! Because I don't understand the question!'

The headmaster yanked open the door of a large cupboard. He lifted something out and leaned it against his desk, covered in a cloth. Richard and Rikki couldn't see what it was, but when he pulled off the blanket, they gasped.

Aparna's Icarus picture had been smashed and wrecked. The glass was broken and a monstrous, jagged scribble had been scrawled across the sky, like black lightning. Worst of all, a filthy word had been written huge and cruel, and Richard shuddered at its obscenity.

'Does the picture trouble you?' said Dr Warren softly.

There was a hideous silence. It was broken by the door opening again, and Miss Maycock stepped in nervously, with a forlorn-looking Jeff. The headmaster nodded, and they both sat down.

'That's terrible,' said Richard.

The teachers looked at him.

'You're jumping to the conclusion that we did that?' said Rikki. 'You think we smashed it?'

'Do you deny it?' said the headmaster.

'Yes!' said Rikki and Richard together.

'I did not do that,' said Richard. 'And if Rikki did it, then . . . then I was asleep. But he didn't do it. Because I haven't been asleep.'

'As I think I told you,' said Dr Warren, 'we have to anticipate times when you will be asleep, Richard. The drugs you're taking are not helping. And it's interesting, isn't it, that the word that's written here is the very word Rikki wrote first on my table? And then on my wall.'

'That doesn't mean anything,' said Rikki.

'Doesn't it?'

'He's lying to us,' said the headmaster.

'Rikki,' said Mr Barlow gently. 'This meeting does not have to be a c-confrontation. There is still time for honesty and even rec-reconciliation.'

Rikki turned and stared at him. 'It's pretty hard, sir, not having a confrontation when someone accuses you of smashing a stupid picture and then tells you you're a liar!'

'You've got some mess on your fingers,' said the headmaster.

Rikki held them up. 'We were clearing up some mess in our locker. Maybe we need to talk about that, Jeff? I don't care, you understand me? I do not care!'

'Rikki,' said Mr Barlow. 'We can avoid c-conflict if we want to. The way to avoid it is to tell only the t-truth. So I want to ask Jeff something – calmly. Jeff?'

Jeff looked up.

'Just before Richard and R-Rikki pushed you. Just before that . . . altercation yesterday. Did you insult him or his family?'

'No.'

'You did,' said Rikki. 'You called our grandad a rotting corpse.'

Jeff gasped.

'Please,' said Mr Barlow. 'I want to hear what you said, Jeff.'

'He said he was glad he'd had a heart attack, and—'

'Quiet!' shouted the headmaster.

Jeff's voice was shaking. 'But I would never, ever say that. I was telling Richard why I didn't want to be friends with him any more. Rikki started doing what he always does. He started telling me I was in love with Aparna. He told me I was a baby—'

'You used the word that's written there!' said Rikki. He was pointing at the picture.

'That's a lie,' said Jeff. 'I don't use language like that!'

'Oh, aren't you an angel?' said Rikki, his voice heavy with sarcasm.

'No,' said Jeff. 'But that language is from the gutter. My father would kill me if I ever said anything like that. And your grandad was nice! I liked him!'

'Liar! You hated him.'

'I used to see him, every day. We used to talk—'

'Wait,' said Mr Barlow. 'Let's keep it calm. Did you hear Jeff say those things, Richard? Is Rikki correct?'

'Yes!' said Richard. Then, as soon as he'd said it, he put his hand over his mouth. 'No!' he whispered.

'What?' said Dr Warren.

'Tell the truth, Richard,' said Rikki. 'He cut up the wings. He smashed the plane . . .'

Richard looked at him and fought for breath. He looked

at his knees, then up at Rikki again. 'I told you, ages ago – no. I told you I would not ever, ever lie for you. You are . . . what are you doing?' He gasped, but tried to continue. He stood up. 'Did we do that to the picture? Why would we do that?'

'Richard,' said Mr Barlow, 'we're going to s-straighten this out.'

Richard put his hands over his face. There were tears rolling from his eyes, and his shoulders were shaking. Rikki stared around the room, but now he looked frightened.

'Jeff did not say anything bad,' said Richard through a sob. 'Jeff is my friend. So is Salome. So is Aparna. We didn't do that to the picture and I don't know what's happening.'

'What about you, Rikki?' said Dr Warren. 'What do you say?'

Rikki laughed suddenly. 'Look,' he said. 'I think this is all pretty simple.' He snarled and stared at the picture. Then he pointed at the obscenity. 'That's what you are, all of you.' He said the word aloud, cruel and clear. He said it again, and the headmaster stood there, open-mouthed.

'Oh, Rikki,' said Mr Barlow softly.

'I think we should end this meeting,' said Dr Warren. 'Continue it elsewhere.'

'Why?' said Rikki. 'Where? That's all we are, all of us.' He said the word for a third time, and then – before anyone could stop him – he took a step forward and stamped hard through what remained of the picture. It was leaning against the desk, so his foot broke the paper and its backing. He swore again and again, as Richard sobbed. Then he stood looking down at the broken glass and splintered wood.

'Get them out of here,' said the headmaster. 'They're off the trip. Isolate them and I'll phone their parents. Doctor Warren – you can take over from here . . . the school gives up.'

CHAPTER THREE

There was a music room beyond the playground, and that's where Rikki and Richard were sent.

Miss Maycock brought them some reading books, and they sat for two hours. Mr Barlow made sure they got a snack and a drink, but they weren't allowed to mix with any other children.

Richard said, 'Excuse me, Mr Barlow?'

'Yes.'

'Can I ask you something?'

Mr Barlow nodded.

'Is there no way . . . If we're—'

'Shut up, Richard,' said Rikki.

'If we're really good and apologize to everyone, is there any way we can come on the residential?'

Mr Barlow shook his head. 'I doubt it.'

'Why would we want to go?' laughed Rikki. 'It's going to be lame. It's going to be the stupidest, boringest waste of time. Don't humiliate us, Richard! Why would we even want to go on it?'

'Well,' said Mr Barlow, 'I d-don't think it would be easy finding a group for you at the moment. I think we've just got to limp towards the end of term.'

'What about the cup final?' said Richard. 'Can we play in that?'

'If it happens,' said Rikki. 'Your memory's going, isn't it? That referee was going to get the match cancelled. We won't be in the team, anyway.'

Mr Barlow was silent for a moment. Then he said, 'It's strange. You d-don't have any problem playing football together, do you? Out on the football pitch, we all work quite well together. Why is that?'

Rikki shrugged.

Richard said, 'I suppose the purpose is so simple. With a football game, you know what you're doing and why you're doing it. All you've got to do is get the ball in the net. We're not all in competition. I mean, I'm not going to make it difficult for Salome when all I want is for her to get a goal, am I?'

Mr Barlow put his hand gently on Richard's chin. He tilted his head back and looked at him in the light. 'There's a s-swelling under your eye, you know.'

'So what?' said Rikki.

'You're bruised, as well, Rikki,' said Mr Barlow. 'That's not from football. What's g-going on? At home, I mean.'

'You're n-not our d-d-dad, Mr Bra-low,' stuttered Rikki. 'You're not even our shrink. If you want to get concerned about someone, get concerned about your own kids. If you've got any.'

Mr Barlow stared at him.

Rikki smiled. 'I've been dying to ask you this, sir. Why do you gob all the time?'

Mr Barlow went to speak, and then stopped. He wiped his mouth with the back of his hand, and looked at Rikki. Rikki picked up a book and started to read it, but Richard was still looking up at Mr Barlow.

'I had a stroke,' he said at last. 'You know that – everyone knows.'

'Please,' said Richard. 'Rikki didn't mean to be so horrible. I don't know why he says stuff.'

'Don't you?'

'No. But it's true – we're hurting each other worse than ever now. I have to hurt him somehow.'

'Can't you talk to the counsellor?'

'No.'

'He might help you, Richard—'

'You're spitting again!' said Rikki. 'You're spitting right in my face!'

Mr Barlow paused again, and licked his lips. He closed his eyes and took a deep breath. 'Rikki,' he said, 'I know it's a p-problem. I convince myself that nobody notices it, but I know everyone does. The reason's simple—'

'Why don't you have your own kids?' said Rikki suddenly.

'I do.'

'How many?'

'I have two.'

'You never talk about them, sir,' said Richard.

'I don't. I tend not to bring them to work, I suppose. My boy's called S-Sam. My daughter is called . . .' He wiped his mouth. 'Her name is Billie. Bryony, actually, but—'

'Why don't they go to this school?'

'You send them to a posh school, don't you?' said Rikki. He laughed. 'You wouldn't want them coming here, meeting people like us.'

'To be honest,' said Mr Barlow, 'I don't see them any more. They're grown up now, but when my wife and I went our separate ways, it was agreed . . . it was ruled . . . that I wouldn't see them. Except once a m-month. And then they moved away, so even that lapsed. They went to Cyprus, and then I had the stroke. A stroke can, in theory, happen to anyone at any age. It's when a b-blood vessel bursts in the brain, and puts a particular stress on some part of it. It can kill you, of course – but I was lucky. The long-term damage was to my right side – you might have noticed that my right arm isn't as g-good as my left. And the c-control of my facial muscles on the right side – it's better than it was, but it's still not good. And the saliva builds up in the right side of my mouth, because the muscles there can't drain it as efficiently as yours can, for example.' He wiped his mouth again with the handkerchief. 'That is the reason I spit, Rikki. I'm sorry it disgusts you.'

'Please help me, Mr Barlow,' said Richard suddenly. 'Please help us.'

'Help you do what, boy?'

Richard shook his head. Yet again, his eyes were full of tears and the book slipped from his fingers.

'Shut up, Richard,' said Rikki. 'Take no notice, Mr Barlow. He thinks he's the only one with problems. He's started wetting himself again, by the way – every bloody night.'

'How can I help you, Richard? Tell me.'

'I can't go on like this,' said Richard. 'It gets worse every day, and just when I think it's getting better, I say something or do something, and I know it's getting worse. Isn't there a drug they can zap me with? – I mean, a better one. I don't want to live like this.'

'There's no d-drug they can zap you with, no,' said Mr Barlow. He pulled out a chair and sat down. 'You have to face your life.'

'Rikki's battering me. I'm battering him—'

'You start it!' cried Rikki. 'I just defend myself, bed-wetter! You're the one!'

'We're not going to last!' wailed Richard. 'And that counsellor . . .'

'What about him?'

'We can't stand him because he pretends, and he fakes it. He doesn't care, and he pretends that everything's going to be all right, when we both know – we all know – it isn't. Ever! He died on the pavement, Mr Barlow! He went cold, so fast!'

'Don't tell him!' said Rikki.

'I was holding him. In my arms!'

Mr Barlow looked from Richard to Rikki, and back

again. He shook his head and put his hand on Richard's wrist.

'I wish I knew what to say,' he said. 'I'm not going to pretend, boy. All I can say is that life is never easy. There are no easy answers and sometimes no explanations, are there? You know that.'

There was a pause, and Rikki suddenly laughed. It was a dry, barking laugh and the contempt in it made the old teacher wince. 'Oh, wow,' he said. He tugged his hand away. 'We've got a philosopher with us.'

'Rikki . . .'

'Wait.' He pretended to search the table for notepaper. 'I want to get down exactly what this wise man just said. What was it? "Life is never . . ." Oh, God – it's gone. You used a really sophisticated word.'

'I said life's n-never easy,' said Mr Barlow. 'We cope, though. We have to.'

Rikki shook his head in mock-amazement. 'That is inspirational. How could anyone walk out on you when you had insight like that? Your kids must miss you every day – they must be lost. You have the secret of life, Bra-man.'

'What do you want, Rikki?' said Mr Barlow loudly. 'Please tell me what you want.'

'To be let go! To be out of here!'

'To die? Is that what you're saying?' Rikki swore. 'Because I need to tell you something,' said Mr Barlow. 'When I—'

'No! Please God, we do not want stories about your . . . kids, or your childhood, or your time in hospital or wherever it was that you saw the light and realized life wasn't easy!' He looked at Richard. 'Don't listen – they know nothing!'

'I knew your grandfather, Rikki. Not intimately, but—'

'Shut up! Shut up!'

'We talked about you, and do you know what he said?'

Rikki was on his feet, holding his ears. 'Shut up, shut up, shut up, shut up! You have no right even to mention him. He was—'

'What, Rikki?' Mr Barlow stood as well. 'What was he? Tell me.'

'He was the best human being in the world. And he's dead, and I wish your stroke had killed you!'

Mr Barlow reached out a hand, and Richard swung the hardest punch he'd ever thrown. He missed, and the chair fell backwards behind him. Mr Barlow went to hold him, but Rikki ducked away – just as the door burst open.

Dr Warren stepped in, and there was an orderly behind him in clean white clothing. The headmaster was behind them, and Richard and Rikki started back, frozen in their panic. The orderly took a step forward and there was a moment of terrible stillness.

'The car's ready,' said Dr Warren. 'Everything's going to be fine.'

'What do you mean?' said Richard.

'We're going to look after you.'

'No you're not.'

'We have an order from the courts. Everything's sorted.'

Richard and Rikki leaped forward then, and bolted

into the corridor. They raced to the end of it, crashing through a fire exit, and the adults tore after them. The playground was full of children, and Richard and Rikki burst into the middle of them. The infants screamed like birds, and wheeled away as the teachers followed. Richard and Rikki doubled back and made for the school field. Before they could get to it, they saw their mother.

She was half running through the school gates, her face a mask of worry and pain – she looked unsteady on her feet, as if she'd been running a great distance. She was out of breath, but managed to call: 'Richard! Rikki!'

Her son shied away from her, across the tarmac, as pupils fled and regrouped, shrieking and howling. Mark was running towards them, while Aparna was rooted to the spot, terror in her eyes. Salome stepped in front of Dr Warren, who tripped as he dodged her, and Richard and Rikki sprinted to the main hall. The orderly lunged for them, and missed by a fraction. The headmaster managed to grab an arm, but Richard and Rikki twisted, jumped and ducked, and were free again, leaping high. They seized the drainpipe, and suddenly they were climbing, hand over hand, as the grown-ups gathered below.

Mr Barlow shouted: 'Rikki! No!'

Dr Warren was shouting too. 'Richard! Rikki! Stay where you are!'

They ignored the cries, and were soon three metres above the playground. Up they went, higher and higher, wedging their feet between the wall and the pipe, as the whole school watched. They reached the top of the building in half a minute and clung to the gutter – it was three storeys high, with a wide, flat roof. In seconds they had swung a leg over onto the edge, and were upside down. They heaved themselves up and round, and then they were standing upright, holding onto nothing. They stood there, swaying, on the very edge of the roof, looking for a place to go – undecided, arms outstretched.

Every face gazed up, and there was a terrible silence.

Like a gymnast, Richard and Rikki simply threw themselves upwards in a wild somersault. They scrabbled at the air, trying to rise, but gravity held them back. They hung there for a moment, and somebody screamed. Then they fell, head first, down towards the unforgiving concrete.

Salome was under them. So was Mrs Westlake and Mr Barlow. Somehow – between them – they caught the falling boy. Rikki's skull jarred against his mother's, but he was gathered in by the shoulders and torso. He was laid gently on his side, his chest heaving, and Dr Warren knelt beside him. He had a sedative ready, and he injected it as quickly as he dared.

Every child watched, in horrified silence.

'Get the car,' said Dr Warren. He could hardly speak. 'This boy needs care.'

'My husband's on his way—'

'No. We're taking him, Mrs Westlake.' He looked at Salome. 'Take your hands off. You can't help him. He needs emergency care now – for his own safety and protection, so . . . everyone back, please. Attempted suicide:

this is just what I predicted.' He picked the boy up, helped by the orderly, and in a moment they were moving.

'No,' said Mrs Westlake. 'You can't—'

'The paperwork's done,' said Dr Warren furiously. 'There's no other option.'

CHAPTER FOUR

They awoke in the Rechner Institute, but everything had changed.

It was a section Richard had never seen before, with red alarm buttons on the walls, and low ceilings. They'd come through the high-security gates in Dr Warren's sleek BMW, and a trolley had been waiting with more, muscular, orderlies. Elevators had swished them up and down until it was hard to remember if they were in a deep basement or high in the sky. The doors opened to the swiping of cards and there was no sign of any nurses.

Mr and Mrs Westlake were there, but some distance away. The consultant was sitting closest, gazing through large glasses. Dr Warren stood behind him, with a file of notes in his hand – and he was dressed differently. His bow tie was gone, and he wore a white coat over a dark jersey. He was holding a set of forms under the nose of a woman seated in a metal chair. There was a silent clock, and the buzz of air conditioners. Monitors flashed, but they too were noiseless.

Richard wasn't sure if he was able to speak or not.

'Something's wrong with Rikki,' he said carefully. His lips felt thick. Rikki's eyes were closed, and his breath came in low, juddering snores. Richard could feel the sedative in his own brain, heavy as sand, and he could hardly lift himself – the bedclothes pressed him to the mattress too. He managed to wipe Rikki's chin gently – he was dreaming, and a small bubble of spit formed between his lips.

'What's wrong with Rikki?' Richard asked.

Dr Warren smiled. 'We've calmed him down a bit,'

'Have you knocked him out?'

'Richard,' said his mother. 'Try not to worry. You're all right – that's the main thing.'

'Why is he knocked out, Mum? Who said they could sedate Rikki?'

'It's a mild dose,' said Dr Warren. 'We can crank it up if we need to, though: we're getting better at judging how the drugs work, Richard. That's a step forward in itself. He'll be out for a couple of hours, so we can all have a talk. You remember Doctor Summersby?'

'No.'

The consultant sat forward and his glasses flashed. 'She's here to help us, young man. I think we need an informed discussion, don't you?'

'Maybe. But it's not very fair, knocking Rikki out – I don't like that.'

'Why not?' said Dr Warren.

'He wouldn't like it, and you know he wouldn't.'

Dr Summersby looked up. 'He's still loyal,' she said softly. 'Rationality's good, and that's the left hemisphere leading.'

'I think it's wrong,' repeated Richard more assertively. 'I wouldn't want you knocking me out so you could talk to him behind my back. And where are we? Where have you put us?'

'Richard,' said his father, 'it's only for a short time.'

'Am I in prison?'

'No! Of course not. You said it yourself – things can't go on like this, didn't you? You nearly died today, and we had that fight yesterday. We had the fire – which we never properly talked about . . . now this. So the doctors are going to look at some options, and—'

'Dad, I don't even know what happened!' cried Richard.

'Then we'd better inform you,' said Dr Warren lightly. He sat on the bed and Richard drew his feet up, away from him. 'Let's go back a bit – before your rather spectacular dive. Maybe we should start with the arson, Richard? Do you want to talk about that?'

'Not to you.'

'That's what it was. Rikki tried to burn your house down.'

'It was me that tried.'

'Was it? Really? What about the violence at school? We know Rikki broke the painting – had he already defaced it?'

'If he did, he did it when I was asleep. That's what I told the headmaster, and that's the truth.'

Dr Summersby spoke again. 'That is entirely possible. We had a case in Asia with a similar pattern.'

'Dr Summersby was out in Vietnam,' said the

consultant. 'She's an associate surgeon here, and spends a lot of time in our research ward. She's been to-ing and fro-ing a little . . . but she's back with us now and has some very good news.' He leaned forward, and smiled. 'We think we have a solution to all this, Richard – if you're brave enough. If you're ready to move fast, and take a chance.'

'We're at the critical stage, Richard,' said Dr Summersby. 'I've seen it before.'

'What stage?' said Richard. 'I don't understand you.'

'You're experiencing symbiotic enmity. It's a competitive process between cranial zones. There's a refusal to empathize with other people – it's similar to your friend, Eric, and we've been developing strategies for exactly these kinds of crises.'

Richard stared at her.

'Intervention is now possible,' she said.

Dr Warren smiled. 'The counselling failed, Richard,' he said. 'Rikki refused it, while you tried to make it work. He's not easy to live with any more, is he?'

'He's not so bad.'

'Really?'

'He's me. I'm still alive.' Richard closed his eyes again, and felt his mother's hand on his. His parents seemed curiously distant, and he couldn't work out why – it was as if they'd been told not speak. 'I just don't know where I am, Mum – where have you put me?'

'You're in a private suite, Richard,' said Dr Warren. 'We can take care of you here, and get things sorted once and for all. We have a team ready—'

'It's a mental hospital, isn't it?'

'No!'

'Then why are there no windows?'

'You're here for your own protection,' said Dr Summersby. 'Only special people get to come here—'

'You cut up monkeys, don't you? Eric told me!'

'Richard!' said his mother.

'I'm not one of your monkeys. I want to wake up Rikki! He's the one who needs help right now, so—'

'Why do you want him with you?' said Dr Summersby. 'Let him go.'

Richard stared at her again, and for a moment he was lost for words. She held his gaze, unblinking.

'Why are you so anxious about him?' she said.

'I just told you,' said Richard at last. 'He's me.'

'Is that what you feel?'

'Yes!'

'But he's poisoning you,' said Dr Warren. 'The drugs only slow things down, especially as he fights against them. He's taking over, isn't he? That can't be good.'

'I don't know what you mean.'

'He wants to destroy you, Richard – it's as simple as that. He made a pretty emphatic attempt this morning, and there was nothing you could do about it.'

'That's not true!' Richard tried to sit up, but couldn't. 'We work together. He's me, and I'm him, and that was clear right from the start. You told *me* that!'

'Richard,' said the consultant, 'We've read your diary here, and—'

'My diary?'

'Yes.'

Richard gaped. 'How did you get that?'

Mr Westlake sat forward. 'They asked us for it, son,' he said quietly. 'We didn't feel we had a choice—'

'But, Dad . . . I write private stuff in that.'

'I know, Richard, I know.'

'How could you just give it to them?'

'It's routine procedure,' said Dr Warren. 'You mustn't be so sensitive, and you mustn't blame your parents. We have legal responsibilities, you see. The last thing anyone wanted was police involvement, so we all worked together and kept it friendly.'

Richard closed his eyes.

'The diary's a fascinating aid to the diagnosis,' said Dr Summersby. 'It's allowed the team to move forward.'

'There's a team?'

'Oh yes.'

'And they all read it. You sat round and read my diary—'

'There's blood on it,' said Dr Warren. 'We were obliged to read it.'

'So you took it out of my drawer, did you? What else did you take? What else have you stolen, Doctor Warren? You inject Rikki and knock him out, and I know why you do that – it's because he's smarter than you, and saw through you from the start. You hate him, so you've kidnapped us. You couldn't deal with Rikki, so you're finding other ways now. That's what this is about!'

'Paranoia,' said Dr Summersby softly. 'Very common.'

'Who's paranoid? How am I paranoid?'

'Richard,' said Dr Warren. He wasn't smiling. 'Nobody here hates Rikki.'

'You do!'

'Emotions like "hate" play no part in diagnosis.'

'You're *scared* of him!'

'He's a destructive intruder. There comes a point when he can be indulged no longer.'

'Please,' said the consultant. 'The clock is ticking, and the panel will be with us in a few minutes. I think we should move to the briefing suite.'

'Good,' said Dr Warren. 'Let's go.'

'I wonder if I should take over at this point?' said Dr Summersby. 'We can show you some photographs, Richard, and lay out the options.'

'I want to wake up Rikki,' said Richard. 'This affects him!'

'No,' said Dr Warren.

A male nurse appeared right on cue. He was pushing a wheelchair, and in a moment the sheets were pulled back and Richard felt strong arms lifting him. His parents were ushered to the side, and a door he hadn't seen slid open. He was lowered into the chair, reversed, and turned. A long corridor stretched out in front of him, and he was rolling down it under pale blue strip lights. All he could hear was the thundering of wheels.

CHAPTER FIVE

They came to a cinema.

It seemed dark after the glare of the corridor, and a large screen dominated one wall. Around this hung several television monitors, leaning in on hydraulic arms. Cables looped between them, and a satellite dish stood blank and white on a rack of electronics. A technician whispered into a microphone, and as soon as the door closed, the television sets started to glow.

Dr Summersby moved onto a platform, and Richard was aware of Dr Warren just behind him. Rikki's head still lolled against his ear, and he could feel spittle down his neck. Another door opened, and his parents stepped through.

'I want to go home!' said Richard.

'I know, love,' said his mother.

'What do they want with me? Let me go!'

His father took his hand. 'Give them a chance, son. That's all we ask. Nothing will be done without your permission.'

'What do you mean, Dad? Permission for what?'

His parents sat on either side of him, and Dr Summersby peered into the gloom. 'Can you hear me?' she said. The technician raised his thumb. 'Is Professor Reed with us?'

'Patching him in. Any minute.'

'OK. And—'

'Doctor Tibbitts is online too, standing by.'

'OK. Richard . . . let me explain,' said Dr Summersby. 'You're about to meet our emergency team. They've all want to talk to you, because they've been following your case, just like me. Sorry, there's a buzzing . . .' A microphone amplified her voice and pushed it out of several speakers. There was a squeal of static, and each television slowly resolved into a human face. The faces hovered, blinking. Dr Summersby pressed a key on her laptop and the screen behind her burst into a multi-coloured grid. 'This is the age of technology,' she said. 'Professor Reed?'

'He's through,' said the man at the desk.

'Edmund Reed is one of our top surgeons, Richard—'

'Hello?' said a voice. 'I can see you, but I can't hear anything.'

'You're loud and clear, Ed,' said Dr Warren. 'Julius is with us too – so's Fergal.' The heads nodded and smiled, then all at once the faces rolled upwards, disappearing at the chin. Foreheads returned, and then staring eyes. The images settled again, grinning.

Richard clung to his father's hand, as Dr Summersby continued: 'We've discussed your situation,' she said. 'As I said before, your case is not unique, and—'

'I'm not a case,' hissed Richard.

'I'm sorry?'

'Shh, dear,' said his mother. 'Let her explain.'

'I'm not a case!' said Richard again. 'I'm just a . . . boy, and I'm not sick or mental. I don't know who any of you are!'

Dr Summersby smiled. 'We understand your sensitivities,' she said. 'When I said the word "case", all I meant was that we've had a very similar . . . example of your situation, out in Asia.'

'A successful procedure,' said one of the televisions. 'Richard, I'm Mr Feeney, and I can tell you, right now, that we're ready to go on this. Butterfly's doing well, and—'

'*Very* well,' said Dr Warren. 'Let's show him, Fergal.'

'Sure.'

'He needs to see the miracle – it's important, Richard.'

Dr Summersby continued her explanation. 'Edmund led the surgery for Butterfly, and it taught us all a very great deal about properly timed intervention. So . . . let's get right to the point.' She pressed another key and the grid on the main screen broke up into a host of thumbnail images.

'How are you feeling, Rikki?' said one of the televisions.

'Julius, this is *Richard*,' said Dr Warren.

'Oh, right. Hi.'

'We thought she was a mutation,' said Dr Summersby. 'At first. That was the logical diagnosis, because there are a lot of nerve agents left in Vietnam. That's the legacy of war, of course, and some of those poisons lay dormant for years. Then the water supply gets contaminated, and before you know it—'

'Two-headed pigs,' said Dr Tibbits. 'Two-headed dogs. Mutations sprouting everywhere. But the little girl—'

'I'm not a mutation,' said Richard through gritted teeth.

'You're not what? I can't hear you, son.'

'Nor can I,' said the screen opposite. 'I can just about hear—'

'I'm not a mutation!' cried Richard. 'There's nothing wrong with me!'

Dr Summersby was nodding. 'You're not, of course. You're a very sensitive young man,' she said quickly. 'And you're right to be picking us up on our language too. You're not a mutation, Rik— Richard. You are a . . . fully functioning, ultra-normal schoolboy, and your teachers speak very highly of you.'

'So do I,' said Dr Warren.

There was a smattering of warm laughter, and Mr Feeney leaned forward into his screen. 'You're not the problem at all, Richard,' he said. The voice was suddenly loud, and the face was all nose and glasses. 'Everyone knows that, my friend. We want that secondary cortex removed, once and for all. You deserve a normal life, same as everyone.'

'Yes, but—'

'We've found a way, at last. OK, there's a level of risk—'

'Rikki!' said Richard. 'I need you, man! Will you wake up, please?'

'Shh!' said Dr Warren.

'Show him the pictures,' said the consultant.

'Be patient, love,' said his mother. 'We agreed to sedate Rikki. We all agreed—'

'Wake up, Rikki!' shouted Richard. 'I need you! We're in a madhouse!'

'He's right here with you,' said Mr Westlake. He put his arm round his son's shoulders and held him tight. 'He'll be awake soon, Richard. Let these people show you what they have in mind – go with us that far. Please.'

Richard laughed. 'You hate him too, Dad, I know you do.'

'I don't hate him, son. How can I?'

'He's me! He's me, and I'm him, and . . . Oh God, you can't just cut out the bits you don't like! Where's Grandad?'

'Look,' said the consultant loudly. 'I think it's best that we outline the treatment, and take it from there. The schedule is tight.'

'The funding's through, isn't it?'

'Oh yes.'

'Then we're flying tonight. Show him the first slide.'

A thumbnail burst open, and two little Asian girls appeared, laughing with delight. They filled the room, and Richard blinked at the brightness. They were seven or eight years old, in pigtails and ribbons – and the whole room was transformed by their energy. Richard gazed, and it took him a full five seconds to realize that while there were two faces and two radiant smiles, there was only one pair of shoulders. His mouth fell open, for it was a single child. Like him, she had two heads, sitting neatly on one slender torso.

'That's Butterfly, Richard,' said Professor Reed. 'We airlifted her from Ho Chi Minh a month ago: the Vietnam experiment.'

'Butterfly?' said Richard.

'Yes.'

'Is that her real name? Why did you call her that?'

'I don't know,' said Dr Tibbits. 'Because she was cute as a butterfly, I guess. And none of us could say her real name. Anyway, that's not the issue. We got her down to Brisbane, where Ed runs a neurological unit just like this one. Show him some more.'

Images clicked and slide followed slide. The child was holding a cat. She was sitting in a chair. She was standing again, in school uniform. The smiles were still dazzling.

Dr Warren said, 'Now look what we did. This was the result of teamwork, and – as I said – the implications are huge. The behaviour changed *totally*.'

The next picture showed a child in pyjamas. She was in a wheelchair, and one of the heads had shrivelled. It was as if somebody had let the air out of it.

'That was three days after admission,' said Dr Summersby. The television faces nodded and smiled. 'The radiation therapy was instantly successful – more than anyone would have believed.'

'It was amazing,' said Mr Feeney. 'We'd found where to target it, right?'

'We bombarded the parietal lobe first,' said Professor Reed. 'That was the big decision . . . show him the next one.'

The screen melted into another huge close-up, and the child's eyes were suddenly closed. She was held in some kind of clamp, and two discs hovered just above her temples.

'My God, she was a tough cookie.'

'Brave, as well,' said Dr Tibbits. 'Never complained.'

'She had endurance, Richard,' said Dr Warren. 'There were some minor complications, of course there were. Temporary paralysis, loss of speech. But we've learned from those experiences, and we want to try again. We can help you lead a normal life – the extremes . . . the rage. The death wish. They'll be all in the past.'

The image changed again, to a side view, and Dr Summersby took over again. 'I moved in on the prefrontal cortex,' she said. 'That closed down the danger areas. We induced strokes, effectively, Richard – in a very targeted fashion.'

'Tiny explosions,' said one of the screen doctors.

'It's safe, and it's controlled—' added another.

'What it does is implode the second head, while giving the other brainstem stimulants that allow it to re-adjust back to the original, happier pathology. It's a bit like re-programming a computer – cleaning out a virus. You can imagine how good it feels.'

'I'm feeling sick,' said Richard.

'We burn out the complications. It's like—'

'A kind of re-booting. You'll feel renewed and invigorated.'

'Butterfly after six days.'

She pressed a key, and Richard's mouth fell open again. The little girl was in bed, and her neck was bandaged. She was staring at the camera with dead eyes. Her lips were swollen and parted, as if she was trying to speak. Dr Summersby clicked again, and Richard saw the second head, the size of a deflated football. The neck had been severed just below the Adam's apple. The eyelids were tight shut, and it was biting its own tongue.

'Let's hold it there,' said one of the televisions. There was a buzz of static again. 'We're learning all the time, naturally, because that second head can teach you a hell of a lot.'

'I'm going to be sick,' said Richard. 'Let me out, please!'

'Hang on, just—'

'Cut the slides, please. He's seen enough.'

'This is wrong!' cried Richard. 'Let me go!'

He tried not to look at the screen, but it was too huge to avoid. Another slide had appeared, and in his effort to close it down the technician flashed up yet another. Butterfly's second brain had been removed from the skull. It sat on a slab of white marble, wired into what might have been a battery. When the slide flipped again, red tissue had been divided into neat slices, and Richard could stand it no more. He scrambled to his feet, pulling himself away from his father. A hand closed around his arm, but he managed to haul himself over the chairs in front and shake it off.

'Richard, wait!' said Dr Warren.

'What's happening?' said somebody. 'Is there a problem?'

'Doctor Summersby—'

'I'm getting out!' shouted Richard. 'Come on, Dad – they're not touching Rikki!'

'Hold him!' cried Dr Warren. 'He's over-stimulating.'

Mr and Mrs Westlake were on their feet too, moving to the aisle. The cinema lights came on, and an orderly in a white coat moved quickly to the doors.

'You're not doing that to me!' hissed Richard. He dodged back along the row, but a second nurse was approaching fast. A third had appeared through a curtain, and Dr Warren was talking into a mobile phone.

Richard vaulted another block of seats, but there was clearly no escape, and he could hear an alarm ringing. The nurses were closing in, and one was holding his father back. Richard leaped again, and found himself surrounded. He tried to get back the way he'd come, but suddenly they were on him, and he was lifted high in their arms. He screamed for help, and heard his father's voice, shouting back – he heard his mother crying out, but he couldn't see them for the cinema was spinning.

'Dad!' he yelled. He was twisting like a fish. 'Get them off me! Get them—'

He managed one mighty kick, and then he tried to punch, but his arms were held too tightly. They had his ankles and his knees, and he was lowered quickly to the ground, locked against white coats.

The shouting was constant now, and his mother was hysterical. Richard howled out again, squirming and twisting, but the hands that held him were merciless and impossibly strong. They'd restrained patients three times his size, and they knew exactly where to grip.

'Careful!' said someone.'

'You got him?'

'I've got him. Hold still.'

'Put him back. Not too far. Doctor Warren?'

His shoulders were bent backwards, and Richard could feel hands on his jaw. He was staring into the eyes of an orderly who was concentrating hard, and he glimpsed the hypodermic as it passed his nose. They were going for the neck. He tried to buck and curl, but it was hopeless. He felt the sting, and he couldn't move a muscle. Still people were shouting, but now the voices were taking on strange echoes, as if in a swimming bath.

'Please!' he cried.

'He's a fighter, this one,' said a voice in his ear.

'Oh, please!' said Richard quietly. 'Don't . . . please . . .' He tried to sit up, but they were pressing him down, and he couldn't speak loudly enough.

Dr Warren was high above him, studying his watch, and then Dr Summersby moved in beneath them all, kneeling. She had a second hypodermic, and Richard couldn't get away from it. She stung him in almost the same place, right in the throat as Rikki's head rolled sideways, mouth open. There was another tiny pricking, just under his chin, and all sound started to fade. He glimpsed the ceiling, blue with a bright, white lamp in the centre – he thought it was the sun, for a moment, bursting out of a beautiful sky. He strained towards it, for he could hear engines roaring. A fighter-jet was hurtling towards him, about to smash through the walls.

Then it was blackness. He crashed into a darkness so thick it simply extinguished him.

PART FOUR
FLIGHT

CHAPTER ONE

'Wake up,' said a voice.

'No . . .'

'You did fine, boy. Just take your time.'

Something was buzzing in his ears, and the light was dim. There was a drain in his mouth, and he could feel pressure on his chest.

'Rikki?' said Richard. 'Are you there?'

'Yes.'

'Thank God. Where?'

'I'm right beside you, brother. As you might expect.'

'You're still with me? They're after you, Rikki – I couldn't stop them . . .'

'Nobody's dead yet. We're in a bad way, though – and we haven't got much time. You've got to wake up, OK? We've been waiting for you.'

He felt a pair of teeth bite gently into his ear lobe. The pressure increased, and there was a twinge of pain. Then the teeth released him and he heard a sound he hadn't heard for a long time. It was laughter.

'Relax, OK?'

'Where have they put us?' said Richard. 'I don't think I can move.'

'We're in the dungeon. They're getting us ready for the big separation.'

'Rikki, I can't move my head. Where's Mum and Dad?'

'They were thrown out,' whispered Rikki. 'Sent home. So stay as calm as you can, all right? There was nothing they could do for us – Warren's got all the paperwork he needed, and he wants me in a jar. We have to get our energy back, 'cos I'm not sure we can even walk at the moment.'

'They've drugged us.'

'They're filling us up, and screwing us down. What floor are we on, Eric?'

'Basement three,' said a small voice. 'High security, so they say.'

'We're underground. Summersby's taking her chance, Richard. They've got the lasers all set up and the surgeons are coming.'

'Where?'

'Look around you. Focus! Can you move your head, even a little bit?'

'No.'

'Move your eyeballs, then.'

Richard let his eyes wander, and the shapes above him gradually resolved themselves. He was held in a vice, and all around his head stood grey, metallic snouts – there were six of them, at least. They were on complicated stands and levers, so they could be swung and tilted. Little red lights gleamed and flashed, and each snout tapered to a single tiny nostril that was aimed right at his skull. They were ranged over both his head and Rikki's, and he realized they were attached to wires and tubes that coiled around his neck and chest. His shoulders felt bolted to some kind of frame, and his temple was squeezed between steel plates.

'This is the end, isn't it?'

'No. We've got an exit strategy, as Eric will explain.'

'Eric? You said Eric a second ago—'

'He's with us, OK? Up on the cupboard, working out the wiring. He's going to save us, Richard.'

'Why would Eric be here? You're hallucinating!'

'Not me. He's going to spring us, but you have to stay calm. They were going to zap him too – don't you remember? Our school's right behind them.'

A lamp clicked on, and Richard saw a shape high above him on some kind of cabinet. 'I'm up here, Richard,' said a voice. 'Don't shout, OK? I'm taking the batteries out of this, and then I'm going to try and unwrap you.'

Richard strained his eyes, and saw that there were shadows everywhere – there were bars around his bed, and they threw stripes across the walls. The long snouts were reflected in huge ceiling mirrors, and he suddenly felt he was falling. The voice had come from in front, so he focused on a tall metal box beyond his toes. Up on the top, side-lit by a shaded bulb, he could see the figure of a child, sitting cross-legged. The side of the face gleamed, and he saw eyes, shining with excitement, and a bright, unmistakable smile.

'It *is* you!' whispered Richard. 'Eric . . .'

'They moved me in on Friday. Shhh! They took me into care, same as you. You've got nothing to worry about, though – I've dismantled their little communication pack, and we have a plan.'

'But why are you in hospital? Are you sick?'

'Look at my head.'

Eric put his cranium down, and Richard saw that it had been shaved: there wasn't a tram-line or a dreadlock to be seen. Eric was as bald as a baby, and looked about eight years old. He jumped down onto the bed and moved close to Richard.

'I told you, didn't I?' he said, chuckling. 'They were going to fry the badness out of me. It's what Doctor Warren wants to try – and Mum signed the forms after what I did to Mr Barlow.'

'Mr Barlow? What did you do to Mr Barlow?'

'I battered him unconscious.'

'What? How?'

'I hit him, Richard. With a fire extinguisher. They threw me off the residential, right at the last minute, and I just lost it. I couldn't stop myself.'

'Why Mr Barlow, though? Did you hurt him?'

'I think so. He was unconscious.'

'Look,' said Rikki. 'All that can wait—'

'OK, but I got to get your drips out first. Let me check the doors again – you stay there.'

Richard lay still, utterly confused. He heard the sound of bare feet and was aware of a door buzzing open, then closing again. Eric was back, leaping the bars nimbly, and he felt quick, careful fingers working at his wrist.

'We can't take any chances,' he said. 'They checked you about five minutes ago, so we should have a window of twenty to thirty. This is going to hurt, all right?'

Richard winced as something was drawn from his flesh. Then he felt hands at his nose, and there were tears in his eyes as something pinched and pulled.

'God, Eric!' he said. 'You stink of cigarettes.'

'Yeah, I'm sorry.'

'Are you smoking again?'

'When I get nervous. Yeah . . .'

Eric spun the wheel nuts of a clamp, and Richard felt his skull easing back onto a mat. 'We're cutting it fine, OK? They want Rikki for full-on dissection. They're just going to take him now, whatever the risk – they want to see inside. I heard them planning it.'

'Tell him,' said Rikki. 'Get the other clamps off.'

'You ready to listen?' said Eric. He was sitting cross-legged, close to Richard's chest. He reached up, flicked a couple of switches, then heaved some kind of brace from the boy's foreheads. Then he peeled a plaster from Rikki's temple and pushed one of the metal nozzles away. He smiled happily. 'You're nearly free!'

'They showed me pictures,' said Richard. 'But what did you hear?'

'This place is hell.'

'What do you mean?'

'I've been in and out for a while,' said Eric. 'You understand that, don't you? I know my way round pretty well, and I got myself one of these passes.' He held up a plastic card on a loop of cord. 'Found it under one of the computers in reception. They think I'm a cute kid, so nobody takes much notice. For a high-security place, they're pretty slack – which is lucky for all of us. I get pretty much anywhere – up in the lifts, down to the pool. They've got a ward full of weirdos, level five. Today, though, I was just roaming, and I think, *What I wouldn't do for nicotine!* I'd had another session up on the same floor as Doc Warren, so I doubled back and saw where he keeps his jacket. You know he's a smoker?'

'No,' said Richard.

'He's trying to give up, but he can't when he's excited. And he's real excited at the moment, because of his plans for Rikki. So I figured he'd have cigarettes.' He removed more sticking plaster and gently withdrew a plastic probe. 'Do you think you can sit up now? I got to get more wires off you.'

'We've got to stand up,' said Rikki. 'Get on with the story.'

'OK,' said Eric. He drew a couple of bolts on the bed-frame and let down the panel of bars. Then he lifted Richard's arm and draped it over his. In a moment, Richard and Rikki were sitting forward, with Eric behind. 'I crawled into Warren's office, OK? I'm doing a Nailhead manoeuvre – me and Mark learned it together. I'm crawling in, just after a fag, all right? – and I hear voices from the inside office. I hear your names mentioned: "Rikki and Richard". So I freeze, and listen harder. I thought you were there, maybe, and I could leap in and say hello – so I got in close, and I peep in on the fat guy with the specs. He's one of the team, I think.'

'Our consultant.'

'Sit up straight,' said Eric. 'They got plasters all round your head – sensors all over you.' He started peeling and pulling. 'Anyway, I'm still in the office. Doctor Warren's right opposite, and there's the woman with the scary face. Dracula's wife.'

'Summersby,' said Rikki.

' "Just do it," says the fat guy. "Get it done." "That's the way," says the woman. "In Vietnam we just took the risk." Doc Warren speaks then, and says, "What if he dies on us? What then?" and Summersby says, "They're insured. So are we." '

'You heard her say that?' gasped Richard.

'That's what she said – those were her words. Then she says, "We need the Rikki brain. I want it!" '

'Rikki, I can't believe this!' hissed Richard.

'Yes, but Doctor Warren took over, then,' said Eric. 'I'm just giving you the gist, OK? "Let's get the sequence clear," he says. "Soon as the team arrive . . . get him straight to the lab." '

'It's an outrage,' cried Richard. 'Mum and Dad, what do they say?'

'They're being lied to,' said Rikki. 'Warren's going to tell them they had no choice. We're on our own, Richard.'

'Try and stand,' said Eric. 'You need to get the circulation going.'

'I'm going to kill him,' said Richard.

Rikki laughed. 'I knew you'd be cross,' he said. They struggled onto their feet. 'It was my reaction too, Rich. Which is not exactly surprising, is it? But it makes me love you even more.'

'They're not going to do it,' said Richard. 'They will touch your brain over my dead body. You understand? We are totally together on this.' He staggered forward, and leaned against a chair.

Eric was right at his side. 'Don't speak for a moment,' he said. 'Get your breath. We're going to get out of here, and survive, Richard: that's the plan. Now see if you can get to the door.' He took some of his friend's weight, and helped him walk. 'Me and Rikki talked about this while you were asleep. I'm going to call Spider, and make sure he's waiting for us. He's got wheels, so if we can get out through the gates, he'll take us away. And we're going down to Wales.'

'Wales?' said Richard.

Rikki was nodding, though the pain of using his legs was making him wince. 'We've had the idea of the century, brother. You're going to be so impressed.'

'What's happening in Wales?'

'It's where the school trip's going! Don't you remember?'

'We hide on the bus,' said Rikki. 'Stowaways!'

'Keep moving,' said Eric. 'Go round the bed. Where are they *not* going to look for us?'

'Many places.'

'Most of all, school. They'd never dream we'd go back to it.'

'So we go on the trip?' said Richard. They walked once round the room together. 'Is that what you're suggesting?'

Eric was shaking his head, giggling. 'Not exactly. You remember when the bus leaves?'

'Sunday,' said Richard.

'And you remember the brochure?' said Rikki.

Eric took Richard's hands and put them against the wall. 'Push,' he said. 'Get your strength back. Keep moving your feet – like you're jogging.' Then he quoted from memory. '*It's the last frontier. It's tough enough for the SAS – is it too tough for you?*' He went behind Richard and Rikki and massaged their shoulders, pounding life back into them. '*Can you handle life in the untamed wilderness?*' he hissed. '*Where man meets his inner self, and finds out what he's made of?*'

'You think we could hide out there?' said Richard. He was breathing deeply.

'The bus will have a roof-rack,' said Rikki. 'We tie ourselves to it. Soon as we get near the camp, we jump down – head for the hills and disappear. Build a log cabin, or find a cave. Live off the land.'

'Hunt wild animals,' said Eric. 'Bag ourselves a deer and rabbits. Get fish from the stream – it's all in the survival book! And you see, nobody will think we'd go where the school is going. So it's the best idea we ever had: and we survive.'

Richard turned to face Eric. 'Look,' he said, 'you hit Mr Barlow with a fire extinguisher. How do you know the residential's even happening? And I don't know why you picked on him . . . he's a nice guy!'

Eric nodded. 'I knew you'd hate me for it, Rich – but . . . I was in a red mist and he was the one who told me the news. He said I wasn't going, and I just lashed out – because they'd promised it to me.'

'It'll be cancelled, then—'

'No. They *are* still going – Mark told me. The headmaster wanted to cancel, but there were too many complaints. So he's leading it himself.'

'Did you hurt him?' said Richard.

'Who?'

'Mr Barlow!'

'I think so. He went down like a sack, and had some kind of . . . seizure. They called an ambulance, but I didn't hear where they took him.' He paused. 'I think we'd better get moving. Do you feel ready?'

'Yes,' said Rikki.

Eric froze. 'I've just thought of a problem. How do I call Spider?'

CHAPTER TWO

They didn't have a phone.

There was one on the wall, and they thought about trying it. After a brief discussion, however, they agreed that it would be connected to some switchboard, and if they went through that, they'd be asking for trouble. Eric offered the solution.

'Warren's office again,' he said. 'He'll be out in the labs, right? So his coat's going to be exactly where it was, with everything we need – money as well.'

'No,' said Richard. 'We could get caught before we're even out of the hospital.'

'We have to take risks!' cried Rikki. 'That's how it is now, so we might as well get used to it. What's the time?'

'Sixteen twenty-seven,' said Eric.

'You think he'll be here so late?'

'Rikki,' said Richard, 'he's planning to cut your head off. You think he's going to knock off early?'

Rikki nodded. 'You're smarter than you look, boy.'

'We need to think together,' said Richard.

'We always did. But you've got to stop worrying, OK? Or I'll have to punch you out.'

'Don't threaten me, Rikki!'

'Guys?' said Eric. 'Do you do this all the time?'

'What?' said Rikki and Richard.

'It must be so frustrating, you arguing like that. I mean, do you argue about what socks to put on, and that kind of thing?'

Richard blushed. 'We see eye to eye on most things,' he said. 'He doesn't mean half what he says.'

'Don't I?' said Rikki, genuinely puzzled.

'You think you do—'

'But you say I don't. And you *know* that?'

'Yes.'

'Wow.'

'Look,' said Eric. 'Just get yourselves dressed. I got you my spares, and I wear baggy stuff. You might be OK.'

Minutes later, Eric had opened the first door, and was padding down a bare, white corridor.

'Four thirty is a tea break,' he whispered. 'Not everyone goes, but the place is definitely quieter. You stay back, all right? There's a guard round this corner.' He trotted silently forward, peered left and right, then beckoned Rikki and Richard.

They moved fast, and hid behind a locker.

'Gone,' whispered Eric. 'I tell you, they don't miss their biscuits.'

He went on again, checking for obstacles. He waved,

and Rikki and Richard followed. It was a slow journey, and they had to pause twice because of footsteps. On one occasion, they had to jump into a cupboard as they heard a trolley coming towards them. Moments later it had rolled by, and they continued to the elevators.

'What is this place? Really?' said Rikki.

'I don't know for sure,' said Eric. 'They're doing experiments, but I don't know the details. Whatever it is, it's dodgy.'

'You're telling me.'

'What floor?' said Richard.

'The top. That's the monkey house too.'

'We never saw monkeys,' said Rikki. 'And we've been there, twice.'

'You go through to the back.'

'And your card thing gets us anywhere?' said Richard. 'It does the lift?'

'It did a little while ago. We just have to hope.' Eric swiped it, and pressed in a code. The light above the doors went from white to red, and the word 'error' appeared on the keypad.

'Blast. Maybe they changed it.'

'How many goes do you get?' said Rikki.

'I don't know. Maybe I got confused. My brain's malfunctioning, don't forget that—'

'So's ours,' said Richard.

'Go *slow*,' hissed Rikki. 'They wouldn't change the code, surely – not in a few hours.'

Eric pressed the numbers again, and they held their

breath. The lift seemed to be thinking hard. Then, after a few seconds, it made its decision, and the doors slid open. They pressed 'six' and up they rose, the sweat clear on their brows. Seconds later, they stepped out onto thick carpet.

'You recognize this?' said Rikki.

'Yes,' said Richard.

'Be brave. We're a long way from home.'

Turning left again, they moved past offices. They scuttled to an open door right at the end, and recognized Dr Warren's consulting room. The fish were still swimming lazily, and there was the scent of coffee.

'I can't see him,' said Richard.

Eric had crawled in already and was up on one of the easy chairs, peering forward. 'He's out the back,' he hissed. 'I can hear his voice. His jacket was right here on the chair . . .'

'Maybe he's wearing it.'

'We'll have to find out.' He slid to the ground and crawled back to Richard. 'The lab's at the end, OK? Then you get to the drug stores – I got a map in my head, but it's not going to be easy. You ready for this?'

Richard and Rikki nodded. 'Of course.'

Eric lowered his voice still further. 'I'm going to do pages eighty-seven to ninety-three: *surreptitious infiltration*. I just wish Mark was here.'

'You nervous?'

'Course I am – you should be too. Just do as I say, all right?'

Rikki and Richard nodded, and Eric rolled noiselessly

across the office floor, disappearing behind the long sofa. Seconds later he was somersaulting through the doorway, and ended up in a crouch halfway up the narrow white corridor. From there he beckoned Richard and Rikki, and as they arrived behind him, he dropped onto his belly.

'Do what I do,' he whispered. 'And get ready for surprises.'

The boys moved forward like eels, rippling their chests and knees in a noiseless advance over the linoleum. As they inched forward, they could hear the doctor's voice more clearly, and a strange, watery bubbling. There was the distant cheeping of creatures and the monotonous hum of a generator. When they got to the next doorway, there was the unmistakable sound of monkeys chattering.

'My God,' said Rikki. 'You were serious.'

'I don't joke,' said Eric. He turned and ducked into the main laboratory, rolling sideways. Richard and Rikki followed, and they were soon lost in a forest of steel struts beneath heavy benches. The air had a chemical smell and the generators were louder. At the far end of the tables, they could see a pair of shoes at floor level, and the bottoms of trousers. Dr Warren's voice floated towards them under a babble of squeaking. Eric led them forward, absolutely silent, and they heard a familiar chuckle.

'That's him!' said Richard.

'Shh!' hissed Eric.

'Honestly, Mrs Westlake,' said the voice. 'He's quite calm at the moment. Composed, even – I've just come from the ward. He was reading his book, totally at ease.

He's a good lad.' He paused, and the boys pressed forward again, straining their ears. 'You know, I really think tomorrow will be better,' continued Dr Warren. 'He needs his sleep, and tomorrow we can all have a nice long session in the lounge, chat everything through again. I'm going to pop down again in half an hour, give him his cocoa. I'll call you right back – you must not worry. He's being much more reasonable, knows there's no other way, and—' He stood up, and the boys froze. The shoes took a few slow paces, and halted again. 'Rikki's been a handful, yes.'

'Swine!' said Rikki.

'Shhhh!'

'But I genuinely think Richard's had enough of him now. Between you and me, he's ready to say goodbye, but doesn't know how to – that's so often the problem. He wants to be free, you see. He wants a peaceful life . . .'

'I'm going to kill him now,' hissed Richard.

Rikki put his hand over his mouth and they crouched, trembling with rage. 'We'll do him together,' said Rikki. 'Don't worry. We'll find a way!'

'I love you, Rikki!' said Richard, removing the hand.

'I love you too, brother. Always have.'

'You're weird as hell, but—'

'It's your fault, you bring out the worst in me!'

'Guys!' hissed Eric. He seized the two throats and peered from one face to the other. 'You've got to shut up now, OK? And get ready to move. The doc's jacket's on the stool, so I'm going to launch what's called a *distraction assault*. Stay close, and keep your mouths shut.' He put his nose closer to Rikki. 'You've seen nothing yet.'

Richard raised his thumb and Eric released his grip.

Again, the boy rolled, but this time he moved at right angles to Dr Warren's shoes and was soon on all fours in one of the laboratory's empty aisles. His head swivelled, taking in distances, and he allowed himself one vertical movement so his head, like a periscope, rose above the work surfaces. When he turned to Richard and Rikki again, there was a thin smile on his face.

'Trust your hunches,' he said. 'Plans come unstuck if you think for too long.'

'Is that from the handbook?' mouthed Richard.

'The Bible – yes.'

Eric led the way back to the first doorway. In a moment, shielded by a set of fridges, he was standing, and the air was suddenly thick with the smell of animals. The chirps and squeaks had risen, and they could hear anxious panting and high-pitched cries. Cages were rattling too, and there were bleeps and buzzes coming from shelves overhead.

'Are you ready?' Eric said.

'No,' said Richard.

'You've got to be.'

There was a row of deep aquaria, and as the boys peered into them, white rabbits gazed back in silent terror. They were in the grip of clamps and straps, their paws outstretched. In the dim light beyond were creatures the boys couldn't recognize: creatures wrapped in plastic, with tubes sprouting from their middles, joined to tangles of wires. They could see computers, and there was the soft chattering of printers. Eric moved forward, pulling Richard behind him. They passed row upon row of rats, the snouts twitching, the eyes staring.

'It gets worse,' whispered Eric.

'It can't,' said Rikki.

'Don't stop.'

The room opened into another laboratory, and at the far end was the chimpanzee called Molly. Her brain still glistened under violet lights, and her single eyeball widened in terror as the boys approached. The creature was losing her fur, and they could see where the tubes went, pumping her lungs. She strained against her restraints, and another printer chattered furiously, while paper chugged under the needles.

'What is this place?' said Richard.

'It's where they want to put me,' said Rikki in a small voice. 'It's obvious, isn't it? Look over there . . .'

They saw then that Molly's brain was not the only one on display. Along a bench to her right, there were rows of dishes and jars, and they all foamed with yet more cables and bulbs. Some brains floated in bright liquids, and some stood on glass. Some were punctured by forests of pins, while others were smooth under neon lights, the blood vessels pulsing as tiny pumps kept them alive.

'How many are human?' said Rikki. 'My God, Warren wanted me the moment he saw me.'

'We have to keep moving,' said Eric. 'I know what

you're thinking, but we can't help Molly. There's more, though – back here.'

'More what?'

'Monkeys. We'll open the cage, all right? That's the distraction. You stay back, and get ready to run.'

Richard and Rikki were numb and trembling, so Eric had to push them into position. He got them past Molly, and turned them towards a long chamber that ran the length of the wall. It was made of tough Perspex, reinforced with steel mesh, and there were rows of air holes drilled along the top. Inside was foliage, and half a tree. Under that stood several food bowls and a mess of torn bark and damp straw. Finally – in a corner – three silver-grey monkeys huddled together, forlorn and afraid. They'd seen the boys coming, and were trying to hide. Bright eyes stared from the little pink faces, and the biggest showed its teeth in a snarl of pure terror.

The door was bolted, and the bolt secured with a plastic tie. It took Eric a moment to pull it free, and then the case yawned open. The first monkey twisted round and saw its chance. It was out in seconds, but its friends were less certain. Eric, Richard and Rikki stood back, opening the door still wider. At last, the other two scampered up to their leader onto the shelves above. They gazed about them, uncertain and disorientated. When they saw Molly, though, they were seized with a new panic. They shrieked as if they'd been electrocuted and shot upwards, swinging onto the light fittings. As they jumped, a tank crashed to the floor in an explosion of glass. A tray of tools was dislodged and the boys heard Dr Warren shout in alarm.

'You ready?' said Eric.

'No!'

The three monkeys screamed again and leaped to the next light fitting, which swung madly under them, chains clattering. The boys heard the crash of furniture as Dr Warren sprang from his stool and raced towards them.

Eric was poised, and the boys moved together, doubling back in the opposite direction. Eric vaulted a workbench and grabbed the precious jacket, then they were rolling back into the corridor as an alarm sounded. They dived into the empty office, and in seconds they were on their feet, moving briskly through the door. The lift arrived as they came into the lobby, and Eric had his card ready in both hands.

As the doors opened, however, an old lady was revealed. She stood staring out at them, a young nurse right behind her.

Somehow, Eric managed to smile. 'Nurse Mills!' he squeaked. 'How, er . . . are you?'

Richard and Rikki wiped the shock from their faces, and slipped the jacket on. They thrust their hands into the pockets and did their best to look casual.

'Hi,' said Richard.

'Oh,' said Eric. 'It's Mrs Jermy, right? You come for your counselling?'

'I have,' said the old lady.

'Eric,' said Nurse Mills. 'Should you be up here? Richard . . . Rikki?'

'We were seeing Doctor Warren,' said Rikki. 'Just finished, and the alarm went off.'

'What's happening?'

'No idea.'

The old lady gazed at Richard and Rikki, trying hard to focus. The alarm was now bleating in short bursts all down the corridor, and there was another explosion of glass somewhere behind them.

'I guess they've had an emergency,' said Richard. 'We've been sent back to the ward.'

'You'd better hurry,' said Nurse Mills. 'What floor are you on now?'

'Ward six, floor three.'

'Go straight there, please. There'll be a lockdown, I imagine.'

'Sure. See you.'

Moments later, they were on floor three, and had turned into a toilet. They locked themselves in a cubicle, where Eric leaned against the door. He was sweating, and his face was grey.

'How on earth did you know that patient's name?' said Richard.

'I met her yesterday,' said Eric. 'She used to be an opera singer, or thinks she did. She was singing to me – there's a ward full of them. Total crazies. Warren's zapping all of them, bit by bit. He turns them into vegetables.'

'I say one thing, Eric,' said Rikki. 'You think fast.'

'Look, guys!' said Eric. 'We've got serious business

ahead. You've got to concentrate now, and cut the chat. Let's see what we've got.'

They emptied the jacket pockets and laid things out on the toilet seat.

'The phone's basic,' said Eric.

'Money,' said Rikki. 'ID, too – could be useful.'

'Keys,' said Richard, noticing a big bunch with 'BMW' on the tag. 'We better not take those.'

Eric chuckled. 'Honestly, Rich . . . you're an innocent boy.'

'What do you mean? I've seen his car, and he'd go crazy if we took the key.'

'Something Spider taught me,' whispered Eric. 'If you want to screw someone, take their wallet, phone and, most of all, every key you can find. Leaves them helpless. Look at this, too – I bet these are his passwords . . .'

'Nice,' said Rikki.

'Just call your brother,' said Richard. 'We ought to move before that lockdown takes place.'

'Sure.' Eric turned the phone on and started clicking. 'I just hope he's got the motor working, boys. I was doing the fuel pump for him last Thursday and didn't finish . . .'

Richard and Rikki waited.

'By the way, we'll have to pay him,' he said.

'Pay Spider?' said Richard. 'You have to pay your own family?'

'He does nothing for nothing. We get on great, don't get me wrong – but he's always broke. I help him out when I can.'

Richard went through the bank notes. 'Is sixty enough?' he said.

'Should be. Depends what mood he's in – he can be a . . . He's picking up, hold on . . .'

Minutes later, the deal was done, and the boys crept out of their cubicle. They were about to exit when the main door was swung violently open, knocking Eric full in the face. An elderly man lurched inside, his head swathed in a turban of bandages. He turned, bewildered. His pyjamas were loose over hunched shoulders and he had trouble focusing.

'I'm so sorry,' he said. 'I thought this was vacant.'

'We were just finishing,' said Rikki.

'Can we get past, please?' said Eric, clutching his nose. 'We're in a bit of a hurry . . . sir.'

'Yes,' said the man. 'So am I.'

Richard and Rikki stared, their eyes wide with shock.

'I'll get out of your way,' said the old man politely. He looked confused again, and put out a hand, as if to touch Eric. Then his attention was taken by Richard and Rikki, and he peered short-sightedly from one head to the other. 'Don't I know you boys?' he said.

'Oh God,' said Rikki. 'You're gonna have to hit him again.'

'Just run,' said Eric.

'No, wait,' said the old man. 'We've met before, I know we have. But I can't place the faces . . .' Everyone stood still, as he shook his head wonderingly. 'I just can't recall your names. Give me a clue.'

Finally, Eric spoke. 'It's me, Mr Barlow. I'm Eric.'

'Eric!' The old man smiled. 'Of course you are!'

'I didn't mean to hurt you – honest. I'm more sorry than you'll ever know, so please don't tell on us. If you tell on us, they're going to kill Rikki. You don't want that, do you, sir?'

'Oh my word – Rikki . . .' said Mr Barlow. His smile got broader. 'It's coming back to me. Richard too – the most interesting boy I ever taught. An incredible mind.' He lowered his voice. 'They've got you as well, have they? I'll tell you something, boys . . . this strikes me as a very bad place. I didn't want to come here, but they don't listen! That Warren fellow won't let me leave, and . . . they say they can cure me. Cure me of what? There's nothing wrong . . .'

He looked, nervously, over his shoulder.

'I've decided to escape,' he hissed. 'I just wish I had a plan.'

CHAPTER THREE

The alarms sounded as Dr Summersby checked the radiation doses. She was in her own laboratory, cross-referencing long, complex calculations, so she hardly noticed the noise at first. When the wall phone buzzed, however, she was jerked back to reality.

'They've gone,' said a voice.

'Doctor Warren? Who's gone?'

'Richard and Rikki – you haven't been down? You haven't seen them?'

'No, but I can hear the siren. What's—'

'Where have you been, then? We've got three primates loose – I've spent the last twenty minutes chasing them, and . . . I get down here and the boy's gone. I'm in theatre now, and the bed's empty.'

'That's not possible. How?'

'I don't know. We're looking for another boy as well – Eric Madamba. He might be their accomplice. The wiring's torn to pieces.'

'They can't get out, can they? The exits are controlled?'

'Every door's locked, and we've got the patrols sweeping upwards.'

'Have you checked the cameras?'

'Not yet! I've got the three monkeys out as well, so half the staff's looking for them. They're scrolling back the tapes but it takes time.'

'This is bad.'

'I've lost my bloody jacket too, and it's got keys, phone – everything. Can you call me, in about five minutes?'

'Why?'

'I might hear it ring!'

'I'll come to your office. You should have sedated them!'

'You wanted them conscious.'

'This is a disaster.'

'It has to be Eric – I'd bet money on it. I should have put him under lock and key. Apart from anything, they're old friends, and if they realized what the schedule was . . .'

'They can't have done, surely. Where are the parents?'

'I persuaded them to stay home, but—'

'But they'll be in tomorrow.'

'Yes.'

'That gives us eighteen hours, and we don't know where they are. The radiation alone takes twelve. Did *they* let the monkeys out? Is that possible?'

'I don't know. And I need to find my jacket – there's a lot of private stuff in it.'

'This is not good. Not good at all . . .'

★

Richard put the finishing touches to Mr Barlow's disguise. They'd found a porter's uniform in the next door service cupboard, and had taken their old teacher round the corner to what appeared to be a laundry room. The green overall was a little large, but the wellington boots fitted perfectly. Eric unwound the bandages, wincing as he did so: there was an enormous, mulberry-coloured bruise over the old man's temple.

Mr Barlow had heard their story, and could not have been more co-operative. 'We have to fly,' he said. 'Sometimes you just have to trust your instincts, that's what I'm learning. Wish I'd learned it years ago – what day is it?'

'Sunday,' said Eric.

'OK. We'll get you outside, and then we'll call your parents, and—'

'Mr Barlow, sir—'

'They want to retire me! – can you believe that?'

Eric opened the lid of a large laundry basket, and got one leg over. Then he stopped. 'What's happened to your stutter, sir?' he said.

'Stutter? Oh, that's a thing of the past, boy. That crack on the head cleared quite a few tubes, I can tell you. I feel stronger than ever. But they're making me resign, or trying to! They say I'm no longer fit to teach.'

'Mr Barlow, can you bend down?' said Richard. 'Your cap needs straightening. Then you get us to the lift, OK? Have you got the pass?'

'Sorry, I'm . . . not being very helpful, am I? I wasn't popular, you know, boys – after that television nonsense.

I was supposed to kick you off the team, Richard, but I said to him, "Not on your life! What's wrong with a bit of controversy?" The headmaster's a complete coward, you know.'

'Mr Barlow—'

'And a hypocrite. He and that Warren fellow are as thick as thieves – some kind of control fetish, I think. I should have stood up to them properly. How do I look?'

Eric took his hand. 'You're looking good, sir. Are you sure you're ready?'

'Can we go?' hissed Rikki. 'Let's move it!'

'What's the destination?' cried Mr Barlow. A smile flashed across his face and his eyes went dreamy. 'Takes me back, this does,' he said with a chuckle. 'I was at a little prep school in Sussex, boys, and oh my, the pranks we used to get up to with the laundry baskets. We had a tuck-shop monitor—'

'Shut up, Mr Barlow!' said Rikki loudly. 'You're screwing it up!'

Mr Barlow jumped. 'I'm sorry,' he said. 'You're right to correct me. Ground floor it is, and—'

'Then get your skinny arse moving!'

Eric, Richard and Rikki snuggled lower and hauled sheets over their heads.

'I'm going to buckle in you in,' whispered Mr Barlow. He closed the lid and pulled the leather straps tight. In a moment, the basket was sealed. 'We don't want anyone prying at this stage – and the thing about a prank is it's got to look authentic. Are you comfortable, boys?'

Rikki swore savagely.

'Yes!' cried Richard.

With that, Mr Barlow held the door open with his foot, and started to heave the load out into the corridor. A security guard walked past, talking loudly into his radio, as the sirens wailed. 'No sign on six,' he said. 'Put a man by the incinerators, Ted. Where the animals get dropped: that's our most vulnerable area.'

A voice crackled back, and the guard moved swiftly on.

All Richard, Rikki and Eric could see now were the white walls of the hospital corridor, with the occasional flicker of running feet. They were aware of Mr Barlow's green trousers, for he was dragging the basket behind him. It slid slowly along, and turned a corner. Ten seconds later, they heard the 'ping' of a lift, and the buzz of opening doors.

'There's no room for that,' said a voice.

Rikki and Richard recognized it instantly. It was the rich, authoritative tone of the fat consultant. They could see the grey cloth of an expensive suit. 'You'd be better off using the service elevator – we're in something of a hurry.'

'Out of order, guv,' said Mr Barlow huskily.

'Dammit. Doctor Summersby, can you squeeze up a bit? Get the doors closed.'

'Bring the back end round a bit.'

'Sorry, darling,' said Mr Barlow, pushing his way in. 'The wife's ill, so I'm in a hurry too—'

'What floor do you want?'

'Main exit, please, mister.'

The boys were now looking at a pair of knees under a black skirt and white coat.

'Oh,' said the woman quietly. 'I need to call Doctor Warren. The fool's lost his mobile.'

'Really?'

'He's panicking too.'

'Try him in a minute – you won't get reception in here. Where's your van parked?'

'Van?' said Mr Barlow. 'Oh, ground floor, guv. Same as usual.'

'You might yet be delayed, I'm afraid. I've just authorized extra security checks at all exits. We're on red alert, as you can see.'

'That's a shame, that is – my old mum's expecting us, and she gets so confused.'

'Have you got your pass?'

'Oh yes.'

'Then I'd use the door by the service elevator, but you'll have to lug that down a flight of stairs. That's the back way into the car park.'

'What floor?'

'This one. You'd better be quick – and watch out for monkeys. They bite, so keep your distance.'

Seconds later, the boys felt the basket swinging forward, and there was a minor crunch as they landed again. The dragging resumed, as they slithered briskly up a new corridor. Feet trotted past in the opposite direction, and they heard an alarm bell ringing.

'That was brilliant, Mr Barlow!' hissed Richard. 'We tricked them!'

'Where he taking us, though?' whispered Rikki. 'You think he knows what he's doing? I think he's cracked.'

The basket stopped abruptly, and was suddenly turned. They heard the creak of a door, and then they were dragged over a ramp. Eric's head jarred against Richard's.

'Mr Barlow!' cried Rikki. 'Let us out now!'

They became aware of a face, close to the basket. 'I'm afraid it's going to be a bit bumpy, boys. Hold on tight, and I'll—'

The boys had no time to do or say anything, because the basket was suddenly shoved hard and keeled over at a dangerously steep angle. Rikki and Richard found themselves rolling onto Eric, who just managed to hold them off. Then there was a back-breaking thump.

'Mr Barlow, please!' shouted Richard.

'Shhh!' said Eric – but then a knee pushed his face hard against the basket's side. There was another thump.

'We're on the stairs!' said Rikki. 'He's thrown us down the bloody stairs!'

They heard Mr Barlow's voice. 'It's one flight, don't worry!' And as he said it, he lost his grip. Eric just had time to shout as the basket teetered up on one end, and then everyone lost all sense of what was up, down or sideways. They somersaulted, bracing themselves against floor and lid, and seconds later smashed down onto the flat ground.

Running feet followed. 'I'm so sorry about that, boys. You slipped out of my grasp.'

'Get the lid open!' cried Rikki.

A mobile phone was ringing.

'We're nearly there!' said Mr Barlow. 'Dig in and stay low. There's a door with a kind of . . . I think I have to swipe this card thing. Stay quiet.'

The phone kept ringing, but where it had fallen nobody could tell. They heard an electronic sound, and the swish of an opening door. Then they were dragged forward and dropped another step. Eric's head crunched against Rikki's again, and a phone dropped out of his pocket onto the sheets. It was vibrating, flashing and ringing all at the same time.

Rikki snatched it up and pressed green. He wiped blood from his nose. 'What?' he said. 'Who is it?'

A voice replied, 'Doctor Warren? You've found it, I presume?'

Rikki froze. Alarms were still sounding in the distance, and they could feel cool air sweeping through the basket.

'Who is this?' said Rikki slowly.

'It's Doctor Summersby. Where are you?'

'I'm not Doctor Warren,' said Rikki.

'Who are you, then?' said Dr Summersby. 'Have I got the right number? This is Doctor Summersby calling Doctor Warren – is this his phone?'

The lid of the basket was lifting now, and the three heads looked up at a nervous Mr Barlow.

'I do apologize,' he said. 'You boys are rather heavier than I thought.'

'What boys?' said Dr Summersby. 'Who am I talking to?'

Eric was scrambling up towards the steel bars of a fence. 'Spider!' he yelled. He put two fingers in his mouth and gave a shrill whistle. 'Spider!'

Mr Barlow helped Richard and Rikki to their feet, as the tinny voice floated from the phone. It was more agitated than ever. 'Who is this?' cried Dr Summersby. 'Is this Doctor Warren's phone or not? This is very urgent!'

'OK, listen, Doctor Death,' said Rikki quietly. His voice was full of menace. 'You're speaking to Rikki Westlake, all right? And I know what you're up to, Summersby, because I'm smarter than the lot of you. We know what this place is about, and your career is finished – you can tell Warren too. We're going to get you exposed and prosecuted. Kidnap—'

'Rikki, wait—'

'False imprisonment, attempted murder . . . and the abuse of innocent animals. We've photographed everything, and you're all going down.'

There was a short silence.

'I think we need to talk,' said the voice.

'What about?'

'Are you in the Institute still? Let me find Doctor Warren—'

'Ha! We're on the roof. We're going to jump and you'll be in every newspaper in the world. You should see our suicide note – it reveals everything!'

'Stay where you are, Rikki – stay on the roof! We'll straighten things out. I promise.'

'You've got sixty seconds, brain-thief.' Rikki grinned, and cut the call. 'That's bought us some time,' he said.

Eric was back. He pushed everyone into a corner of the yard and they huddled in the shadows of a delivery platform. 'We've got problems,' he hissed. 'Spider's here . . . but he can't get in. They don't let people in without a pass. There's police around too.'

'What's goin' on, guys?' said a voice. A thin teenager in denims was peering through the bars. His pale face looked anxious. 'What kind of trouble you in?'

'Shall we just climb over?' said Rikki.

'I'm not sure I can,' said Mr Barlow. 'We're sitting ducks here, though.'

'We'll have to try!' said Eric, looking up at the barbed wire. The railings were smooth and high, and a camera sat far above them on a post. 'Spider – help us!'

Richard laughed and grabbed Eric by the shoulders. 'Eric!' he cried. 'I've got a better idea. You took the keys, didn't you? And we know what car Warren drives. It's that one there – look! The black one, sticking out.'

A powerful sports car was parked just a few metres away, and the BMW logo was clear on the bonnet. Eric grinned, produced the remote and pressed it. As if by magic, the sidelights flashed. He pressed again, and they heard the clicking of the door-locks.

'Can you handle a sports car?' said Rikki.

Eric's eyes were glittering. 'Spider can,' he said. 'Wait and see . . .'

CHAPTER FOUR

Dr Warren was up four flights of stairs in less than a minute. He crashed his way out onto the hospital roof, two guards wheezing behind him. A quick scan suggested the rooftop was deserted, but there was a large water tank that could be a hiding place. The men split up and approached it from opposite directions. Thirty seconds later, it was clear that their prey had fled.

'Gone,' panted Dr Warren. 'Dammit . . . they're fast.' He walked to the nearest wall and looked down into the car park. There was a police car manoeuvring in as the gate rolled open, its blue light flashing. A black vehicle waited politely for it, then moved quickly past, onto the road.

'They're letting people through,' he said. 'I thought you said the exit was sealed?'

'It is, sir,' said one of the guards.

'Well, look at that!' He pointed as the gate rolled shut again. The black car had paused to let someone clamber in, and now it was revving loudly. 'Who's in charge down there? Radio down and tell them to seal all exits!'

'Come in, Gamma-Foxtrot,' said the guard. 'Up on the roof, Brian. Looking down at gate four with Doctor Warren. Seems you're letting vehicles through?'

There was a crackle.

'He says they're only letting top brass out, after—'

'Keep it shut!'

'. . . after they show passes.'

'Tell him to check carefully. Did he check the vehicle that just left? We're dealing with very clever children!'

The guard radioed down, and there was another burst of croaking static. 'Bit of confusion, sir,' said the guard apologetically. 'He wants to know *your* location.'

'What do you mean? I'm here, with you.'

'Yes, but he sounds a bit anxious. He says you just left – they've just let you through!'

'What are you talking about?'

'He says how am I talking to you up here, when you drove out just half a minute ago? Black BMW. Smoked-glass windows—'

'What?'

'He checked the pass, Doctor. It was all legit, so he waved you through.'

Dr Warren felt the blood drain from his face. He looked down again, and wondered how he'd missed something so obvious. The black car was his own, and he could see it still, smoke pouring from its exhaust pipes. He could hear the engine roaring, and even as he watched and drew breath to yell, the driver let out the clutch so hard that the back wheels spun screaming on the tarmac. Horn blaring, the vehicle shot forward like a rocket, fish-tailing wildly down the Institute drive.

Dr Warren turned. His lips were dry, and a film of sweat had broken out over his whole body. To make matters worse – as if the nightmare had only just started – he saw three more figures emerge from the rooftop door, freeze for a moment and then scamper to the wall. He had no time to shout: the monkeys were out, and their instinct was to get high. The leader made a leap for the Institute's reception mast and clambered quickly upwards. Seconds later all three were at the very top, huddling together as the breeze ruffled their fur. They gazed down with wide, excited eyes – savouring their freedom.

'Wot's the plan, bruv?' said Spider, smiling grimly.

The boy's fingers were light on the steering wheel. He'd found easy-listening rock on the car's powerful sound system, and was finding out just how efficient the transmission was. The acceleration in third gear was joyous.

'School,' said Eric. 'Green Cross.'

'Who's after you?'

The car's tyres squealed round a roundabout, and Spider plunged the vehicle down into second. Everyone was pressed back into their seats as the vehicle catapaulted forwards, nought to fifty in three seconds, outside lane.

'They want Rikki's head,' shouted Eric, over the noise. 'We're going to double-bluff them – make for the hills.'

'Tell me the enemy,' said his brother. 'Let me deal with 'em.'

'Everyone's against these boys,' cried Mr Barlow. 'They've made good decisions, though. All they need now is for their luck to hold.'

Spider increased his speed, and was soon weaving through the traffic. 'You're gonna need tools,' he said.

'No time,' said Eric. 'And we've got the Nailhead book—'

'I'd say drop by Mojo's place, pick up a Glock—'

'No,' said Eric. 'We're going into hiding, Spider, and you mustn't tell anybody.'

'I won't tell no one,' said Spider. 'But I think Zed would be in. Hundred-fifty, he'd swing you a shotgun and some ammo—'

'We don't need guns,' said Eric. 'We're going to ground, and they're never going to find us . . .'

'Then stay in the squat, mate. Leela's had the baby now—'

'Listen,' shouted Rikki. 'We know what we're doing! We're going to get the bus down to Wales – stow away on the roof, and—'

'Don't tell all the plans!' said Richard.

'He can to my brother!' said Eric. 'You wouldn't tell, would you?'

Dr Warren's phone was ringing. 'Hi,' said Rikki. 'Shhh! Turn the music down.'

'Is that you, Rikki?' said a voice.

'Is that our counsellor? Whose phone are you using, head-hunter!'

'Never mind whose phone I'm using. I want you to turn that car round . . . that's my car you're in – correct?'

'Correct,' said Richard and Rikki together. They were both smiling broadly. Mr Barlow put his thumbs up and sat back. Spider was touching ninety, blasting his horn.

'The police have been informed.'

'Good.'

'I need my phone back.'

'We're looking after it. It's a bit old-fashioned—.'

'Rikki, you are being pursued and you have no chance of getting away. I can promise you that if you turn the car round, you will not be in trouble. And that goes for whoever is driving too. Is Mr Barlow driving, by any chance?'

'I'm driving, buddy,' said Rikki.

'Look, Rikki, please!' said Dr Warren. 'You have to trust me now, more than ever before. Any fears you have, or any misunderstandings . . . are going to be central to our discussion – which will be face to face, with your parents, with your headmaster, with—'

'A face-to-face discussion with Doctor Two-Face Warren?' said Rikki. 'That's going to be so confusing. Have you found your monkeys yet?'

'Rikki, listen to me!'

'I know what you're up to, and I knew from the start. You don't want individuals, do you? – you want everyone the same. But I'm going to squiggle you out, once and for all. I'm *me*, Doctor Warren – and you can't change me!'

'I don't want to. I want to understand—'

'I'm what I am. You have no right to kill me.'

Richard took the handset. 'You're not touching

Rikki, all right? That's what you want to do, and it's not happening.'

'Richard, don't you need help?' said Dr Warren. 'Be honest—'

'Not from you – never!'

'Richard, think about this logically, and stop the car. Give us your location and we'll get someone straight to you. Are you on the motorway yet?'

Richard smiled at Rikki, and his voice changed. 'Yes,' he said meekly. 'How did you know?'

Rikki stifled his laughter and Eric grinned from the passenger seat.

'You're too smart for us, Doctor Warren.'

'This is Richard still, isn't it?'

'Yes.'

'I can tell by your voice – and I can tell you're being rational. Now, please . . . can you tell me exactly where you are? Rikki's leading you astray again – what junction are you approaching?'

Richard bit his lip and put the phone against Rikki's ear. 'We're . . . heading north,' said Rikki in the same crest-fallen voice. 'We're just coming up to some . . . motorway services. If we turn ourselves in, you promise we can talk, sir? You *promise*?'

'Talking is the priority, Richard – it always was. You must have joined the M2?'

'Yes. Doctor Warren, the only reason we ran was because we were scared!'

'You saw the chimp, didn't you? You saw Molly?'

'Yes.'

'Everything we do is legal and responsible. Research, Richard – she's taking part in a legitimate transplant test—'

'We got so scared, sir!'

'That's still Richard, isn't it? Richard?'

'Yes,' said Rikki.

'Is Eric with you?'

'No. He went home.' He let a sob escape his lips. 'We just didn't know what to do, and we woke up in that big, nasty bed! We were missing our mum, and our dog, and . . .'

'Pull into the services,' said Dr Warren in his most understanding voice. 'I blame myself for this. I should have explained everything far better. So tell whoever's driving to pull off the motorway, and I will come to you in person. We're going to sort this out together, and reconnect.'

'We're pulling off now. Thank you, sir!'

'What's the name of the services? If it's the M2 it should be . . . Hussett Lane, with the big Shell garage. Is that what you can see?'

'Yes,' said Rikki. 'We're coming up to it. We'll wait at the Shell garage. Pump number eleven.'

'Good boy. And tell Rikki not to be frightened. He was never in danger – nor was Eric.'

'I love you, Doctor Warren,' said Rikki.

'Love's important. Keep the phone on – keep it safe.'

'Please hurry . . .'

They turned the phone off at once, and the car sailed on towards the sunset. An hour later, Spider was cruising familiar streets. He turned left, picking his way through the back roads, and he rolled to a halt at the rear entrance of Green Cross School.

Eric leaped out, and checked they were alone. He shook his brother's hand.

'Where does this doctor-dude live?' said Spider. 'He's the enemy, right?'

'Right,' said Eric.

'Have his wallet,' said Richard, passing it over. 'There's cards as well – everything.'

Spider grinned, and flipped it open. 'Stay in touch, bruv,' he said to Eric. 'I'm going to pick up some mates and do a bit of business.'

'Will you trash the car?' said Rikki.

'Oh yes,' said Spider.

'What else?'

'We'll sort him.' He revved hard and closed his eyes in ecstasy. 'We'll zip out to his place, see what's flammable. Crash and burn, Doctor Warren. You're going down . . .'

CHAPTER FIVE

The school was in darkness.

For an awful moment they thought the arrangements had changed, and that the bus had gone. Then, as they crept round the building, they saw it at the far end of the playground. The headmaster had just locked the main school doors, and the driver was stubbing out a cigarette – their timing could not have been better. The vehicle's interior lights were dim and the excited passengers, supervised by Miss Maycock, were drawing the curtains over the windows.

The roof rack looked heavily laden.

'This is goodbye, boys,' whispered Mr Barlow. 'Good luck, both of you.'

Eric took his hand. 'This is your trip, sir. I think you should come.'

'I had looked forward to it, Eric – you're right. But I'm not really equipped, and . . . I do have responsibilities. At least, I do.'

Eric drew him gently into the shadows. Rikki and Richard were just behind, and even as Mr Barlow protested, they moved quickly to the back of the bus. The engine spluttered into life, and in seconds Eric was up on the roof itself, dangling from the ropes of a large tarpaulin. Richard and Rikki pushed, and Eric pulled. It was a struggle, but at last they got their teacher onto the bumper and up the ladder, Then they wormed their way in amongst the tightly packed luggage.

'I'm going to slow you down, boys!' protested Mr Barlow. 'Reconsider!'

'We're a team now,' said Eric. 'All for one. One for all.'

With that, they were moving. They heard a chorus of goodbyes from the parents below, and the horn blasted twice. In a moment, they were over the speed bumps and out of the gates. They felt another gear-change, and they were moving faster into the night.

Rikki used Dr Warren's phone as a flashlight, and they soon had several rucksacks open. It was a tight space to work in, of course, but the bags could be turned and restacked. They built themselves a little igloo of luggage, and the plastic made a tight, secure roof that protected them from the weather. They found three sleeping bags, and even an air bed for Mr Barlow. They found good torches too, and warm clothes, though Richard felt slightly anxious as he hauled on Jeff's brand new coat. That didn't seem right or fair. They pocketed several stashes of sweets, drinks and biscuits – one thoughtful parent had packed a flask of hot coffee which they shared immediately. As the bus made its way out of town, they curled up cosy and snug, feasting happily.

'We better make plans,' said Rikki. 'What time do we actually arrive at this place?'

'I'm afraid I can't remember,' said Mr Barlow. 'I'm finding that my short-term memory has taken a bit of a battering, but—'

'I know,' said Eric. 'Me and Mark read that schedule so many times I got every single detail. O-six hundred, arrive at camp. Six-fifteen, secure camp, with allocation of equipment and provisions. Six-thirty, full kit inspection, followed by open-fire breakfast . . . briefing at o-seven hundred.'

'What's for breakfast?' said Rikki. 'Remember that?'

'Eggs, bacon and beans. And SAS hot chocolate.'

'Wow, Eric. You are cool.'

'What's *our* plan, though?' said Richard. 'We can't just jump down and expect a welcome. We're going to have to stay well out of sight.'

'They're going to notice the bags have been mucked around with,' said Rikki. 'I vote we go straight to the mountains.'

'I remember the terrain,' said Mr Barlow. 'It was way back, when I was a boy—'

'How long ago was that?' said Eric.

'How old are you, Mr Barlow?' said Rikki. 'Are you Victorian?'

'No, Rikki. I'm fifty-seven, and I was in the Scouts for six years. So it was forty-five years ago, or thereabouts. That was why I set up the residential, you see. It brought back all my childhood memories – we had such a wild time. The chap who runs the centre now is new to the job, keen to make a go of it, so—'

'And it's in the middle of a wilderness?' said Eric.

'The Adventure Centre isn't,' said Mr Barlow. 'But the countryside's close by. We went hiking, and I remember getting hopelessly lost. Every now and then you'd get scared out of your wits by jets – it's where the pilots did their training, you know. There's a famous rock in the sea, where the pilots practised.'

'I know,' said Richard.

'That's where we'll go,' said Rikki quietly. 'Say no more.'

'They used it for those . . . what do you call them? "Arrested landings". Aircraft carriers. You know all about that too – don't you?'

Richard looked at him. 'I want to get so lost,' he said. 'As lost as I can, for as long as I can. I'm going to survive, sir.'

'Hide for ever,' said Rikki. 'And you're not going to die, are you, Mr Barlow? You're not going to conk out on us?'

'I hope not, Rikki. I'm feeling good.'

'You're not looking it. I'm joking . . .'

'I think we need sleep,' said Eric. 'We're going to have to be wide awake tomorrow.'

Rikki nodded. 'True. We're going to need our energy.'

They turned off their torches and curled up against the wall of luggage around them. The bus was heading west, and it rocked gently at a nice, steady speed. In a short time, Mr Barlow and the boys were all fast asleep. Richard and

Rikki dreamed of aeroplanes, as usual, and found themselves hurtling through dark skies, clinging to wings, gazing from cockpits, hunting for the sun.

Dr Warren, however, had become a truly desperate man.

He had commandeered an ambulance and driven all the way north to the M2 service station. Needless to say, he found no trace of the children or his car. A massive traffic jam delayed his return, and when he got back to the hospital, it was after midnight. The police were waiting for him, and he felt sick with fear.

Three rhesus monkeys had been spotted in a local park, he was told. A large crowd of animal-lovers had gathered, making it impossible to recapture them. It was assumed they were now deep amongst the trees of a nearby forest. An investigation into the Institute's licences would follow: that was inevitable. More importantly, there was a personal matter to be dealt with, and the officer told him to sit down. Dr Warren braced himself again, but it was still a terrible shock. His house had been vandalized – the attack had been mercilessly efficient. His wife and little Nathaniel had escaped, thank God, but only with what they could carry. Three fire crews were still at the scene, damping down the ashes.

'Anyone got a grudge against you?' said the sergeant.

'No.'

'These animal rights people, you know. Vindictive lot. We have found the car, apparently. That's just been confirmed.'

'And the children,' said Dr Warren hopefully. 'Are they in it? Have you got the boys?'

'No.'

'We've got to find them! It's terribly important.'

'Hmm,' said the officer, checking again. 'BMW, upside down in the old quarry. That's where they hold those all-night races, of course – someone's should have thought to check there, hours ago. They love the sports cars. Was it the three-series convertible?'

'Yes.'

'Fuel injection, I imagine. A lot of poke, those new ones. Brand-new, was it, sir?'

'Yes. Officer, we need to find the boys.'

'Anything valuable in it? You said your had a lot stolen.'

Dr Warren felt faint again, and his stomach lurched. He closed his eyes. 'Oh God,' he said. 'Yes. I keep a hard drive in the glove compartment. All my notes, all my . . . confidential files. It's my backup. If they found that . . .'

'Confidential stuff?'

'Yes. They've got my phone too. They could cross-reference. Oh God.'

Dr Warren stood up and pressed his hands to his temples.

'Don't give up, sir,' said the sergeant. 'Never say die. That's the old SAS motto, I think. *Never say die*.'

Dr Warren stared at the man. 'I don't think that's . . . right,' he said. 'That's not the motto I know.'

'No?'

'No.'

'Live and let die? *Do* or die? Something similar.'

'*Who dares wins*,' said Dr Warren quietly. He said it slowly, pausing on each word. 'That's the SAS motto, now you come to mention it. It's when . . . combat is required. When you're really up against it, and you think you've lost everything. I remember, now: *Who dares wins* – when you need to fight back.'

He looked at the telephone.

'You don't look at all well, sir.'

'I'm not. But I need to make a rather private call. Would you mind?'

The officer left and Dr Warren dialled Dr Summersby's office. Summersby answered on the first ring.

'We've got to find them,' he said. 'Whatever the cost.'

'How much do they know? Everything?'

'We have to assume so. They have access to every single document.'

'Can we limit the damage? I can start moving things—'

'No point. My hard drive was in the car. We have to assume they took it, and we have to find them.'

Dr Summersby was silent. 'It might be time to leave.'

'No. Wherever we go, they'll ruin us. We have to find the children, and silence them.'

'How?'

'They're on the run, aren't they? We can follow – we can be quick. The police are here now, in my office—'

'You're talking to the police?'

'Of course I am. And I'm thinking fast, Summersby: we need to stand together. If the children are running, then the police will start looking for them – they're minors, after all, and the parents are going to be desperate. They need their medication, do you understand me? That's what I'll say. I'll go back in there now, and insist that we move heaven and earth to find those boys, because otherwise they won't survive. They need the drugs we've been prescribing – do you follow me? I'll say we have to get to them first, for their own sakes, and we need to administer . . . a complex prescription. Complex. Can you get what we need?'

'What do we need?'

'Something heavy. We need to close them down for ever, and we both know it. Rikki and Richard, Eric too. There's no other way.'

'You know what you're . . . suggesting?'

'What's the alternative? Do you have one?'

There was a long silence.

'Vulnerable children on the run,' said Dr Summersby at last. 'We'll put out an appeal. We'll have to be in the front line, though. Then we might just do it.'

'Use trazodone. Mix it with the roxanol – codeine, if you want. Just make sure the roxanol's concentrated. Three hypodermics, all right? Four – one as a backup. And absolutely no mercy. Massive doses.'

'I'll get my bag.'

'We can win this. But we need to move fast.'

PART FIVE
SURVIVAL

'Those on the run have just one duty, and that's to themselves. Trust yourself, and trust your mates.'

Chris 'Nailhead' McGinty – *Alive and Uncaught – SAS Survival Handbook (Introduction)*

CHAPTER ONE

They were ready for the drop at four-ten the next morning.

They'd taken three of the best rucksacks, and crammed them with the most useful gear they could find. Eric, Rikki and Richard put on good, coarse trousers, snug-fitting boots and woolly hats. The rain was falling heavily. Mr Barlow had found boots and a coat, but beneath it he was still in a porter's uniform. Dawn was breaking faintly as they inched down the back of the bus. Mercifully, the roads were quiet, and when the driver paused to turn through the village, they leaped to the ground and scuttled into the shelter of a nearby front garden. Behind the hedge, Eric had a map open immediately. It wasn't long before they found their location.

Mr Barlow did first recce, and was back in three minutes.

'There's a phone box,' he said. 'I suggest we call a mini-cab and ask it to drop us by the viaduct. We can walk into the hills from there.'

'No, sir,' said Eric. 'We've got to assume we're being

looked for. If the police have our descriptions, that driver's going to be straight onto them.'

'We're hardly conspicuous,' said Richard. 'We just look like we're off on a trek. I vote for the minicab.'

'Richard,' said Rikki, 'how can you say we're not conspicuous?'

'We're not.'

'Ah,' said Mr Barlow. 'He's got a point.'

'We've got two heads,' said Rikki. 'We've got two heads sticking out of Jeff's bright red waterproof jacket: isn't that going to burn itself onto the retina?'

Richard nodded. 'I forget sometimes,' he said.

'I don't notice either,' said Eric. 'You look normal to me.'

'Turn round,' said Mr Barlow. 'There's a Plan B sitting right behind us.'

The boys turned and followed the line of their teacher's gaze. Three bicycles stood against the porch of the house, and Mr Barlow was already crawling slowly towards them.

'I'm not condoning theft,' he whispered, as he lifted the first one upright. 'I would never, under normal circumstances, be so . . . free with other people's property. Desperate times, however, call for desperate measures.'

'Agreed,' said Rikki. 'But can you ride a bike?'

'Of course,' said Mr Barlow.

'I can't,' said Eric. He smiled a forlorn smile. 'I can handle a truck, but I never learned to cycle.'

Minutes later they were skimming through puddles towards open country. Eric sat on the handlebars in front of Mr Barlow, map-reading by torchlight. Rikki and

Richard were behind, surprised at the speed their old teacher could sustain. The road curved and rose steeply – the hills were visible now, towering out of the chilly mist. Mr Barlow flicked down his gears and rose up in the saddle. Soon, they were climbing fast, light-headed with anticipation.

At the Clifden Adventure Centre, however, there was only early-morning disappointment.

The bus had pulled into a miserable-looking industrial estate, and when it stopped on the concrete forecourt beside three badly maintained storage huts, everyone assumed the driver was lost. There was a hand-painted sign, though: 'Clifdon'. The 'o' had been re-shaped into an 'e'. The whole place was in darkness – and the site looked derelict. The children and their teachers clambered down, stiff and weary, and hunted for a bell or knocker. They couldn't find either, and the front door was heavily padlocked. Miss Maycock tried the number on the centre's leaflet, but all she got was a recorded message: '*Your call is important to us,*' said a slow voice. '*Leave a message, if you please, and—*'

'This is intolerable,' said the headmaster. 'If this is Barlow's organization, then we're in for a difficult week.' He looked at Miss Maycock and added, 'We're well rid of him, my dear. He'd lost the plot.'

Miss Maycock smiled nervously. 'He did his best, I thought. The children loved him.'

'No loyalty,' said the headmaster. 'And a questionable sense of discipline.'

'Shall we get the bags off the roof?' said Miss Maycock. 'It might keep us warm if we're doing something.'

'No,' said the headmaster. The rain was getting heavier, and the class huddled under a plastic awning. 'I think we'll wait until the place is open. If there's no one about we'll have to drive straight home again.'

Forty minutes later, a man in overalls arrived to open the property next door.

'You kids waiting for Bob?' he shouted.

'We're waiting for the camp leaders,' said the headmaster. 'They appear to have forgotten we were coming.'

'Oh, that's Bob for you. I've got his home number – I'll give him a bell.'

They waited another hour and a small, noisy car arrived. A fat man in a baseball cap wound the window down, and there was a half-hearted cheer from the damp children. 'Mr Barlow?' said the driver. 'You all from Green Street?'

The headmaster moved into the rain so as to communicate more easily. 'Barlow's indisposed,' he said through the narrow gap in the window. 'I'm Mr Prowse, headmaster of Green *Cross*. We've been waiting a very long time.'

'I'm sure we said this evening,' said the man. 'Five o'clock, Monday afternoon—'

'Monday *morning*,' said the headmaster. 'We've driven through the night, and we're freezing.'

'It's not a problem – it's all ready for you. It's going to be a bit chilly, though – the central heating takes a while. What are you going to do for breakfast? Have you had it?'

'Of course we haven't,' said the headmaster angrily. The rain was soaking through his jacket, and there were gusts of wind that rocked him back onto his heels. 'Breakfast is supposed to be served about now – *by you.* We've got schedules printed.' The children were huddled together, staring with anxious faces.

'Not a problem,' said the man. 'Not a problem at all! There's a café round the corner that does take-away, so what I'll do is get you all inside and sorted, and we can send out for some bacon butties. Pig of a day, isn't it?' He clambered out of his car, opening a huge umbrella as he did so. 'We were hoping you'd cancel – it's set to get a lot worse than this.' He searched the pockets of a tight-fitting tracksuit. 'Listen up, kids!' he cried. 'I'm Captain Colin. Not my real name, but I don't use that, for operational reasons. Now, where's the little varmint?'

He extracted a large bunch of keys and chose a small grey one – then he pushed through the pupils to the bar and padlock.

'We put lasses on the left, lads on the right. Showers? Well, I'm afraid we've had problems . . . we had a block go down just last week, so you'll have to organize some kind of . . . rota. This is a stiff little beggar . . .' He fought with the lock, and at last it fell open. 'Nobody's been in for a month. You going to get unloaded? I would say wait till the rain eases off, but you've heard the forecast, have you? I hate this country – it gets worse and worse. Come on in – welcome to Clifden!'

The door was stuck, but he managed to force it open.

He pressed various switches, but the lights remained obstinately unlit.

'Oh no,' he said. 'We've got some kind of drain on the electrics, same every bloody time. I turn stuff off . . . hang on, I've got a couple a coins.'

There was a slot meter just above his head, and he pushed some money into it. The children cheered weakly again as fluorescent tubes flickered down the damp corridor.

Fifteen minutes later, they had the tarpaulin off the bus roof, and Miss Maycock was handing down the bags. A human chain ferried them inside to a small dormitory lined with bunk beds.

'There's a lot of . . . sweet wrappers up here, Headmaster,' she shouted. It was hard to hear her for the rain on the roof. 'Orange peel too!'

The headmaster closed his eyes. 'We'll pass you up a bin-liner. This really isn't the time to be worrying about litter!'

Salome was halfway up the ladder, assisting. 'Some of them have come open, sir. There's stuff all over the place.'

'Oh, this is intolerable. You were asked to seal your bags properly. This is what you get if you don't obey basic instructions. I'm not arguing about it, Salome – get the bags inside, and we'll see what's missing. Quick as you can, please! Eleanor – lift it, don't drag it!'

The job was soon done, and the children stood around their bags, shivering. It seemed that almost every rucksack was unzipped, and a lot of equipment was now very wet. The room they were in seemed colder than the forecourt, and the carpet had a puddle in its centre. The ceiling sagged.

'I must say you've come well-equipped,' said the captain brightly.

'We just followed the kit list,' said Jeff.

'Why the tents, though? We don't have a garden.'

'For the camping.'

'Camping where? Where d'you want to camp?'

Several children pulled out their copies of the leaflet. Carla read it to him: '*Night hike followed by two days under canvas, in uncharted SAS training territory. Make sure you have the gear.*'

'Not in this weather, love,' said the captain.

'What do you mean?' said Mark. 'What's weather got to do with it?'

'We do the camping in August, over in the back field. If it's sunny, that is. We're not insured any more. I think you've been looking at some of last season's leaflets, haven't you? We've had problems with the website – my brother-in-law got a bit carried away. Oh, and just a small thing . . . we don't allow gas stoves. Fire officer banned them in his last report, and you can see his point – it's all wood and paper, this place. You drop one of them, we'd go up like a Buddhist monk.'

'So how do we cook?' said a child. She had a portable stove in her hands.

'You don't,' said the captain.

'So how do we eat?'

'The pizza place. Just by the bowling alley. We do have a microwave, but that's been playing up in the damp – lad got a nasty shock last month, ended up in Casualty.'

'Look,' said the headmaster, 'we're here for an Outward Bound adventure. What activities have you organized? This is a . . . disaster.'

'Activities? Loads!' said the captain. He laughed. 'Don't worry, you're not going to get bored at Clifden.'

'Rock climbing?' said a boy. He was holding a coiled rope.

'Yes. There's some boulders by the skateboard park.'

'White-water rafting?' said Carla, her nose in the leaflet. 'Life jackets supplied.'

'Leisure Centre, Thursday mornings – but you do pay a supplement for the jackets. You don't need them, really. It's very shallow.'

'You mean a swimming pool?' said Jeff. 'Rafting, in a swimming pool?'

'Wave machine,' said the captain. 'We had some old folks down here last year – they loved it. They didn't stay here, though – they used the Holiday Inn.'

'We've been ripped off,' said Salome. 'This is a total waste of money.'

'Oh, hang on a minute, love,' said the captain. 'You've only just got here, let's not get negative. We can do a camping simulation, if you like. Put the tents up inside, if you want to – get some string.' A telephone was ringing. He moved across the room to answer it. 'Captain Colin?' He paused. 'Oh.'

There was a silence, as everyone listened to an urgent-sounding voice on the other end of the line.

'Twenty minutes ago,' said the captain. 'I've just let them in – they look like drowned rats. OK, no problem – I'll hand you straight over.' He put his hand over the receiver, and grinned at the headmaster. 'Police,' he said.

'What about them?' said the headmaster.

'I thought they wanted me for a sec, but it's you – they've been trying you all night. Your mobile's switched off, and some kids have gone missing.'

CHAPTER TWO

Ten miles away, Mr Barlow and the boys had stopped for a rest.

They were high in the hills now, and though the weather was foul, they were warm and happy. Perhaps it was their high spirits that led to a grave tactical error, for it was at this point that Rikki turned Dr Warren's phone on.

According to Nailhead McGinty: '*The real enemy to survival is over-confidence.* Never *let your guard down . . .*'

The phone rang immediately. 'Hello?'

'Rikki,' said Dr Warren. 'Where are you?'

Rikki thought fast. 'We're at the motorway service station. Where are you?'

'We both know that's not true. We've got to stop playing games.'

Richard grinned and took the phone from Rikki.

'You're breaking up,' he said. 'Reception's bad.'

'Where are you?' hissed Dr Warren. 'We've been up all night! – everyone is looking for you! Your parents are . . . beside themselves, and the police—'

'We're in your lovely car, on the M1 northbound.'

'That's a lie, Rikki!' He paused, and brought his voice under control. 'My car's been found, and it's a write-off. So is my house.'

'Oh dear.'

'You cannot get away.'

'We saw the lab, Doctor Warren. We're going to put you in jail.'

'I've done nothing illegal, but you boys . . . don't you realize how dangerous this has become? Answer me this: are you still in London?'

'Yes.'

'You're going to be prosecuted for theft, vandalism, arson – attempted murder. As your doctor, I can protect you, but I need to see you and talk – one to one. Is Mr Barlow with you?'

'No, sir. He went home.'

'So he was the one driving. Rikki – listen. That is Rikki, isn't it?'

'Yes,' said Richard.

'Let me speak to Richard, please.'

'Why?'

'Because . . . I think he's less prone to extreme behaviour. I need to talk sensibly, because there's a very great deal at stake now and I want to help you.'

'OK,' said Richard. 'I'll hand you right over.'

'Hi,' said Rikki softly. 'This is Richard. I'm so sorry about the house – that was Rikki. He's a bad boy, Doctor Warren!'

'Richard, I'm glad to hear your voice.'

'I'm glad to hear yours.'

'Rikki's putting you in grave danger – I think you realize that. Have you got my portable hard drive? It was in the car—'

'I've got it here. Rikki took it.'

'Keep it safe, I beg you. Right now you have to free yourself from his influence and give yourself up.'

'I know, Doctor Warren. He's just . . . taken over completely – like you said.' He slapped his knee, and Richard squealed in a theatrical way, stifling his laughter. 'Ow! He just . . . hit me again. He's desperate!'

'Listen to me and stay calm,' said Dr Warren earnestly. 'You can dominate him, but you have to take control of the situation. Give me your location.'

Rikki put his hand over his own mouth and made the sounds of strangulation. 'Please help me!' he cried.

'Where are you, Richard?'

'That was Rikki, trying to silence me . . .' He faked breathing problems. 'I don't know how long I've got! We're trying to restrain him, Doctor Warren!'

'Where are you Richard?'

'We got the tube! We're at, er . . . King's Cross Station.'

'Why there?'

'We're hiding out, but . . . oh, Doctor Warren, you're the best doctor in the world. I know you can help me.'

'Give me your location!'

'Will you be there for me?' said Rikki.

'I will always be there for you,' said Dr Warren. 'We've both learned a lot.'

'I just need understanding—'

'And a little help from my friends.'

'I *am* your friend.'

Richard choked back the laughter. 'I want to come home, sir!' he cried. 'We're by a kind of . . . brick wall, beside platforms nine and ten – we found a kind of gap—'

'Is Eric with you?'

'You're breaking up, Doctor Warren! Help me – there's a steam train coming in, and a kid with little round specs—'

'Stay on the platform!'

'It's getting smoky!'

'Don't move from that platform.'

'Hurry!' wailed Rikki and Richard together.

They switched the phone off, and collapsed back on the soaking grass, howling with laughter.

'He's going there!' snorted Rikki. 'I don't believe it, but he's going there!'

Mr Barlow said: 'That wasn't wise, boys. I've got to say it.'

They looked at him, and sat up. 'Why not?'

'I know it was . . . perhaps what he deserved. But I'm fairly sure that if the police are on our tails, they can find out what transmission mast was used to service that call. They're going to know exactly where we are.'

'Is that true?' said Eric.'

'Damn,' said Richard. He sat up. 'I didn't think.'

'Blast it,' said Rikki.

'We're an idiot,' said Richard. 'That was really dumb.'

'No point crying about it,' said Mr Barlow. 'We'd better make a decision. Do we give ourselves up now – or press on? We can always strike a bargain, you know, or—'

'Talk to the police?' said Eric.

'Yes.'

'No way,' said Richard.

'We've just started, sir!' said Eric. 'This is the beginning.'

'We're not going home, Mr Barlow,' said Rikki. 'If you want to go back to your lonely old life, that's your affair. Die if you want to, but we're serious.'

'I can see what courage you've got, but—'

'We're hiding out,' said Richard. 'We've got everything we need, and we're disappearing. And you should stay with us, sir – you know you should. What have you got to go back for? Let's have an adventure.'

'Boys – they will comb this area,' said Mr Barlow. 'Children aren't allowed to disappear.'

'They won't take me alive,' said Eric.

'Nor me,' said Richard and Rikki together.

'We've got the handbook too,' said Richard. 'Eric knows what he's doing.'

Rikki smiled. 'They can hunt as long as they want,' he said. We'll give them a run for their money, and we'll do whatever we have to do.'

'Very well.' Mr Barlow thought hard. 'The first thing, then, is to hide those bikes. Then we get off the path, and do some cross-country work. Let's make it difficult for them.'

The boys stood up and touched fists again. 'Operation Survival,' said Rikki.

'Bring it on,' said Eric.

They moved the bicycles into the trees, and buried them in the foliage. Then they hauled on their rucksacks and checked the map. A narrow track went north-north-west, towards a mountain that appeared and disappeared in swirls of mist. Eric took a bearing, and they all drank water.

'To higher ground?' said Eric.

'Of course,' said Rikki.

They adjusted their hoods, for the rain was harder, and put their heads down for a long trek through the deluge.

Forty minutes later Chief Inspector Mantz updated his Child Protection Unit. A team of officers was crammed into the station's main briefing room, and the mood was serious.

'Axton Hill transmitter, ladies and gentlemen. South Wales. Which is all very interesting . . .' He clicked a switch and the screen behind him was filled by an enormous map. As he pointed, the image resolved itself into a larger scale. Soon, those watching could see contours and footpaths. 'That's where they are,' he said. 'They followed their pals.'

'The residential was important to them,' said Dr Warren. 'It's a form of egomania – they just want to fit in.'

'They've not been seen, have they?' said the inspector. 'I would imagine they took fright at the last minute.' He clicked, and a photograph of Mr Barlow came onto the screen. 'This, we believe, is their leader.'

The officers stared. The doctors said nothing.

'He's a clever one. He's not touched his credit cards, and he's not hired a vehicle. We don't know the details, but it's my hunch that he's kidnapped them. Bit of a desperado, is our Mr Barlow – estranged from his own kids, apparently. Doctor Warren here did a consultation, and he says Barlow sees these youngsters as surrogates. We're pretty sure he won't harm them, but I'm taking no chances. We've got mountain rescue waiting for us, and the good news is there's a unit of commandos down there too, on a training exercise. There's red tape to cut, but everyone pulls together when it's kids. I think they're going to help us, and if so, we could have those boys safe before nightfall. I want that teacher in custody.'

He clicked, and his audience saw icons of forked lightning over heavy clouds.

'The downside is the weather. It's set to get worse, ladies and gentlemen, and the terrain is ultra-hostile. These kids don't have equipment, and they've got no training whatsoever. We've got to expect dehydration and hypothermia. Demoralization's going to kick in as soon as they get wet, and we have to remember something else. According to their doctors, these youngsters are without their medication, and without it . . . they won't last. We can expect seizures and spasms and . . . what was it?'

'Heart failure,' said Dr Summersby.

'Heart failure,' said Mantz. 'We need to keep our medics close.' He stared around the room. 'I predict panic. The children will give up as soon as it's dark. They won't be able to light a fire. They'll get hungry – and they will cease to work as a unit. That's when catastrophes happen . . .'

Every officer nodded.

'Let's get them back to the clinic. Where they belong. That's where they can be properly looked after, and . . . excuse me one moment.' He opened his mobile phone. 'Mantz.'

Those watching saw the inspector's eyes narrow. They saw the tip of his tongue lick a heavy upper lip and the mouth set into a hard, firm line. He clicked the phone shut, and looked up.

'Just received reports that two bikes have gone missing. Village, right by that transmitter mast – first crime in forty years. It's a lead and I'm following it.'

'Helicopter's ready,' said a man at the door.

'Do you want dogs, sir?' said someone else.

'Yes.'

Chief Inspector Mantz was loading papers into his briefcase. 'We're going down now and I want everything. I want frogmen. I want satellite surveillance, and I'll want a second chopper ready over that mountain. They're close to the sea, so I want the coastguard informed. And I want to speak to Lieutenant Kirby again about the commando unit. I've got a bad feeling about this, so let's get moving.' He looked at Dr Warren and Dr Summersby. 'I want you right beside me,' he said. 'You say they trust you?'

'I believe they do, Inspector,' said Dr Warren.

'They'll need you now, my friend. What about the parents?'

Dr Summersby shook her head. 'I'd keep them back, Inspector. They might make things worse, and it's important we have time alone with the boys. We're going to need to do fast, emergency checks—'

'We don't want hysteria, that's for sure.'

'Then leave it to us, sir.'

'We have what we need,' said Dr Summersby.

'Good. I'll let you make the first contact, and advise us. Stay close.'

CHAPTER THREE

Back at the Clifden Adventure Centre, things had got worse.

The headmaster had been taken to the local police station, leaving Miss Maycock in charge. Captain Colin had brought in two boxes of cold bacon sandwiches, and then he'd led a forty-minute singsong. Soon he was telling stories about the interesting things he'd done 'undercover'.

Salome got a note to Jeff, Aparna and Mark – all members of the original 'Tiger Team' – and they slipped out the back to a small storage shed. They shut the door, and turned on their torches.

'I'm going to deck him in a minute,' said Salome. 'This is desperate.'

'What do we do, though, huh?' said Mark. 'I can't stand much more of him, either – he said we'd do charades later. I hate charades!'

'It's a joke,' said Jeff. 'Except it's a joke that isn't funny.'

'We have been seriously and totally ripped off,' said Salome. 'Abseiling in the Leisure Centre – if you're over fifteen and your parents are with you . . . it's a disgrace!'

'I wish Rikki was here,' said Mark. 'He'd sort him out.'

There was an uncomfortable silence.

'That's true,' said Salome. 'Rikki was insane, but he didn't put up with this kind of garbage.'

'Eric wouldn't, either,' said Jeff.

Mark nodded. 'Eric saved up all his own money for this. We were practising things from that handbook! It's all wasted.'

Jeff clenched his fists. 'They're probably sitting in that Rechner place,' he said. 'They'll be crying their eyes out. God, I wish they were with us.'

'How would they sort this?' said Salome.

Jeff grinned. 'Rikki would tell that jerk what he thought of him.'

'Too right,' said Mark. 'And I tell you what Eric would do: he'd just take off into the woods by himself. Have an adventure of his own – and I'd go with him!'

'Is that what you're suggesting?' said Salome.

'I don't dare. Not without Eric.'

Aparna sniffed, and everyone looked at her. She was perched on a small box and had – as usual – been listening in silence.

Salome sighed. 'Give us a suggestion, Aparna. Save the day before I smack that fat loser and end up in jail.'

Aparna nodded slowly. 'I agree with Mark,' she said. 'I think we should do what Eric would do, and climb that mountain.'

Mark laughed. 'Which one?' He opened his leaflet and the familiar face of an SAS officer stared at them, a grey crag looming over his shoulder. 'Are you talking about this one here?'

'Yes.'

'That's out of bounds,' said Salome in disgust. 'Off-limits!'

'Look,' said Aparna. 'I can't stand this. We have the equipment, don't we? I know it might seem dangerous and we might get into trouble. But these people have lied to us, and we've all been looking forward to a proper adventure. Something's wrong, so let's do it.'

'The headmaster would kill us,' said Jeff.

'I hate Mr Prowse,' said Aparna. 'Who cares what he thinks?'

Everyone gasped. 'Aparna!' said Jeff. 'What's got into you? Think of the rules we'd be breaking – we could get expelled.'

'You don't break rules!' said Salome. 'Ever.'

'No,' said Aparna. 'And this time I'm going to.'

'This needs thinking about,' said Jeff. 'Your parents would go ballistic.'

Aparna stood up. 'It doesn't need thinking about, Jeff. I've thought about it. I've been thinking for ages – all I do is think, and I'm tired of thinking.'

She pushed the door of the shed open and strode back through the rain to the huts. In a moment, she was in the dormitory and had hauled her rucksack from under a bunk. The others followed, utterly astonished. From the next-door room, the captain could be heard going over the supper order again.

'Onion rings are extra,' he cried. 'Listen! Shut up! Onion rings are two pounds fifty . . .'

Aparna picked up a sweater and stuffed it into the bag. Then she was sitting, pulling on her boots. Nobody said a word, but all eyes watched her. She worked methodically, without any hesitation, and in a few minutes she was zipped into her waterproofs, gloved and hatted, with the rucksack towering over her head.

'I'll go on my own,' she said quietly. 'You don't have to come.'

'You're crazy,' said Jeff.

'I want to climb that mountain.'

'Look,' said Salome. 'It's pouring. If we wait till tomorrow—'

'I'm going,' interrupted Aparna. 'We've got to, and I'm leaving now. You're cowards, all of you!'

'I've lost my coat,' said Jeff. 'Half my stuff's gone missing.'

Mark said, 'I think she's right. Let's get out of here before we go crazy.'

'Something bad's happening,' said Aparna. 'I hate this place – Rikki would set fire to it, with that slob locked inside. I'm not staying a single night here – we need to be on that mountain, out . . . out in the open.'

They managed to persuade her to wait for three minutes. In that time they packed everything they thought they'd need, and then all four slipped back into the yard. It was getting dark, for a storm was rising over the very rock they were heading for. That didn't stop them, though.

They clambered over a fence, and ran in single file down an alleyway.

Five minutes later the estate came to an end. They ran past some cottages into a copse. Beyond the trees, a muddy footpath took them straight across fields, and within ten minutes they'd come to the wilderness.

Mr Barlow, meanwhile, was feeling better than he'd felt for years.

He had been gathering wood, and now had a nice supply of dry kindling. He moved back down the slope, aware that the daylight was fading fast. To his right he heard a pair of owls, and he paused. It was an old Boy Scout code he'd taught them: Rikki and Richard were the owls, and Eric the raven. He was the woodpecker, so he put a hand to his mouth and gave the answering call. The raven cawed from way off in the trees, which was reassuring.

Mr Barlow walked carefully back to camp. Both tents were up, of course. They were beautifully disguised by a skeleton of tree branches, overlaid with ferns. A ring of stones had been set up in the mouth of the larger one, around a pit – Eric had dug it according to Nailhead McGinty's instructions and diagrams (Chapter Six). The cooking implements were carefully set out, ready. They had chosen a low spot in the woods, partly for shelter, but also so that the wood smoke would be dispersed among trees. They had also set up snares.

Mr Barlow poured milk and a little water into a

saucepan, and covered it. A voice behind him said, 'Don't move.' He swung round with a cry, and there was Eric grinning down at him.

'Ha! You didn't hear me?'

'I didn't hear a sound, boy!'

'It takes a while, but you've just got to be really, really careful. I think I could creep up on a deer. Or a rabbit.'

'I'm sure you could. You were silent as a ghost.'

'Shall I light the fire?'

'Would you mind?' said Mr Barlow. 'I've never been good at that.'

Eric squatted, and was soon laying a nest of twigs over a handful of tissues and dry leaves. He'd dug an air vent, so it blazed hot and fierce. They heard Richard and Rikki long before they saw them, because they were dragging a heavy piece of deadwood. Mr Barlow put the grill over the flames, impressed again at the boys' care in constructing such an even, stable fireplace. Within minutes the milk was boiling, and he was mixing in the chocolate powder.

Night fell slowly, and there was a rumble of thunder. The rain eased off, then burst down again, and they sat happily munching. There was a good supply of food and water, because they'd robbed so many of the bags on the bus – and the bag-packers had genuinely thought they'd be living rough. After a thick vegetable soup, they mixed powdered potato and warmed up two cans of beans. They fried sausages in a small pat of butter. Then they brewed more hot chocolate, and shared an enormous packet of digestive biscuits.

'Are you scared, Mr Barlow?' said Eric.

'Me? No.'

'You look worried.'

'The face is a deceptive thing. I'm happier than I've been in a long time.'

'You enjoy teaching, don't you?' said Rikki. 'I thought you loved us.'

'Yes, I do. Of course I do.'

'Even me?'

'Especially you – and I don't know why.'

'What will you do without us, then?' said Richard. 'What do teachers do after they get sacked?'

'There are many ways of earning a living,' said Mr Barlow. 'And I was definitely getting stale.'

'They might arrest you,' said Eric. 'You should have handed us in, really, shouldn't you?'

'I'll plead temporary insanity,' said Mr Barlow.

'We need a better plan,' said Rikki. 'They will come looking for us – you were right about that, sir. They'll be right on our tails.'

'We need a strategy,' said Richard.

'Yes,' they said together. 'Let's assume—'

'What?' said Richard.

'What were you going to say?' said Rikki.

'You go first,' said Richard. Their heads were pressed together, because they were sharing the hood of Jeff's coat.

'I was going to say that we need to assume the enemy knows where we are,' said Rikki. 'Because of us using the mobile, which – I agree – was the most stupid thing I've ever done. They are going to assume that we came down to this part of the world so as to be with our friends. Would that be correct?'

Everyone nodded.

'In that case,' said Richard, 'they can't be that far behind us.'

'We played right into his hands, didn't we?' said Richard. 'When we were violent – that gave him the excuse he was waiting for! Oh God, why did you throw us off the roof, Rikki?'

Rikki laughed. 'We've been through this,' he said.

'What do you mean?'

'I asked you exactly that question. I'm telling you, I didn't. That was you.'

'That wasn't me. I'm the survivor.'

Rikki laughed again. 'Richard! You're using my words – that is exactly what I said. Now try to remember: I climbed the drainpipe, didn't I? That was me: Rikki. Definitely.'

'Yes,' said Richard. 'I agree. You always think faster than I do – you grabbed the drainpipe.'

'But when we got to the top, I wanted to escape. Your dweeby ways took over again, and you caught me completely by surprise. You just . . . launched us backwards into thin air. I remember thinking, *Oh no, what a loser!*'

'Well, if that was me,' said Richard, 'I was totally unaware of it.'

'Let me ask you another question,' said Rikki.

'Go on.'

'Tell the truth. Did you vandalize Aparna's picture?'

'No!' cried Richard. 'Absolutely not!'

'And you still think I did?'

'Yes!'

'No loyalty, you see? Even now.'

'I don't know *when* you did it – or how. But . . . who else uses that swearword? And who else has a big thing against Aparna? Nobody.'

'Why do you have a thing against Aparna?' said Eric.

Rikki sighed. 'I don't know,' he said. 'I suppose she fascinates me. I just want her attention.'

'Eric,' said Richard, 'did *you* smash up Aparna's picture?'

'No way,' said Eric. 'Maybe it was Mr Barlow.'

'Well, it wasn't me,' said Rikki. 'It could have been anyone. People do weird things. Oh, and by the way – Mr Barlow.'

'Yes?'

'Thank you for catching us.'

'Salome caught you.'

'Really?'

'She was there first.'

Rikki looked away.

'She said you were light as a feather,' said Mr Barlow. 'And your mother was there too, don't forget.'

'That's true,' said Richard. 'She came running.'

A silence fell, and Rikki stirred the beans.

'They're going to be worried,' said Eric. 'Your parents are so nice. You should have texted them.'

'What about yours?' said Rikki.

Eric laughed. 'Mum won't even notice I'm gone. *Your* parents love you.'

'They let Doctor Warren knock Rikki out!' said Richard. 'They were considering cutting his head off.'

'Oh, come on,' said Rikki. 'Did they have a choice?'

'Yes!'

'I never made things easy for them. I'm not surprised they . . . thought about it. Especially if Warren told them it was the only way to save you. Dammit! It's so much easier when people are villains. Now you're making me feel bad about them. Why is it easier to hate people?'

Mr Barlow fed the fire carefully. 'Since we're all asking questions,' he said, 'can I ask one?'

The boys nodded.

'It's a bit personal. Are you sure I won't offend you?'

Richard looked at him and swallowed. 'You're going to ask the unaskable again, aren't you?'

'What's that?' said Eric.

'He's going to ask about Danda.'

'Grandad,' said Rikki. 'Grandad.'

'How did you guess that?' said Eric. 'And why shouldn't he ask about your grandad? He was ace – why don't you talk about him?'

'I only ask,' said Mr Barlow, 'because he must have been one of the ones who trained down here. They train commandos in the hills, but out at sea . . .'

Richard was shaking his head. 'Don't tell me. I don't want to know.'

'Out at sea, they trained the pilots for the aircraft-carrier runs. He was a great man, Richard. All I was—'

'No,' said Rikki. He was holding up his hand, and looking at Mr Barlow. 'We like you a lot, sir, we really do. And we will tell you anything you want to know about sex, drugs, rock-and-roll. I will even tell you that horror story about the psycho who nails his wife to the car roof. But please don't ask Richard about Grandad.'

Richard had his eyes down.

'Why?' said Eric.

'Because it makes him blub,' said Rikki.

'Why?'

'I don't know. Richard thinks he could have done something. I don't know what, but that's what he's always thinking, and it's a pain in the arse because people die sometimes. What's the mystery? Leave it.'

It was at that moment that the tripwire Eric had laid sounded the alarm, and everyone looked up. It was a basic Nailhead failsafe, designed to protect the camp against intruders. What Eric hadn't mentioned was that he'd also constructed three man-traps on the main approaches, and one of them had been sprung.

There was a swish of branches. The scream that filled the night air was louder than any bird. It filled the whole valley.

CHAPTER FOUR

Eric had got carried away – even he admitted that.

He'd put a loop of cord around two forked sticks, and jammed them into the soil. The sticks were connected to a sapling that had been bent almost horizontal. Some of its limbs had been lopped to ensure swift and immediate straightening, should the trigger be released. It was a deadly mechanism.

Mr Barlow was on his feet before anyone, reaching for his torch. When he switched it on, the beam revealed an upside-down figure, squirming like a fish on a line. It was dangling from one ankle, and they soon saw that it was Salome, and she was the one howling. Around her stood Aparna, Jeff and Mark, flapping and dithering, blinded by the light.

'Jeff!' cried Richard.

'Mark!' shouted Eric.

Salome continued to scream. In a moment, Mr Barlow was among them and had the weight of the victim. Eric clambered up the sapling, untying his knots, and the party was then helped into the camp, whimpering with fear and shock. Soon everyone was under the tent roof, seated around the fire-hole. The newcomers were wet and frozen, and they were all in tears.

'It is so good to see you,' whispered a shivering Aparna. 'We have been so silly, Mr Barlow! Thank goodness you're here . . .'

'Eric, we got lost,' said Mark. 'We didn't even bring a tent!'

'We were getting really cold as well,' said Jeff, taking a mug of hot chocolate in shaking hands. 'We forgot food too, because we left in such a hurry! I borrowed this cardigan, but half our kit's been lost – my mum's going to kill me. So we just kept going, hoping—'

'We thought we'd die!' said Mark.

'Thank God we found you,' muttered Salome.

The newcomers blinked at their friends in disbelief, and gazed at Mr Barlow as if he had to be an illusion.

This is too . . . amazing,' said Jeff. He paused. 'Rikki. Richard.' He put out his hand. 'You guys have just saved our lives, because we would have been walking in circles all through the night and we would have frozen to death. I am really pleased to see you. I'm sorry we had a falling-out.'

Richard and Rikki shook his hand warmly. 'I think it was me who caused the problems,' said Rikki.

'No,' said Jeff. 'It was me.'

'I just thought you were a boring little suck-up,' said Rikki.

'He is,' said Eric.

'Well,' said Jeff, 'I know I over-react to things.'

'We provoked you,' said Richard. 'We were pretty insulting—'

'I should have sat down and discussed the situation. I got far too emotional.'

'You took a stand,' said Richard. 'I admired you for that. You were protecting Aparna, and—'

'I didn't want protection,' said Aparna. 'He was embarrassing me, and he *is* a suck-up. You bore me to death, sometimes, Jeff.'

'Do I?'

'You always play it so safe.'

'I just do what I'm told. I can change, though.'

'Eric,' said Mark suddenly. He had been distracted by his friend's whittling of a stick, and was staring at the blade.

'What?'

'Is that a, er . . . sorry, buddy, but . . . isn't that my Lockerman knife you're using, huh?'

'Yup. I want to have a few sharp sticks ready, in case we have to do more snares.'

'Right.'

'We're going to need meat tomorrow.'

'It's just that it was in my bag. The knife, I mean.'

Eric smiled. 'Oh! I see what you're saying. Yes, I was going to tell you about that,' he said. 'We were in a situation and we just didn't have too many choices. We stole a lot of stuff – we had to.'

'This is your coat, Jeff,' said Rikki. 'Totally weatherproof – you chose well.'

'And isn't that my tent?' said Aparna. 'I remember you

saying it was too big, Mr Barlow. But, well . . . it's the perfect size.'

There was a long silence. Salome spoke first. 'My God,' she said. She grinned a wide, joyful grin. 'They were on the roof of the bus. Miss Maycock was going on and on about it, but nobody would listen! These guys stowed away to join the residential, and robbed all our kit!'

Richard nodded. 'We were running for our lives,' he said. 'We'd better tell you the whole story . . .'

By the time the tale was told the group was welded together in hurt and fury. They sat closer than ever, as Mr Barlow tended the fire, and Richard and Rikki felt arms around their shoulders.

'I feel sick to think about it,' said Jeff.

'It's disgusting,' said Aparna. 'Well done for saving the monkeys.'

Mark high-fived his friend. 'That was a neat job, Eric,' he said. 'You are amazing.'

'Those doctors,' said Jeff. 'They're out of control.'

Salome was nodding. 'Too right,' she said. 'I know Rikki's a pain. But that doesn't mean they can take his brain out. I mean, we've all got bad bits. You can't just go cutting them out!'

'Just what I said,' said Richard.

'They showed you actual photos?' said Jeff. 'Photos of a kid who'd had it done?'

Richard and Rikki winced. 'That was the closest I came to screaming,' said Richard. 'I'm not kidding – there was this little head . . . it had kind of . . .'

'Don't!' said Mark. 'I don't want to think about it.'

'Well, we'd better keep well hidden,' said Rikki. 'I don't want to end up in a jar being poked about by Warren. He's still after us, don't forget. We've got to be smarter than ever.'

'You're dead right,' said Jeff. 'You say the police know you're in this area. They're going to be looking for *us* now, as well.'

'What do we do?' cried Rikki.

Salome hugged him harder. 'We'll protect you, boy,' she said. 'We'll keep you safe.'

'Then let's work on a plan,' said Eric seriously. 'We can't just sit here saying how angry we feel. *Chapter Four: The hunted man has to be practical. That is probably the ultimate test of his manhood.*'

'I say climb the mountain,' said Aparna.

'Why?'

'That's practical.'

'Go up, though?' said Jeff. 'I was going to say the boring old opposite.'

'We could break through enemy lines,' said Salome. 'Bust through the lot of them, and get back to civilization, and—'

'I don't want civilization,' said Richard. 'Never again.'

'The advantage of climbing the mountain,' said Mr Barlow, 'is that we won't be overtaken. We're also less likely to be surprised. We'll have the advantage of height, and we can probably move quickly. We're all pretty fit, right?'

Everyone nodded.

'There's a cave up there too,' said Mr Barlow. 'Quite a deep one, as I remember.'

'You really know this area?' said Jeff.

'Oh yes. I was telling the boys, I spent a couple of weeks here with the Scouts. I think it's going to be pretty familiar when we start climbing. The quickest way is by water. Then there's a fairly steep ascent up what's called the Devil's Chimney, which is the way I went last time – it's a wonderful climb. Obviously the weather's a problem, but we've got ropes. So as long as we're careful . . .'

'Mr Barlow,' said Jeff, 'why did you book us into that awful Adventure Centre? Why didn't you just take us out here?'

Mr Barlow looked surprised. 'What was so awful about it?'

They told him, and soon everyone was shaking their head, giggling. Jeff did an impression of Captain Colin, and the laughter grew hysterical. They talked about the camping-simulation exercise he'd promised them, and the horrible food – and they were choking, unable to speak. The rain grew heavier and heavier, and the giggling continued – their circle stayed close and warm. At last, Mr Barlow said he had to retire through sheer exhaustion, so he crawled off to the second tent, wishing everyone goodnight. The children curled up close to Eric's fire-hole, snug in their sleeping bags, and whispered as the rain fell.

'Salome,' said Rikki.

'What?'

There was a long silence.

'What?' said Salome, again.

'You know I'm sorry, don't you?'

Salome smiled. 'I know you're crazy. So it's fine.'

Minutes later, they had all fallen into a deep, dream-laden sleep.

CHAPTER FIVE

They did not hear the baying of dogs.

Mountain rescue passed within half a mile, but its leaders were convinced the children would be closer to the footpath. The dogs couldn't pick up any scent because of the storm. A second group had found the two bicycles, and was successful in following tracks for an hour or so – but then they suddenly disappeared, and Chief Inspector Mantz halted them until dawn.

He had arrived just after midnight, and commandeered the Clifden Adventure Centre as a damp headquarters. The rest of the Green Cross children were bussed back home, and a rumour went round that Captain Colin had been arrested – a policeman had recognized him and he'd been packed off to see the Fraud Squad, who'd been hoping to interview him for a number of years. A hotline was now established between the new HQ and the commando base: the red tape had been successfully cut, and a hard-faced soldier – Lieutenant Kirby – arrived by jeep, ready and willing to deploy his sixty-five professionals. The key players considered their strategy as the thunder rolled in.

'Tell us again,' said Mantz. 'Why are these kids running?'

'Well,' said Dr Warren. 'Rikki is a pretty desperate character. You know he'd been certified?'

'No.'

'Oh, he's criminally psychotic,' said Dr Summersby. 'We had him in our secure unit, for his own good. His parents insisted.'

'And the two heads are fighting each other?'

'Oh yes.'

'That's bad.'

'What frightened us,' said Dr Warren, 'was how Rikki simply couldn't restrain himself. He was injuring Richard. He was lighting fires, threatening suicide. I would say he's potentially homicidal.'

'Homicidal?' said Lieutenant Kirby, looking up from his map. 'You think he's a killer, do you?'

'He threw Richard off a school roof.'

'So he's unpredictable.'

'Yes, sir.'

The soldier removed his spectacles. 'This changes everything, Mantz. I didn't realize this was a combat mission. You said recovery.'

Chief Inspector Mantz leaned forward. 'Looks like he fooled us all, Lieutenant. How confident can you be about finding him?'

'Oh, we'll flush him out,' said the soldier.

'When?' said Dr Summersby.

'We'll have him before nightfall. What we have to do is agree the objective.'

'It's to isolate Rikki,' said Dr Warren. 'Always has been.'

'Then what?'

'We'll need to shut him down, sir. I can do that, with Doctor Summersby—'

'My men need specifics,' said Lieutenant Kirby. 'Define "shut him down".'

'Very well,' said Dr Warren. He looked at the two men, and swallowed. 'I'm fond of the boy, and I've tried to help him. But I think we need to use maximum force now – for the protection of the others. I think we should surround them, and seal off the area. Tranquillize if possible – and then Summersby and I can move in to administer proper sedation.'

Lieutenant Kirby stroked his chin. 'Tranquillizers, eh? There's a lot of ifs and buts with these tranquillizer guns. Do we know the dosage?'

'I've got all his records with me,' said Dr Summersby.

'Then I want you in the front line, standing by. The snipers go forward, and we bring you in by chopper, soon as he's down.'

'I like that,' said Mantz.

'Parents?'

'They followed us here,' said Dr Summersby. 'But we're keeping them back.'

'Loved ones can be tricky,' said the lieutenant. 'You don't want family in a war zone.'

The inspector nodded. 'The Westlake parents insisted on joining us, that's the problem. Let's keep them at arm's length.'

The lieutenant stood up. 'I say do it,' he said. 'Fast. Call off the mountain rescue boys, Inspector – we don't need civilians. I want Two-heads flushed out into the open. I'll divvy up the battalion and lead a pincer movement. Have a corkscrew assault faction standing by – this is just the kind of action they'd been hoping for. Doctor Warren, you'd better get your toolkit ready with this good lady, and sort your ballistics.'

'Will the snipers feel comfortable?' said Dr Warren. 'I mean – he's only a youngster.'

'Comfortable about what?'

'Shooting a child.'

The lieutenant stared at him. 'My men do what they're told,' he said.

Mr and Mrs Westlake were waiting in a small, bleak hotel room. They had no information. All they'd heard was that 'preparations were being made', and that the police were 'closing in'. They sat listening to the wind and rain, wondering where their son could possibly be. Nobody was available to speak to them, so their calls went unanswered. 'The matter is in hand,' was the only response they could get.

The press had got hold of the story somehow, and they watched news bulletins in which their own anxious faces appeared. They heard experts speculating about the chances of a child surviving more than twenty-four hours in the worsening weather, and there was film of the Green Cross children returning from the disastrous residential.

It was the lead story on every bulletin: six eleven-year-olds missing, plus an elderly teacher. As dawn broke, thin and grey, Mrs Westlake said to her husband, 'We can't sit here any more.'

'I know, love.'

'I had a dream.'

'Did you sleep? I thought you were awake.'

'I don't remember sleeping, but I had a dream and I can't make head nor tail of it. I want to be moving, Frank.'

'Where do we go? Everyone we've spoken to says sit tight.'

'Why would he jump off the roof like that? I keep turning it over and over. There's something going on – we can't just sit here.'

Mr Westlake stood up. 'Where do you want to go? We'll go anywhere you say.'

'Why did we even consider it?'

Mr Westlake was silent. 'We had to,' he said at last.

'I'll never forgive myself. If we don't get him home, Frank, just as he was, I'll never forgive myself.'

'They're together, still. They'll keep each other safe.'

Mrs Westlake turned to the window. 'He's going to the sea,' she said. 'I don't know why, but I can feel it in my bones. There's a lighthouse – he's going to that, I'm sure of it. It's where Dad was, years ago.'

'Let's get a map. I'll call us a cab – we can go into the town and get the things we need. Is that what's best?'

'Yes.' The rain lashed the glass, but the grey surf was visible, just beyond the beach. Mrs Westlake gazed into space. 'He'll make for the sea,' she said again. 'I can feel it, stronger than ever.' She felt the tears in her eyes again. 'We're going to need a boat, Frank – or we're going to need to find someone with a boat . . . When he jumped off the roof, he wasn't trying to kill himself. I know he wasn't.'

She stopped.

'What was he doing, love?' said her husband. He put his arms round her. 'Say it. Say what you feel.'

'This is going to sound so stupid. But we haven't dealt with it! He didn't want to die. When I had that boy, he wanted life, and he thought he had wings. He wanted to just . . . fly away. Is that so stupid?'

'No. I know what you mean.'

'He wants his grandad.'

'We should never have moved things. We should have waited.'

'We had to make changes. Richard understood that—'

'I'm not so sure. What does talking do? We should have waited much, much longer. He's still in there, isn't he? It's his house, still, and he loved that boy more than . . . Oh, Lord, if I feel it, then Richard must be . . . he must have been in torment.'

Mrs Westlake wiped her eyes. Her husband could feel her heart beating. 'Frank,' she said quietly.

'What?'

'It was a year ago that he died. A year ago today.'

Mr Westlake felt his throat tighten, and a chill rose up through his body. For a moment he felt the old man watching, and though he knew that was ridiculous, he caught a whiff of pipe smoke. There was a flicker in the wardrobe mirror, and he found himself turning to look. It was gone at once, but the smell lingered. He held his wife harder.

A year ago, they had rushed to the hospital. His wife had got there just before him and was with Richard by the time he arrived. The old man had passed, and he heard the whole horrible story while holding Richard in his arms. His brave son, who'd tried so hard and was now carrying something too awful to bear, and so heavy it was crushing the life out of him.

Mr Westlake blinked, and kissed his wife. Then he turned and picked up the telephone. 'I'll call a cab,' he said. His voice was shaking. 'He needs us more than ever, doesn't he? I don't trust them. I trust my son – that's who I trust.'

'We're going to need a boat,' said his wife. 'But I don't know why.'

CHAPTER SIX

The commando unit was split into eight small squadrons. The soldiers dressed for 'extreme conditions', and all weapons were stripped down and oiled. Radios were tested, and a convoy of trucks took them through driving rain towards the mountain.

Unaware of this, Eric supervised breakfast. He made tea from spruce leaves, assuring everyone it would keep off scurvy. Mark checked the rabbit-snares and found that two had been successful. Eric's book was coming apart in his hands, but he held it open as Salome did the cutting and gutting. Soon the thin, pink bodies were turning over the fire, while Jeff made coffee. They still had some bread rolls, so they chewed rabbit-burgers, and finished the baked beans.

They buried their rubbish, and struck camp. Within an hour they'd found the stream Mr Barlow remembered, and they all split up to find timber for a raft. The rain came down in a steady monsoon. Rikki and Richard had insisted on returning their coat to Jeff, so they were wrapped in a spare pak-a-mac Mr Barlow had salvaged from the bicycle he'd stolen.

Eric checked Chapter Five, and lashed the raft-spars. They carried the finished item downstream, and soon they came to a possible launching point. This river, of course, had spent the night absorbing gallons of water from the mountain, and had burst its banks to become a raging torrent. Everyone squatted in a mist of spray, and it wasn't easy to speak over the roar. According to Nailhead, the main thing was to have an edging of rope all the way round the raft, which they could cling to with hands and ankles. Bags would all be strapped to their bodies and steering would be out of the question. The depth meant that they'd be safe from rocks, or so they hoped – they would trust to the physics of water.

The launch was frighteningly sudden. They clambered aboard by forming a human chain, and there was no going back. The last man let go, and a swirl of water took the raft out into midstream. There, the current simply lifted it and shot them forward like a missile.

The children screamed, clinging on for dear life. In seconds, they were plunging down the valley in clouds of foam, the granite whipping past as the water curled and bulged. At last they were spat right through the air, and they thought the raft would split – they felt rocks under them, but they were now going so fast they simply skimmed over the top. Somehow the knots held, and they hit a great elbow of white water where they were turned three times in a full circle, before bobbing on again. The water became brown, and widened out, and eventually they slowed to a brisk, steady sailing. Mr Barlow pointed out two herons and a cormorant.

They came to a sandy bank under a great shelf of yellow stone, and they used a loose pole to ease themselves towards it. They clambered up onto a dry platform and held each other, laughing – astonished that there were no broken bones.

'And there she is,' panted Mr Barlow. 'Steeper than ever. The Devil's Chimney.'

They all looked up at a jagged crevice, rising vertically into mist and forest.

'The thing about this kind of climb,' the teacher continued, 'is that it looks harder than it is. We're not exposed, so we won't get blown off. The rock's actually quite dry, because of the natural shelter of the walls. So as long as we keep our heads and work together, I don't see a problem. Does anyone see a snag?'

Nobody did, so the ropes were salvaged from the raft. Aparna revealed that she'd done a bit of climbing in the Hindu Kush, with her uncles. She supervised the tying of the belay that would keep them in line. Salome was the strongest, and was a regular at her community centre's indoor climbing wall. She went first, therefore, and was soon looping off at appropriate intervals as the rest of the party followed her. They paused every twenty metres or so and gazed out at the cloud.

Every minute, the world changed. Cloud was nudging down the valley, billowing over the river. Cloud was coming up the chimney, almost between their legs. Cloud was also skudding over their heads, sliding down upon them like a great grey lid. There was moisture everywhere

– for the whole mountain seemed saturated – but they felt dry inside their waterproofs, and even warm. Now and then the sun would find a hole to peer through, as if it was checking they were still together. Then a blast of thunder would send everything swirling again, and there was the occasional crackle of thin, cruel lightning.

Jeff laughed. They were balanced together on a narrow ledge, getting their breath back after a particularly tough stretch.

'What's funny?' said Richard.

'Do you remember the scholarship exam?' he said. '*Question seven: Write about an experience of nature.*'

'I didn't do that,' said Salome. 'I'd never really had one.'

'I missed that whole section,' said Mark.

'I wrote a poem,' said Richard. 'God, it was bad.'

'*Do not look for me, God*,' said Mr Barlow in a deep voice:

'For I will look for thee.

The mountains are our home,

And everything we own, is given up for free.'

'Nice,' said Rikki. 'What does it mean?'

'I was never sure,' said Mr Barlow. 'It's Walt Whitman, or someone like him. Very mystical.'

Mark said, 'I'd be a teacher if it wasn't for that boring stuff.'

'Poetry?' said Jeff.

'Yeah. So dull.'

'There's nothing boring about teaching,' said Mr Barlow. 'But I'm afraid I was a very boring teacher.'

'That's not true,' said Aparna.

'Oh, he could be,' said Salome. 'Remember *Great Expectations*? . . . That is the only time I ever actually fell asleep in the classroom.'

'I fell asleep a lot,' said Eric. 'But then I wasn't sleeping at home.'

'I liked school,' said Jeff. 'But next year I'm going to start rebelling.'

'Mr Barlow,' said Rikki. 'Did you notice how we used to call you "Bra-low"?'

'Yes.'

'Did you notice all the spit jokes?' said Eric.

'I'm afraid I did.'

Mark shook his head. 'What were we doing? I feel so bad!'

Salome said, 'You should have screamed at us. You should have . . . battered us.'

'I should have laughed,' said Mr Barlow. 'That's what I should have done.' He smiled and hauled himself upright. 'And that's what I *shall* do from now on, I hasten to add. I'm going to spend a lot more time laughing. This world is too wonderful. We have another two hours at least, by the way – and then it's uphill walking.'

'Did you deliberately choose the hardest way up?' said Aparna.

'No,' said Mr Barlow. 'It was the one my old patrol leader chose. Of course, *he* may have chosen the hardest way up – he had a lot to prove, as I remember. There may well be easier ways, but . . .' He beamed at Aparna. 'Would you want the easy way?'

'No. Yes.'

'You can see the sea from the top, you know. And the Kiduggan Lighthouse.'

Aparna nodded. 'I do know. You see, this is what I painted.'

'When?'

'Icarus,' she said. 'It's what Icarus saw. Isn't it?'

Mr Barlow was right.

After two more hours of strenuous climbing, they came out of the chimney into a bulge of thick forest. There were no paths, but Jeff and Eric took compass bearings and led the party onwards and upwards, for the mountain peak appeared and disappeared. Around mid-afternoon – just as they came to the edge of the trees – they heard an engine.

They crouched down and froze.

A helicopter puttered overhead, coming in low. Eric waved them back, and they retreated. Soon the noise was deafening – it seemed as if the craft was just above the treetops. It lingered, and hunted. It moved left then right. They all peered up, but nothing was visible. Eventually – after several breathless minutes – it moved on and the children, and Mr Barlow, relaxed.

'They're on to us,' said Rikki.

Salome slipped her arm round him. 'They're not going to get you. Don't worry.'

'It's good they've looked around here,' said Eric. 'It means they'll move on somewhere else. It was an Army helicopter, wasn't it?'

'Should we stay in the wood?' said Aparna.

'No,' said Jeff. 'I think Eric's right. If they've got a whole mountain to cover, then they can tick this bit off, and go elsewhere. I think we keep going.'

'Where to, though?' said Mark. It was clear he was getting tired.

They looked beyond the forest, to a cliff of grey rising up to another wedge of cloud.

'I want to get to the top of that,' said Rikki.

'You have to,' said Aparna.

'We won't get up tonight,' said Richard. 'We'll have to camp at the base. How long to get there?'

'It's going to be hard work,' said Eric, 'but I'd say three hours. Everyone warm enough?'

'No,' said Jeff. 'I've lost a glove. My hand's like ice.'

'Use these,' said Mr Barlow, stripping off his own. 'Go on, Jeff, do as I say. I'm warm as toast.'

They took another compass bearing, in case the mist came down again, and set off. In a short while the rain was horizontal, so they trudged close together, listening for the return of the aircraft. They felt the weather was on their side, for the worse the visibility got the more likely it was that the pilot would be forced to give up.

It was Rikki who started singing:

'*One more step along the world I go!*'

He sang out in the rain, and Salome kept the beat on his shoulders. Mr Barlow took up the chant, and sang lustily – it was the hymn Aparna had so often played at the end of assembly. They plunged through the deluge, shouting the words like a football song:

'One more step along the world I go!

One more step along the world I go!

From the old things, to the new –

Keep! – me travelling along – With! You!'

The chorus became a war song, and they roared it together:

'And it's fro-om! The old! I travel to the new! Yes!

Keep. *Me! Trav-ell-ing! Along. With. You!'*

They got to the cliff face, breathless, exhausted, but laughing. They leaned back and looked up at the lightning. The cloud was pouring down, thick as smoke, and the thunder couldn't keep up with the jagged forks that sprang through it – north, south, east and west.

'One hour,' shouted Eric. 'One more at the most!'

'An hour of what, though?' yelled Mark.

'Before the end of the world!' cried Richard.

Eric called back, 'One more hour of daylight. Not that it's . . . very bright, I know. I say we dig in. At the back of these rocks. We don't have much light left.'

'You do the snares,' shouted Salome. 'We can get the tent up.'

'I'll do the fire,' yelled Mark. 'How deep do I go for a firepit, huh? I'm cold, man.'

'I'll help you,' said Rikki. 'Let's check the book.'

CHAPTER SEVEN

Darkness fell, and the soldiers inched closer.

The children began a slow stir-fry, stirring the last of the rabbit into the vegetables. Aparna had brought tinned spinach, sweetcorn and a bag of lentils. They kept adding water, and the food kept thickening. After three quarters of an hour they had a huge pan of the sweetest-smelling stew they'd ever tasted.

'You don't eat meat,' said Jeff suddenly.

'Who doesn't?' said Mark. He was happy again, for the tent was warm. His long arms hugged his knees.

'Aparna! She's a vegetarian.'

'Not today,' said Aparna. 'I can't be – and I wasn't yesterday.'

'I thought it was a religious thing,' said Salome. 'Can you just . . . take a break when you want?'

'I just decided there wasn't much choice,' said Aparna.

'But you're not going to throw up, are you?' said Richard. 'It must taste pretty disgusting – if you only do vegetables.'

Aparna smiled. 'It's fine,' she said. 'It's a bit like banana.'

'Look, Aparna—' said Rikki.

'Here we go,' interrupted Jeff. 'Get ready.'

'No, listen. I don't want to be a bore, but we were arguing about this yesterday. Who smashed up that picture of yours? Because Richard thinks it was me, and I think it was Richard – and probably everyone thinks it was one of us. But it wasn't.'

'I still think it was Mr Barlow,' said Eric. 'He's the real villain.'

Everyone laughed.

'It could have been any kid,' said Salome. 'If Rikki and Richard say they didn't do it, we ought to believe them.'

'But I know,' said Aparna. 'It was me.'

The laughter stopped. Then Mark sniggered, and said, 'Huh?'

'How was it you?' said Richard.

Jeff grinned. 'She's just trying to make everyone feel better . . .'

'What do you mean?' said Richard. 'Let her speak.'

'I think the girl's serious,' said Salome. 'Are you serious, Aparna – or are you joking with us?'

Eric said, 'That was about the nicest picture in the world. You won a prize for it. Everyone says you're going to be an artist, if you're not a dancer, if you're not a lawyer. And you're saying you smashed the glass and wrote all over it?'

'Did you see *what* was written on it?' said Mark.

'Yes,' said Jeff. 'The word Rikki likes so much. It wasn't you, Aparna – that's crazy!'

'I'd had enough of it,' said Aparna softly. She stirred the meal. Mr Barlow made the hot chocolate, as quietly as he could. The hurricane above suddenly lashed at the tent-skin extra hard, and they heard the guy ropes groan. Jeff turned his torch off, and the only light was from the fire in the hole below, and a candle on the ledge. Nobody spoke, and the wind set up a high, sighing moan.

'Tell them why,' said Mr Barlow.

'I don't know if I can,' said Aparna. 'I'd just had enough of it, and I'd had enough of me. I wanted to get Rikki expelled, of course. I knew if I smashed it up everyone would think it was him, and I . . . I'm afraid I hated you, Rikki. Richard. I hated you so much I wanted to kill you. It was me that did all that to your locker too, and messed up your books. I stole all the planes. I cut up the wings-badge because I knew you loved it.'

'What wings?' said Salome.

'What did you do to his locker?' said Eric. 'I'm not understanding this at all.'

'We didn't tell anyone,' said Richard. 'We didn't know what to do, and—'

'We didn't have time,' said Rikki. He looked around at the faces. 'Someone threw stuff in our locker. Trashed it, tore everything up . . . I didn't think it was you, Aparna, but . . . I'm so glad it was.'

'How could you smash up your own picture?' said Jeff.

'I hate . . . everyone always going on about it,' said Aparna. She was staring at her knees. 'Going on about art and how clever I am.'

'You are,' said Salome.

'No,' said Aparna. 'No. You haven't met my sister.' She laughed. 'You haven't met my other sister, who's at medical college and has an offer to train at . . . I don't even know where, somewhere famous. I'm not clever at all – all I do is . . . remember stuff. I've got a good memory. I'm not as clever as Eric. I couldn't catch a rabbit.'

'Oh,' said Eric, 'rabbits are just dopey—'

'I can't be nice, like Jeff. I can be dull. I can be quiet. I can't say stuff, like Rikki. That speech you made, for the TV: that was so terrible and frightening, and brave. You were so angry – it was my dad who clapped you, by the way – he said you were a genius, which made me hate you even more. And anyway, the other thing about that picture was what someone said about Icarus, after Mr Barlow told the story. About why did it have to be a sad ending, and why was it always about punishment and death? I thought, *Why am I doing paintings about death?*' Aparna paused, and everyone waited. 'So I went into reception late, after my music lesson. And I hated you so much, Rikki. That must have been the main thing. I just smashed it with a stone. And in the morning, I'm so sorry . . . I did that to your locker. But I kept the little plane.'

'It's only stuff,' said Richard. 'Stuff can be fixed. I wish I still had the wings, though.'

'They're here,' said Eric. 'They were by your bed.'

Rikki stared.

Eric dug in his pocket, and out they came, damp and forlorn. A piece of sellotape had held them together, but it had come off, and they were in two pieces again. Jeff switched his torch back on, and they looked at the careful embroidery, and the gold thread fraying where Aparna's scissors had sliced them in half.

'I'm so sorry,' she said again. 'I wish they could be mended.'

'They can be,' said Salome.

'Aparna,' said Jeff. 'Are you really sick of yourself?'

'Yes.'

'That's so weird. I'm sick of me.' He laughed.

Mark smiled. 'You imagine what it's like being me, then,' he said. 'I'd rather be you, or Eric. I mean, look at me! Look. I'm just this bug-eyed zero who never says anything worth saying. I'm just this stupid body, in a bunch of clothes that don't even fit me—'

'That's not true!' said Rikki.

'I'm even rubbish at football. I don't care, most of the time . . . but sometimes you just think how nice it would be to be someone else. And be good at something. And be special.'

'I don't get my parents,' said Jeff. 'They never have a laugh. They're so sensible – all the time.'

'You try living with mine,' said Salome.

'Your dad was scary,' said Richard.

'He's not. Not really. Mum's the scary one. But all I do is train and train, and then I go and lose my temper . . . I nearly lost everything over . . . you know, over Rolo. And Dad won't let me forget it.'

'It was a good punch,' said Rikki. 'I'd like to box.'

'I didn't insult your grandad,' said Jeff. 'You told Mr Prowse I'd called him names.'

Eric laughed. 'I remember your grandad,' he said. 'We used to call him *Uncle*. Everyone did. If you called him "sir" or "mister", he used to pretend he couldn't hear you – you remember? He'd put his hand by his ear and say, "What was that? What was that?" And remember him at football practice, shouting his head off! Did he get on your nerves, Mr Barlow?'

'No.'

'He had a hell of a loud voice,' said Salome. 'He was a boxer too, wasn't he?'

'He used to be,' said Rikki. 'He was a middleweight. He only got so . . . frail in the last few years – he was always going on about how skinny I am, but he was the one.' He smiled. 'He wasn't active any more – you know, in the last years. He had some kind of arthritis, which slowed him down. Then diabetes, which Mum said he wasn't really controlling properly. Then . . .'

'I thought he'd forgotten something at first,' said Richard.

'When?'

'The day he died. When he stopped. It was outside the newsagent – I thought he'd forgotten something. He just stopped. And he looked back behind him, or I thought he did. I thought maybe we'd left something in the shop, but then his face changed. I was holding his hand, and he let it go for a second. I said, "Are you all right?" It was that narrow bit of pavement, where the waste-bin is, and he held the wall for a moment.'

Rikki was nodding. 'Yes. Then he went down on his knees, really slow. I got hold of his arm, but he kept going down, and his face was so different, like he was thinking really hard about something. Then this terrible . . . jolt. He was trying to breathe then.'

'You wouldn't believe how quickly he went cold,' said Richard.

'Yes. It was like someone had flicked a switch.'

'I tried to get his collar open, but I couldn't. He was half on his side, and there were people around. They called an ambulance, and then nobody knew what to do. Why don't we learn first aid?'

'Why don't we?' said Rikki. 'We could have saved him.'

'It was massive, though,' said Richard. 'The heart attack.'

Jeff said, 'Do you think he felt much?'

'I don't know,' said Richard. 'I always wonder: what was he feeling and thinking? Did he know that it was all over? Does your life flash past again, or are you just too frightened? Maybe he was asking for help.'

'He was thinking about us, probably,' said Rikki. 'Knowing him. He loved us.'

'You think so?'

'God, I miss him so much because . . . I mean, I know people have to die. I know that. We do it all in science: people die. But it was just me and him there, and I didn't . . . I could've . . .'

'Could've what? What should we have done?'

'I don't know.'

'We couldn't do anything.'

'I know.'

'What then? What?'

'I just wish we'd said something he wanted to hear, and now we can't. I just wish I'd told him I loved him, and said goodbye, because I could have done. Maybe it would have made it better for him, and then maybe I'd feel easier. There's no heaven – I'm never going to see him again, and he was . . . I still can't imagine . . . Did I love him enough? Did he *know*, Richard? Did he know we loved him?'

'Yes,' said Richard.

'God, I hope so. I wish I could believe that.'

Mr Barlow told a story, then – another myth – about a woman who had wept so much in grief that the gods swept her up and turned her into a mountain. The mountain ran with mist and water for ever more.

Mark fed the fire, and after some time they blew the candle out. Then they listened to the weather hammering down, and they dozed. The earth turned, and they crawled into sleeping bags and heard some creature moan, out on the rocks. The moon came close, invisible behind boiling cloud, and pulled at the sea.

After some time, when the earth had turned a little further – Aparna said, 'They're coming for you.'

'Who?' said Jeff.

'Wake up. They know where we are.'

'Who's coming? What are you talking about?'

She was on her feet, shaking the others. It was still dark, and the wind was tugging at the roof. Eric was in the doorway.

'Where have you been?' said Salome. 'What time is it?'

'Nowhere,' Eric said. 'I just had this feeling. We ought to move higher.'

'Me too,' said Aparna. 'We're not hidden at all, are we?'

'I just scouted around,' said Eric. 'I didn't see anyone. But I've got this feeling we should get Rikki and Richard upwards.'

They didn't light a fire. They didn't have breakfast. They struck camp, and did their best to bury all evidence of their stay. They were reluctant to use torches and they hardly spoke. They packed their bags and crawled into the rocks. Then they climbed as quickly as they dared. There was a thin, feeble light in the sky, and they could still hear the muttering of more thunder as it rained and rained and rained.

The top of the mountain was invisible, so they just kept climbing, looking only at their hands and listening to their own breathing.

CHAPTER EIGHT

Jeff's glove had been found just after midnight.

A name-tag was neatly sewn into it: 'Jeff Rawlingson'. It was dry enough to suggest that the children were healthy and fit, and the commandos assumed they were still on the move. The strategy was adjusted and the units called together. They re-deployed, and threw a cordon right around the mountain, following the contour they were on. There would be an advance party of four trackers, backed up by a dozen snipers.

The tranquillizer darts were loaded into the guns. Dr Summersby measured the doses, and checked the hypodermics in her bag.

'First thing in the morning,' said Lieutenant Kirby. 'We'll have him.'

Inspector Mantz and the lieutenant conferred. The children were presumably sheltering in caves, so they would get the chopper out at dawn, and the search would be over. Mantz placed a call to the Westlake parents, and was surprised to find they'd left the hotel.

'They were seen at the port, sir,' said a sergeant.

'Doing what?'

'Asking about boats, sir. They used to do quite a lot of sailing, apparently.'

'Sailing? Now? Get them on their mobiles. Update them. Say we hope to have everyone safe by the end of the day – the doctors are standing by.'

'Right-o, sir.'

'What do they want a boat for?'

'Nobody knows.'

'Keep them under observation, then. We're moving as soon as it's light.' He put the phone down, and checked his maps again. Then Dr Warren and Dr Summersby were driven to the helicopter station.

At 4.30 a.m. the commandos received their orders. They stowed all gear, and in strict formation started up the sides of the mountain. The trackers would make first contact, and the snipers would be ready with fire.

At 6.10 a.m. a scout spotted a bright red coat.

By 6.13 a.m. all the children had been identified, along with an adult answering the description of Mr Barlow. They were negotiating a difficult rock face, moving steadily upwards – they appeared to be making for the summit. There was now the concern that too swift an assault would cause panic, so the soldiers held back and radioed the chopper. Rikki and Richard were in a blue waterproof, and although two snipers got him in their sights, it would have been fatal to take him. They would move in slowly once the helicopter was close.

'Keep your eyes on Two-heads,' said the lieutenant. 'Strict control, men – but take no chances.'

By 6.20 a.m. the cloud had lifted and the helicopter was thundering in. Dr Warren looked at Dr Summersby, who held the medical bag.

'This is it,' she said. 'Do you want to do it?'

'Yes.'

'One dose. He won't wake up.'

The children heard it coming, and there was simply nowhere to hide.

They were on a flat shoulder of rock, huddled together – and the caves were far too shallow to be useful. Mr Barlow searched, wondering how his memory had deceived him – he was sure there'd been a deep recess. He could remember sheltering in it. They scoured the area, but there was simply no way of disappearing. The wind was hammering at them, for they were so exposed, and it was obvious that the pilot had seen them. Their strategy suddenly seemed absurd. They reconvened in a shallow gulley and it dawned on them that this was their last stand. It might even be their last meeting.

'Never say die!' shouted Jeff.

'We can still go up!' said Eric. 'We're not at the top yet.'

It was hard to hear him, because of the wind and the helicopter's rotor blades. The aircraft had backed off, but it was keeping them all under observation. Eric led them up another ten metres, and at last they found an opening between two grey slabs. They put their torches on, and crawled in. The tunnel narrowed to nothing, and they had to crawl out again.

Jeff looked down, and mountains fell away beneath him. Behind a crag, he saw the face of a soldier, gazing up at him. He gripped Richard's arm and pointed, and the man made no move to conceal himself. In fact, he lifted a hand. Then they saw him use his radio.

'What do we do?' said Salome. 'This can't be it!'

'Stand and fight,' said Mark. 'They can't take us if we don't want to go.'

Suddenly there were more soldiers, and they were running. They were on the plateau below, where the children had camped. They were moving in from all visible directions, and the lower part of the mountain was teeming with men.

'Up,' said Jeff. 'Come on. At least get to the top. And we stay together!'

'Why?' said Rikki.

'They're not taking you! If they try it, they're dead!'

'I think we're done for,' yelled Richard. 'But we won't make it easy!'

Mr Barlow said, 'The thing we have to remember is that we took a stand. We took action, and that's something a lot of people never do. You're safe, Rikki – Richard. If we hadn't—'

Whatever he said next was lost in another burst of engine noise. The clouds had lifted for a moment, revealing a silvery sky, and the helicopter burst into it, bigger than ever. It was now so close that they could see the pilot's face – and his mouth as he spoke into his headset. The craft turned, and they saw the wide open doors, and more commandos. They were harnessed at the edge, and one of them was preparing a winch.

'Oh God,' said Richard. 'It's Doctor Warren.'

Sure enough, he was there, in combat clothing. His eyes were clearly visible and he carried a medical box.

Rikki was pale. He said, 'He's come for us, Rich.'

'I know.'

'He said he'd be there for us, didn't he? He said we could trust him, and here he is.'

'You trust him?' said Richard.

Rikki smiled. 'We can't give up now, you know.'

'Rikki,' said Richard, 'I have no intention of giving up, ever. I will never give up.'

'So what do we do? Look – they're going to drop him. And the soldiers are here . . .'

The winch was ready. There was a metallic glint as another rare moment of sunshine caught the harnesses. They could hear a voice, bleating out of a megaphone. 'Stay exactly where you are,' it wailed. The sound bounced off the rocks, and was all around them. 'You are not in danger!' it cried. 'We are here to save you!'

There were more words, but a gust of wind tore them to shreds. Then there was a crack of rifle fire – two quick pops, like bangers – and the children all dropped to the ground. A squall of rain hit suddenly, and there was a rush of cloud. The helicopter turned again, and rose upwards.

'What do we do, sir?' said Richard to Mr Barlow.

'I'm not sure, boy,' said Mr Barlow. 'I'm afraid I've been shot.'

'What?'

'Something caught me in the arm – look. My goodness.' He showed them the back of his arm, and a small dart was sticking out of it, just above the elbow.

'What are they doing?' said Jeff.

'I don't know,' said Mr Barlow. 'But my arm's going numb. I don't think I can . . . I'm not sure I'm going to be any help for much longer. You really must go it alone now.'

Aparna looked at Rikki and Richard. 'You'll have to fly,' she said. 'That's what you want, isn't it? For your grandad.'

Eric was there, beside Rikki. 'Come with me!' he cried.

'Where to?'

'Page one-ninety-two!' screamed Eric. 'One-ninety-two – it's the only way! Come on, Mr Barlow – you can do it!'

'What do you mean?' shouted Richard.

The rain burst over them then, and a bolt of lightning cracked somewhere so close they smelled burning. Jeff held Richard's arm, and Salome held Mark. Mr Barlow was gesturing at a group of soldiers some way below, hoping to keep them back – one raised his rifle and Mr Barlow stood in front of Rikki and Richard with his arms outstretched. There was another crack of rifle fire and the old teacher staggered backwards, holding his shoulder this time.

Eric was yelling something. 'It's Chapter Twenty! The last chapter!' His book was in his hand, the pages flapping madly. Even as he held it, the wind snapped it upwards and it was gone. The rubber bands broke and the pages flew, like a hundred birds, in a cloud around their heads. He snatched at one and looked at it. Then he held it to his chest. 'I've got it!' he shrieked. 'The page I wanted!'

'Follow me!' screamed Aparna. And she was moving, clambering up a channel in the rock. Mr Barlow was on his knees, but they couldn't stop for him – he waved them on, smiling dizzily. The helicopter had disappeared temporarily, and they found a precious patch of shelter. At last, it was the mouth of a proper cave.

'You have to go,' said Aparna. 'You can't hide any more. Let me see the diagram.'

The wind hadn't dropped, but in the cave mouth there was a curious stillness. She had her rucksack on the ground, and was pulling the tent out of it. Eric sorted the poles into different sizes, laying them out in triangles.

Mark found the roll of tape.

Aparna started unfolding the fabric, issuing orders – the precious page they'd caught was weighted under stones, for easy reference. She had Mark's Lockerman ready, and started to slice the nylon. They created an aluminium cube, and Jeff shook out his rucksack, so that more poles scattered over the ground.

'We're insane!' he shouted. 'But it's going to work.'

Mark held the ends, and Eric taped them. Aparna was now working with the edge of the cloth, hooking the eyes and threading them onto the framework. Jeff took the knife back, and hacked the smaller tent in half. Mark held it taut and she continued the delicate threading, as Rikki and Richard watched.

The helicopter was back, suddenly, nudging in closer than ever. Dr Warren leaned out of the door, wondering if he could drop. He put a thumb up, and the helicopter turned slowly. They could smell the fuel, and the noise was unbearable. They could see the commandos' grim, humourless mouths, and this time Dr Summersby had the megaphone.

'Keep still, Rikki!' she cried.

Rikki and Richard had removed their waterproof, and stood freezing in a thin jersey. Then Dr Warren was floating down towards them, the winch unwinding.

'Take that off,' said Eric. 'Boots, as well. Empty your pockets.'

Rikki did as he was told. The whole frame was going over his bare, scarred shoulders now, fitted by many hands. He was covered in cuts and scratches, and his friends winced as they tightened the cords around him.

'Goodbye,' said Aparna. 'Goodbye.'

The two heads – both Rikki and Richard – wore an identical expression. They were frightened, but calm, and it was suddenly impossible to tell who was who. Their hair flew backwards, and their jaws were set.

'Take it easy, boy!' said a voice. Everyone turned to see a commando heaving himself over the rock. He clambered to his feet, smiling – and moved in.

'Take that off, son,' he said to Rikki and Richard. 'It's suicide.'

Salome stepped forward and hit him full on the jaw. It was her finest uppercut, and it knocked the soldier flat on his back. At once, Aparna dragged Rikki and Richard up to the very summit of the rock, and Mark and Jeff held the gigantic wings as the gale raged over them. Another peal of thunder crashed onto the mountain and the lightning struck harder than ever. It seemed to strike the child, for he staggered, and spun, and there was fire all along the metal frame, sealing the fabric. Jeff and Mark clung on, with Aparna – Salome clambered up now and, with Eric, they drew Richard and Rikki backwards.

They pulled him right back, and then the boy with two heads started to run. He ran as fast as he could over the rocks, and then even as he stumbled he jumped the longest jump of his life, right up into the wind. His two bare feet kicked, as hard as they could – and he dived off the edge of the mountain.

He was caught at once in a swirling air current, and blown backwards. He corkscrewed for a moment, and they thought he'd be dashed against the rock. An air pocket sucked him up and righted him, and his wings found some kind of balance. His feet kicked again, uselessly, and they saw how he clung like a child to the framework – no controls, nothing to steer with, just a frail white body under the huge flying machine. The helicopter rose in shock, and Dr Warren was jerked upwards as Rikki and Richard flew underneath him, plunging into clear blue sky.

The soldier who'd been hit by Salome gazed, his mouth bloody, his eyes wide with astonishment. There were soldiers everywhere now, so the mountain seemed full of spectators: they all stared upwards as Rikki and Richard rose higher and higher. Another crosswind took him and he was skimming out towards the sea.

Those on the mountain watched, shielding their eyes. The sun had come out, too bright to look at, and the child flew straight into it.

CHAPTER NINE

It was curious weather.

On the left, there were storm clouds. On the right, there was bright sunshine. The wind caught Richard and Rikki and seemed to push them where the two skies came together. They flew in a huge, calm arc, and one moment they were sprinkled with rain, and the next baked dry.

It was only a kite frame, so they went where the currents took them. The mountain revolved far below, and then there was a glitter of sea as they rose and rose. Perhaps Rikki leaned to the left and it did make a difference? They banked left and were among birds, startled at the intrusion. They banked right and were dropping. They looped round in a spiral, dangerously low, and just as they felt the salt spray, they were rising again.

They flew and they flew.

They practised loops, and they found out how to do rolls. They learned how a bird can rise in an air current and hang motionless. They let the breeze take them right out to the silver horizon, where the world disappeared, and then they drifted back in long graceful arcs. When Richard saw the island, Rikki did too. They saw the lighthouse and they knew it was their destination. At first, it looked like an angry little spike, marooned in the sea. As they came round, however, they saw that there was a beam of light winking out at them. Under the lighthouse was a short plateau of land, as flat as a runway.

They saw one sailboat in the sea, and they somersaulted once above it, for the sheer joy of gymnastics – it was just a little dinghy, with two little people inside it, bracing the sail. They swooped in, then shot upwards again, so the world shrank to a football.

Rikki looked left and saw Richard. He was sitting quiet and calm, at the end of the wing.

Richard looked right and there was Rikki. He too was on a wing, and their eyes locked together.

In those magical seconds they smiled at each other and gazed, unable to tear their eyes away again. Soon, however, they were banking and both knew they were ready for the drop. The island was below them, still marked for the planes that had practised there, and they plunged down towards it.

Mr Barlow had been right.

Pilots really had trained at this very spot for years and years. The water was deep enough for the aircraft carriers, and the island itself had been the perfect length to try the innumerable takeoff and landing manoeuvres – the assisted landings that were so important to the Navy. It was no longer in use. Even the lighthouse was unmanned – but the markings stood out bright white, and there were a handful of rusty sheds and hangars.

The boy approached from the east. He was caught by a downward gust that dropped him faster. He was lost in cloud for a moment, but came through it, and the island was yet closer. Rikki leaned left, and Richard leaned right, and they lifted their legs. The runway was under them, and another gust carried them down, so they floated in, soft as a butterfly. Their running feet came to rest with ten metres of ground to spare.

They removed their wings and stood, breathless – rib-cage heaving. They were shaking all over, burned by the sun. The last thing they expected to hear was a voice, because the island had seemed so deserted – but the voice came loud and clear, and they turned in wonder.

There were men in uniform all around them.

There must have been twenty or thirty – absolutely rigid and still, as if stuck fast in photographs. Their hands were raised to their caps in a crisp military salute, and the world had faded to black and white. In the middle of the island stood a thin, elderly man – slightly hunched and smiling.

He said, 'The perfect landing.'

Rikki blinked, aware that everything had slowed down. Just the turning of his head was in slow motion. He saw the man moving towards him, walking carefully over the grass. There was an extraordinary stillness, as if the wind had been simply sucked away, and the men who saluted still didn't move. Even the grass was still, and the wings lay on the landing strip absolutely motionless.

The man was frail, but determined. He was carrying a flask, and he stopped to unscrew the top. Then he poured steaming coffee into it and smiled again. With difficulty, he got down on his haunches and set the flask on the ground.

Richard and Rikki sat down in front of him. They were on the pale grey tarmac of the landing strip.

'If it was me,' said the old man, 'I'd add something a bit stronger. But you don't need it at your age. There's plenty of sugar in this, and . . . I think you know what's in here. You recognize this?' He pulled a paper bag out of his pocket, and they could see at once that it was full of chocolates.

He sat, with difficulty, spilling a little of the coffee. He was breathing hard, and it was clear that he wasn't used to getting down onto the ground. Once he'd succeeded he relaxed, and Richard and Rikki took a sweet each and looked at their knees. They could not meet his eyes.

Neither could they speak, so they looked down and waited.

'First time I did that was 'fifty-eight,' the old man said. 'The Sea Vampire, which was the training craft then. Not my favourite aeroplane, but . . . serviceable. You'd come in from the east, just as you did – and you had three seconds. It's called the "Icarus Drop", you know. Did you know that? You remember me telling you that?'

He smiled, and took hold of Richard's foot.

'Once you'd done the Icarus Drop they gave you the badge. Have you still got the badge, son?'

Richard nodded.

'You've got it with you? I know you have.'

It was the only thing left in Rikki's pocket – the only thing he hadn't discarded as he stood on the mountain. He produced it. The two halves were one again, as if a magic hand had stitched them. The gold thread gleamed in the sunlight.

'You can wear it now, can't you?' said the old man. 'Wear it on your new blazer, if you want to. You're off to the grammar, you know. You got in. But then we all knew you would.'

They ate another chocolate. They finished the coffee, and there was no hurry. Time was standing still for them.

'You were spotted, of course,' said the man. 'This is a secure area, so, er . . . don't think you've got away. The coastguard took over, and there's people coming for you. But the boat you saw – that should get here first. And that's important.' He put his hand on Rikki's. 'Your mum and dad are in that boat, boy. So I'm going to disappear. You understand that, don't you? You understand I've got to go? It's been a year now.'

Rikki nodded, but the pain was so acute he thought his jaw would break. The tears were also blinding him, and he couldn't lift a hand to wipe them away. He wanted so much to look up and speak. He had so many things to ask and say, but his airway was blocked. He could only sit, and listen.

Richard was the same.

'I know you've got questions,' said the old man. 'I can't let you speak, love. If you speak, the spell will break – just like that. Do you understand? It would all be over – and it is nearly over. So let's just . . . enjoy the last of it. I'll tell you some things. I'm not going to blub, all right? I am not going to make an exhibition of myself. I'm going to tell you some things, and then it really will all be over. Number one is that people die. We die, Richard, Rikki. We clear the ground. We don't want to, usually. I didn't want to and I didn't expect to, but that was how it was – and if I'd had a choice, I wouldn't have done that to you, my love. Why it happened like that, I do not know. Why you had to endure that, I do not know. There was nothing you could do. You know that, don't you?'

Richard nodded, and he felt his grandad's hand on his chin. Rikki felt the same, and they managed to look up at last, and meet the old man's clear, pilot's eyes.

'You've got to be strong when we go. Don't let the dead take you with them: stay with those who need you. Take comfort, son. From the time we had. Are you listening? And you have to accept . . . you have to accept that I'm just not there any more. I'm in you, and part of you, and in that way I'm never going to leave you. You're stronger for that, even though . . .' He wiped his eyes. 'Oh, I know how lonely it is.'

Richard managed to nod. Rikki was simply crying.

'What you're doing can't go on, son. You know it can't. You're too precious to be broken like this, and you're breaking up others. You've got too much to do. Too many friends. You've got your mum and dad to look after. School, Rikki. You're going to a good, wonderful school. You can be whatever you want – and I'm not asking you to forget me. Think about me – always think about me. Look in the mirror, and you'll see me. But not over your shoulder any more, because I'm not coming back. I'll be in your eyes, looking right back at you. You understand?

'You have to get on now: get on with things. People die, and the time they have is precious for that reason, isn't it? And you know what I'm saying is right, because it's what you think when you're sensible.' He pushed up with his hands. 'Help me up, lad.'

Richard stood up with Rikki. They didn't think they were going to be able to, but they did. They managed to wipe their eyes, and they even managed to hold a hand out to their old, dear, dead grandad, who seemed lighter than ever as they held him – translucent, almost, as if he might float away.

He put his arm round the grandsons he'd loved, and laughed. He pulled them together.

'Don't speak,' he said. 'Not yet. I want to tell you one more thing, and then . . . look. Your parents are here. I want you always to remember that I loved you.' The old man put his hands on the two heads. 'No man had a better grandson than you. How do you think I feel, watching you destroy yourself? No man *could* have had a better grandson. Why was I so lucky? Come here.'

He hugged Rikki to him. Richard managed to get his arms up, and around the old man's shoulders.

Rikki felt it first: a kiss, firm on his forehead – and it was like another lightning bolt. Richard felt it too – a blast down his spine and into the soles of his feet. He thought he would faint, but he clung on with Rikki and he felt the man's hands squeezing them back together. There was such strength and pressure, and for a moment there was intolerable pain. He glimpsed his grandad's own, twisted face, using every atom of his last strength, and he felt Rikki's rage and courage burn inside him.

Rikki gasped, and felt the heat of Richard's love and wonder – and then they knew it really was over. Without needing a mirror, they knew: a year had passed, and they were whole again. They were one, and could at last wipe one pair of eyes.

Rikki and Richard spoke together. 'Goodbye, Grandad,' he said.

As he spoke, the spell broke, and the child was alone on an abandoned airstrip.

He turned. He saw his mother and father, some distance away – at the far end of the runway. They walked, and then they were running. Their son started walking towards them – and, of course, in a moment he too was sprinting towards his parents. They met in the middle and threw their arms around each other.

And that is how they were restored to each other.

EPILOGUE

I'm going to dash this off fast because I'm supposed to be at the gym with Salome, helping her train and being her personal punch bag – and I don't want to dwell on stuff, anyway. We're at the end, as you must have guessed. And the beginning too.

The soldier she hit is not pressing charges, which is lucky. He was so amazed he got smacked by a girl that he's saying nothing about it – there's no comeback from that. Our beloved headmaster got a boot so hard up the you-know-what that he went flying into early retirement (where he wanted to send the Bra!) – and nice Miss Maycock got a full-time job because of what they call 'continuity'. That's what we all need, they say, for the last few days of our very last term before the big, wide, scary world. Continuity. They asked Mr Barlow to come back too, but he's getting ready to go travelling.

I told him he should look up his poor abandoned

kids, and patch things up with Mrs B – she might be lonely and sorry, and they could all be happy together in Cyprus. He said he'd give it serious thought, but I think he's going to head off to some wilderness and do all the crazy things that he should have done in his teens. He recovered from the tranquillizers, of course – he said they made him feel nice and fuzzy. They had to carry him off the mountain, though.

'I'll be sending you postcards,' he said – but where he hopes to send them, I don't know. Because of course, all of us are splitting up. There are five schools around town, and we get scattered now, like a bunch of sweet little seeds. Where will we land? Will it be on stony ground, or nice, rich, fertile soil? Will we grow straight and tall, or crooked and bad? Who knows . . .

And I am pleased to confirm that Dr Warren has officially lost everything.

Dr Summersby legged it, straight out of the country, while the Rectal Institute is facing the biggest investigation in the world – it made the national papers and there were big demonstrations, and I was on TV at last (just three seconds, in the background, looking outrageously handsome). We all made statements, and Eric's brother produced the hard drive he'd found, which – along with the phone – showed exactly what that very nasty man hoped to keep secret. Those poor old animals are being taken care of, so we were told, and the whole place is closed.

A few more loose ends, and I must be gone.

Jeff and Aparna are best friends again. But she's going to an all-girls school, so that's going to be difficult. Except she might not be: she's told her parents she's not, anyway. Jeff's developing attitude too – one step at a time, and I help him along the best I can, giving him tips. Aparna just laughs at us both. How we didn't see that coming is beyond me. She's a dangerous girl now, and everyone's scared of her.

Eric's fine, and still wants to join the Army – more than ever, in fact. He's going to repeat the year, and says he's ready to work hard for the qualifications he needs. He got so much praise for all that survival stuff that I think it changed him. Mark, as well – the commandos loved both of them, and they stayed a week at the training camp as a special reward. Mark got his head shaved, and they spent all their time doing assault courses and rifle-range stuff. Learning to be men.

We're happy, I think. All of us.

Can I tell you about the last football match

we played? I've got to, because you might have forgotten, but Green Cross did make the cup final – that awful ref never dared to complain. It took place in the very last week, against arch-arch-rivals Dundonald Primary. They're a school like us: same size, same kind of kids, and they wanted to win even more than we did. By half time we were one down, and Jeff was feeling bad because it was an easy save and he muffed it. But the great Barlow (supercoach) had come back for just that game, and he had a meeting with us there on the touchline, and he worked his magic. He reminded us of a few things, and we just got it together and played like a dream. We played for each other and Eric equalized after ten minutes.

Who scored the winner?

It shouldn't matter, because we all did, and you can see it, if you want – see the last page. We won a silver cup, and got to dance around the pitch holding it. We got to show it off in school assembly, and we were in the local paper. We even got a special dinner, which was our end-of-term party, and the very last thing I'm going to mention. Mr Barlow made a speech that had everyone in tears, because he told us he loved us. There was so much hugging and crying I couldn't see straight, and then suddenly it was over – all over. Finished.

We opened the doors, and there were our parents waiting to drive us home . . .

Let me tell you, friends: you have to fight to survive.

Aparna and Jeff, for instance: they fight all the time. They can't agree on anything.

Which makes me think maybe they're the closest. Because I know the people we love most are the people we fight with – I see that now, and I never saw it before. I think the day you stop fighting is the day the world ends, and that's when it's over.

It was an amazing term, and I have no problems now looking in mirrors, because it's just as he said. I see his eyes, looking into mine, and I'm going to live up to his memory, or try to.

Lots of love, and thank you for reading . . .

R.W.

xx

ACKNOWLEDGEMENTS

I wrote this book during my last year in Manila, so I'd like to thank my friend Jane Fisher for her encouragement. Dinah, Rob, Nikki & Rob, Trav and Rachel were also very kind and supportive. While the story never changed, details did. I'd like to thank Susan Wardell and John Childs for helping with a few facts. I'd also like to thank my family, for constant support, as well as the children of Dundonald Primary School in Wimbledon – especially Year Six, looked after so ably by Harvey McGavin.

Lesley Burgess, Michael Gee, Annemarie Shillito, Sam, Abigail and Louie North, and Chris Mantz let me use their houses. Jane Turnbull was with me on every page, and the David Fickling team: David, Hannah, Bella, Tilda and Linda were tireless in offering ideas and challenges. Sue Cook was a superb copy-editor, and it must be time to record a real debt of gratitude to Sally Riley, for all her hard work.

There are ghosts in this book, of the children I've taught. So thank you to Max, to Paolo, to Mustafa, to Alice, to Ben, to Sam, to Billie, to Adam, to Miles and to

Katkat . . . and the many others who may or may not see fragments of themselves.

Finally: thank you, Joe and Katie, my next-door neighbours. You offered advice, and you gave me the idea in the first place.*

*To view that final goal, log onto www.andymulliganbooks.co.uk. Click on 'The Boy with Two Heads' and follow the links.

Read on for a sneak peek of

1

My name is Raphael Fernández and I am a dumpsite boy.

People say to me, 'I guess you just never know what you'll find, sifting through rubbish! Today could be your lucky day.' I say to them, 'Friend, I think I know what I find.' And I know what everyone finds, because I know what we've been finding for all the years I've been working, which is eleven years. It's the one word: *stuppa*, which means – and I'm sorry if I offend – it's our word for human muck. I don't want to upset anyone, that's not my business here. But there's a lot of things hard to come by in our sweet city, and one of the things too many people don't have is toilets and running water. So when they have to go, they do it where they can. Most of those people live in boxes, and the boxes are stacked up tall and high. So, when you use the toilet, you do it on a piece of paper, and you wrap it up and put it in the trash. The trash bags come together. All over the city, trash bags get loaded onto carts, and from carts onto trucks or even trains – you'd be amazed at how much trash this city makes. Piles and piles of it, and it all ends up here with us. The trucks and trains never stop, and nor do we. Crawl and crawl, and sort and sort.

It's a place they call Behala, and it's rubbish-town. Three years ago it was Smoky Mountain, but Smoky Mountain got so bad they closed it down and shifted us along the road. The piles stack up – and I mean Himalayas: you could climb for ever, and many people do . . . up and down, into the valleys. The mountains go right from the docks to the marshes, one whole long world of steaming trash. I am one of the rubbish boys, picking through the stuff this city throws away.

'But you must find interesting things?' someone said to me. 'Sometimes, no?'

We get visitors, you see. It's mainly foreigners visiting the Mission School, which they set up years ago and just about stays open. I always smile, and I say, 'Sometimes, sir! Sometimes, ma'am!'

What I really mean is, *No, never – because what we mainly find is stupp*.

'What you got there?' I say to Gardo.

'What d'you think, boy?' says Gardo.

And I know. The interesting parcel that looked like something nice wrapped up? What a surprise! It's stupp, and Gardo's picking his way on, wiping his hands on his shirt and hoping to find something we can sell. All day, sun or rain, over the hills we go.

You want to come see? Well, you can smell Behala long before you see it. It must be about two hundred football pitches big, or maybe a thousand basketball courts – I don't know: it seems to go on for ever. Nor do I know how much of it is stupp, but on a bad day it seems like most of it, and to spend your life wading through it, breathing it, sleeping beside it – well . . . maybe one day you'll find 'something nice'. Oh yes.

Then one day I did.

I was a trash boy since I was old enough to move without help and pick things up. That was what? – three years old, and I was sorting.

Let me tell you what we're looking for.

Plastic, because plastic can be turned into cash, fast – by the kilo. White plastic is best, and that goes in one pile; blue in the next.

Paper, if it's white and clean – that means if we can clean it and dry it. Cardboard also.

Tin cans – anything metal. Glass, if it's a bottle. Cloth or rags of any kind – that means the occasional T-shirt, a pair of pants, a bit of sack that wrapped something up. The kids round here, half the stuff we wear is what we found, but most we pile up, weigh and sell. You should see me, dressed to kill. I wear a pair of hacked-off jeans and a too-big T-shirt that I can roll up onto my head when the sun gets bad. I don't wear shoes – one, because I don't have any, and two, because you need to feel with your feet. The Mission School had a big push on getting us boots, but most of the kids sold them on. The trash is soft, and our feet are hard as hooves.

Rubber is good. Just last week we got a freak delivery of old tyres from somewhere. Snapped up in minutes, they were, the men getting in first and driving us off. A half-good tyre can fetch half a dollar, and a dead tyre holds down the roof of your house. We get the fast food too, and that's a little business in itself. It doesn't come near me and Gardo, it goes down the far end, and about a hundred kids sort out the straws, the cups and the chicken bones. Everything turned, cleaned and bagged up – cycled down to the weighers, weighed and sold. Onto the trucks that take it back to the city, round it goes. On a good day I'll make two hundred pesos. On a bad, maybe fifty? So you live day to day and hope you don't get sick. Your life is the hook you carry, there in your hand, turning the trash.

'What's that you got, Gardo?'

'Stupp. What about you?'

Turn over the paper. 'Stupp.'

I have to say, though: I'm a trash boy with shorts. I work with Gardo most of the time, and between us we move fast. Some of the little kids and the old people just poke and poke, like everything's got to be turned over – but among the stupp, I can pull out the paper and plastic fast, so I don't do so bad. Gardo's my partner, and we always work together. He looks after me.